PENALTY PLAY

Boston Rebels
Book 5

JULIA CONNORS

Cover Design by Qamber Designs
Developmental Editing by Meanie Yu, Made Me Blush Books
Line & Copy Editing by Amy Pritt
Proofreading by Elizabeth Solomon, and Alyssa Nazzaro, Hundred Proof Services

*For anyone who ever felt the need to make themselves small
in order to fit the mold of someone else's expectations . . .
this is your world, take up all the space you need.*

Author's Note

Penalty Play deals with topics that may be sensitive for some readers, including body insecurity issues, death of a parent (in the past), an emotionally abusive parent, and pregnancy loss (in the past, and not the female main character).

For a full list of content warnings, please visit my website: juliaconnors.com/penalty-play

Chapter One

MORGAN

"If there's one thing in life I excel at, it's attracting assholes," I say with a sigh.

Across from me, Alessandra Jones lifts one of her perfectly arched dark eyebrows, her full lips tilting up into a soft smile. "Please don't tell me this is about Carter."

I groan, leaning back in my seat as I cover my face with both hands and shake my head.

"You didn't give him another chance, did you?" she asks. I can hear the well-deserved judgment in her voice. AJ is the general manager of the Boston Rebels, the first female GM in the NHL, and an all-around badass who would never let anyone treat her the way I somehow keep letting guys treat me.

My hands fall from my face. "He was so apologetic and insisted that he really wanted to make things work this time." I hear how ridiculous *this time* sounds as it rolls off my tongue. How many times do I need to let him walk all over me before I finally learn my lesson?

I probably shouldn't be gossiping about my love life with my boss, but she's become a good friend over the past few months and I need *someone* to talk to about the text I just received.

She rests her elbows on her desk and folds her arms over each other as she leans in. "All right, what happened this time?"

"He's been texting me about how much he misses me, how he was wrong to let me go, and how he now knows we were so good together . . ." I pause, swallowing through the thick lump in my throat as I think about how honest his lies sounded. He told me exactly what I wanted to hear, and I was so desperately gullible that I believed him. "So last week I went to dinner with him, and I ended up spending the night at his place. He left for a weeklong business trip and just got back today. And about two minutes ago, I got a text from him saying that he thinks we're better off keeping things casual."

"Morgan." Her voice is sympathetic but chiding. It's the tone you'd use when you're telling someone they should have known better. Which is fair, because I absolutely should have.

"I know. It's like a repeat of June all over again." I met Carter earlier this summer, and he'd love-bombed me to the extreme. He wanted to see me almost every night, flew me to Miami while he was there on business because he couldn't be apart from me, bought me gifts—and then, with no warning and no provocation, he ended things.

This time he didn't end it, he just doesn't want a relationship. I'm good enough to sleep with, but not good enough to be his girlfriend, I guess.

"You deserve so much better than to be some guy's booty call," AJ says.

"How am I supposed to know when a guy doesn't mean any of the things he says, though? There were no red flags. He just came off as this really great guy, who was really into me . . ."

"Until he wasn't?" AJ offers up the truth I don't want to admit.

"Yeah. But then his apology was so sincere and his interest seemed so genuine."

"Sometimes it can be really hard to tell," AJ says with a small shake of her head. I know her first marriage wasn't a good one, and her ex-husband ended up being the douchiest of douches. "But when someone shows you who they are, *believe them.*"

"Yeah, maybe my issue is that I'm too willing to give people second chances." I shake my head, a little sad about the thought of people being unable to redeem themselves. "I can't help but want to see the good in people."

"I'm not saying you should never give someone a second chance. Look at me and McCabe. If we hadn't given each other a second chance, we wouldn't be where we are now."

I smile as I think about our team captain and our general manager, who last season seemed to hate each other over something that had happened years before when they were both with a different team. Now AJ, McCabe, and his baby girl, Abby, are the perfect little family.

"What I am saying, though, is that if someone *repeatedly* shows you they're not trustworthy, you need to let them go.

No matter how good it seems when you're together. No matter how good it *could* be." She pauses, shakes her head as she looks at me, and says, "You are so good at giving other people excellent advice in similar situations. Maybe you just need to stop and ask yourself, 'What would I tell a friend in this instance?'"

I huff out a laugh. "None of my friends are single anymore, so I wouldn't need to give that kind of advice. But I know what you mean, and I'll try that next time." I push down any lingering emotions I have about what I thought Carter and I could have together, determined not to be some guy's doormat again. From now on, I'm going to embrace my inner badass like AJ. "Okay, sorry. We're not meeting to discuss my love life. What's up, Boss?"

AJ cringes a tad at my use of the term, as if she doesn't like thinking of herself as everyone's boss. That might be part of why she excels in her role. She never tries to throw her weight around—she just leads quietly and confidently, and everyone from the team's owner to the players respect the hell out of her for it.

"I'll wait until Patrick gets here to jump into the nitty gritty of it, but before that, I wanted to say how thankful I am you're stepping into this role. I know you have your own clients and your own PR company, and that this is just temporary, but I *really* appreciate you stepping in for Tatum while she's on medical leave."

"Well, the Rebels just officially became my biggest client."

I'd helped AJ and the Boston Rebels with a PR situation toward the end of last season. Then I'd agreed to come on part time to help revamp their social media vision and put a plan into place for executing it.

When their social media manager, Tatum, found out she needed to have back surgery and would have a long recovery, I agreed to fit this into my already busy schedule.

Behind me, there's a knock on the door and I turn as Patrick Patrona, the VP of Marketing and Public Relations, walks in. On his heels is a young woman with pale blonde hair and big brown eyes.

"Morgan, this is Natalie. She's doing one of her co-ops for Northeastern and will be our social media intern for the rest of this year."

"So nice to meet you," Natalie says, extending her hand to shake mine. "I'm looking forward to working with you."

"Oh, I'm just filling in for Tatum for a few months," I say, glancing at Patrick. No one mentioned needing to manage an intern as part of my job responsibilities.

"Natalie will be reporting to me," Patrick says, clearly noting the question in my expression, "but she'll be looking to you for guidance about our social media vision. We'll also need to talk a bit about some of the upcoming press releases we've got scheduled, and figure out how we want our socials to build excitement around our announcements."

I glance between Patrick and Natalie, where they stand to my right, and AJ on the other side of her desk, to my left. "I just want to reiterate the expectation that I'm coming on part time. It sounds like you're asking me to do Tatum's full-time job, including training an intern, while also working on PR that was beyond the scope of her responsibilities . . . in fifteen hours a week?"

If there's one thing I learned in the course of earning my MBA and starting my own company, it's to set clear expectations.

"Morgan's right," AJ says before Patrick can respond. "We need to make sure we're clear about what we need her to do, so she can delegate the rest."

I glance at Natalie, who looks like she's caught in the crossfire *and* in over her head, even though this is a perfectly civil conversation about boundaries. Oh boy.

"We'll make sure to keep it manageable," Patrick says to AJ. "And ensure *you* are free to manage the players, not the PR staff."

AJ huffs out a laugh. "Patrick, how long have we worked together? Is there any part of this organization I don't have my fingers in?"

He shakes his head with a soft laugh. He doesn't seem to think she's overstepping, it's more like he's thankful she found me and brought me on in this role.

Even though I know I don't have enough time in the day for this project, when you get the opportunity to work with someone truly amazing, someone you want to learn from and emulate, it's hard to say no. AJ is that person for me. Plus, having the Boston Rebels on my roster of clients is certainly not going to hurt my future business growth. It's only for a few months, after all.

"Great," AJ says, then turns to me. "So once you're back from Bermuda, we can start?"

I press my lips between my teeth and give her a sharp nod. Bermuda is the trip that's been looming on my calendar all summer, ever since my mom announced her plans to marry a man I've never even met and insisted that I be her maid of honor. Again.

"Yeah, next week should be fine. I fly back on Monday."

"Great, we'll see you here on Tuesday, then. In the meantime, we'll get Natalie all caught up on the social media vision you created and the strategy we're using to execute it. You should go relax and have a great trip." AJ must notice my grimace because she says, "C'mon, it's Bermuda. How bad can it be?"

And my god, I wish she hadn't asked that question, because now all I can think about is how much I don't want to go.

I say my goodbyes and, as I head out of AJ's office, my phone buzzes in my purse. I pull it out to see that my mom has texted.

At least AJ isn't here to see *this* grimace, because the article my mom has shared with me makes me dread this trip even more.

MOM:

Not the weather report we were hoping for!

Staring back at me, under the headline *Bermuda Preparing for Tropical Storm This Weekend*, is an aerial map of the Atlantic showing the potential path of the tropical storm, with Bermuda right smack in the middle of it.

Chapter Two

AIDAN

After shooting off the text to one of my few close friends, Ronan McCabe, I set my phone down and look around at the piles of boxes stacked in my living room. A year ago, I broke my hand in a bar fight I wasn't even trying to be part of. When it became clear that I'd be out for the whole season, I rented out my place in the city and moved back to the beach town south of Boston where I spent most of my childhood.

But "coming home" felt a lot more like showing up in a place I'd outgrown long ago. I've never been great about "staying in touch," except with my childhood best friend, Liam. And since I've played for three different NHL teams over the years, I've lived all over the country. Each time I move, I start over. I don't know why I like to leave the past in the past, but I do. I barely even see my stepdad, who is my only family, now that he lives in Miami.

I've unpacked four boxes, collapsed the cardboard, and taken it down to the dumpster behind my brownstone before McCabe replies to my text.

> MCCABE
>
> Oh wow, you're alive? Nice to hear from you
> after a year.

Okay, so maybe I'm *really* not good at keeping in touch.

> AIDAN
>
> Sorry, you know I'm shit with replying to
> texts.

> MCCABE
>
> How are you with reading them? Because if
> you've read any of the messages I sent you
> over the past eleven months, you'd know
> that I've got a baby and can't just run out for
> a drink. And I assume you know that AJ and
> I are together? She moved in this summer.

I know both of these things, of course, in the same way you know things you've only heard about—superficially and without much detail.

Should I have driven back into the city and met McCabe's baby? Yeah, probably. But I was in constant pain and not good company.

Should I have reached out when the news broke that he and AJ were dating? Or when the Rebels lost the Stanley Cup? Or when I knew I'd be returning to play this season? Yes to any and all of those.

AIDAN

Okay fine, I'm a shit friend.

You sure AJ can't stay with Abby, so we can catch up?

I'm proud of myself for at least remembering his baby's name. I do follow him on social media, so I've seen some photos—most notably the set of photos that he and AJ released right after they went public with their relationship a couple months ago. Abby was in most of the pictures, but she didn't at all resemble the newborn photos he sent me last September.

MCCABE

The ONLY reason I'm saying yes is because I'm your captain and feel obligated to let you know what you're walking into at training camp.

Training camp is still two and a half weeks away. I know him well enough to know that this means he thinks I'll need time to adjust to whatever he's about to tell me.

———

"Don't give me that grumpy-ass look," I say as McCabe slides into the opposite side of the booth at The Neon Cactus, a bar in Beacon Hill where he suggested we meet. I've never been here, but with its shellacked wooden walls littered with neon signs and old posters, not to mention the Christmas lights strung around the perimeter of the room, it has a certain old Boston charm to it.

He's about to reply when a waitress walks up. "Hey, Sandy," he says.

She nods, seemingly unaffected by the fact that Boston's star hockey player knows who she is. "McCabe."

"You know what you want?" he asks, turning his head toward me.

"What do you have on tap?" I ask Sandy.

She looks like she's barely restraining herself from rolling her eyes. "About forty kinds of tequila."

My brows scrunch together at her reply. "You don't have *any* beer on tap?"

"It's a tequila bar," McCabe says, sounding pissed off that I don't know this. He always sounds pissed off, though. "You want beer, you can have it in a can."

"Uhh . . ." I pause, and then throw out the name of the first beer that comes to mind because I'm unusually flustered by how foreign this all is . . . me at a new bar with my best friend who I haven't talked to in nearly a year, who's conversing with the waitress like he's here all the time, and now ordering a margarita instead of a beer.

Once Sandy leaves, McCabe levels me with a stare. "Nice of you to grace me with your presence after going dark for a year."

How can I explain that this last year was the hardest of my life? That one surgery after another left me in constant pain, that I was unwilling to take any of the hard drugs they offered me after the way my own father succumbed to his addiction to painkillers which finally killed him? That moving "home" was the worst decision I could have made, that not having hockey in my life for the first time ever almost killed me?

"Yeah, sorry about that."

"What the fuck happened?" McCabe grits out the question through his clenched jaw. The way he looks even more annoyed than usual has me wondering, for the first time, if my not being around this past year was hard on *him*.

We're both pretty quiet guys, both kind of gruff in a way that can easily trespass into asshole territory if we're not careful. We both played for other teams before coming to the Rebels, and while he was here for a bit before me, our similar personalities had us ending up as friends by default. I respect the hell out of the guy and what he can do on the ice, but sitting here now, I realize that maybe I never really knew him that well off the ice.

"I got hurt. You had a baby." I shrug. "We were both busy."

"What the fuck were you *busy* doing for the last year?"

"Besides the three surgeries, the constant physical therapy, and being in a shit ton of pain the whole time?" I ask, crossing my arms over my chest as I lean back in the booth. His gaze focuses on the raised scar across the back of my left hand. It's not as swollen as it once was, but the surgeon told me it's unlikely it will ever fully fade. "Not much."

Just wallowing in my own self-pity for the first half of the year, and clawing my way out of it in the second half. The only things that got me through it were needing to be there for Liam when tragedy struck his family, and knowing that returning to the Rebels was what lay on the other side.

"You couldn't have returned a single one of my texts?"

"I wasn't in a good headspace," I say, and he tilts his chin as his eyes narrow in on me.

"Are you *now*?"

Is that concern I hear in his voice? "I'm good."

"What changed?"

I don't really want to get into it, so I say, "I got cleared to play for the season."

McCabe doesn't look like he wants to let that go. "Are you sure you're good now? Because if you're not, there are options—"

"I'm fine," I say as Sandy slides a turquoise can of beer in front of me. It's from a microbrewery on the South Shore, and I'm pretty sure I still have a six-pack of them in my fridge at the beach. Then she sets McCabe's margarita in front of him. It's in a rocks glass, with half a jalapeño and a slice of lime wedged into the ice. *What the fuck kind of drink is that?*

"Thanks," McCabe says as she turns to leave.

"So, there were things you wanted to tell me about the team?" I ask as he takes a sip of his drink.

Setting it down, he looks back at me and says, "Yeah. There have been a lot of changes, and a lot of talk about where you might fit into it all now that you're coming back. I'm not going to sugar coat it . . ."

I swallow and nod that he should continue. I'm not used to getting a talking-to by my team captain, nor am I used to McCabe taking on this role. For the past few years before I was injured, he was kind of resentful of being captain. It was always our goalie and unofficial captain, Colt, who'd sit you down and have "the conversation."

". . . you're kind of an asshole, and that's not the vibe of the team."

"Wow." I don't say anything else just to see what he says next.

"Some of the new guys—Jenkins, Reid, and Hartmann,

specifically—have brought a different energy to the team. Wilcott's done a great job building camaraderie among the players," he says, and that sounds exactly like something our coach would focus on. He's the fatherly type, the kind you want to play well for because you don't want to disappoint him. "AJ's focused on another Stanley Cup—"

I cough out a laugh and say, "Among other things."

It's the kind of thing that would have made McCabe laugh a year ago, as much as he is actually capable of laughing.

"Not fucking funny, man." The words are tense, his tone harsh, and I know I just crossed a line I shouldn't have. "She and I have our personal and professional boundaries firmly in place. But if you so much as say one disrespectful thing about her, I will absolutely go apeshit on your ass. As your captain, of course."

"I have nothing disrespectful to say about her." I hold my hands up so he'll calm the fuck down.

In fact, AJ is the only one in the entire Rebels organization who I felt actually cared that I was gone. She checked in with me regularly, sent me take-out gift cards when I had each surgery, had our team doctor, Olivia D'Angelis, make a house call to check on me once I was done with my final round of PT, then made sure I came in and got cleared by the athletic trainers and Dr. D once my surgeon cleared me to play.

"Good. Keep it that way."

"Tell me about the new guys," I say, hoping to glean a bit more about what I'm walking into at training camp. I'm really looking forward to getting back on the ice with my team. I just have to get through my stepdad's wedding in Bermuda first.

"I mean, you know who they all are. Drew Jenkins replaced Piatza when he retired, and has settled into being the Center on our first line." There were rumors of Jenkins "replacing" me as the team's unofficial enforcer when I went onto injured reserve, but he's hardly spent any time in the penalty box this season, unlike when he played for Colorado.

"Zach Reid is the chillest guy in the world," McCabe continues, referencing a new defender who was traded from Philadelphia. "He alternates between the first and second line defense, depending on where Wilcott needs him. And Luke Hartmann . . ." He pauses, letting out a gruff laugh. "He's still a bit green—"

"Yeah, I watched Game 7." Like the rest of the world, I saw him choke when Colt got injured in the third period. The whole team played like shit that period, but there's no question that it was Hartmann who lost us the Cup, which is all kinds of awkward since his family owns the team.

"We're over that and focused on *this* season," McCabe says, the warning tone in his voice telling me that this isn't something to bring up, especially with Hartmann. "Anyway, Hartmann's actually a really great player and an even better teammate, once you get used to the whole golden retriever shtick."

"Golden retriever?"

"He's like the most loyal guy ever and is always trying to make sure everyone else is okay. You know, the opposite of you." He says it like he's joking, but it's the kind of joke that hits too close to home.

My hand flexes around the beer can I'd just picked up,

and the air is filled with the sound of crinkling metal. This isn't the "welcome back" I'd been hoping for, even though I know it might be the one I deserve after the way I disappeared for a year. The phone calls and texts I didn't return have obviously not been forgotten.

"The thing is," he says calmly, "this isn't the same team you left, and I want to make sure you don't try to make waves when you come back."

"The only waves I'll be making are on the ice," I tell him.

"About that . . ." He glances down into his drink before he looks back up at me. "It looks like you'll be starting on the second line."

"The fuck?" I should be grateful AJ's even bringing me straight back to the team rather than sending me to our AHL affiliate, but this still stings.

"Walsh moved up to the first line to take your place," he says, like I haven't watched every single game this season and don't know this. "And it looks like Coach wants to keep the line together. You know, since we made it all the way to Game 7 that way."

I try to relax my jaw, because I'm clenching my teeth together so hard I'm going to give myself a headache. I knew this was a possibility. Strategically, it makes sense. Why would Coach mess with a good thing? But I know, with every fiber of my being, that I belong on the first line.

"The good thing," McCabe continues, "is that the second line is also really strong, and putting you on it means we'll basically have the equivalent of two first lines."

"Look at you with the rose-colored glasses," I say. If McCabe was on the second line—no matter how good it is— he'd be pissed as hell. Just like I am.

"What can I say? I'm a bit more of an optimist now. We should have won the Cup last season. You coming back gives us an even better shot at it this year. I have a good feeling about this."

I'd like to have a good feeling about this season too. Instead, now I feel like I have to prove myself all over again, over a decade after going pro. And the worst part is, at thirty-three, I'm not sure if I have it in me to claw my way back to the first line again.

"And, even though you're a dick for disappearing for the past year," McCabe says, "I'm glad you're back."

Chapter Three

MORGAN

The best thing about flying into Bermuda is the way you get to watch the ocean go from deep blue, to bright turquoise, to pale turquoise as the plane touches down.

"Welcome to Bermuda," the flight attendant's sunny voice comes over the speaker as we taxi toward the terminal, "where the local time is 2:30 p.m. It's a hot and humid ninety-two degrees Fahrenheit outside, and it looks like you're going to get about another few hours of sunshine before the storm rolls in. There is a weather advisory, so please stay alert and follow all local guidelines as the island weathers the oncoming storm. Your Boston-based crew will be turning around and heading back shortly, but it was our pleasure to fly you down here. Stay safe!"

As if I wasn't already dreading this trip enough, the tropical storm in the Atlantic that looked like it was going to miss

Bermuda a few days ago, is—as the article my mom sent informed me—now barreling straight toward the island.

I had hoped they'd cancel the wedding because of the weather, but no such luck. The storm is not expected to stay long or do major damage, but the only thing about this weekend I was looking forward to was spending some time at the pool and the beach, and now today and tomorrow morning look to be nothing but driving rain and wind. My mom is convinced that everything will be just fine for her wedding tomorrow night.

As the plane turns toward the gate, I turn airplane mode off and wait for my phone to connect to the local network in Bermuda. People in the few rows ahead of me are already deplaning before my phone connects, and the screen is flooded with text messages. This is what happens when the Wi-Fi on the plane is down for the whole flight. I'd planned on getting some work done on the way down here so I could clear my plate and be ready to start with the Rebels after the long weekend, and now I feel more behind than ever.

EVA

Guess what? Gigi and I might get to come
home from the hospital as early as Monday.

AUDREY

Amazing! Anything we can do to help you
get ready for that?

JULES

Yeah, we're around if you need us.

EVA

LOL, I don't even know what I'm walking
into at home. Luke said he put the crib
together, so at least she'll have a place to
sleep.

I snicker to myself thinking about how, when my friend
Eva was hospitalized for preeclampsia weeks ago, Luke's
teammates, their girlfriends and fiancées, and me, pitched in
to create the nursery of her dreams. She has no idea what she
and her baby girl are coming home to! Luke would do
anything for her, and she doesn't even suspect this surprise. I
still don't think she's quite wrapped her head around just
how much that man loves her.

MORGAN

It'll all come together. I just landed in
Bermuda, but as soon as I'm back in
Boston, your place is my first stop!

JULES

OMG, I just saw the weather. Please stay
safe, Morgan.

MORGAN

I'll be fine. It's supposed to blow through in
less than 24 hours. I'm really not looking
forward to being trapped at a hotel with my
mom and my new stepdad who I've never
even met. But at least it's just for the
weekend.

Speaking of, I should probably go read the text from my
mom that I saw in the massive list of notifications that
appeared on my home screen when my phone connected.
But the line of people in the aisle is moving, so I drop my

phone into my over-the-shoulder bag and stand to grab my carry-on suitcase.

Once I'm in a taxi for the short ride to the hotel, I click back into my texts to catch up with the others I missed. There are two from my mom, whose flight is supposed to arrive a couple hours after mine—just long enough that I didn't have to politely offer to wait for her at the airport.

MOM

Hi honey, unfortunately our flight from Miami just got cancelled because of the storm. We're getting rebooked for tomorrow morning, and we'll hopefully arrive right after the storm moves out to sea again.

Maybe you can track down Danny at the hotel and get to know your new stepbrother. His flight arrived earlier today.

I snort out a laugh in the back seat, and the taxi driver glances at me in the rearview mirror but says nothing. I can think of zero reasons I'd want to get to know my soon-to-be stepbrother, when he'll just be added to the list of all my former stepsiblings in six to nine months.

The first time my mom got remarried after she left my dad and me, I gained a stepsister. She was my age and we got along great. As an only child, I loved gaining not only a sibling, but a friend. Then summer hit and we went on vacation together. Her dad and my mom fought the whole time, and it was impossible for us to not side with our own parent.

By the time they got divorced, I realized it wasn't worth investing all the time and energy into developing a relationship with my stepsibling if the marriage itself wasn't going to last a year. Which they never do. Not the past three, anyway.

Aside from a few quick hellos while on video chats with my mom, I haven't even met Max, my mom's plastic surgeon and now my future stepfather. So it's hard to say if this one will last, but if past precedent holds, there's no point in becoming emotionally invested in him or his son.

I'm still trying to decide how to respond to my mom's text when we pull into the circular drive of the pastel pink hotel. I love the way so many buildings in Bermuda are painted with bright pastel colors, accented by white stone roofs.

At the front desk, the receptionist who checks me in reminds me about the impending storm and tells me that they're expected to lose power at some point tonight. "Only two of our restaurants will be serving dinner tonight: the White Elephant, which requires a reservation and has a shirt and tie dress code, and our cliffside bar, which offers a wide menu with a more casual atmosphere and doesn't take reservations. Would you like me to make a reservation for you?"

"No, thanks. I'll just grab something at the bar," I say.

"Okay. I'd recommend going on the early side because, if we do lose power, we'll have to shut down our kitchens."

"Thanks for the heads up," I say, turning to wheel my suitcase across the lobby. It's a good thing I packed a few protein bars in my bag just in case. I hate eating alone, but it's better than the alternative, which was dinner with my mom, future stepdad, and soon-to-be stepbrother.

———

My hair is windblown with strands stuck to my face by the time I make it the short distance under the covered walkway between the lobby and the bar. The hotel sits on a point overlooking a bay, and on a clear day, I'm sure the view from this glass-encased bar is spectacular. Right now, there's nothing but dark clouds and driving rain. I can barely see the edge of the cliffs, much less the water beyond.

"Our tables are full right now," the host tells me, "but there are a few seats left at the bar, and we serve a full menu there if you don't want to wait."

"The bar is great," I say, and head that way. There are two open seats right in front of me, one at each corner of the bar. As I get settled on a barstool and take the menu the bartender hands me, I'm thankful to be sitting here and not alone at a table. I love people-watching and, as I turn my head to the left and scan the restaurant, I notice the view from here is great for that.

But when my head swivels back to the right, I realize the formerly vacant seat next to me is now occupied. The guy now sitting there is objectively hot. A sharp jaw, chiseled cheekbones, an olive complexion with a deep tan, and eyes that are a kaleidoscope of brown with flecks of green and amber. His dark hair is short but unruly, and his pale pink lips curve into a smile when our eyes meet.

"Any idea what's good here?" he asks. I struggle to respond because it's like he stole the breath from my lungs with his good looks and easy smile.

"Uh, I'm not sure. I haven't even looked at the menu yet."

"Let's ask the bartender, yeah? The staff always know the best food on the menu." He gives me a conspiratorial wink, like we're in on some secret together. Like we're . . . here having dinner together?

The temptation to look over my shoulder and make sure he's not talking to someone behind me is nearly overwhelming, but I resist. He's clearly talking to me, I just don't know why.

"Sure," I say, and give him a smile as I set the menu on the bar in front of me.

"Can I get you something to drink, lovely?" the bartender asks me as he approaches, entirely ignoring the hot guy to my right.

My eyes flick to my neighbor before I look back at the bartender and ask, "What's your favorite cocktail on the menu?"

"Most people come to Bermuda and want a Dark 'N' Stormy or a Rum Swizzle," he says, and his biceps flex as he picks up two glasses from a rack that looks like it was just pulled from the dishwasher and uses a towel to dry them off. "You can get a Dark 'N' Stormy anywhere though, so I'd go with the Rum Swizzle as long as you like a fruity cocktail."

"Sure, let's do that," I say. Normally I'd order something boring like a vodka tonic, because I know these fruity drinks are loaded with calories and I try to keep strict tabs on what I eat. I wish I had the kind of body that didn't act like it was in starvation mode, storing every calorie I eat. But I've accepted that counting macros and watching calories are just part of my life if I want to stay even remotely fit.

He turns to leave when the guy beside me calls out, "Yeah, I'd love a Dark 'N' Stormy, thanks for asking."

My chest shakes with laughter as the bartender turns

back toward us, gives him a small salute, and then proceeds down the bar.

"Oh, he *likes* you," I say with a laugh.

"I think he doesn't like that I'm sitting next to you."

"What makes you say that?" I'm not looking for flattery, I'm actually curious.

"Maybe the way he was so obvious about it, calling you lovely, and completely ignoring me even though we were talking when he walked up."

"Hmmm," the noise rattles around in my throat as I glance down the bar where the guy is making our drinks. He glances up, his blond hair flopping back from his face as he looks over and gives me a wink.

"You still not sure he's into you?" the guy next to me says with a laugh.

I turn toward him then, putting my full back to the bartender as I say, "He's not my type."

"Oh yeah, what's your type?"

A little over an hour ago, while I was holed up in my hotel room, AJ sent a text: *Find a hot guy and have a vacation fling, and then never think about Carter again.*

What are the odds he'd sit down right next to me? I send a silent *Thank You* out to the universe, then say, "I like them tall, with dark hair."

He folds his muscular forearms over each other on the bar and then leans toward me, nudging my arm with his elbow. "Where would you ever find someone like that?"

Chapter Four

AIDAN

Was there another seat available at the opposite end of the bar when I arrived? There sure was. But I noticed the way the bartender was eyeing the cute girl currently sitting next to me, and the way she was completely oblivious to him.

It's not in my nature to go for a woman when there's competition. I'll take the sure thing over the girl I've got to fight for any day. There are too many willing women in this world to waste my energy like that. But something told me that this one would be worth it.

"So what are you doing at the bar alone?" I ask her.

"I was meeting people here and their flight was cancelled. You?"

"Same. I heard some guy at the front desk say that any flight arriving after three today was cancelled because of the storm."

She glances across the bar, where the wind is already bending the palm trees. "Think it will get much worse?"

"I mean, I wouldn't want to land a plane in this. But it's not going to destroy the hotel or anything."

"Do you land many planes?" Her voice is teasing, and there's something about the way she lifts her eyebrow, like she's looking to call me out on my bullshit, that makes me want to know her better.

"Not many, no."

"But some?"

"Occasionally."

I have my pilot's license, and I fly just enough to maintain it. It was something I got because I had a fear of flying when I was younger, and my stepdad thought that if I flew a plane myself and understood how everything worked, I'd get over the fear. I did it just to prove to myself that I could, and it worked. Which is a good thing, because once I started playing hockey in college, I was on planes all the time and that hasn't stopped since.

She lifts the Rum Swizzle that the bartender set beside her a few minutes ago, and pulls the straw between her lips. They're full and pouty in a way that has my gaze instantly focused on them. She takes a sip, then lets her lips part so the straw falls against the side of the glass before she looks up, running her tongue along the seam between her lips, and saying, "Wow, that's good."

Does she have any idea how fucking sexy she is? She's not like the toned, practically plastic women who normally chase my teammates and me during the season. The ones who zoom in on you the minute you walk into a bar, giving you "take me home and fuck me" vibes.

No, this woman is soft. Her strawberry blonde hair is up in a clip, but loose tendrils fall on the sides of her face, and she keeps tucking them behind her ears. She's got a light smattering of freckles across her cheeks and the bridge of her nose, and her eyes are a bright blue. She's curvy and lush, and the V of her sundress highlights the crease of her cleavage. But it's her full lips, and the way they turn up at the corners when she talks, that have me mesmerized.

"What do you do when you're not flying planes?" she asks, but it's a question I'd like to avoid.

"I've been out of work for a while with an injury."

She nods, and it's clear that she's curious but not going to push. I don't ask her what she does for work.

"And do you have a name, my poor injured friend?" Her cheeks push up with a smile that lights up her whole face as she taunts me and her shoulders relax. I love the way she smiles, the way her whole body changes when she does. I want to see her do it more often. When I don't respond right away, she says, "Or do I need to guess?"

"Guess my name?" My chuckle rumbles out of me as I lift my drink in a mock toast and say, "Go right ahead."

She tilts her head to the side and chews on her straw before taking another sip of her drink. "Nicholas."

"Why Nicholas?"

"I don't know, you look like you could be Greek? Or maybe from somewhere else in Southern Europe. Nicholas feels like a catchall name that could work anywhere."

My shoulders shake with silent laughter. "Sure, Nicholas works."

"What about me?" she says, with a slow bat of her eyelashes. "What should my name be?"

Oh, this is a fun game she's inviting me to play. No names means no strings, just how I like it.

I take in her creamy skin with a very light tan, and the softness of all her features. Somewhere under all that softness, I suspect there's a toughness to her—not physically, but emotionally. I don't know why, but I feel like she has more life experience than she lets on.

"Amy," I say decisively.

"Why Amy?" Her eyebrows dip as she looks down at her drink.

I reach over and tilt her chin up so she's looking at me. "I don't know, it just felt right."

With my knuckles bent under the point of her chin, my thumb strokes the smooth line of her jaw. I run the pad of my thumb over her lips as a promise of what's to come. The way her breath hitches before her lips curve into a sly smile makes me think we have the whole night ahead of us.

———

"How old do you *think* I am?" she asks, later, in response to my question. Her eyebrows lift and she blinks at me, those dark lashes descending over her blue eyes.

The sensualness of her curves, the air of flirty self-confidence, and the success she's already had in her career make me think she's got to be older than she looks. "Well, with college and an MBA under your belt, not to mention owning your own company . . . My guess is at least thirty?"

She huffs out a small laugh and says, "Sure, thirty sounds good."

It's amazing how many times we've used that "sounds good" phrase over the course of the last hour, as we've chatted and created stories about each other that may or may not be true while eating dinner.

According to her, I'm a thirty-two-year-old dentist named Nicholas, and I live in New York City but my parents are originally from Greece and own a Greek restaurant in Brooklyn. The scars on my left hand are from a freak accident with a dental tool, which kept me out of work for the past few months.

According to me, she's a thirty-year-old from Chicago. I was originally going to go with a flight attendant, until she mentioned the accelerated online MBA she finished over a year ago. Now, I'm trying to work out her background.

"I think you grew up in the suburbs, and then after college you couldn't wait to start your life in the city."

With her elbow resting on the bar, her chin is propped up on her hand, but I don't miss the small smile behind her curled fingers. She tilts her head slightly and says, "I *do* love the city."

"I'm thinking you're in project management. I could see you being very bossy," I say with a wink.

Her tongue curls up as she runs it along her top lip. "I bet you'd like that, wouldn't you?"

It's not something I normally enjoy, but with her, I bet it would be fun. "Maybe we should find out."

Her lips part, but I'm left hanging there, waiting for her response, because the lights go out and the entire restaurant is bathed in darkness. The silence that descends in the room only accentuates the sound of the wind roaring outside.

"Hold on, folks," the bartender, who long ago gave up his

flirtatious endeavors, calls out. "We've got emergency floodlights."

A moment later, the space is lit up with shockingly harsh white lights that have everyone squinting and using their hands to shield their eyes.

"Your servers will be around to have you sign off on your bills with your room numbers," he calls out again, and then the chatter of the remaining diners left lingering late into the evening starts up again.

"Seems like they've done this before," Amy says.

"I'm sure they have. I don't think tropical storms and hurricanes hit Bermuda often, but I'm guessing they prepare for this."

We finish our third round of drinks as we wait for the bartender to bring over the paper slips with our orders, and when we list our room numbers, she's giggling as she says, "Of course we're like three rooms away from each other."

"Here," I say, putting my hand on her lower back when she steps down from the barstool. "I'll walk you back."

She gives me a look that I can only describe as a smirk. "Walk me back to . . . ?"

I press my hand to her lower back, positioning myself on the outside to hopefully block some of the wind and rain, before we step outside. "That's really up to you. I'm sure our rooms are both equally comfortable."

Her chest and neck flush before she turns toward the door. We rush along the side of the building under the covered walkway that leads back to the hotel, trying to avoid the wind that's blowing in sideways while also trying not to slip on the wet concrete.

By the time we make it into the lobby, we're both

drenched but laughing. From there, we head back out under another covered walkway lit by floodlights. All the rooms open to these outdoor walkways, which I'm sure is a great feature when there's not a tropical storm bearing down on the island.

We head up the two flights of stairs which are thankfully encased inside brightly painted stucco walls, and then we're out onto the third-floor hallway. My room comes up first.

"This is me," I say, nodding toward my room. "Want to come in for a nightcap?"

"I think three drinks is enough for you, my lightweight dentist friend," she says with a laugh, as she taps my breastbone with her finger. I understand perfectly. Three drinks is enough for *her*. She's not drunk, but I get the sense that one more drink might send her into that territory.

I capture her hand in mine, holding it to my chest as I pull her closer. "How about just coming in, not for a drink, then?"

"Sounds perfect," she says.

Chapter Five

MORGAN

"Your room is neater than I'd have expected for a single guy," I say, trailing my finger along the row of clothes, hung and organized by garment type, in the closet. "Wait, you *are* single, aren't you?"

The look of horror that must pass over my face has him chuckling. "Very single, I assure you."

"When's the last time you were in a relationship?" I ask casually, walking past him and heading toward the windows at the far side of the room. The curtains are still open but you can't see anything but the river of rain running down the large panes of glass.

"About ten years ago."

That has me spinning back toward him. I know that the identity I crafted for him at the bar is fictitious, but I can't see any obvious reason the real-life man standing in front of me wouldn't be taken. "Why?"

"I'm not really the settling down type."

That has me rolling my eyes. "You and every other guy who makes it to thirty unmarried."

"Hey," he says, his voice dropping so it's low and sensual. "My life isn't conducive to a long-term relationship."

That has me all kinds of curious, but I don't pry. My dentist, Nicholas, absolutely has the kind of life that's conducive to a long-term relationship. So much so that there's no way he wouldn't be married with kids already. Which means *this guy*, whoever he is, is the much better choice for a vacation fling.

"Well, that makes you kind of perfect for right now," I say, stepping toward him. He meets me halfway. "Doesn't it?"

"Whatever you need right now is exactly what I'm here for." He says it with the confidence of a man who always gets what he wants.

I tilt my head up toward him, and a shiver runs up my spine. The air in here is cool and crisp, a sure sign the air-conditioning was still working until the power went out.

"What do you say we get out of these wet clothes?" I don't know where this streak of confidence came from, but it's probably derived from the realization that I can be whomever I want to be right now and never have to see this guy again.

The only light in the room comes from the outdoor flood lights shining through the transom above the door. In the dim space, his hands run up and down my arms, like he's trying to chase away the chill. Then he turns, taking a few quick steps across the room and disappearing into the bathroom before returning with two folded towels in his arms.

Gently and without words, he turns me so my back is to him, and tugs down the zipper on my dress. It crests my shoulders and falls to my waist. He presses his lips to my shoulder and trails kisses along the ridge of muscle to my neck, where he nips at the skin, raising more goose bumps. This time, though, they're from my entire core clenching in anticipation, not the chilly air. I've never done anything like this before.

His hands meet the fabric at my hips as he slides the dress over them, and he hisses out an appreciative "Damn," as the fabric falls to the floor. I'm normally incredibly self-conscious about my body. My skin is firm and taut and damn near perfect, but every part of my body is larger than I'd like.

I want the kind of body positivity that I know most of my generation has, but my teen years were spent hearing "you have such a beautiful face," which—combined with my mom's casual remarks about hitting the gym more often—has left me with deep insecurities that won't go away no matter how ridiculous I know they are.

But, as if I knew he'd appreciate me exactly as I am, it never once occurred to me to be self-conscious in front of this man. The fact that there's very little light in this room helps, too.

He drags the thin straps of my thong over my hips and it also falls to the floor. A gentle tap on my arms and a soft spoken "Up" prompts me to lift my arms so he can wrap a towel around me. I tuck one corner under the edge of the towel where it rests across my breasts and step out of the fabric of the dress pooled at my feet before turning to face him.

Squatting at my feet, the muscular curve of his thighs fully on display between the hem of his khaki shorts and his knees, he fists my dress in his hand and looks up at me with hunger in his eyes. He stands and drapes my dress over the wooden chair at the built-in desk on the wall behind me, before hanging my thong off the corner to dry.

His eyes are on me as his fingers come to the buttons of his collared shirt, and there are butterflies making a ruckus in my belly as I imagine how he'll look without clothes. I can tell he's muscular, but not overly bulky.

"Here." Stepping toward him to close the small distance between us, my voice is huskier than normal when I say, "Let me."

His hands fall to my hips and his fingers curl into the towel as I glance down at his shirt and start undoing the buttons. The sound of our breathing grows heavier in the silence of the room, the occasional howl of the wind and rain outside serving as background noise while my skin heats under his gaze. I feel his eyes on me without even looking at him to confirm it. As I undo the last button and then slide my hands along his chest to push the shirt back over his shoulders, his breath catches and he dips his head to press a kiss to my hair where it meets my forehead.

I've never done this before—never had sex with a stranger—and I consider telling him that. But then he's shrugging out of his shirt and tossing it aside as he undoes his belt and the button and zipper of his shorts with alarming alacrity, before dropping them to the ground.

And then it's my breath that's hitching as I catch sight of him in his boxer briefs. He's only semi-hard and still huge, and I'm wondering whether or not to be insulted that undressing me hasn't gotten him more excited, until he says, "God, you're fucking gorgeous." Then he takes my towel, pulling it free from me.

His touch is unhurried as he gently dries every drop of rain left on my skin. This is not the frantic rush of a man desperate to have sex, it's the practiced hand of someone who knows he has all the time he needs and is planning to maximize every moment.

Once he's done with my body, he wraps a corner of the towel around his fingers and pats my face dry. The motion is tender, as is the way his hand moves to the back of my head, tugging me closer until there's barely a hair's breadth between us.

I'm not sure what it is about the moment that has a lump forming in my throat. Maybe it's the way he's not trying to rush me for his own pleasure. Maybe it's the way his gruff voice and striking looks didn't prepare me for the gentleness of his touch. Maybe it's that having sex with a stranger is new territory.

Whatever it is, it's an emotion I don't really want to deal with right now, so I clear my throat to make the lump go away. His eyebrows dip as he gazes down at me. "Having second thoughts?"

"Not a chance. But you're still soaking wet, and it defeats the purpose of drying me off if you're just going to get me wet again."

The way he snickers in response and says, "You'll be wet, all right," makes me laugh too. It's the break in the heaviness of the moment that I so desperately needed.

Reaching past him, I grab the dry towel where it sits on the end of the bed, and go about drying him off. My heart is pounding as I run the towel over his muscular frame. The white terry cloth is a stark contrast to his deep olive skin and the smattering of dark hair across his chest. When the towel hits his abs, he flexes and lets out a low laugh, and my eyes are stuck on the eight-pack he's sporting, even as he quietly says, "Sorry, I'm a bit ticklish."

I glance up, my eyebrows lifted slightly in surprise. "Are you now?" I don't know why this very natural reaction is surprising to me, but there's something about a guy who's easily over six feet, with ropes of muscle wrapping around his entire body, letting out what's damn near a giggle.

"I am." His fingers skim my sides, from my hips up along the sides of my breasts. "You're not?"

"Not really," I say, conveniently leaving out that my feet are so ticklish that I die laughing any time they're touched. It makes pedicures incredibly awkward.

His voice is gruff when he asks, "Am I dry enough for your liking?"

Realizing that I only dried his arms, chest, and abdomen before I stopped to stare at his body, I reach up to his shoulder and turn him around to dry his back. "I'll let you know when you are."

When my fingers dip into the waistband of his boxers, he lets out a hiss of air, then a groan as my fingers move to the front of his hips so I can pull the elastic out enough that it won't catch on his dick. As soon as I've pushed them down to his knees, he's reaching behind him and grabbing the towel from my hands and pushing his own boxers off his legs. There's no trace of the gentleness he showed me, just quick efficiency as he dries himself off before turning to face me.

As tempted as I am to look down and see if he's as big as I suspect, my stomach flips as nerves take hold. I keep my eyes focused on his chest.

He steps so close that the evidence of his arousal is

pushing against my stomach. When he brings his hands to my neck and gently tips my chin up with his thumbs so I'm forced to look at him, I finally exhale. It's not only longing that I see in his eyes, there's a softness, too. Not nerves, like he probably sees in my eyes, but a tenderness I'm still not expecting, even though he keeps revealing it.

"Are you sure about this?" he asks. "Because it's not too late to change your mind. It's never too late . . ."

I close my eyes, breathing deeply and enjoying the way he smells earthy, like rain, and spicy, like the ginger and rum from his drink. "I'm sure."

"Look at me," he says, and my eyes fly open. "Are you really sure?"

I nod, thankful that he cares enough to ask twice when most men I've been with didn't even bother to ask once.

With his gaze locked on mine, his hands slide down my shoulders, and the sensation of his rough palms moving over my smooth skin sends a shiver of anticipation up my spine. He continues his perusal of my body, his hands skimming the sides of my breasts on their way to my ribs and down to my hips. Then he's pulling me against him, tethering us together as he dips his head and his lips meet mine.

His kiss is slow and gentle, like he's taking care to make sure he's not rushing me, but as I loop my arms around his shoulders, my lips part for him and then he's invading my mouth like he's done waiting. The growl that escapes as our tongues clash has me lifting a leg and wrapping it around his hips. His hands are on the back of my thighs and he lifts me like I weigh nothing.

My core lines up perfectly against his hard length, and I lock my ankles together behind his back, enjoying the way my clit presses against him and how his cock throbs at the contact. He thrusts his hips slightly, just enough to give me pressure on my clit, and my hips move in response until we're a tangled mess of kisses and moans.

With his deep kisses and constant movement against my clit, the pressure builds quickly and my core is clenching, reminding me that it needs to be filled. But then he's turning and taking a step toward the bed before kneeling on it and laying me on my back.

He trails kisses down my jaw and along my neck, and then his hands are behind his back, unhooking my ankles where I've locked them in place. He brings my feet to each side of him on the bed, so my knees are bent and, as he sits up, I'm on full display in front of him.

He trails his thumb along my seam and groans. "So beautiful, and so wet for me."

I want to make a joke, to bring back the easy banter from the bar, but that girl is gone, choked out by the very real anticipation of having sex with this stranger. This stranger who is running his thumb through the slickness coating me and then circling lightly over my clit, just enough to have my back arching off the bed, while he gazes down at me with a devious look in his eye.

While continuing the pattern with his thumb, he bends forward, resting his other elbow at my side and cupping my breast with his large hand. He brings his lips to my nipple and sucks me into his mouth while running the tip of his tongue back and forth across my sensitive peak.

The moan I let out as my back arches off the bed again isn't sexy, it's guttural and raw, and an honest response to the way he's pleasuring me right now. It seems to spur him on, because his thumb plunges into me and leaves me gasping as his teeth rake over my nipple. And then he's kissing his way down the underside of my breast and across my stomach as he scoots his body down the bed.

When his face is almost at the junction of my legs, I startle and half sit, using my elbow to prop myself up. "You . . . you don't have to do that."

He glances up at me. "I want to."

"But—" I've always gotten the sense that guys find going down on girls kind of . . . pointless? Or just something to suffer through before having sex?

"I've been wanting to know what you taste like for *hours*. Ever since you crossed your legs at the bar and your dress slid up your thigh. All I could focus on was the flash of pink lace underwear I saw before you pulled your dress back down. I wanted to know what your legs would feel like, clamped around my head as I brought you right to the edge—"

"Oh god." My breathing is so ragged I nearly have to gasp out the words.

He sits up on bent knees and stretches forward, reaching beyond me. And then he's lifting my upper back and sliding pillows behind me so I'm propped up.

"What are you doing?" I ask.

"I get the sense that this is new for you. So, I want to be able to see you so I can make sure you're enjoying it."

"You actually *want* to do this?"

"Have I not made that clear?"

"I just . . . I didn't think guys liked this."

"I'm sorry," he says, running his thumb along my jawline.

"Real men like to eat. So I don't know who you've been with before, but they clearly weren't men."

My chest shakes with honest laughter because I think he's hit the nail right on the head. I haven't had sex with that many guys before, but they all feel like fucking children compared to the man in front of me.

He pushes my knees apart until I'm wide open in front of him, and even in the darkness, I can see him focus his gaze on my pussy. "Now, if you can stop trying to convince me I don't want to do this, I'd really like to know what you taste like."

I gulp and nod, hoping that he's so focused on my arousal that he doesn't notice the way I get a double chin when I look down at him. But then he's using his thumbs to spread me, and dipping his head to taste me and provide pleasure like I've never experienced. I'm no longer thinking about my own insecurities. I'm thinking about the way he's toying with my clit, sucking it between his lips while he runs his tongue over it, the way he sinks two fingers into me and my entire core contracts around them. And when he moans in response, the vibrations almost send me over the edge.

Then my hips are moving to meet the thrust of his fingers, and his tongue is working my clit with an unimaginable level of expertise. My back arches again as I hiss out, "Yesss." My hands fist the comforter beneath me as my core clenches. I try to relax because I can feel the orgasm right beyond my reach and I'm too tense to let it take over.

As if he knows exactly what I need, he lifts his head. He meets my eyes as his fingers stroke along my inner walls, and says, "I'm going to need you to relax."

I lick my lips, letting myself exhale and release a bit of tension.

"Just like that," he says, his gaze never leaving mine as he puts his thumb on my clit while his fingers continue working me. "Now, are you going to keep breathing so I can go back to tasting you?"

I nod and he smirks in response before dipping his head back to my pussy. But his eyes never leave mine, like he's making sure I stay relaxed enough that I don't hold off my own orgasm.

To be honest, that's what normally happens. I get so in my head about things that it's hard for me to come. But instead of making me feel like it's a problem, here he is, coaching me through it.

When he curls his fingers slightly and increases the pressure on my clit with his tongue, I focus on exhaling instead of holding my breath and tensing up.

That's all it takes for the heat that's built around his fingers to spread through my body like lightning, and this time when my back arches and my limbs go rigid, he moans against me.

I bite down on my lower lip to stifle the moan because otherwise I'm afraid it'll come out as a yell, while the intense waves of pleasure ricochet around my body and my pussy grips his fingers with a rhythm I've never known.

When I finish, my body melting into a puddle of jelly, he smirks at me and says, "Good girl."

I huff out a quiet laugh. "You worked hard for that one."

"Didn't feel like work at all." He scoots up the bed until he's propped on his elbow and hovering above me. "But I'm really going to make *you* work for the next one."

Chapter Six

AIDAN

She's far too cute and mature to be as inexperienced as she seems. It makes me wonder if it's actually inexperience, or just shitty sexual partners, that have left her feeling like I wouldn't want this—wouldn't want *her*—as much as I obviously do.

The way her eyes widen when I tell her I'm going to make her work for the next one is a total turn-on, if I'm being honest. I definitely wasn't getting innocent girl vibes from her at the bar, but here in bed she's like a different person, less confident, but more willing to be bossed around. I'm not sure which version I like better.

"The *next* one?" Her voice is timid and she shakes her head slightly. "I can't really do that . . . twice in a row."

I press a kiss to the bridge of her nose, "We should probably test that theory just to make sure."

"No really, I don't want you to feel bad if I can't come

again. I never can." She looks up at me with those big blue doe eyes, concern written all over her face.

"No pressure at all. I won't feel bad if you don't. And if you do, it'll be a bonus."

Her lips turn up slightly at the corners and I'm relieved to have taken away the pressure she might otherwise feel to "perform." However, I'm *determined* to be the one to show her that she can have multiple orgasms. Since I'll never see her again, I want to be remembered as the first guy who ever made her come twice in a row.

"Okay," she says, and then shocks me by reaching between us and gripping my shaft, sliding her tight fist along me and circling the head of my cock with her hand.

"Fuuuuuck," I grit out the word, unprepared for how amazing this feels. It's been way too long since I've been with anyone. It's just been me and my hand for the last year—not for lack of opportunity—but if there's one thing my stepdad taught me, it's that you don't shit where you eat.

Ember Cove is far too small of a town to sleep around casually. It's a lesson that was hammered into me my first summer in the NHL when I came home for a visit, had sex with a girl I went to high school with, and then ran into her the next morning at the coffee shop *and* the grocery store the following day. I quickly realized I didn't need that level of awkwardness in my life, and I never made that mistake again.

"Hey." The word is tinged with concern, and as my eyes snap back to the gorgeous girl beneath me, I realize her eyebrows are dipped in confusion. "You okay?"

"Never been better," I say, leaning down to kiss her. But

she stops me by moving her free hand to my chest and holding me in place as her eyes scan my face.

"You sure? Because you just looked like you were either completely lost in thought or having an out-of-body experience. And I've barely touched you so I don't think it was the latter."

"Sorry," I chuckle and give her the smile that most women can't resist. Somehow, I don't think it quite works on her. "Got lost in my head thinking about how good that felt."

"You sure you weren't lost in your head picturing someone else?"

Ouch. The fact that that's the first place her mind goes says all it needs to say about her past experiences.

I roll to the side so I'm laying next to her, and pull her with me onto her side so we're face-to-face. I brush my fingers into the tendrils of her hair and push them back off her face, then rest my palm against her cheek.

"I absolutely was *not* picturing someone else. It's . . . just been a while since I've done this."

"Had a one-night stand with a stranger in a hotel room?" Her voice is teasing, as is the way she drags her finger up my chest before curling her hand around the side of my neck.

"Had sex." I don't know why I'm even telling her this, except that I don't want her to feel like she's not good enough and I was picturing someone else instead. "So, your touch? It almost undid me."

"Oh yeah?" That teasing tone she uses makes me want to fuck her so hard she won't be able to find her voice, much less mock me with it. "And what do you look like when you come undone?"

I know my smile is wicked when I say, "I think we should find out."

This time, when my lips meet hers, it's not soft and sweet like after I'd undressed her. No, we're like two people desperate for each other. The drag of her hand along my cock, the taste of her cum still on my tongue as I kiss her, the way her ample tits drag along my chest as she moves to give herself room to stroke me . . . all of it has my body on fire.

Reaching down, I pull her top leg over my hip and find her cunt, still soaked from her orgasm. When my fingers dip inside her, there's no hesitation on her part. She moans into my mouth and presses her hips to meet each thrust, over and over until she's begging me for more.

"Let me grab a condom," I say, rolling away from her. I rip the foil packet and roll it on quickly before I'm back, guiding her onto her back and spreading her legs as I line myself up with her entrance.

I want to be face-to-face for this. I want to see her eyes when I slide into her, watch the way her tits move with each thrust, see her face when she has that second orgasm she doesn't think she can have.

She's tighter than I'm expecting, and the way her lips part in a small gasp as I enter her makes me cautious. I move slowly, letting her adjust.

"I'm not going to break," she says, but I can't tell if she's assuring herself, or me.

Pressing my hips forward slowly, I slide in deeper. "I sure as hell hope not."

But somehow, the thing that runs through my mind is: *I'm more worried about* you *breaking* me.

I have no idea where the thought comes from or what it

even means. This is one night, that's it. For some reason, though, I wish it could be more. Which is ridiculous, because I don't do *more.*

Not even when the flirting is as fun as it was at the bar. Not even with the almost reverent way we're handling each other's bodies. Not even when the sound of her moan, as she wraps her legs behind my back and pulls me deeper, has my dick throbbing for her.

Caring about people is just giving them a chance to leave you.

So tonight will have to be enough, even though that word —*more*—is on repeat in my brain. It's probably just because I liked the way it sounded when she was begging me for more. So that's what I'll give her . . . more of my body.

It's all I'm capable of giving her. There's no way I'm ever doing a relationship again after the last one reinforced what I already knew: the people I love always leave. But if I *were* going to be into someone, it would be someone like her.

She traces the muscles along my spine lightly with her fingertips and then wraps her hands up over my shoulders, pulling me down to her as she tilts her chin up so we're face-to-face.

"Give me a sec," she says, her voice breathy and her eyes wide. Up close like this, with her hair spread beneath her, she looks so goddamn innocent. Smooth, round cheeks with the freckles I can't see in the dark. Wide eyes and full lips.

I press my lips to her forehead. "You doing okay?"

"Just . . . so full."

"We're almost there," I assure her, running my thumb along her jaw.

Her laugh sounds more like a cough she's choked on.

I brush my lips across her forehead again, whispering, "Relax. We're so close, just a little more."

I don't know if she's this tight because it's just how her body was made, or if it's because she's tense or nervous. Either way it feels amazing for me, but I want it to feel good for her, too.

I might be a selfish prick in real life, but I'm incredibly selfless in the bedroom. It takes absolutely no work for me to get off, but where would the pleasure in that be, if my partner didn't also enjoy it? Might as well just come in my fucking hand if my partner isn't also having a great time.

I raise up slightly on one elbow and let my eyes adjust to the difference. I hate not being able to see every inch of her. I wish we had more light, so I could watch the way she responds to my touch, to my movement, as I trail my other hand down her neck, along the ridge of her shoulder, and down the side of her breast.

She sighs as my hand cups her breast, and I lick my lips at the way she spills over my palm and fingers. When I run my thumb over her nipple, she takes a ragged breath and tilts her hips up, taking more of me. It's unbelievably difficult to take it this slow after not having sex for a year, but it's probably the best choice right now, otherwise I'd likely embarrass myself. Because there is absolutely nothing about my own hand that is a suitable substitute for this, right here, with her.

"Yes." She hisses out the word as the pad of my thumb scrapes against her nipple again, and she thrusts her hips up again until I'm fully inside her.

I pause momentarily, making sure she's comfortable. She bites her lower lip as she looks up at me, and raises an eyebrow like she's asking why I stopped. I lean down, brushing my lips across the bridge of her nose. "You good?"

"I'm good. You?"

"Literally never been better."

Her laugh has her breast bouncing against my palm, and my thumb dragging across her nipple again. The laugh turns to a moan, her eyes half-closed as she licks her lips. And when I slide out slowly before pushing back in, her jaw drops open with a breathy sigh, and she opens her eyes again, locking her gaze on me.

The naked lust staring back at me ratchets up my own need, and when she drops her feet to the mattress beside my thighs so she can lift her hips to meet me thrust for thrust, it's hard to hold back. But I'm determined to give her that second orgasm.

My fingers gently twist her nipple until she's moaning again, and then I dip my mouth so my lips brush against her earlobe. "Your little moans are making it hard for me to hold back."

She runs her arms along the sides of my rib cage and then wraps them around my lower back. "So why hold back, then?"

Sliding an arm under her lower back, I lift her lower body enough to slide one knee up and then the other, so I'm sitting on my heels with her thighs draped over my quads. This new position gives me better access to her body, even with me leaning forward above her.

I trail a hand up her abdomen and between her full breasts, spreading my hand against her collarbones and slipping my splayed fingers along either side of her neck and over her jaw, before I push my thumb between her lips. She lightly nips the pad before sucking it into her mouth and swirling her tongue around it. When I bring my thumb back down between our bodies and glide it over and around her throbbing clit, now soaked in her own spit, her back arches farther off the bed.

"Fuck, yes," she whispers, and then I don't let up. I fuck her while lavishing plenty of attention on her clit, working her back toward that orgasm. And when I lean forward, trailing my tongue across her breast, her moans grow louder and more frequent. I suck her nipple into my mouth with a deep pull against my tongue and she comes undone.

The words she's uttering blend together with her moans. Her brows are furrowed above tightly closed eyes and then her lips part in a gasp followed by what looks to be a silent scream. I sit up just enough to watch the pleasure wrack her body while her core pulses around me. The moment her eyes open, I'm scooping her up, pulling her chest against mine to hold her tightly while my own orgasm rips through me. My face is buried in her chest, which muffles the loud groan I let out, and her fingers thread into my hair, holding me to her as my body convulses.

With her body still tightly wrapped around mine, she sighs and says, "I think I'm dead."

The stubble on my chin and cheeks scrapes lightly against her breasts, and I can't contain my smile. "You felt very much alive to me."

"Nope," she says, her body softening to the point she feels limp. When I lift my head, her eyes are closed. "Pretty sure that orgasm killed me."

"As the second one should," I whisper, gently lifting her off my lap and laying her back on my bed. Her breathing is even and slow when I get up to dispose of the condom, and when I return from the bathroom, she's curled onto her side right in the middle of the bed.

I don't cuddle after sex or spend the night with women because that always leads to expectations of something in the future—expectations I'm not willing to meet. I should scoot her over or lie on the far edge of the bed. But I don't. I lie on my side next to her, slipping my arm around her almost protectively as I pull her against me and let myself drift off to sleep beside her.

———

The knocking on my door startles me out of a deep sleep, and I'm sitting up almost before I've even opened my eyes. I look around in confusion at my empty hotel room. Amy's no longer in my bed. Her dress and underwear are no longer hanging on the chair. And the level of disappointment I feel is shocking. Her slipping out while I was still asleep should be a relief—the perfect non-awkward ending to a night of no-strings sex.

There's another knock and I glance at my phone to check the time, but it's dead. I slip on a pair of shorts and pad across the rug to the tiled hallway in front of the door. Peeking through the peephole, I find Max's smiling face.

"C'mon, Danny." His voice is muffled by the door. "Daylight's ticking." For an older guy, Max has nearly limitless energy. Must be why each of his new wives gets younger and younger.

I swing the door open to find him standing there in khaki

shorts—the unofficial uniform of Bermuda—and a polo shirt.

"You don't look ready for golf."

"You can't possibly be serious. You just landed and you still want to try to make that tee time?"

"I'm getting married tonight, but first, I'm spending the day at my favorite place with my favorite person."

I lean against the doorframe, crossing my arms over my bare chest. "Shouldn't your bride be your favorite person?"

"I promised you when your dad died that you'd always be my favorite person."

"I'm not a kid anymore," I say with a sigh. Max does not truly seem to grasp this fact. "I don't need to be your favorite person."

"Too bad." He reaches up and ruffles my already messy hair. "You still are."

"Well I don't want to crush your dream, but we got at least six inches of rain overnight. There's no way the course is open."

"But the driving range is." He says, like it's the best news he's ever gotten the privilege of delivering. Given his job as a renowned plastic surgeon, that seems unlikely. "C'mon, put some clothes on and let's go spend the day together."

See, this is the thing about Max. You can't possibly *not* like him. Even when he wakes you up from a dead sleep after you stayed up half the night fucking a girl you may never forget, and you just want to go back to bed but he's not letting you . . . you still can't not like him.

Trust me, I've tried.

Chapter Seven

MORGAN

My eyes burn when I crack them open to find bright light streaming through my windows. I'm asleep on top of my bed, and must have been too tired or too hot to get under the covers when I snuck back to my own room in the early hours of the morning.

There's pounding on my door, as though someone has knocked a few times and is frustrated that I haven't answered yet. A small part of me worries it might be Nicholas, or whoever he really is, upset that I snuck out of his room. But when I push myself off the bed and look through the peephole in the hotel room door, my mom stands there looking equal parts peppy and annoyed.

I guess her flight got in okay this morning. I swing open the door and force a bright smile onto my face. "Hi, Mom!"

She lets out a deep sigh as she sweeps her highlighted blonde hair off her shoulder. "Oh good, she lives." Her eyes scan my face and track down my body, taking in my rumpled dress from last night that I never changed out of. "Rough night?"

"Sort of. I got caught in the rain coming back from dinner, and didn't get much sleep because of the storm." Damn, that lie came a little too easy. At least it's partially true.

"That's okay, our spa day and a good makeup artist will do wonders for those bags under your eyes and your puffy face."

The way she says it so cheerfully, like she's trying to convince herself that she can somehow change the way I look so I don't ruin her wedding photos, is an instant reminder of why I see her as infrequently as possible.

At least this time, with her flight delay and the wedding happening tonight, the weekend will be over before I know it. I should be thanking the weather gods for their intervention, because last night was *exactly* what I needed. And if my phone hadn't died in the middle of the night with no way to charge it, I'd text AJ and tell her she was absolutely right about having a vacation fling.

Best sex of my life, with a hot guy I'll never see again and who therefore can't disappoint me. Less than twenty-four hours into the weekend, and I'm already winning.

"With the power outage, is the spa even open?" I ask. Honestly, I hope that it is because my whole body is sore from last night's activities, and the massage my mom said she booked sounds perfect.

"It is," she confirms. "They have a generator, and they're expecting power to be restored to the rest of the hotel before tonight, so it shouldn't impact our wedding dinner. I did have to talk to the wedding planner when I arrived about the condition of the outdoor space, though. It's absolutely unacceptable to expect that I'll be getting married with palm fronds and flower buds littering the ground."

I try not to laugh, I really do. But the amused giggle slips out anyway. My mom's eyes narrow in response.

"Sorry, it's just that, you know . . . tropical storm cleanup probably takes a while."

"It wasn't like it was a hurricane," she says with a dramatic eye roll as she walks into my room, forcing me to step back in the narrow hallway to accommodate her entrance. "I still can't believe they cancelled our flight and then we arrived to the resort looking like this."

"Well, I certainly hope they apologized for the inconvenience," I say as I close the door. When I turn to face her, she's looking at me like she's not sure if I'm being sarcastic or if I genuinely expected either the airline or the hotel to apologize that a tropical storm dared to interrupt my mother's plans.

"One would think," she says, then sighs. "Why don't you get changed and clean yourself up so we can head to the spa."

I try not to shake my head as I gather up a change of undergarments and clothes and head into the bathroom. I used to let my mom, and her small, cutting remarks—like *rough night* and *bags under your eyes* and *clean yourself up*—get to me. It's not like anything she's said isn't true, it's that the remarks are unnecessary. Looking in the bathroom mirror, I can see how much of a wreck I am. I didn't need her commentary on it.

At least the fact that she's always made negative comments about my appearance taught me to do better. I'd never want to make anyone feel the way my mom constantly makes me feel.

Two more days.

"You look beautiful," my mom says, as we stand under the overhang of the open bar. Now that it's not raining, the glass doors have all been slid open along a huge track that leaves two entire sides of the bar wide open, nothing but the spectacular view of the bay beyond the balcony. The bright turquoise water becomes a lighter aqua as it approaches the shore and meets the pale pink sands that Bermuda is famous for.

"Thanks," I say, truly grateful that she didn't follow up with a remark about how much better I look now that a hairstylist and makeup artist have gotten their hands on me.

The hotel's wedding planner standing next to my mom curves her hand behind her ear and takes a few steps forward to peek over the balcony that runs along the edge of the room.

"There's the music, and it looks like we're ready to go. Morgan, you're going to go first. Be careful on the wooden path that leads along the cliffside because it may still be a bit slippery from all the rain. And then once you walk under the moon gate, you can take your place to the left of the officiant. Make sure to leave room for your mom. She'll follow about thirty seconds behind you."

I roll my shoulders, which are sore from the way the massage therapist tried to work the knots out while simultaneously asking me why I was so tense.

"Will do," I say. I'm so flipping proud of myself at how I resist the urge to tell her how familiar I am with this process since it's the third time I've done this with my mom.

I give my mom a small, encouraging smile and then turn to walk down the path. Even though this experience is old hat at this point, it's the first time I will be meeting my future stepfather and stepbrother at the wedding itself. Even if my mom's flight hadn't been delayed a day, meeting them the evening before the wedding would still have been weird.

I navigate the beginning of the wooden path carefully so I don't slip in my heels. Had I known I'd be traversing slick wooden slats, I wouldn't have chosen three-inch heels with a single wide fabric strap across my toes.

The palm trees block my view of the deck until I'm at the bottom of the walkway. In front of me is one of the circular stone archways, or moon gates, that are built around Bermuda. Beyond it, I see the officiant standing at the farthest point of the round deck, and to the right of her I see the tan linen pants and matching brown shoes of two men, but their bodies are blocked by the thick stone arch and the flowering hibiscus plants that extend from the opening back around the edge of round deck where the wedding will take place.

Beyond them, there's nothing but the beautiful water with shades of blue I'd never seen before coming to this island. It's so serene, it's hard to imagine that a tropical storm blew through here last night.

As I take the final step to the moon gate, a chill runs up my spine and trails its tentacles along my skin. But the air is humid and hot, the soft breeze too warm to cause a chill.

It was probably a quick shot of anxiety, I tell myself,

because it's a familiar enough sensation. The nerves about meeting my new stepfamily, combined with my resentment at having to give up the long weekend that could have been spent back in Boston with friends, is enough to trigger that feeling.

Luckily, it's fast and fleeting, and by the time I walk under the stone arch, I'm composed as I turn my head to the right to give my stepdad and his son a smile. But my smile freezes in place, awkward and rigid, as I struggle to breathe.

Because next to the handsome man with silver hair, who I already know is my mom's future husband, Max Heinberg, stands the man I spent last night with. Who is apparently *not* a dentist named Nicholas, and is in fact my new stepbrother, Danny.

What. The. Actual. Fuck?

The adrenaline rush hits my body as the realization takes hold. My skin flushes, I break out in a cold sweat, and the desire to run nearly overwhelms me.

Instead, I veer off to the left where I know I'm supposed to stand. When it comes to weddings, I've done this way too many times to mess up. At this point, I'm a goddamn professional.

I am *not* going to ruin my mom's wedding with a major freakout. No, I'll be too busy quietly dying inside. With any luck, I'll be fully deceased by the time this ceremony is over, so I'll never have to deal with the realization that last night, I had sex with my future stepbrother.

Chapter Eight

AIDAN

My gaze is focused on the moon gate while a string quartet just in front of it plays the opening notes of a song, and I focus on not letting any emotions seep into my expression. I know myself well enough to know that the resting bitch face comes out if I'm not careful, and the last thing I need is to ruin the wedding pictures by looking pissed off during the ceremony.

There is absolutely no doubt that I do not want to be here. My stepdad knows this; I can tell it by the way he puts his hand on my shoulder and gives it a squeeze. I glance over at him, giving him a nod and hoping it conveys that I'm here for him, while hiding that I don't want to be.

It's not that I don't want to see him happy. That's actually all I want. But I want that happiness to come with someone who doesn't look like my mom. I want him to settle down with that person because he loves *her,* not because he's still in love with the woman she looks like.

I don't want him to forget my mom and the years they shared together. But I do want him to move on, so he can be happy in the present.

I glance back toward the moon gate, and my gaze travels up to the bar that's perched at the edge of the cliff. God, I wish I could rewind time and go back to last night when I sat down next to "Amy."

I'd give anything to relive last night. To spend hours exploring her body, to relish being with a woman for the first time in so long. Even knowing I'd still end up here, where I very much do not want to be.

Even though we went into it knowing it was a one-time thing, last night was anything *but* casual sex. There was a connection there I haven't felt since Hayley. My teeth involuntarily clench as I try to clear my thoughts. She is the last person I want to think about right now.

At the top of the hill I notice two women standing on the deck that surrounds the bar. One is in a dark blue dress, her hair pulled back off her face, with a clipboard in her hand. The other is in a white knee-length, form-fitting dress with a short veil attached to her blonde hair, blowing in the gentle breeze.

Something about this whole wedding feels off. Max normally introduces me to the women he's dating well before he actually proposes. This time though, he proposed within months of them going on their first date. If their flight hadn't been cancelled, last night would have been the first time I met her—in person, at least. I don't really count the few video calls with Max, where Anne popped into the frame to say hello, as "meeting" her.

If she wasn't standing there in a white dress and a veil, I

wouldn't even have recognized her. That's how little time I've spent talking to her.

My mind goes, again, back to the woman from last night. I wonder if I can get out of the post-wedding dinner early and find her? I know what her room number is, but I'm not quite desperate enough to go knock on her door. Accidentally running into her would be perfect. Maybe I can park myself in the lobby with my phone, pretending like I'm waiting for someone, and run into her there.

I'm so engrossed in the memory of her, and the way it feels like she's possessed my thoughts, that when I catch a glimpse of strawberry blonde hair just above the hibiscus flowers and beyond the moon gate, I almost think I've conjured her out of thin air.

It can't be her, though. That wouldn't make any sense.

The curve of her hip, clothed in flowing pink fabric, comes into view, followed by a perfect pair of breasts squeezed together in the low-cut dress above a small cluster of flowers held at her waist. It's then I realize I'd know that body anywhere—in the darkness, in the light . . . maybe even if I was blind.

What the hell is she doing here?

And then the pieces fall into place. Our parents' cancelled flight, us both ending up at the bar alone. Going back to my hotel room together, the way my bed still smelled like her this morning. Those flowers in her hand as she steps beneath the stone archway, the smile that freezes on her face as she glances toward us, the absolute panic in her eyes.

Oh fuck, did I just sleep with my stepsister?

———

The ceremony goes by in a blur. Aside from remembering to hand Max the rings, I'm not sure I process any part of what happens, because I'm way too focused on *her*.

I know her name is Morgan, but I just want her to be Amy.

I want her to stop avoiding eye contact.

I want to know if she's freaking out like I am.

I want to know if she's filled with regret right now.

I *should* be filled with regret, but honestly, the memories of us together last night that are flashing through my mind don't lead me anywhere near regret . . . they fill me with longing. Which is absolutely the last thing I should be feeling right now.

I watch as our parents finally kiss at the end of the ceremony, and my gaze slips past them to Morgan, whose cheeks turn pink as her eyes meet mine. She glances away so quickly I can't read her expression, and I wonder for a moment what she saw in mine.

But then the recessional music starts up, and the officiant congratulates our parents. Max turns to shake my hand, and then Anne turns and gives me a hug while Max hugs Morgan.

We didn't talk about this part—about whether the ceremony would just end here, or whether I was supposed to walk my stepsister back up the walkway to the hotel. Desperate to have a few moments to talk to her without our parents around, I opt for the latter, hoping she follows my lead.

Stepping forward, I hold my elbow out, lifting my eyebrows at her to indicate we're about to exit together. Like a dutiful bridesmaid, she steps up next to me, sets her hand in the crook of my elbow, and we step away from my parents.

"*What. The. Fuck?*" she whispers, with added emphasis on each individual word.

I can't help but chuckle at the way her thoughts mirror my own. But instead of lightening the mood, my chuckle has her fingers curling and her nails digging into my arm.

"Did you know who I was when you sat down next to me at the bar last night?" Her words are an angry stream as she glances up at me.

"Why the fuck would I have hit on you if I knew you were going to be my stepsister?" I keep my words low so we can't be heard over the music, but they come out sounding gruff like I'm annoyed. I'm not annoyed, I'm enthralled.

"Who knows why guys do half the perverted shit they do?" She shakes her head. Her lips part, and I'm anxious to hear what she'll say next, but from behind us, Max's amused voice rings out.

"Hey kiddos, you don't have to run to dinner. They'll hold the table for us."

I groan, thinking how painfully awkward this night is about to get.

Chapter Nine

MORGAN

Accidentally saying "orgasm" instead of "organism" to my hot lab partner during my college biology class. Walking in on my boyfriend getting a blow job from my roommate senior year. Showing up to my first day of work after college only to discover I had a pair of underwear stuck to the back of my skirt. Hitting on my business school professor, who was giving me all the right signs, only for him to tell me I was way too young for him. Trying to catch the eye of a cute guy at a coffee shop, running into a post with a hot cup of coffee in my hand, and getting first-degree burns on my chest instead.

Those are only *some* of the highlights in the catalog of awkward or embarrassing things that have happened to me over the past decade. But nothing, and I mean absolutely nothing, will *ever* top sitting next to my one-night stand at the post-wedding dinner for our parents.

"So, when are you officially headed back to work?" Max

asks Danny, seemingly trying to steer the conversation into familiar territory given that every time anyone asks him something, Danny responds with clipped, one-word answers.

His hand flexes open and his fingers splay wide on top of his beige linen trousers beneath the table. We're seated so close our knees would be touching if I hadn't crossed my legs to prevent it.

"I'll catch you up later," Danny says, and my gaze flits up to his face. I'm surprised that he didn't respond with "yes" or "no" given the stilted conversation thus far. His casual tone reminds me so much more of the man I got to know last night than this rigid and unengaged person I've sat next to for the past fifteen minutes. "Morgan and I chatted for a bit at the bar last night," he continues. Heat rises on my neck and spreads up to my cheeks as he says my name. "I don't want to bore her by repeating myself."

He glances at me then, and our eyes lock before his gaze slips down my face and to my quickly reddening neck. When he continues his perusal down toward my chest, the flush spreads.

I rest the elbow closest to him on the table, bringing my fist under my chin, to block his view. All I can think of right now is there's not much of a difference between how he looked at me last night and how he's looking at me right now —and I need to shut that down.

Stepbrother, I remind myself.

"Oh look, Max," my mom says, excitement lacing her voice as she sets her menu down on the table, snapping our attention and focus back to her. "They have oysters on the half shell. Let's get some! Morgan? Danny? Do you guys like oysters?"

"Not a fan," Danny says.

I sigh. "I'm deathly allergic to shellfish . . . remember?"

"Oh my gosh, of course!" she says, and playfully bonks her forehead with her palm as if we didn't have this conversation at the engagement party before her *last* wedding, when she'd given me an appetizer that included chopped clams and almost killed me. A shot of epinephrine and a trip to the emergency room were not how I planned to spend that evening. "Well, no oysters for you then!"

I focus on relaxing my shoulders because I can tell I've tensed up at the memory of those events . . . which I obviously can't share with our present company.

"Should we even get oysters if Morgan's allergic?" Danny asks, concern lacing his tone.

"Well, we're not going to force feed them to her," my mom says with a giggle that borders on maniacal—a sure sign she's uncomfortable. Mom does not like being called out like this, no matter how kindly. "You're fine with *other* people eating them, right, honey?"

"Sure, let's just keep them away from me," I say with a lightness I don't feel.

What I *do* feel is the weight of Danny's gaze on me, like he recognizes the wrongness of this whole conversation—of my mom not knowing that I'm allergic to shellfish and insisting they be served on a table I'm eating at—and wants to know if I'm actually okay with it.

The thought of him caring more for my well-being than my own mother has a lump forming in my throat, and I have to remind myself that not wanting me to die is *not* the same as actually caring. I've been known to glom onto a little detail like that and conflate it in my mind to mean something it doesn't. And that's not a road I'm willing to go down again . . . especially not now, with my stepbrother.

Fuck my life.

My friends always say I have the most shit luck of anyone they've ever known, and I'm sure they'd find this whole thing hysterical. Hell, if it were happening to anyone *but* me, I'd probably find it funny, too.

Danny must mistake the slight shake of my shoulders as I try to hold the laughter in for something else, because he runs his knuckles along my outer thigh beneath the table. When I glance at him, his eyes are narrowed on me. "You sure?"

"Positive," I say, shifting in my chair so his hand falls away. The glide of his knuckles along the thin fabric of my bridesmaid dress brings back too many memories of last night, and dinner with our parents is the last place I want to be when envisioning us together.

The waiter returns to take our order, and we fall into conversation that lasts through dinner, most of which my mom dominates. Max seems content to let her talk, and maybe he's even amused by her vivaciousness. Mom can be great in small doses. I'm curious to see what happens when that dose builds up to toxic levels, and what happens to their relationship when it does.

My mom wasn't always like this. She was always a bit insecure and clingy, always needing external validation. My childhood was a happy one, though.

I was ten years old and had just hit puberty when things started to shift between my parents. At the time, I was incredibly focused on how my body was changing, how my friends' opinions of me seemed to be shifting as my body developed before theirs, and how my mom was suddenly so critical of me. So maybe I wasn't attuned enough to figure out *why* things changed between my parents—why my mom suddenly became too much for my dad to deal with—right then.

"What do you think, Morgan?" Mom asks, and my gaze snaps to her. Luckily, I think she can tell that I was lost in my own thoughts, because she prompts me, "Boating tomorrow sounds fun, right?"

"Sure," I say through a fake smile, not even a little surprised she's forgotten that I'm terrified of the open water. I don't want to remind her because, after the oysters, I'm afraid I'll make her look bad in front of her new husband. "I love boats."

I can tell from her bright smile that adding my love of boats doesn't trigger any memories for her. Next to me, I feel, rather than see, Danny tense up, like he can tell I'm lying even though my mom has no clue.

"It's not a very big boat," he says, "we'll just take it over to St. George's. Then there's a really nice private beach we can go to, and a shipwreck we can snorkel around if we want. It's all within the bay, so the water is pretty calm."

"Sounds lovely," I say, hoping my voice doesn't convey my anxiety. As long as there are life vests and I can see the shore, I'll be fine.

"Perfect way to spend your twenty-seventh birthday, right?" Mom says.

I clear my throat. "Twenty-eighth."

Max laughs and rubs my mom's shoulder, saying, "There's

no way anyone would believe you have a twenty-seven-year-old daughter, sweetie, much less one who is twenty-eight." The irony of him being her plastic surgeon is probably not lost on anyone at the table.

In fact, if Danny's clenched jaw is any indication, I'd say he hasn't missed the irony at all. I watch him as he looks at our parents together, and it occurs to me then that his name doesn't fit him at all.

Danny is a happy-go-lucky name. Maybe that name would have felt right last night—though not half as well as Nicholas, if you ask me.

But tonight? This rigid man, who seems to alternate between pissed off and concerned, does not seem like a Danny. There's a darkness there, an underlying resentment, that I didn't see last night. I wonder if he has the same kind of relationship with his dad that I have with my mom? Maybe this is as hard for him as it is for me?

Mom's eyes flit back and forth between us as she takes her napkin from her lap and sets it on her empty plate. "Who feels like a little dancing? There's a club at the hotel right up the road."

A laugh escapes even though I don't mean it to. Mom's always accused me of being an "old soul," and I always remind her that someone has to be. Sometimes I wish I could be a free spirit like she is. But in my mind, "free spirit" is just a polite way to say "selfish." The kind of person who puts their wants above everyone else's needs, even their own child's.

"I wish I had the energy for that," I say. "You kids have fun."

Mom laughs and says, "We're the kids?"

Max presses a kiss to my mom's temple and says, "You make me feel like a kid again."

Once again, I wonder how long he'll be enamored with that aspect of her before he realizes she's technically an adult, but never really grew up. My best guess is that Max is nearing sixty. He's already raised his son, and while my mom might make him feel young right now, he'll tire of her eventually.

Six months. I give it until between Valentine's Day and St. Patrick's Day before it all falls apart. Unfortunately, I've gotten exceptionally accurate in predicting these things.

"I'm out too," Danny says from beside me.

"Well, if you two are going to be complete downers," Mom says with a giggle, "we'll just have to go without you. C'mon, Max," she says, pulling him up, "take me dancing."

"Charge dinner to my room," Max says to Danny as my mom pulls him away.

"My god," Danny mutters as he watches them make a spectacle of leaving. My mom is holding Max's hand up above their heads. Her white dress and her bouquet, and his boutonniere pinned to his lapel, make it clear they just got married. Everyone around them is clapping as they make their exit.

"They're going to be *loads* of fun this weekend," I deadpan, and he huffs out a laugh in response.

"Are we going to talk about what happened last night, in light of us now being related?" he asks as the waiter approaches the table and puts the bill in Danny's outstretched hand.

I don't know how I didn't anticipate this question. I guess

I just figured he'd spend this weekend pretending like nothing had happened, the same way I planned to.

"We're going to forget that happened," I say. *"In light of us now being related."*

He glances over at me with a smirk as he picks up the pen, writes down what I know to be *his* room number, and scrawls an illegible scribble for a signature.

"You're going to forget, huh?" He lifts an eyebrow. "I'd like to see you try."

He's not wrong that forgetting the best sex of my life would be difficult, but it's the cockiness that grates at me—the way he casually assumes that I've never had anything better, with anyone else. Joke's on him though, because the bar is extremely low.

"It's already forgotten," I say, standing as I drop my napkin on the chair, pick up my phone, and hightail it out of the restaurant so quickly I'm hoping he can't catch up.

Joke's on me this time, though, because when I glance over my shoulder, he's sitting at the table. He's not trying to catch me, and he's amused that I'm running.

Chapter Ten

AIDAN

I don't know what I regret most: letting her walk away or sleeping with her in the first place. Why does the first person I'm truly attracted to in *years* have to be my fucking stepsister?

I sit at the table for a few minutes after she turns to make sure I'm not following her. I don't want to be a creep about it, and with my fast stride and our rooms being only a few doors away, I would easily catch up to her if I didn't wait it out. I have no idea if she'd want that or not, but it's better for both of us if I don't find out.

When I finally leave the restaurant to return to my room ten minutes later, I realize that no one ever mentioned to Morgan when the boat is leaving in the morning. I know that Max knows, so I'm not worried about him and Anne getting there on time. But does Morgan even have any idea where to meet us, or when?

Her mom will probably tell her, I assure myself as I approach her room. And as much as I feel like it's none of my business, I've gotten a good sense of who Anne is and what her priorities are over the past few hours. And for some reason, Morgan is not on that list. With cell service still out on the island, it's not like her mom can text her about it.

The mental image of Morgan waking up to an annoyed knock on her door, only to find out she's supposed to be on the boat already, has me passing my room and coming to a stop outside hers.

She pulls the door open with confusion on her face, and a thin tank top and a tiny pair of shorts hugging her curves. *Fuck.* Everything about her body is a turn-on for me. The way every inch of her soft skin practically glows, the deep crease between her tits, her wide hips expanding from her narrower waist, and the way her thighs are thick and smooth.

I try not to let the memory of them wrapped around my head last night totally cloud my judgment, but seeing her braless and in barely any clothes has me forgetting what I'm doing here. All my brain can think about right now is how much my body wants hers.

"Yes?" she asks, crossing her arms over her chest to hide the fact that her nipples are hard and fairly visible through the thin fabric. Unfortunately, all that does is emphasize her cleavage.

And now, my dick is hard just from the sight of her standing here, wearing her pajamas. I try to remember the last time I felt this way about anyone—not just the physical attraction, but the desire to be in her presence—but I come up empty-handed. There hasn't been a single person since my college relationship fell apart.

"Did you really knock on my door just so you could stand here scowling at me?"

God, I love that annoyed tone. Flirting with her at the bar last night was fun, but I bet fighting with her would be even better.

I shove my hands in my pockets, hoping that pushing the fabric forward will hide the tent in my pants. "I didn't know if you knew when and where we're meeting tomorrow morning?"

"Morning?" she says with a heavy sigh.

"Yeah, the marina said they usually get thunderstorms in the afternoon since it's summer, so I booked the boat starting in the morning."

She tilts her head as she studies me. "*You* booked it?"

"Yeah. Sort of as a wedding gift. Thought it would be something nice to do that wasn't just sitting at the pool or the beach all day, listening to our parents yap. I've . . . done this a few times."

I don't know what makes me offer that up, since I have no idea if she knows this is my stepdad's third marriage since my mom died.

She huffs out a laugh. "Yeah, I've done this a few times, too. Three, to be exact."

She leans against the doorframe, one eyebrow lifted like she's waiting for me to tell her how many times Max has been married. This feels like something we should have known about our new stepparents before the day of the wedding.

"Also three."

Her eyebrows shoot up into high arches on her forehead

and she clears her throat. "Okay, so what time does the boat leave tomorrow?"

"We're pulling out from the dock at nine."

"Why so early?" The question is practically a groan.

I chuckle at that. I got so used to being up by five every morning for hockey practices when I was a teenager and in college that, even as an adult, I have a hard time sleeping much later, unless I'm up really late, like last night. "Not a morning person?"

"With enough caffeine, I can be. Otherwise, no."

"I'll make sure we're stocked with caffeine," I say. I should turn and leave, but for some reason, I can't make my feet move. Even with this borderline hostility that's rolling off her right now, I just want to spend more time with her. So, I lift my hand and rest it against the top frame of the door, leaning into her space. I don't miss the shiver that shakes her shoulders or the way goose bumps prickle the skin across her chest and her upper arms. "Want to invite me in?"

"You're my stepbrother," she says, the last word leaving her mouth in disgust.

"All the more reason we should get to know each other better." I give her a wink, and now she looks even more pissed off. Why do I like that so much? I just want to keep annoying her to see what her reaction will be. It's juvenile, but I don't care.

"I think we did plenty of getting to know each other last night," she says, and reaches for the door but I stop it with my free hand.

"I disagree. Why are you so hostile right now?" I say it as if I can't tell she's deeply uncomfortable with the turn things have taken here, as if I'm not intentionally trying to push her just to see how she responds.

"Oh, I'm sorry. Is there some sort of *how to act after you accidentally fuck your stepbrother* playbook I should be following?"

"It's not like our parents will be married for long," I say. "He'll drop your mom in a few months when he realizes she's not a suitable replacement for *my* mom."

I hear how wrong that sounds the minute it's out of my mouth, and the horrified look on her face confirms that it was not the right thing to say. No matter how much Morgan doesn't seem to like her mom, and even though it seems like her mom puts her dead last, Anne's still her mom.

So when she reaches out, plants her hand on my chest, and pushes me backward while muttering "Goodnight, Danny," I don't fight her on it. Instead, I head to my room, trying to work out whether I should say something to make it right when I see her tomorrow.

———

The way Morgan storms down the limestone steps built into the hillside above the marina has me pressing my lips together to hide a smile. She's pissed off and not hiding it well. At least she's not late. In fact, she's made it here before our parents, which is saying something since Max's default mode is "on time is late."

Her strawberry blonde hair is back in a clip like it was that night at the bar, and she's wearing oversized sunglasses. Her white knit cover-up is made up of loosely linked stitches that hide nothing beneath, and the tie at the center leaves a deep V from her collarbone to her waist completely open, exposing the yellow string bikini beneath. Every step she takes down those stairs has her tits bouncing and, glancing around, I see that I'm not the only guy who's noticed. In fact, almost everyone is staring at her, which makes me feel unreasonably territorial.

I want to call out and tell them all to put their tongues back in their mouths, but instead, I turn away to adjust myself. I need to get my shit together before she or our parents notice me sporting a semi every time I so much as look at her.

But fuck, did she really have to show up here looking so gorgeous? And why didn't I anticipate how difficult it would be to see her in a bathing suit, knowing what she looks like naked?

I turn back toward her as she walks down the dock, but instead of taking the small step from the wooden platform onto the boat deck, she stops.

"What's wrong?" I ask.

She takes a deep breath, exhaling as she pushes her sunglasses on top of her head and squints against the bright sunlight that shimmers off the turquoise water. She crosses her arms over her chest as she says, "Both our parents have food poisoning."

A laugh bursts out of me, and her shoulders shake as she tries to hold hers in. "Think it was the raw oysters?"

"Probably. And the smell that was coming from their room when I stopped by on my way here . . . " She makes a gagging noise. "So anyway, I just wanted to tell you they aren't coming. So I'm going back up there," she nods toward the cliffs, "and taking a nap by the pool."

I reach out before she can turn, circling her wrist. "No fucking way. This island is far too beautiful to sit by a pool when you could be out exploring."

"Danny." She lets out a deep sigh. "I just want to relax at the pool."

Without thinking, I step up onto the dock, bend and throw her over my shoulder, then turn back toward the boat. She squeals and struggles against me, demanding that I put her down.

"Stop squirming or you're going to fall in," I say as I step back onto the boat, but our combined weight all at once has it rocking violently.

She gasps and freezes, and I step to the center of the boat to balance the weight. Once we stop rocking, I set her on her feet and push her backward into one of the white seats.

"Asshole," she mutters.

"Brat," I spit right back, but the word has no bite. Why do I like this side of her so much?

"You didn't have to manhandle me. I could have easily gotten on this boat myself."

"Yeah, when you turned to walk away, it *really* seemed like you were getting on the boat," I say, turning away to untie the rope from the cleat at the edge of the dock. I push off, then head to the helm and sit in the seat behind her so I can start the motor.

"Where are the life jackets?" she asks right before the engine roars to life.

"Every seat has one under it, just lift the part you're sitting on," I say, remembering how the guy who rented me the boat showed me that along with some other features before she arrived. "Wait," I say as the boat slowly moves away from the dock. "Why do you need a life vest? Can you not swim?"

"I can swim. I just hate boats."

"Oh, so that *was* sarcasm I heard in your voice last night?" I feel a bit bad about throwing her over my shoulder and bringing her onto the boat if she's scared. At the same time, I'm selfishly not willing to let her get off. Instead, I'll help her stay comfortable so she realizes that boats are not, in fact, scary.

"I guess." Her cheeks get a little pink, like she's embarrassed she wasn't better at hiding it, or that her mom didn't pick up on her hints. Does Anne actually know *anything* about her daughter? I think about how close Max and I are, and wonder how I'm closer to my stepdad than she is to her own mother.

"So, let me help you get over that fear."

"I didn't say I was *afraid* of boats, I said that I don't like them."

"Okay," I say, wondering if there's actually any difference. I keep the boat at a slow pace as we head toward the channel that will take us over to St. George's, the small town that was the site of the first permanent British settlement in Bermuda. "Tell me what you don't like about them."

"I don't like that when I get off a boat, it feels like I'm still on it and then I feel seasick."

"That happens to me too," I admit. "I've got Dramamine in my bag. It helps a ton. What else?"

She looks away and then says, "I don't like being too far from land. I want to know that if something happened, I could swim back to shore."

"Okay, we'll stay close to the shore."

"No." The shake of her head has some of her hair falling loose from her clip and hanging to frame her face. "I don't want to ruin the experience."

"This is a twenty-foot Boston Whaler with a single engine. It's not like we're taking this thing out on the open ocean. We're just going to take it up the channel to St. George's Harbour, walk around the town a bit, then come back to Castle Harbour. There's a beach out on Frick's Point that's only accessible by boat unless you own one of the mansions on the cliffs above it. And there's a shipwreck not too far from there, if you're feeling adventurous. We'll never be more than swimming distance from shore, and we're in a protected bay the whole time. You're safe. I promise."

She glances over at me, her eyebrows dipping as she likely tries to work out why I threw her over my shoulder and made her come with me, and why I'm now trying to reassure her. I don't really want her to know that it's because getting to spend the whole day, just with her, has already made the second half of this trip so much better than I expected it to be.

She shrugs out of the cover-up she's wearing, and clips the life vest around her chest. "All right. Since you *promised.*"

"Hey, you want to hold this steady for me," I say, nodding down to the wheel, "so I can put the Bimini up?"

"What the hell is a Bimini?" she says with a laugh, as she grabs the silver support pole to balance herself while moving from the front of the boat to the helm, while I explain about the fabric cover that will give us some shade from the intense sun.

I nod toward the two to-go cups of coffee sitting in the

cupholders near the steering wheel. "You said you weren't a morning person, so I got you coffee. How do you take it?"

"That's . . . unexpected. Thank you," she says. "Milk and sugar."

I don't want to think too much about why she sounds genuinely surprised at this small gesture, so I tell her to take the cup on the right. Then I rush to explain a bit about the different parts of this particular boat, while snapping the Bimini in place.

"You seem to know a lot about boats."

"I grew up in a beach town," I tell her. "My best friend's family owns the local marina, so I spent a lot of time on boats growing up. Don't worry, I have my boating license."

"Didn't know that was a thing," she says. "And you have a pilot's license too? Or was that all bullshit the other night?"

I huff out a laugh as I watch her sip her coffee. "No bullshit. I'm a man of *many* talents."

Chapter Eleven

AIDAN

"No shade to St. George's," Morgan says as we pull up to the private beach on the point, "but that sleepy little town was a waste of time when we could have been here instead."

"Yeah, I see why everyone says to go into Hamilton instead. Maybe we should head there tonight?"

She pulls her full lower lip between her teeth, and I have to glance over at the two boats anchored off the shore, so my body will stop reacting to every aspect of hers.

I honestly didn't think this whole day through. The way she looked, sitting at the bow of the boat with the wind whipping around her as we navigated the channel on our way to St. George's Harbour. Walking side by side on the narrow sidewalks of the town like we were a couple. The way I felt seeing her in my ball cap after she pulled it off my head and insisted she needed it to hold her hair off her face more than I did since I was under the shade of the Bimini.

And then, as we rode across Castle Harbour, she sat at the bow in nothing but her bikini and my hat, slathering sunscreen on herself. Her fear about being out on the water seems to have faded, but I've kept the boat at a reasonable speed just to make sure she's comfortable.

"I'm probably busy tonight," she says.

Ouch. "Oh yeah, doing what?"

"Packing. My flight leaves really early tomorrow morning."

Knowing that she's brushing me off right now makes me wonder if it's because she's giving herself the same kind of reminders as I am. Based on what she said last night about not knowing how to act after finding out she'd fucked her stepbrother, I'm guessing that's the case. But, there's always the potential that she's not interested, despite our chemistry the other night.

I cut the engine so we don't get any closer to the shore. It's amazing how quickly the water changes depth and color here as the islands—essentially a collection of coral reefs in the middle of the Atlantic—jut out of the water.

Coming around the helm, I head toward the bow, wanting to get the anchor down while we're still far enough away that we won't drift into the other boats anchored nearby.

Morgan moves aside, watching me as I pull the anchor out, hold it by the chain, and toss it toward the shore, then pull slightly to make sure it's hooked into the sand below. "Are we swimming to the beach?"

"We're shallow enough right here that I think you can just walk in."

She snorts out a laugh. "Says the guy who's over six feet tall."

"Happy to throw you over my shoulder again if necessary."

She looks like she's going to say something, then thinks better of it, but it's hard to tell for sure with her sunglasses on and the brim of my hat shading most of her face.

"You'll be too busy carrying the cooler and our bags," she says, finally.

She bends forward to grab her bag from the deck, and goddamn, that bathing suit barely covers half her ass.

I don't know why I'm so attracted to her—why every curve of her body has me turned on, why her laughter makes me feel lighter, why her smile makes me happy. Her generally sunny disposition is a brightness that I've never thought I wanted in my life.

And that you can't have, I remind myself.

I turn away, annoyed that I have to keep reminding myself that she's my stepsister and I shouldn't want her . . . that I *don't* want her.

This isn't because I've fucked her. I've fucked a lot of women without the desire for a repeat performance, without being unable to focus on anyone but them afterward.

Stepsister. I grind out the reminder in my head.

I grab the soft-sided cooler that's packed with drinks and lunch and set it on the seat with a bit more force than necessary. My voice is terse when I say, "I'm going to jump in. You can hand me the cooler and our bags and I'll carry them to shore."

"Yes, sir!" Her tone is mocking, but goddamn do I like those words coming off her lips.

I step in and the water only comes up to my chest, so I take my aviators off and hold them above my head while I dunk under. Then I stand and shake my head to get the excess water out of my hair before putting my sunglasses back on. When I look up at Morgan, she's taken my hat off. Her hair is loose, falling in long waves well past her shoulders, but with her sunglasses still on, I can't tell if she's looking at me or the beach.

She lifts the cooler, using her knee to brace herself on the edge of the boat as she bends to lower it to me. From my vantage point, I have a fantastic view of her almost spilling out of the triangle top of her yellow bikini. To stop myself from thinking about how her breasts felt in my hands, how her nipples peaked under my thumbs, I focus on balancing the cooler on my shoulder and holding the two bags she passes to me above my head so they don't get wet.

She's right about her needing to swim to shore, and once we're there, our towels spread out on the beach far away from the two families that are also here, she pulls bottles of premixed cocktails, flavored waters, containers with dips and finger foods, and individually wrapped sandwiches from the cooler. Then she glances up at me, smirking as she says, "This is a fancy- ass picnic."

"Today was supposed to be my gift to our parents. The boat trip, lunch on the beach, snorkeling . . ."

"And then they got sick, and now you're stuck with me."

I like it so much better this way, I almost say. "Bummer for me, I guess," I say instead, to which she laughs and pokes me in the side, telling me I'm a jerk.

After we eat, she's eager to get back in the water. "Let's go explore that cave carved into the cliffs," she says, pointing to the opening just off the beach. It's much larger than the smaller cave behind us, which is barely big enough to stand in.

The water's shallow in the ocean cave, and we stand there waist-deep, keeping still while brightly colored fish swim all around us. The water is so clear that we can see them without putting on our snorkeling masks and sticking our faces in the water.

As the waves lap at the rough coral arches around and above us, Morgan clears her throat. "Last night, when you said that Max will drop my mom in a few months, when he realizes she's not a suitable replacement for your mom—"

"I'm sorry," I blurt out, bringing my hand up to run it through my hair. The fish, alarmed by my sudden movement, scurry away. "I shouldn't have said that." And I definitely shouldn't have waited for her to bring it up before apologizing. But we were having a relatively nice, and less hostile, time today without our parents around. I didn't want to bring that tension back.

"But what did you mean?" she asks, her eyes scanning the water like she's watching the fish that are no longer there.

I reach out, tilting her chin up so she meets my gaze. "At least look at me if we're going to talk about this."

Her tongue darts out between her lips, wetting them, and she gives me a slight nod. "Okay. So, what did you mean?"

I let my hand drop back into the water, but take a small step closer to her. The light shining through the triangular opening of the cave illuminates the water, but our upper bodies are in the shadows and I want to see her clearly.

"Max married my mom when I was in middle school—"

"What?!" The word is half surprise, half confusion.

"After my dad died—"

Her gasp echoes in the cave. "Max isn't your biological father?"

"No. He was one of my parents' closest friends. He and my dad met in med school, around the same time my parents got engaged. They all stayed close friends. He was always around when I was a kid, basically like an uncle."

Her voice is quiet and concern is written all over her face. "What happened with your dad?"

"He had rotator cuff surgery to repair an injury that never healed right. And then he got addicted to the opioid painkillers he was prescribed. It was . . ." I pause to gulp down my emotions, ". . . messy."

"I'm sorry. That must have been so hard." Her blue eyes are dark in the dim light as she looks up at me.

"It was." I want to say more. I want to tell her how he was a whole different person by the end. But I don't trust my voice not to crack with emotion, so I just nod. I'm not sure why I even want to open up to her about this, except that it feels like she'd understand.

"So your mom married Max, and then?"

"And then she died my freshman year of college."

"Holy shit, Danny. That's terrible, I'm sorry." Her hands find my waist and give me a supportive squeeze, and all I want to do is pull her close and wrap my arms around her. But I don't trust myself not to kiss her, and she's made it clear that's a line we're not crossing again.

"Yeah. The thing that sucks the most about it is that they were so happy together. And then she was in a head-on car accident late at night. It was an elderly man driving the wrong way on the highway. She swerved to avoid him, but he clipped the back of her car and sent it spinning into the trees just off the side." I can't bring myself to describe the way the car flipped over as it spun.

"My god." She breathes out the word so quietly it's almost a whisper. "And Max has been trying to replace her, as you called it last night, ever since?"

I chew the inside of my cheek and give her a curt nod. The women he dates always look the same. Golden blonde hair with light highlights, blue eyes. Maybe he just has a type, but the resemblance is usually so close it's hard to imagine that it isn't intentional. I asked him about it once, which didn't go particularly well, so we've never discussed it since.

"I didn't even realize he was your stepdad. I . . ." She glances away, toward the pitch-black end of the cave. "I don't even know if my mom knows. She's always referred to you as his son."

"I *am* his son. He adopted me after he married my mom, and the only reason I don't call him 'Dad' is because he didn't want to take that title away from my father."

She swallows and her fingers curl into my sides. "And you've had to watch him marry multiple women who looked like your mom?" Her jaw is tense, like she's gritting her teeth against whatever I'm about to tell her.

"Yeah. And it never takes long for him to realize that they aren't . . ." I trail off as she drops her hands from my hips, not sure what to say or how to say it. *Good enough?* ". . . her."

"So he just, like, lures women into marriage for their looks?" Her voice is critical, and in some ways perhaps it's justified, but my protective instincts kick in.

"I don't think he *lures* women into anything. He's a catch," I say, thinking about his good looks, kind nature, and lucrative career as a surgeon, "who wants to be caught. I assume he just wants to be happy?"

Her laugh is a scoff. "By finding a replica of your mom? I hope he's talked to someone about that, because that sounds an awful lot like *transference.*"

My brows dip. "What's that?"

"It's when you unconsciously redirect your feelings, desires, and expectations from an important person in your past to a new person. It usually happens after a traumatic loss."

My stomach dips at how accurate that description is to what I've watched Max go through since my mom died. I've always thought of these rebound relations as him trying to replace her but maybe, instead, he's just trying to find someone to fill that void.

"Why do you know this? Are you a therapist or something?"

"No, but I majored in psychology, and that's basically Psych 101. So, you don't think this thing with our parents will last?"

My bark of laughter is so loud and sharp that it echoes off the walls and the water, repeating the sound around us in a way that's almost eerie. "No."

"Because my mom isn't good enough for him." It's not a question. Deep down, I think that this is the conclusion she's already come to and is just looking for my confirmation.

"I don't know your mom well enough to know the answer to that. But based on what I do know, she's not going to last."

She grits her teeth, and as I watch her trying to keep her expression neutral, I wonder if she's battling between knowing I'm right and feeling like she should defend her mom. Though based on what I saw of their relationship last night, I can't imagine why she'd feel the need to defend her.

She clears her throat and looks out toward the opening of the cave. "There are some clouds moving in. If you want to snorkel at that shipwreck, we might want to do that before those afternoon storms."

Chapter Twelve

MORGAN

I poke my head up out of the water as another wave crashes over my snorkel. I glance back toward the boat and note that it's moved farther from us than it was when we jumped in the water. I can see the taut line of the anchor chain, but the waves are moving the boat around for sure.

"Danny," I call out when his head pops up, and he looks over at me, pushing his mask up to his forehead as he does. "The waves are getting a bit choppy, I'm going to swim back."

He glances up, and I do the same. The white puffy clouds that were covering the sky when we rode across the harbor —which is separated from the open sea by small islands—are now gray. The air is cooler as the wind has picked up.

"Fuck. Yeah, let's go."

I'm extra thankful I decided to wear the life vest while snorkeling out here, given how hard I have to push through the waves to make it back to the boat. The waves aren't that big but they feel angry, like the sea is churning.

He holds onto the side of the boat as I go up the steps on the back, then he follows me onto the deck. I flip the steps up as he rushes to the bow to bring the anchor up. Of course, with us so far from it and the boat pulling the chain, the anchor doesn't budge when he tries to reel it in. The wind whips around us, as though trying to carry his words away when he calls out something in my direction.

It's obvious I can't hear him, so he walks back to me. "I'm going to have to jump in and dislodge the anchor from whatever it's stuck on. See how the wind is pushing us back toward that island? Once the anchor is loose, there's a good chance the boat will be pushed back into the reef, so here's what we're going to do . . ." At the helm, he starts the engine and shows me how to accelerate slightly once I notice the anchor is loose.

"Won't I just bring the boat right into you?"

"You're only going to give it enough juice to keep the boat in place, not to move it forward. You're basically just preventing it from going backward into the reef."

My stomach churns. I don't know *anything* about driving a boat, and I'm terrified I'll run it right into him and kill him, but equally terrified of drifting back into the reef and becoming the next shipwreck in the harbor. Especially because there's nothing but jagged pieces of rock-like coral dotting the water and smooth cliffs of solid rock behind us, and the closest beach to us is the one we just came from. Which looks *very* far away from over here, where we're separated from it by hundreds of yards of choppy waves. I'm fairly sure I could not swim over there even if my life depended on it.

I grab a larger life vest from the seat behind me and loop my arm through it in case Danny needs it after he dives for the anchor. With the way the sky is darkening, I'm worried that he's not going to be able to see the bottom to find the anchor once he's in the water.

"Okay, show me what to do again."

He steps behind me, places one of my hands on a lever on the dashboard, and the other on the steering wheel. His head dips low, near my ear, as he reminds me how to accelerate just enough to hold the boat steady, and what direction to turn the wheel to keep us moving away from the reef and cliffs behind us.

"You're doing great, hold it just like this," he says, then presses his lips to my temple before he returns to the bow, pulls his mask back down over his face, and jumps toward the anchor.

I can tell the minute he's pulled it free because the boat is pushed backward a little, and I accelerate a tiny bit to hold us in place. I scan the waves in front of the boat but he's not there, which has me freaked out. But I can't leave the helm to look for him, or the boat's going straight back into the rocks. *Fuck my life.*

I'm taking shaky breaths, trying not to panic, but I don't know what I'm going to do if he doesn't come up soon. And that's when the rain starts. It comes down in sheets and the waves get choppy enough that one of them crashes over the stern. I glance behind me, and there's water on the deck. *Oh my god, I don't know what to freaking do here.*

How did this beautiful day turn into this so quickly?

When I glance back at the bow, the anchor is sitting on it, and then the chain is thrown up onto it as well. And then Danny must swim around to the back of the boat, because the stern dips down and when I glance back, he's on the deck rushing to the front. "Give it a little juice to move us away from this island while I roll the anchor in," he calls as he rushes past.

I do as he says, feeling instantly relieved and a whole hell of a lot calmer now that he's back on board. He reels the anchor in quickly, and then he's back next to me, pulling the Bimini back and securing the blue canopy behind us.

"What are you doing?" I call out, annoyed that the one thing that was sort of blocking the rain is now gone and I'm being pelted by it.

"This thing would be ripped off the boat by the wind the minute we start moving if we left it up," he says, as he comes up behind me, putting an arm around each side and covering my hands with his. "All right, we're going to drive this together."

"What?" There's panic in my voice, because *why?* "This seems like something I should leave to a professional."

"So you can sit there by yourself and freak out? No way. C'mon." His words are practically a growl. I lean my head back against his chest, reminding myself that this is a very inopportune time to find this bossy man so damn sexy.

He guides us out into the harbor, away from the rocks, and I can feel him turn his upper body to the right, back toward the marina, and then to the left, toward the private beach we just came from. "I don't want to chance going the distance all the way to the other end of the harbor with the waves picking up like this," he says. "I think our best bet is to go back to the point, and beach the boat. There was that smaller cave right on the beach. We can get some shelter there until the storm passes."

"Okay," I call out over the wind. "Will you put a life vest on?"

"Will it make you feel better if I do?"

"Absolutely. If anything happens . . ."

"It won't," he says, but he drives the boat a little farther out and then holds the wheel steady with one hand while slipping the extra life vest off my arm with his other. "You're driving while I get this thing on."

"Do I just . . ." I ask, but before I can even finish the question, he's already got his hands back over mine.

"All right, let's see what this single engine can do." With a rumble of laughter, he opens it up and we're speeding across the short expanse of water at a far faster rate than we traveled before, which makes me realize just how slow he was going earlier to keep me comfortable on the boat.

Now, though, the speed is the thing keeping me comfortable, because with each moment that the beach comes closer, I feel safer. Even with the loud howl of the wind, the rain lashing at my face and arms, and the boat bouncing in the choppy water, I feel safe because his arms are around me and he's taking me to shore.

My skin stings from the elements, but as he slows the boat near the beach, I feel a palpable sense of relief. On the ride over here, we watched several windsurfers leave their boards on the sand and hop into a larger boat that arrived to pick them up. There's no one else there now though, nor have we seen any other boats on our ride over. We are well and truly alone out here.

A huge crack of thunder has me startling, but Danny curls his body around mine protectively. "I'm going to slow us down so we can beach the boat. We can't risk putting the anchor down and swimming to shore with thunder in the area."

No sooner do the words leave his mouth than a huge, forked bolt of lightning streaks across the sky on the other side of the point. It's out in the ocean, but that doesn't mean we're safe in the harbor.

The minute the bow hits the sand, he tells me to jump out and get away from the water. Then he drives the boat up a little farther, moves to the back of the boat, pulls the motor up, and returns to the bow. I watch from ten feet away as he pulls the anchor out and drags the chain up the shore. "Best not lose the boat," he yells over the wind, "you never know what the ocean will do in a storm."

He stalks toward me across the sand, grabs my hand, and pulls me up the beach toward the small cave we barely bothered exploring before we ate lunch. It's not a large space, nothing like the one off the water that we watched the fish in, but it's dry and just a bit quieter. From here, the sound of the rain and the wind is comforting, not terrifying.

"Holy shit," I say, pushing my hair off my face as he steps up in front of me. I lean forward, resting my head on his chest and wrapping my arms around his waist. My heart is beating so fast that I swear I can feel it against my rib cage.

He brings his hands to each side of my neck, and I can feel my pulse pounding against his palms. "You're trembling," he says, his voice quiet and concerned.

"That was . . . terrifying."

Chapter Thirteen

MORGAN

I focus on slowing my breathing, but as he tilts my head back and looks down at me, his eyes studying me intently, everything in me kicks up a notch—my pulse, my breathing, my lust.

Nooooo, I tell myself. *You just had a near-death experience. This is adrenaline, nothing more.*

But the way he's looking at me, the naked longing I see in his gaze, has me convincing myself that this could be a good idea.

"The only thing scary about that was the fear that something might happen to *you*." The second the words leave his lips, his mouth crashes into mine, and I don't pull back. Instead, I wrap my arms around his shoulders and push up on my toes, parting my lips and letting him invade my mouth.

Our kiss is frantic, just like my heartbeat, and he moans into my mouth as he pulls me against him. The hard length of him is pressing right into my belly, and has my core clenching with need. His fingers fumble at the back of my neck as he unties the strings of my bikini top and peels the wet fabric from my breasts, and then he's kissing his way down my neck and chest until his lips are clamping around my nipple.

The moan that crawls up the back of my throat is impossible to contain, and the sound of it ricochets around the cave. Danny responds by flattening his tongue and dragging it over my nipple, again and again, which only winds me up more. The intense need I feel for him is raw and desperate, and when a quick glance toward the opening of the cave assures me that no one else is around, I give in to the desire.

Hooking my thumbs in the straps at my hips, I push my bottoms down my thighs.

Danny drops to his knees in the sand and looks up at me, groaning as he says, "Fuck, I've needed this. Are you sure?"

I nod, so keyed up that I can't even speak. He slides my bikini bottom down around my ankles, then lifts my leg over his shoulder and buries his face between my thighs. I watch his chest expand, and then he's saying, "God, I missed the smell of you," before his tongue is on my throbbing clit, toying with me.

Then he tilts his head back, looking up at me. "I want to watch you play with your tits."

"So demanding," I chide, but my hands are cupping my breasts and my thumbs are stroking over my nipples before I can even consider refusing him. I'm pretty sure I'd do anything he asked of me right now, as long as it results in an orgasm. Because the truth of it is, no one has *ever* made me feel the way he does, and I'm pretty sure he knows it.

"Fuuuuck." He grinds out the word between clenched teeth as he watches me. I love the way he looks at me, with nothing but appreciation for my body. "I could come just from watching you."

"How about instead you make *me* come," I tease, my voice husky with longing, "and then we can worry about you."

He brings his hand to his lips, spits on two fingers, and then his face is back at my center, his tongue running along the seam of my opening before he plunges his fingers into me.

It's harsh and deep, a relentless pace that has me gasping and moaning, and then he pulls my clit between his lips, sucking while he strokes me. And that's all it takes for the pulsing between my legs to spread through my core. I reach both arms in front of me to brace myself on the walls of the cave because my legs are shaking so much I can barely stand. The orgasm rips through me in an intense wave of heat and pleasure, and I ride the sensations until they're over. It's then that I realize I've got my leg basically wrapped around his neck.

"Oh shit," I gasp, as he stands. "I'm sorry, I was strangling you."

"You weren't, but if I had to die, my face in your pussy would have been the way to go." He glances quickly at the opening of the cave, checking to make sure we're alone just like we both did a few minutes ago, and then drops his swim trunks.

My lips part, my jaw dropping open slightly as I take in the sight of him. I know how he feels, but I could barely see him in the dark hotel room the other night, and I'm not prepared for this view. The hard lines of sinewy muscle that wrap around every part of his body like tense cords, the way his hip bones stick out below his waist, and the enormous cock that juts out from his body like it's seeking mine. No wonder I felt so full.

"See something you like?" His voice is teasing but thick with lust as he steps toward me.

"It's okay, I guess," I say as I look up at him and bite the corner of my lower lip. My internal dialogue could not be more different than the words coming out of my mouth, and he looks down at me like he can read my mind.

I take a slight step back as he steps closer, so he grabs my hips and pulls me to him. "I need to remember what it's like to be inside you. I want to feel the slick walls of your pussy sliding along me right now, pretty much more than I want to breathe. But I obviously don't have a condom, so if you don't want to—"

"Oh, I *want* to," I say. There's nothing I've ever wanted more, actually. "Are you sure it's safe?"

"I'm positive. And I won't finish inside you, I promise."

I have an IUD so I'm not worried about getting pregnant, but it's probably better if we don't cross that line too. I nod, then I'm lifting my leg and wrapping it around his waist, pulling him toward me as he slides his feet apart in the sand to line himself up with my entrance. I tilt my hips up to run myself along the length of him, using my cum to coat him. He presses his forehead to mine, groaning and saying, "Fuck, Morgan. You're . . ." He threads his fingers through my wet hair, pushing it off my face. "So. Fucking. Gorgeous."

And then he pulls back, wraps his hands around the backs of my thighs, and lifts until my legs are wrapped around his waist and he's nudging my entrance. I can tell he's trying to go slow like he did last time, but I don't want slow, so I wrap my arms around his shoulders, tighten my legs around his waist, and sink onto his cock.

Our simultaneous groan fills the cave, and then our grunts, moans, and the slapping of skin every time our bodies meet overtake the raging storm outside. I flex my hips into him with each thrust, and the way he's sliding along my inner walls has me feeling things I've never felt before.

He buries his face in my chest, which is right at eye level with me wrapped around him, and then he steps forward, pressing my back against the cave wall. I hiss in pain as the sharp fragments of dried-out coral—the foundation of the entire island—come into contact with my shoulders. He spins us around and leans his upper back against the wall to give him leverage, but keeps his hips far enough out that my legs don't scrape.

"You're going to scrape up your back," I say.

"Don't give a fuck," he says with another deep thrust, and then his lips clamp around my nipple and he presses into me over and over, his body slapping my clit each time he bottoms out, until the feelings of pleasure are overwhelming.

The walls of my pussy clamp around him, but I don't realize what's happening until the spasming waves spread from there. I've never had an internal orgasm before. Not from a man, or even my best toys. So I'm unprepared for the feeling, the way little pinpricks of electricity zap inside me, the way every muscle in my core clenches in pleasure, the way the intensity has me crying out as I'm throbbing around his dick.

I ride out the orgasm as I grind against him, and the minute I'm done, he's pushing me back enough to pull out and then pulling against him with his cock trapped between us. I feel the hot release of his cum as it shoots onto my stomach, and I bury my face in his neck, enjoying the sensual feel of raw sex with him. My body wants to do that again, but he whispers, "Fuck."

It's not a word of pleasure this time, it's a word of warning. And then he's pulling me from him, dropping my feet to the sand, and bending to pull his swim trunks from the ground. As he uses the inside of his trunks to wipe his cum from my stomach, I hear it too. The rain has stopped, and the motor of an approaching boat is loud.

"Step into the shadows there," he says, nodding his head toward the opposite wall as he pulls his trunks on. "I'll distract them so you can get your bathing suit on." Then he presses a kiss to my forehead, mutters an apology, and walks toward the opening of the cave.

Is he apologizing for mauling me in a cave, or for having to leave as soon as we finished? But as I watch his retreating back, I think maybe it's better if I never know the answer to that question.

It'll make it easier to remember that this can't keep happening, and to forget him once we leave this island.

Chapter Fourteen

AIDAN

I'm about to knock at Morgan's hotel room when singing comes from the transom window to the left of her door. If her setup is the same as mine, that's the bathroom window above her shower, and it's cracked open. I stand there for a moment listening, truly shocked at how good her voice is. There's faint music in the background, so I assume she's singing along, but I know this song and I'm convinced she's singing it as well, if not better, than the original artist.

When the song ends, I rap my knuckles on her door a few times, laugh softly as she mutters under her breath, and then lean up against her doorframe when she opens it.

Her eyebrows scrunch together in confusion, as if she didn't already tell me she was busy packing tonight. "What are you doing here?" she asks.

"I made a dinner reservation for us."

She's wearing the same matching tank top and shorts set

she had on last night—so thin they might as well be sheer, which would be less of an issue if she were wearing a bra. "I already told you I wasn't having dinner with you tonight."

"Except I forgot today was your birthday, and now I feel like I have to make it up to you. So I made dinner reservations in Hamilton."

"I'm exhausted, Danny. I need to pack . . ."

I glance beyond her, at the open suitcase on her bed with rows of neatly folded clothing inside. "Funny, it looks like you already have."

"Okay, fine," she says, crossing her arms and dropping her voice into a bossy tone that I like way more than I should. My dick springs to attention instantly. "I'm not *interested* in going to dinner with you."

"Why not?"

She groans and then says, "You're my stepbrother. This is already awkward enough."

I'm tempted to make a joke about how she didn't seem to mind earlier today in that cave. But the moment she walked out, she was all cool indifference, as if it had never happened. It was like I got to watch all her defenses come back up as we chatted with the guys from the marina who had come to retrieve the windsurfing boards that were left on the beach during the storm. And then she barely spoke as we rode back to the hotel in our boat.

"Listen, if we're never going to see each other again, we might as well have one more night together."

"Make it sleezy, why don't you?"

I push open her door, and she steps back willingly. The fact that she makes no attempt to prevent me from entering is all the permission I need. I glance at the few dresses still hanging in her closet as her hotel room door swings shut behind her, and grab one that's a bright coral with tiny buttons down the front.

"This one's nice," I say, turning and holding it out to her. "Either I can force you into it, or you can get dressed yourself. The first will be more fun for me, so think about how you'd like to proceed here."

A sound rattles in the back of her throat—half groan, half growl—and she rolls her eyes as she takes the hanger from me. "My god, you're bossy. I'm only going because you remembered it's my birthday."

"I feel bad that I didn't remember first thing this morning," I say as she walks past me and digs around in her suitcase before pulling out some nude-colored undergarments.

"Yeah, well," she says as she turns back toward me, "at least you remembered."

She goes to move past me, headed into the bathroom to change, but I plant my hand on the wall opposite me so my arm blocks her. "Does that mean I'm the *only* one who remembered?"

Why does that thought haunt me?

"With cell service and the internet down on the whole island, I have no way of knowing if anyone else remembered."

"But your mom didn't?" I say, thinking about how Morgan stopped by there on her way down to the boat, and again on her way back to her hotel room.

"I assume she was too busy throwing up to think of it," she says, her voice tight.

I'd stopped by there about half an hour ago, and our parents were both feeling marginally better, so I told them

I'd order them some soup and bread and have it delivered to their room. By tomorrow they should be recovered . . . just in time for Morgan and me to both be gone. At least they can enjoy a few days of their honeymoon.

Morgan slips by me and closes the bathroom door behind her, and as I walk into her room, I glance down at the open suitcase on the bed. The triangle top of her bikini is folded neatly right on top. I consider taking it as a memento of our time together, but even I know that would be wrong. Instead, I take a seat in the chair in front of the sliding doors that go out to the balcony. She's back out of the bathroom, dressed and ready, in less than ten minutes.

Her lips shine with a juicy pink lip gloss, and dark eyelashes frame her bright blue eyes. But once my eyes leave her lips and travel down her body, the goddamn dress is all I can focus on. It clings to every curve in a way that's damn near sensual, and the deep V of the neckline should be illegal for the way it highlights her cleavage.

My fists curl around the armrests of the chair as I glance back up at her face. She's fucking smirking at me, like she's reminding me that I was the one who picked the dress and she doesn't feel bad about the way it's affecting me. "You ready?"

I clear my throat, mentally calculating the odds that I'm going to spend all night being jealous of other guys looking at her. Pretty sure those odds are one-hundred-percent. "Ready."

The way the column of Morgan's throat moves as she takes a sip from her champagne flute is a damn near erotic experience, which is how I know that I've probably had enough to drink.

As dinner was wrapping up, she'd told me to "be resourceful and find a place to go out for another drink," while she ran to the bathroom. The way she scooted out of the booth across from me, turning sideways to slide between the tables and letting her ass drag along my arm, felt very intentional. The tables were close together, but not that close.

The waiter recommended a ritzy club at a hotel near ours, which I figured might be the one Anne took Max to last night. The irony wasn't lost on me, but we came here anyway and she insisted on French 75s for her birthday, explaining that it's her favorite drink even though she hates both gin and champagne.

"I knew going out after dinner was a good idea," she says with a giggle as she turns and presses her back against me on the dance floor, our hips swaying together as she grinds herself against me.

"I couldn't agree more." I trail kisses across her shoulder and up the side of her neck, before saying, "But what do you say we get out of here?"

She glances over her shoulder at me as she presses her lower back into my dick. I wish it was her ass, but the height difference between us makes that impossible, even in the strappy gold heels she's wearing. "You're not having fun."

I bring my mouth right to the shell of her ear and say, "I'm having a great time. But I'd be having more fun if we were alone."

She leans her head back on my chest, her eyes glassy with longing when she says, "Danny . . . we can't."

With my hands on her hips, I spin her so she's facing me, and her lips part in a slight gasp as I lean down toward her. The way she wraps her arms around my shoulders and presses up on her toes to meet me is all the assurance I need. I delve into the kiss like we aren't in the middle of a crowded dance floor. My hands roam her body while our tongues tangle together. She lifts one leg up along the outside of my thigh, like she's about to wrap it around my waist and climb me. Which I'd love—if we were anywhere but here.

I pull back, and she looks dazed as she stares up at me.

"We're going. Now." I take her drink out of her hand, then wrap my other arm around her waist as I lead us toward the door. I set the glass on the last table before the exit, and then we head down the driveway of the hotel.

Before we get to the street, Morgan pulls me to a stop. "I can't walk this fast in heels," she says.

"Easily solved," I say, about to pick her up and carry her back to the hotel.

"I also . . ." She moves toward me, her hand trailing up my chest and wrapping around the back of my neck as she pulls my head down close to hers. ". . . can't wait until we get back to the hotel."

"You . . . can't wait?" I'm trying to determine if she's using that expression literally, when her eyes slide to her right. I follow her gaze to the dark area against the high stucco wall that separates the grounds of the hotel from the street. It's completely shaded by some trees and there are large bushes beneath that would hide us from view.

"That's risky, Morgan."

She groans, and says, "You shouldn't have gotten me so worked up if you weren't going to deliver."

"Is this the alcohol speaking?" I ask, cupping her jaw in my hand and turning her face back toward mine.

Her eyes are clear when she looks back at me. "This is my body, needing yours. My underwear is drenched, and I'm *aching* for you."

She steps close enough that she can slide her hand between our bodies, cupping my dick in her hand as she runs her palm along my zipper.

My inhale is nearly a gasp. "Jesus, Morgan. I thought you just said this couldn't happen again."

"It *shouldn't*. But we both know it *will*. So don't make me wait, or I might change my mind by the time we walk back to our hotel." She glances over her shoulder to make sure no one is around and then drags me between the wall and the bush that borders it.

Chapter Fifteen

AIDAN

We find ourselves in an open space surrounded by a semicircle of tall flowering shrubs and covered by the shade of several large trees. Soft rays of light stream between the overhead branches, filtering the street lights standing on the other side of the tall wall. It's our own secret garden, but there's no time to appreciate it because Morgan is pulling me to her, wedging herself between my body and the wall, holding me to her with a leg wrapped around my ass.

I brace myself from falling into her by planting a hand on either side of her head. "Someone's eager." My voice is teasing, but there's a question in there too.

She said this wasn't going to happen again, and now she's offering herself up to me. Mentally, I'm running through the drinks she had at dinner and the club, trying to figure out if she's drunk. She seems maybe a little tipsy, but she ate a full meal with those two drinks at dinner, and only had the one at the club, so I'm pretty sure she's making coherent choices right now.

"So eager," she purrs as she fists my collar and pulls my face to hers. "This is the last chance we have. If we do see each other again after this, it'll be at some awkward family dinner or something."

"I think we both know there will be no family dinners."

Tonight, we should have toasted to our parents' impending divorce. It may be months away, but the way they were bickering in the hotel room when I stopped by before dinner made it seem like they might already be laying the groundwork.

"Good, then fuck me like this is goodbye."

I don't know why that request makes me angry. Maybe it's because there have been too damn many goodbyes over the years, and not enough people who stay. But Morgan was never going to be someone who'd remain in my life, and there's no way this could ever be more than the vacation fling it is.

I don't even know anything about her besides the fact that the sex is fantastic and being around her makes me . . . happy? But she's kept some distance intentionally, and maybe that's what pisses me off—that I might be open to more, might want to see her again, while she clearly isn't of the same mindset?

Doesn't matter, you're supposed to be focusing on nothing but hockey this season, I remind myself. *No distractions.*

She pulls me to her, closing the small gap between our bodies, and I channel all my frustration into that kiss, into the way I aggressively tug at the fabric of her slinky dress where it clings to her hips, sliding it up to her waist, into the way my fingers move her soaked thong to the side so they can trace the silky skin between her legs. And when she moans into my mouth, the feeling reverberates in my throat and sends me right over the edge of my own control.

My body acts on instinct as I pull the strap of her dress and bra down over one shoulder so her breast springs free, then bend to lavish attention on her nipple while my fingers sink into her wet cunt. She lets out a guttural moan in response, and it's too loud in the quiet night. I glance up, giving her a warning look and mumbling, "Quiet."

"I need you inside me," she whispers. "I want to come on your cock, not your fingers."

I'm about to ask *Why not both?* when voices approach from the other side of the wall, and I realize that we probably shouldn't spend too much time out here.

"Hands on the wall, spread your legs," I whisper against her cheek.

"Yes, sir." She says it playfully, like she did earlier on the boat, but there's nothing playful about my body's response. My dick throbs against my zipper. As I fish a condom out of my wallet, she turns, spreading her legs as she bends forward slightly, planting her hands on the stucco wall. There's just enough light that the tan lines from her bikini bottom are visible as she tilts her peach-shaped ass up.

God, there's so many things I want to do with her, but there's no time to explore her body. The drag of my zipper is audible in the quiet moment we've carved out under these trees, and I roll the condom on in what has to be record time. But our quiet is interrupted as more voices pass by on the other side of the wall, and that's its own kind of thrill.

Fisting myself in one hand, I lean forward so my upper

body is along hers, my chin resting on her shoulder as I plant my hand above hers on the wall. I trail the tip of my cock along her slit until I'm rubbing it against her clit. Her resulting whimper is quiet and I can tell she's holding in sounds that, in any other situation, I'd want to hear.

"How hard do you want to come?" My breath trails along the shell of her ear and her body convulses in a shiver.

"So hard." Her voice is barely audible.

"You going to be able to keep quiet for me?" I ask, increasing the pressure on her clit as I slide the head of my cock back and forth over it.

"Yes." The word is a breathy sigh leaving her lips. "Please, Danny . . . "

I almost correct her, almost insist she use my full name and not my childhood nickname, because there's nothing childish about the way I want to fuck her right now. But then she whimpers, "Please . . ." and the way my dick aches to feel her again supersedes any desire to get into a conversation about my name.

I push off the wall and use one hand to hold her hips in place while I line myself up with her entrance, and then I thrust into her hard and deep. She gasps quietly at the invasion, so I pause, giving her a moment to adjust while I drag the other side of her dress and bra down to free both of her tits. I pluck at her nipples, and her hips press back into me, her core clenching around my length.

"That's right," I whisper. "You can take it."

"Yes," she hisses out.

I pull back and slam into her, setting a punishing pace that has her gasping quietly with each thrust, but the way her body is moving in rhythm with mine, meeting me each time, tells me those aren't gasps of pain. I move one of my hands to her neck, sliding my palm up until my splayed fingers and thumb press into the space beneath her jaw.

I pause, leaning into her and pressing my lips to the back of her head as I whisper, "I'm going to make you come so hard, you'll see stars."

She turns her head to glance over her shoulder at me. Her eyes are wide and her black pupils have nearly overtaken her blue irises. She licks her lips as she gazes at me and nods.

"I won't hurt you, I promise," I say as she turns to face the wall again, then tilts her pelvis to give me even better access while she clenches her core around me.

I stand fully, giving myself some space between our bodies so I can focus on giving her that orgasm she's so desperate for. I've never had this much of a physical connection with anyone. And I can't get enough of her feistiness and the way our conversation flows naturally when it's just the two of us. I want more time with her because it feels like this could develop into more than just sex, if the circumstances were different.

But they aren't.

With one hand gripping her neck and the other still toying with a nipple, I pull out and push back into her, setting a slightly slower pace and focusing on hitting that spot inside her that I know will drive her wild. I can tell when I've found it by the way a soft moan rattles against my palm, and that's when I add some pressure around her neck.

She hisses out a "yes," and I smile at the satisfaction of knowing her body this well already—knowing what will feel good, knowing that she trusts me to deliver.

Her entire body is moving in tandem with mine as she

pushes herself back toward me with each thrust of my cock along the slick walls of her pussy, and I can already tell she's chasing her orgasm. I know it in the way she huffs out a breath with each stroke of me inside her and the way every muscle in her legs and ass are flexed.

Tightening the pressure on her neck just slightly has her arching her back and moaning against my palm, so I bring my other hand from her breast to her mouth, pushing two fingers in. She sucks them in greedily, sweeping her tongue around them. My balls tighten in response, and I'm not going to be able to hold on much longer.

I move my fingers to her clit, sweeping them over and around the swollen bundle of nerves until her legs are shaking. Then, I fuck her hard and fast, keeping the pressure on her clit until she's bucking wildly against me as I release the pressure on her neck, letting her gasp in oxygen.

"Oh fuck," she whispers, followed by a groaned out "Yes!" that's too loud given the people that we've heard walking along the wall or up the driveway to the hotel.

Her legs are shaking so violently that I'm half afraid she's going to collapse, so I wrap my other arm around her waist to hold her up as I bury myself inside her. I come so fast and hard that I have to hold in my groan as I watch her turn her head to the side and bite her own arm to keep herself quiet while her core squeezes me over and over, pulling out every drop of my release.

When we finish, we both slump forward. Her head rests on her forearms where they're folded against the wall, and my forehead rests on her shoulder.

"Holy shit." Any other words are lost—the kind that could

tell her how amazing that felt, how I've never had a connection like that with anyone else, how perfect she is.

But then she sighs and says, "That was . . . fun. But it's probably good we're never going to see each other again."

Ouch. I know we only ever intended for this to be a vacation fling, but after the feelings I was just having as we finished, it stings.

I'm about to ask why it's good we're never going to see each other again when she adds, "I'm not sure I could look you in the eye after what you just did to my body."

I slip out of her, quickly removing the condom and tucking myself back into my pants. Then I turn her toward me and back her against that wall, leaning in close. "Like hell you can't."

She rests her head against the wall, gazing up at me. "You know what I mean." She starts to look away but my hand is already on the side of her face, guiding her back to look me in the eye.

"No, I don't," I growl out the words. Is she upset? Did I hurt her? "So please explain."

"That was . . . amazing. But the way I was just so desperate for you is—"

"Also amazing."

"I was going to say 'a little embarrassing.'"

I slide my palm along her jaw and sweep my thumb along the ridge of her cheek. Her skin is flushed, I can feel the heat pouring off her, and I don't know if it's from the orgasm or whatever embarrassment she's feeling. "Why the fuck would you be embarrassed by great sex?"

"I don't know," she says, but even in the soft filtered light streaming through the branches above us, I notice her cheeks flame.

Has someone made her feel ashamed of the way her body responds during sex?

"Morgan, the way you respond to me is *why* the sex is so good." I bend my head forward, letting my forehead rest on the top of hers when I admit, "The best I've ever had."

"Me too," she whispers, and I hate the sad notes I hear in her voice. "But now we're both leaving. Speaking of which," she says, moving her head so I have to lift mine as she pulls the straps of her dress up over her shoulders, then reaches down to fix her thong before sliding her dress back down over her hips, "walk me back to the hotel?"

I clear my throat to try to rid it of the lump that's forming there. I'm never emotional like this, especially not about women. I should be glad we're going our separate ways. Things would be too messy otherwise, and I don't do messy.

"Yeah, of course." My voice is rough as I turn away, hoping the disappointment isn't evident on my face.

Chapter Sixteen

MORGAN

I'm sitting in the large living room of the posh high-rise condo Eva shares with her husband, Luke, surrounded by some of my closest friends and my cousin. And even though I made Jules bring me straight here from the airport so I could see Eva on the day she brought her baby, Gigi, home from the hospital, I'm distracted thinking about Danny.

About how I managed to sleep with my stepbrother, before I knew who he was, and how I let it happen again—twice—even after I did.

"Oh!" Lauren's voice snaps me out of my own thoughts, which may have wandered while she was talking about a vacation she just took. "Speaking of which, how was your mom's wedding?"

I feel my cheeks turn pink as my friends all look at me, and hope they think it's a sunburn flaring up. "It was . . . eventful."

"Oh no," Lauren groans. "What happened?"

"We never even heard from you the whole time you were gone," Jules adds.

I explain about the tropical storm knocking out power that first night, and how cell service and Wi-Fi remained down the next two days.

"Oh my god, please tell me you met a hot stranger at the bar and had wild sex with him to get over that douchebag you were seeing earlier this summer," Audrey says, and I love the protective way she doesn't even mention Carter by name.

My friends don't need to know that I let him back into my life again before this vacation because they'd probably hunt him down if they knew he was just using me for a hookup. I bite the inside of my lip as I wonder if I essentially let Danny do the same thing, while convincing myself that *I* was the one keeping it casual between us.

"Basically, yeah," I say.

"And?" Jules asks.

"And then the next morning, my mom's flight came in and the two of us spent the day getting ready for the wedding. And that evening, when I walked down the aisle, guess who was standing there next to my new stepfather?"

"No!" My friends all gasp at once.

"Yeaaaah," I say, drawing out the word. "My new stepbrother." It sounds even worse coming out of my mouth in front of my friends than it sounded all the times I reminded Danny of our new connection.

"No fucking way," Audrey says through a laugh before sweeping her long, dark hair back behind her shoulders.

"Oh my god, Morgs," Lauren says, using the nickname only she and her sister, Paige, call me. "Only you!"

"I have the most shit luck of any person on the planet," I groan and shake my head.

"So what did you guys do?" Eva asks. I can only guess that she is trying to imagine the shitstorm of awkwardness that ensued.

"Swore it would never happen again, and then tried to avoid each other as much as possible." Even as I say it, I know it's not true. We kept being drawn toward each other, and we didn't fight it very hard. I'm disappointed in myself, to be honest. As someone who specializes in PR and fixing people's messy lives, I knew better than to step into a messy situation like that myself.

"So *did* it never happen again?" Jules asks, her voice revealing how much she wants the details of this situation.

"Uhhhh . . ." My tongue darts out as I lick my lips and look away, out the wall of windows that overlook the Back Bay and the Charles River. What the hell is wrong with me? Could I possibly make it more obvious? "There may have been a slip-up," *or two*, "but it's fine. I'll probably never see him again. I doubt this marriage will last any longer than my mom's three other marriages after she left my dad."

Eva balks at my mom being married five times, and Lauren asks, "But what if they *do* stay married?"

"You know my mom," I say, waving off that idea. "They won't. The weird thing, though, is this guy—my stepbrother—it's like he doesn't exist. I Googled him on the flight home and couldn't find anyone with his name that looked anything like him."

"That's odd," Audrey says, and asks for his name as she reaches for her phone.

"Believe me," I say, "if he existed, I would've found him. Social media is literally my job."

I glance down at my phone, thinking about how the minute the plane took off this morning and I was able to connect to Wi-Fi for the first time in days, I immediately searched for Danny online.

And, according to the internet, he doesn't exist. I even went back to some earlier texts with my mom to confirm that his last name is Heinberg, but whether I search for Daniel, Dan, or Danny Heinberg . . . I came up with nothing conclusive.

It occurred to me after about half an hour of searching that, since Max was insistent that Danny not call him "Dad," so as to not try to replace his father, maybe he didn't change his last name when Max adopted him? I have absolutely no idea what his biological father's name was, and no way to find out unless I ask my mom to ask Max.

"Why don't you just ask your mom for more info?" Jules asks.

"And make her wonder why I'm asking? No, thanks. Plus, he'll be easier to forget if I can't stalk him online."

"*Would* you stalk him online?" Eva asks, an eyebrow lifted as she brings Gigi up to her shoulder to burp her now that she's finished breast feeding.

What would they think if they knew how long I'd already spent searching for him? Maybe it wasn't internet stalking—yet—but if I had found him online, the temptation would definitely be there.

"I mean . . . I might be curious and go looking, which would be bad. It might have been the best sex of my life, but he's my stepbrother. And to be honest, he was kind of an asshole anyway."

Even as I say it, I know that isn't quite accurate. He had the air of an asshole after the wedding, for sure—but given that we'd just found out we were related, maybe he was processing. But the way he was concerned about my allergy at dinner, took care to keep me comfortable on the boat, made me feel safe in the storm, took me out for my birthday after my own mother forgot it . . . would someone who was *truly* an asshole do that?

"Why'd you sleep with him if he was an asshole?" Jules asks, but my friends know as well as I do that it's a rhetorical question. Dating assholes is sort of my brand.

"Did I mention how hot he was? And he wasn't really an asshole until our parents showed up. Just bossy as hell, which, to be honest, kind of worked in the bedroom."

Eva chuckles and her eyes get a far away look that has us all staring at her.

"Something you'd like to share?" I ask, thankful to divert the conversation away from me and Danny.

"Uh, no."

"Oh, come on," Jules says to Eva. "You're still newlyweds. You should be having good sex all the time. The rest of us are."

"Except me," I say, because me being the single one is kind of a running joke.

"You just said you had the best sex of your life in Bermuda," Audrey reminds me.

"Which is why it sucks that it can't happen again." I tuck a strand of my hair behind my ears. "Not that I even know how to find this mystery man."

My friends start throwing out suggestions, and I just laugh. I already know that the only way I'm going to find out any more information about him is if I ask my mom a few questions—which my pride and my sense of self-preservation will not allow me to do.

"You think I didn't already think of all those things? Honestly, it's best if I just put him out of my mind."

"Put who out of your mind?" Luke's voice comes from behind me, and we all turn to find him standing in the entryway in his sweaty workout clothes. I notice how they cling to his muscles, and even though Luke is bulkier than Danny, it still makes me think of my stepbrother's muscular frame.

"No one," I say quickly, because I have no desire for Luke to know about my dalliance with my stepbrother.

Then I pick up my phone and shoot a text off to Eva, Lauren, Audrey, and Jules, reminding them not to share these details with their significant others. Especially now that I'm working for the team part-time, I don't need to be known as "that PR girl who slept with her stepbrother."

———

I drag my ass into the Rebels' practice facility, where their corporate offices are, bright and early the next morning. I've got my second coffee of the day in my hand, and I'm hoping the caffeine hits my bloodstream soon. I stayed up way too late last night, doing exactly the kind of internet research I promised myself I wouldn't do.

But searching through everything I could find about Max online still didn't reveal anything about his stepson's identity. Who doesn't have some sort of a digital footprint these days? Is Danny really just that private?

I'm so busy wondering about this that I almost run right into Lauren walking down the hallway with Tucker Hartmann. I've never met him in person, but I know he's the CEO of the Boston Rebels.

Lauren introduces us, and because my brain is only half functioning at this early hour and I can't think of anything to say, I blurt out, "You're Luke's brother."

"You know Luke?" he asks.

"Uh, yeah," I say, suddenly uneasy about the role I played helping to fabricate a believable backstory for Luke and Eva's sudden marriage earlier this summer. "I'm really good friends with Eva."

"Morgan is good friends with *all* of us," Lauren says, and it comes out like a warning.

I take a gulp of my coffee, praying that it helps jolt me awake so I can figure out what's going on here. I hate mornings so much.

In response, Tucker laughs and says, "Noted."

Lauren looks over at me and says, "Like all the Hartmann men, Tucker's a perpetual flirt."

I have heard this reputation repeatedly, but since Luke's the only Hartmann I've met, and I've only ever seen him have eyes for Eva, I've never seen it in action.

"Hey, that's not fair," Tucker says. "Luke hasn't flirted with anyone but Eva in years."

The Hartmanns own the team, and it's hard to imagine their patriarch, Frank Hartmann, being a flirt. His bushy white mustache and round pink cheeks give him a jolly old grandpa aura, but who knows what he was like in his younger years.

But Tucker, standing here in his stylish suit, his brown hair fashionably messy and a devilish grin on his face? Yeah, I can picture him being a flirt quite easily.

"Why do you look like you're only half awake?" Lauren asks me when I don't respond. She puts her hand on my back and guides me down the hall as she and Tucker continue walking.

I groan. "It's not even 9 a.m. yet. Being at work this early should be criminal."

Lauren laughs and tells me I've worked from home for too long. She, on the other hand, has worked here for the past two years—first in their marketing department before being promoted to the Director of Marketing—after years of being a stay-at-home mom to her twin girls.

"All right, get to that meeting before you're late. Tucker and I are meeting in my office," she turns and points down the hall, "right down there to the right, if you want to stop by afterward."

After saying our goodbyes, I turn toward AJ's office and her assistant tells me to head on in. I find her sitting at her desk and Patrick sitting across from her next to an empty seat. I wish Patrick wasn't here yet, because I'd really love to dish about the Bermuda trip with her before we get started. She's like everyone's no-nonsense big sister—she'll spew some wisdom and set you straight without trying to spare your feelings in the process. I can always count on her for completely objective and reliable advice. Then again, should I tell my boss I slept with my stepbrother? Perhaps not.

Patrick turns toward me as I sit down, gives me a brief

smile, and says, "All right, first things first, training camp starts for the rookies next week." I take a notepad out of my bag as he starts listing off his vision for what he'd like to see on the social media front for the rookies, and I take notes.

My mind is already spinning with different ideas, approaches to introducing each player that are more innovative and fun than what he's asking for. But I'll need to think about how to best broach my ideas with him, and I don't want to do it in front of AJ because I know she'll support me and he'll capitulate to her. I want him to say yes because my ideas have merit, not because one of my friends says he should do what I'm suggesting.

Once he's done going over all the rookies, he asks, "Do you know Aidan Renaud?"

"I know *of* him. My dad is his agent, but I've never met him. He was out with an injury all last year, right?"

I used to go to all the Rebels games with my dad when I was a kid. But then I was in New York for four years for college, and in Park City for another three years after that. I moved back to Boston with Lauren a couple years ago, but since her husband, Jameson, is also an agent and former player with season tickets, I usually offered to watch her twins for home games so she could go with him. I've only been to a handful of games since moving back, and most of them were this past year while Renaud was out with his injury.

"Yeah," AJ confirms, "his injury was more severe than his original diagnosis of two broken fingers. He ended up having several hand surgeries, and he's coming back this season. He's an exceptionally talented player, but he's volatile as hell on the ice and with the media. He needs a whole PR makeover." She huffs out a laugh.

"I'm going to need a little more info than that," I say. Patrick launches into a list of all the times Renaud has lost his temper and said the wrong thing to the press, a few times he's done stupid shit off the ice that still made the team look bad, and the fact that he's one of the biggest brawlers in the league.

He sounds like an asshole, exactly the type of guy who gives hockey players a bad name. I know that's the kind of thing AJ hates, so hopefully he gets his shit together.

"This season will be about me working with him on that last part," AJ says, "and you two figuring out how to make him look better to the public. He'll be on a short leash this year and is up for a contract renewal at the end of the season. I'd love to have lots of reasons to keep him. He's got so much talent, and if he could just harness it for good, it would be a no-brainer. Instead, he's exceptionally good at giving me reasons to trade him."

I chuckle, thinking about how the same was true of team captain Ronan McCabe, whose animosity toward AJ was legendary until last season. Now, they're practically married.

"All right. Make him look good. Will do."

"Here's his file," Patrick says, picking up a manila folder that's sitting on AJ's desk in front of him. "I'll need you to put together a media profile on him. He'll be here this afternoon, so we're hoping to introduce you to him then and give you some time to interview him about his return to the team. Then Natalie will stop by to shoot some pictures of him at the rink. I'll need you both to spend some time at training camp next week, too. He'll be there early to work with the trainers because he's coming off injured reserve and is getting back into the swing of things."

Patrick hands me the file, right as AJ says, "I'm so relieved that you're with us part-time now, Morgan. I know our social media is in good hands."

"Thanks," I say, wondering if that means she didn't feel that way with Tatum running things. I'd been working with and coaching her prior to her medical leave, and things were getting better—but not as quickly as they should have.

I flip open the manila folder and glance down as Patrick explains what information I'll find in there. But I'm no longer listening.

Every single bit of my focus and effort is being spent on making my lungs work and keeping my expression neutral. Because right here in my hands, staring back at me, is a man with shaggy dark hair, dark brown eyes with flecks of green and amber, and a full beard. But even with all the excess hair, I recognize him immediately. *Danny.*

Chapter Seventeen

AIDAN

Walking back into the Rebels practice rink is not unlike pulling on an old favorite pair of skates —ones that used to be so comfortable they felt like an extension of your own body, but after not wearing them for so long, they're stiff and foreign. Everything's the same, but it's not.

Life goes on without you. It's a painful lesson, but a necessary reminder.

McCabe warned me that I'd feel a change in the team dynamics, but I didn't expect to feel it the moment I walked into our practice facility. It's not just the way new flags hang over the ice, denoting the Rebels as the conference and division champions last season—it's like the vibes of the place are different and I can't quite figure out why.

I take the turn from the upper spectator level around the practice rink and scan my ID card at the reader on the wall next to the set of double doors leading to the hallway that houses most of the Rebels staff offices. One floor down are the training rooms and locker room, and one floor up are the leadership offices. I head down the stairs for my meeting with one of our trainers and our team doctor, but as soon as I exit into the hallway, I see my GM waiting outside the training room door.

AJ is wearing beige slacks with sky-high heels and a cream colored sleeveless top. Her dark hair is slicked back into a low bun. All business, as usual. Try as I might, I still can't picture her and McCabe together, but maybe it's because all I can think of when I see her is the way he always grumbled about her on our flights home from games.

I wonder if we'll still be seatmates like we had been the past few seasons, or if that's another thing that has changed in my absence? I should have thought to ask him when I saw him last week.

AJ's head snaps up as she hears me approaching, and she gives me a slight smile and a nod of her head. "Renaud, welcome back. I know you're about to meet with Jared and Dr. D, but we need to have a quick chat first." She turns toward one of the smaller conference rooms that are used for one-on-one meetings down here and pushes the door open before gesturing me in.

My stomach twists, wondering how I've already done something wrong when I only just stepped into the building a few minutes ago.

"Have a seat." AJ pulls a chair out for herself, nodding toward the one at the opposite side of the table for me. Once we're both seated, she rests her elbows on the table, crosses her forearms, and tilts her chin as she assesses me. "At the outset, I want to say that I'm glad you're recovered and are back to playing this year."

"Thank you. And I appreciate that you didn't send me back to the AHL first. I'm ready."

"I know you are," she says. "Some players have an innate ability, and others have to work really hard at it. I know you've always been the former, but I need you to try to be more of the latter, too."

I feel my face contort in confusion. She's saying that I have an innate ability as a hockey player, so much so that she didn't think I needed time in the minor leagues to get back up to my previous ability after a year off. But also, that I need to work really hard at it?

"Come again?"

"Ledderman let us know that he's retiring. Effective immediately." Anthony Ledderman has been with the Rebels for a long time; his tenure is second only to Colt. He's not even close to the most talented player on the team, but he puts his head down and does the work. He's also incredibly levelheaded, especially when everyone else on the ice gets worked up. He's held me back from fights and talked me down when things got heated, more times than I can count. But he pulled a groin muscle last season, was out for a few games, then came back too early and reinjured himself right before the playoffs. He was supposed to be back this season, but it sounds like maybe he didn't make a full recovery.

"I'm sorry to hear that," I say, unsure what this has to do with me.

She lifts an eyebrow, like she's waiting for me to make some sort of connection to what she's said and how it relates to me. But Ledderman plays defense, and I know she's not going to ask me to switch positions.

And that's when it hits me—Ledderman is one of our alternate captains.

My jaw drops open slightly as I hold my hands up in front of me. "Noooo."

"Your name has come up before," she says.

"I am not captain material," I tell her.

"That's what McCabe said, and look at him now. Sometimes, all people need in order to reach their potential is an invitation."

I think about the several seasons McCabe has been captain and how resistant he was to step into the leadership role management wanted him to play. But something clearly changed over the past year, and I don't think it was only because of his relationship with AJ.

"I think I'll have enough to worry about just getting back to playing. I promised myself there'd be no distractions this season."

"And you think that being an alternate captain would be a distraction?"

How do I tell her that being an alternate captain would demand a skill set I don't have. I'm not optimistic, supportive, or sometimes even rational.

"My whole career I've been an enforcer."

Captains are measured and calm. Enforcers are shit stirrers who set the tone of the game by physically intimidating their opponents. Captains are the ones talking to the referees about penalties, while enforcers are the ones being sent to the sin bin in the first place.

"There's no such thing as an official enforcer anymore,

Renaud. And if you paid attention this past season, you would have noticed that the Rebels had the least amount of time in the penalty box of any team in the league. And that took us all the way to the finals."

I cough out a laugh. "Where Hartmann choked."

"Easy to say from your couch, right?" She clears her throat. "*Our team* fell apart at the end. Every single player on the ice that night bears some of the blame. And Hartmann is the only one who had a legitimate excuse."

I'm tempted to flippantly ask if she has to say that because he's the owner's son and the CEO's brother. But McCabe warned me that things had changed, so I hold my tongue.

I'm sure Luke Hartmann is a good guy, but when our team needed him most, he wasn't a good goalie. And *that's* the metric that should matter.

"What we're focused on *this year*," AJ continues, "is coming back stronger. And to do that, we need every single player not only giving his all, but giving more than he's ever given before. For you, that means working harder than you're used to working—"

"I'm not afraid of hard work." There's no way AJ doesn't know this. In fact, aside from the team doctor, she's the only other person who knows the grueling recovery I went through in the last twelve months so that I could be back on the ice again this season.

"—and stepping up in ways you haven't before. I need you *on the ice*, Renaud. That means I need you to be levelheaded out there so you're not spending as much time in the sin bin as you do on the ice. Understood?"

"Understood," I say, my voice definitive, even though I'm extremely conflicted.

Hockey is a violent sport, and the fights are part of what makes it fun for fans. My willingness to lay someone out when needed is one of the things that helps prevent the other team from playing dirty.

But AJ getting caught in the middle of a fight in the stands while holding McCabe's baby last season may have changed her perspective on things a bit. Or maybe her perspective was already changing? Drew Jenkins was a known brawler when he was in Colorado, but very rarely got in a fight after being traded to the Rebels last season. Did she give him this same talk last fall?

"I need you to be a leader on this team."

I sit back in the cushy chair and cross my arms over my chest. "Why me? There have *got* to be better options." Like maybe someone who wasn't just out for a whole season?

She presses her lips between her teeth briefly and then shrugs. "There are certainly other people who'd jump at the opportunity to wear the *A* on their jersey. But wanting that distinction, and being the right person to serve as the alternate captain, are two entirely different things. Show us that you're the kind of player who's right for that role, Renaud . . ." She trails off, like there was something else coming after it, and my mind is spinning with the possibilities. But the only one that feels right is *or else.*

My chest shakes with a laugh, because this is AJ's special brand of leadership: making you believe you can be better than you are. But the problem is, I'm a great hockey player precisely *because* I'm a physical player. I'm the guy who lets his emotions get the better of him out there on the ice, because my emotions are the fuel that lights a fire in me, making me push myself harder.

Asking me to tamp down my emotional responses on the ice, to lead instead of fight—that's like asking me to be a worse player, instead of a better one. Isn't it?

"I see those wheels turning," she says, leaning back in her seat as she rolls her chair away from the table. "And I suspect you're asking yourself the right questions right now."

"Which are?"

"How you can play at the level you've been playing at, if you have to rein in your emotions out on the ice."

Goddamnit. Is she a fucking mind reader?

"But the answer leads right back to where we started," she continues as she stands. "You need to be the kind of player who has to start working hard at it. Because if you take physical intimidation out of your playing style, I suspect you're going to have to put a bit more effort into your other strengths."

"Ouch." I stand, mirroring her position.

"Listen, Renaud, you're a very good player who has the potential to be great. You're also not getting any younger and basically shattered your hand a year ago. If you're getting in fights all the time, the risk that you'll reinjure your hand increases dramatically. And if you're out on IR again, you might as well retire at the end of the season with Colt."

Well, shit.

"If you want longevity in this league, not to mention on this team, you're going to need to make some changes to how you play." She lifts a shoulder and an eyebrow before saying, "The choice is yours. I'll see you in a couple hours in my office. Have a good workout."

———

Two hours later, freshly showered and with a recovery shake in hand, I approach AJ's office. The workout my trainer, Jared, just put me through has my body feeling sore in ways it hasn't in a long time, but at least it gave me something to think about besides my GM's ultimatum. Or ultimatums, plural, actually.

AJ's assistant, Colleen, isn't at her desk, but the door to the office is wide open and McCabe, Colt, and Walsh sit chatting with AJ on the couches and chairs in the seating area near the wall of glass that overlooks the practice rink. It's only then that I realize that AJ sought me out earlier so she could have a private conversation with me about my future with the team, and now, more than ever, I appreciate her discretion.

My teammates greet me with more enthusiasm than I probably deserve, and then spend the next ten minutes catching me up on what's changed since I last played for the Rebels. It's a lot of what McCabe already told me, so I spend my time watching the dynamics instead—how Colt, who was always our unofficial captain, sits back and lets McCabe take the reins; how Walsh peppers comments in about the new players, and their strengths and weaknesses; how McCabe actually sounds like he gives a shit, whereas before he was the grumpiest fucker that ever played hockey.

AJ opens her mouth to say something but a knock on the door behind me stops her, and then Colleen's voice rings out, "Morgan's here."

My stupid, hopeful heart beats harder just at hearing that name, even while I know it's not *her*.

"Hey, I forgot you started working here!" Colt says, jumping up from his seat and striding past me.

I turn in my seat, only to see him wrapping his arms around *my girl*.

My stomach clenches as he pulls her into a quick hug before he lets her go, stepping back enough for me to see her. She's standing there in an ivory dress that's fitted on the top before flaring out just past her hips. The heels of the strappy wedge sandals make her calves more pronounced and remind me just how sexy her legs are when they're wrapped around my head. With her freckles and her strawberry blonde hair flowing loosely past her shoulders, she looks like a literal ray of fucking sunshine.

"She's worked here since the playoffs," McCabe grumbles.

What. The. Actual. Fuck.

"Nooo," Morgan says, drawing the word as she looks back and forth between AJ and McCabe. I can tell she's holding in a smile. "I did some work for AJ during the playoffs, and then agreed to come on as a consultant for the team. Now I'm stepping in to *actually* work here for a few months, because Tatum is having surgery and you all need someone to run your social media."

"What about your PR company?" Colt asks. "You just leaving all your other clients to come work with us?"

"I'm doing a favor for a friend."

A quick glance shared between her and AJ lets me know that AJ is the friend in question . . . and none of this makes any sense. AJ is well over a decade older than her. How are they friends? And how does she know McCabe, Colt, and Walsh?

Most importantly, why has she not even acknowledged

me? In fact, she's directed her attention at everyone in the room *except* me, which means she's not surprised to see me here. She's intentionally ignoring me.

Finally, she turns toward me, holds her hand out, and casually says, "Hi, I'm Morgan. You must be Aidan," as if I didn't just have her coming apart in my hotel room, in a cave during a storm, and against a wall outside a hotel just this past weekend.

There's a slight emphasis on my name as it rolls off her tongue—not enough that anyone else would notice, but I can tell she's pissed. It's like when we saw each other at the wedding, only a hundred times worse. Because not only have I not stopped thinking about her for the last two days, but now, in addition to being related, we apparently work together.

I'd convinced myself that I could forget about her because I'd never see her again. But this is another hit I didn't see coming.

Chapter Eighteen

MORGAN

The minute the elevator doors close, he turns toward me, backing me against the wall and stepping so close I'm forced to tilt my head back to look at him.

"What the fuck?" His words are a low growl, but there's hunger mixed with confusion in his gaze, and I have to force my body to fight its natural reaction to him.

"I'm having the same thought right now, *Danny.*" Any trace of the friendliness and professionalism I presented in AJ's office is gone.

The only reason I was able to hold myself together back there was because I'd had two hours to mentally prepare. If I hadn't seen that picture of him ahead of time, there's no way I would have been able to keep that first interaction professional.

"It's a childhood nickname. No one calls me that but Max, and a few of my friends from home," he says, and while I've never heard of Danny being used as a nickname for Aidan, I guess it makes sense. So he didn't technically lie to me about his identity, he just left out some very important details. Which, to be fair, I guess I did too. "Did you know who I was, back in Bermuda?"

The scoff rips out of my throat so quickly it surprises me. "No. Being my stepbrother is bad enough, but if I knew we'd be working together—"

"You sure?" He drops his head toward me, his voice low and . . . angry? seductive? I'm not sure I can tell the difference right now. "Because even being my stepsister didn't keep your clothes on—"

His words are like a slap across the face—a sharp and painful reminder of how easily I'd given myself over to him despite all the times I said we couldn't go there again. Those ugly feelings from yesterday, the ones that made me feel like I let Danny use me just like I'd let Carter use me, rear their ugly head again. So, I clap back.

"Fuck you," I spit out, my words an angry whisper shout in the small elevator.

"Is that an offer?"

"God, you're such an asshole. I will *never* make that offer again, especially since you're one of my dad's clients—"

"What?" His head rears back. "You're Carson Kaplan's *daughter?*"

"The one and only," I say. "Oh my god, and do you know what the worst part is? I came home from Bermuda and told all my friends I'd had sex with my stepbrother, thinking I'd never see you again."

"Why is that an issue?"

"Aside from the fact that they're all going to know it's you?"

"Why would they know it's me? It's not like I'm going to meet your friends."

"You already know some of them! Lauren, the head of marketing? She's my cousin. Drew's fiancée, Audrey, Colt's fiancée, Jules, Hartmann's wife, Eva? Three of my best friends. AJ? Also a good friend of mine."

I watch him connecting the dots but can't tell how he feels about it. "I don't know Audrey, Jules, or Eva—"

"Exactly, because you've been MIA for the last year. Meanwhile, these people, including your teammates, are like family to me."

"You don't have to tell *any* of them I'm your stepbrother."

"What? How would I hide that?"

"I think we can easily keep that piece of information to ourselves until our parents' inevitable split."

"But . . . I'm a terrible liar."

"The way you just pretended like you had no idea who I was back in AJ's office means we both know that's not true. I think you can lie just fine when it's convenient for you."

"There is absolutely nothing fucking *convenient* about this situation," I say as the elevator dings.

"Any other lies you told me in Bermuda that I should be aware of?"

"I didn't tell you a single lie in Bermuda . . . unlike you." I think about the way he redirected the conversation at dinner after the wedding so that Max wouldn't talk about him being a hockey player. Makes me wonder what else he might have lied about.

I push past him, heading straight to the elevator doors

and turning slightly to fit through them before they're even halfway open. I can feel him close on my heels as we walk along the rubber mats that line the rink, and while there's no one nearby, I still drop my voice very low when I say, "We're done talking about this."

"For now." His words ring out like both a threat and a promise.

I easily slip back into professional mode when I note that Patrick and Natalie are at the end of the rink, waiting for us. "So, as part of my role here, I'll be doing a media profile on you. And, if I'm being honest, what everyone wants to know, your teammates most of all," I say, letting my gaze slide his way, "is where you've been for the last year."

Having the last two hours to prepare has allowed me to dig into his injury and return, look at what fans had been saying, and send off some texts to my friends' significant others asking what I should ask Renaud.

It all yielded one clear question. As McCabe put it: *Why the fuck did he go MIA for the last year?*

So now, what I really want to know is how Aidan Renaud went from an all-star hockey player to a recluse over the past twelve months?

I can tell by the way his jaw flexes that the mention of his teammates has annoyed him.

Good. Because while they might be *his* teammates, they're *my* friends.

I've only been back in Boston for a couple years, and I've spent that time carefully building friendships with women I admire and respect and men who know how to treat a woman right. If he thinks he's going to waltz in here and insert himself into my circle of friends, he'll need to reconsider.

"I moved back home. Everyone knows that."

"And home is Ember Cove?" I reference the small town south of Boston that, until today, I didn't even know existed.

"Done your research, I see."

"I've done my *job*." I try to emphasize that this is work, not me looking into *him*. He doesn't need to know that I spent hours yesterday trying to track down who he was. "So, you've been less than an hour south of Boston, but couldn't be bothered to keep in touch with anyone or even come to a game?"

When he hisses out an exhale through his clenched teeth, I know I've struck a nerve, just as I intended. The only way I'll get through this is to keep my armor on and my defenses up.

"Hey," Patrick says with a friendly smile, as we approach. "Sorry, we're a bit early for the photos. I know you probably haven't had time to fully finish the interview," he says to me, before turning toward *Aidan*—a name that's going to take some time to get used to—shaking his hand, and welcoming him back. "Mind if we just shoot some pictures real quick and then we'll get out of your hair?"

"I think I've got enough to get started, and something I ate for lunch isn't sitting well." I rest my hand on my belly and wince, even though the only thing going on in there are hunger pangs because I was too anxious, after learning Danny's real identity, to actually eat lunch. "I'm going to head out. I'll follow up with you if I need more info, Aidan. Thanks for your time."

I turn and flee, barely making it outside before I'm dry

heaving into a metal trash can. It's not the hunger pangs causing this. It's the realization that there's no way I'm going to be able to avoid him—and the uncertainty about whether I truly want to—that's making me sick. So when I hop in my car, I head to the one place guaranteed to make me feel better.

———

On the bluestone patio surrounding the pool at my dad's house, I sit on a chaise lounge with my laptop open on my legs. I've written up the skeleton of what will eventually become a press release about Renaud's return to hockey, and a bare bones social media profile that will need a lot more work before it's ready.

But right now, I still have way more questions about Aidan Renaud's return to the Rebels than I have answers, and it's my own fault because I ran away instead of asking those questions. To be fair, I didn't really want to puke in front of him, my boss, and the intern who is reporting to me until Tatum returns.

"Imagine my surprise, coming home from work and finding your car in the driveway," my dad's deep voice booms from behind me, and I turn to find him walking out onto the patio from the living room. "How was going into the office today?"

I tell him a bit about my day, leaving out any mention of my previous connection to Aidan—not only because I'm *never* telling my dad that I slept with my stepbrother, but also because we talk about my mom as little as possible.

When they divorced, she didn't even fight my dad for

custody. She just quietly moved across the country, leaving us both behind. She's moved several times since then, always because she needed "a change of scenery" after her latest divorce.

Dad would never tell me not to have a relationship with my mom, but he also hates the way she constantly disappoints me. I appreciate that he gives me the space to figure it out.

I keep my voice as casual as possible when I say, "I can't quite get a read on Renaud. It seems like he has a pretty big chip on his shoulder. What's his deal?"

Dad's belly laugh is exactly what you'd expect from someone of his stature. He's six feet tall, with a big bald head, a dark auburn beard he keeps neatly trimmed, incredibly broad shoulders, and a Santa-like belly. I've got my mom's height and coloring, but my "big boned" structure and the touch of red in my hair are definitely all from Dad. Sometimes I wonder if my mom's comments about my body are because I remind her too much of him?

"You're writing an article about him," Dad says, "so obviously I'm only going to say good things about my client."

I roll my eyes as I glance over at him, where he's pulled up a chair from the dining table that sits under the massive wooden pergola. "This isn't investigative journalism, Dad. My job is to make him look good. But since I'll be working with him on crafting the story about his absence last season, I'm genuinely curious what type of person he is."

Dad blows out a long, slow breath between his lips.

"He's a damn good hockey player, but he can be a dick. You're right about the chip on his shoulder. I've worked with him since he was in college, and he's always had it."

I can't help but think about what his life was like then. His dad dying when he was younger, his mom dying while he was at college. That would put a chip on anyone's shoulder, wouldn't it? Maybe hockey was his escape, the same way singing became my escape when my mom left?

"What can you tell me about his background?" I ask, wondering if he knows as much as I do.

"Not much, seeing as how he's my client. Sorry, kiddo. You're going to have to dig into his story on your own. He'll tell you what he wants you to know."

His comment makes me think he knows at least as much as I do about Aidan's past—most likely more.

Wait, does he know that Aidan's stepdad married Mom? No, I assure myself, *he obviously doesn't, or he'd have said something.*

I haven't told him anything about the wedding, aside from the fact that it was happening, nor do I intend to. And I especially don't intend to tell him that I've slept with one of his star hockey players—the one with the bad attitude who the rest of the league loves to hate.

Dad and I have always been close, and I don't like lying to him, but we're both better off if he doesn't know the truth . . . and so is Aidan. I'd hate to see what Dad would do to Aidan's career if he found out. This is a contract year for him, and if Dad knew what happened between us, he'd make sure Aidan was playing hockey in Sweden by the end of the season. And that's if he were feeling generous.

His phone rings, as shrill and loud as it always is, because he refuses to miss a call . . . ever. He glances down at it, then stands and says, "It's Liam Walker. This might take a while."

Dad doesn't represent many athletes outside of hockey, and I don't know exactly how it happened, but landing the football star as a client years ago—right as he was developing into a well-respected quarterback—was a major coup.

But tragedy struck the Walker family earlier this year, and Liam decided to take the season off to stay home with his son. It's a decision that hasn't sat well with some Boston football fans who were used to annual division titles and regular appearances at the championship game. But personally, I can't imagine being in his shoes, and I'm sure he made the choice that was right for him and his family.

"Okay, I'm heading home soon anyway," I tell Dad, as I close my laptop.

Dad bends to give me a kiss on the top of my head then turns, answering the call as he walks inside. The screen door slams behind him, and I bend my knees up to my chest before wrapping my arms around my legs. I sit, curled up like this, watching the pool sparkle as the wind kisses the top of the water, and listening to the birds chirp as they flit between the thick row of hydrangeas that line three sides of the pool.

But the peaceful setting doesn't prevent my mind from immediately turning back to the surly hockey player I exchanged heated words with today.

I've known him for less than a week, and already I can't stop thinking about the different versions of Aidan Renaud that I've already seen—a fun and flirty stranger the first night I met him, then my broody and hot stepbrother following the wedding, and now, a hockey player with a chip on his shoulder.

All of it leads me to wonder: *Who is Aidan Renaud? And how am I ever going to survive him?*

Chapter Nineteen

AIDAN

"It's good to see you," my agent, Carson Kaplan, says as he reaches across his desk to shake my hand before taking a seat and gesturing that I should do the same on the opposite side of his desk.

I sit, quietly studying him as he folds his hands on his desk in front of him. His short auburn beard ripples as he says, "How is everything going with the Rebels?"

"Hard to say," I tell him, "since we haven't practiced yet."

"But you've seen your teammates, right?" There's concern in his voice, like he's worried about how I'll settle back in with the team.

"Yeah, I had a meeting with AJ, and McCabe, Colt, and Walsh were all there. I'm going out with a bunch of them tonight," I say, thinking about how confusing it was when I was added to a group chat called *Rebels Fam*, and it took me about twenty texts to figure out who the three unknown numbers were. Turns out it was Drew Jenkins, Zach Reid, and Luke Hartmann—all of whom I'll be meeting for the first time tonight.

"Good. I suspect you know that the key to successfully transitioning back onto the team this season is highly dependent on reestablishing ties after going dark for the past year. That's what AJ is going to be looking at—as much as your game—when she decides whether or not to renew your contract. You do still want to stay in Boston, right? That hasn't changed since we last talked?"

"I definitely want to stay." The thought of starting over again feels a lot more daunting in my mid-thirties than it did in my twenties. I'm settled here. Boston is my hometown, and getting to play here until I retire is the dream.

"All right. It'll be well into the season before she's ready to talk about contracts, so I think the key here is for you to put your head down and focus on being the best player and teammate you can be."

Obviously. "She wants me to take the alternate captain position now that Ledderman is retiring."

Carson's bushy auburn eyebrows lift in a way that reminds me of Morgan when she looks surprised. Their faces are very different, but she has some of her dad's coloring and expressions.

Sometimes it feels like the universe is trying to fuck me, and this is one of those times.

Of all the people staying in Bermuda that weekend, I had to sleep with the one who was about to be my stepsister, works for my team, and is my agent's daughter? The first two things are minor hiccups compared to the last. Carson is not a man to be fucked with, and if there's one thing I know without needing evidence, it's that he's overprotective of his daughter.

"Are you going to accept?"

"I don't know. I'm a bit confused about her rationale. She said my name had been brought up for the position before. But it seems kind of weird to start the conversation by telling me that the team has changed a lot over the last year, and end it by offering me a leadership position when I'm coming back to a team with different dynamics than when I left."

"Why do you think she's offering it?"

"I suspect she's looking for ways to keep me in line. To make sure I fight less—"

Carson's loud bark of a laugh interrupts me. "That's kind of what you're known for."

"Yeah, well I don't think it's what she's looking for anymore."

"Makes sense, with the way the Rebels' style of play is changing. You know the stats, I'm sure."

"I do. AJ mentioned the Rebels had the least amount of time in the penalty box last season . . . when I wasn't around." It's hard to know whether she meant that it was *because* I wasn't around, or if it was simply reflective of a shifting approach to winning.

"Honestly, she's probably also looking for ways to protect her investment. You're no good to that team if you hurt your hand again." Carson pauses, then says, "I think you should take the alternate captain position. Show her that you're coming back more committed than ever."

I nod. "I know. I just can't stop thinking that this feels a bit like a setup. Like she's giving me enough leeway to mess up, because if I take the position and end up in a few fights on the ice, she'll have reason enough not to keep me."

"Even if you don't take the offer, that could be a reason for her not to keep you. If you *do* take it, it could be extra motivation for you to clean up your act and demonstrate some leadership skills you've had no need to tap into in the NHL. You were the captain of a D1 team in college, so it's not like you lack the skills."

I shake my head, and unclench my fists like I often have to force myself to do when I'm extra tense. "College was an entirely different game."

"Sure," Carson says with a shrug. "But the skills needed to be a leader on any hockey team are pretty consistent."

I glance out the window of his office high above Copley Square, taking in the view of brownstone rooftops lined up on the few blocks between here and the Charles River.

"So?" he says. "You going to do it?"

"I need to think about it more . . . get out on the ice with my teammates and see if it feels right."

"Keep me posted," he says, and I think we're done here. But as I set my hands on the arms of the chair, ready to stand, he adds, "By the way, my daughter mentioned interviewing you for some social media and PR about your return to the team."

I give him a nod that I hope hides my shock. I hadn't thought she'd mention us knowing each other. Then again, he'd obviously know his daughter is working for the team, so of course we'd meet eventually. As long as she didn't tell him about Bermuda, there's no harm in him knowing we work together.

"Morgan's got ambition and a work ethic to match. But

she also has a strong need to help people, especially an underdog. And I would never want to see her taken advantage of," he says, eyeing me up and down. "I'm sure this goes without saying but I'm going to say it anyway. No distractions, Aidan . . . just like we talked about this summer. That *especially* goes for women, and *most especially* the young woman I raised."

"Understood," I say. The word is calm and reassuring, nothing like the chaos I'm feeling inside. I need him on my side as we enter contract negotiations this season, and he's telling me point-blank to stay away from his daughter.

If he knew what had already happened between us, I'd have a broken nose and be looking for a new agent.

"So I can trust you to make *responsible* choices this season?" Carson asks, his eyes narrowing on me. The man is shrewd, I'll give him that.

"For sure." I look him dead in the eye when I say this, because despite what's already happened between Morgan and me, I'm committing here and now to not allowing it to happen again.

It doesn't matter that I haven't stopped thinking about her since that first night together in Bermuda, or that every time I jerk off I'm picturing her. It doesn't matter that if the circumstances were different, I'd want more than just those days in Bermuda with her.

Because none of that can happen again . . . every time I consider it, the universe throws another obstacle in the way. I'll just have to figure out how to be around her without wanting to be *with* her. There's no other option now.

———

"I can't believe Ledderman is going out like that," Drew says, shaking his head as he sets his glass on the table.

"Not like he can play with a pulled groin," Colt says. "And thirteen years on the team . . . at some point you just have to admit that your body can't take it anymore."

Hartmann turns toward Colt, and runs a hand through his hair. "You trying to tell us something?" The kid looks a bit nervous, and after the way he choked last season, I'm not surprised.

"Nah, you're stuck with me until the end of the season." I'm a little surprised Colt doesn't come back with a barb about not being able to retire because he doesn't have a reliable backup goalie—something I heard him say to our other goalie, who Luke replaced. Even Colt seems more chill now.

"Unless AJ finds you standing on another chair," Drew says.

My eyebrows dip in confusion as everyone else laughs. I have no idea what they're talking about. McCabe must notice, because he says, "You had to be there."

Then Walsh says, "Just imagine Colt standing on a chair, trying to hang a mobile on a ceiling above a crib, while he's still in PT for his knee, and AJ walking in and telling him to get his ass off the chair or she'll put him back on IR."

"Whose crib was this?" I ask, trying to figure out if Colt has a baby I don't know about. Pretty sure he and his agent's little sister Jules just got engaged a few months ago, so I don't think she had his baby.

"Gigi's," Luke says. "We were getting the nursery ready."

"And AJ was there, because . . . ?" I'm trying to wrap my mind around AJ spending time with any of her players outside of official team activities. It's not like her at all.

"Because *I* was there," McCabe practically growls at me, like how dare I question our boss hanging out with the people who work for her.

"We were all there," Zach says, "and our girlfriends had just come from throwing Eva a baby shower."

I nod my head like this all makes sense, but mentally I'm trying to reconcile how everything feels so different now. Everyone is so settled, and I'm . . . the same as I've always been.

Images of Morgan flash through my mind. Not just the chemistry we had in Bermuda, but the way we laughed together and how it was so easy to talk to her that I started divulging things I don't normally discuss, like my dad's addiction or Max's Stepford brides. But I push the thoughts of Morgan away because I promised myself, and her dad, that I wouldn't go after her.

Though, if Colt's best friend and agent could forgive him secretly dating his baby sister, could Carson ever be okay with Morgan and me?

I don't even know where that thought comes from. I don't want a relationship, and she sure as shit doesn't seem to want anything to do with me after our conversation the other day. But somehow, thinking about her always leads me to wonder if something more serious could develop between us.

The guys are all looking at me like they're waiting for me to respond, and I'm not sure what they want me to say. "Uhhh, so when was your daughter born?" I ask Luke.

"A few weeks ago, but she and Eva were in the hospital for a while, so they just came home on Labor Day."

The same day Morgan and I both flew home from

Bermuda, separately. She mentioned Eva being one of her best friends, and I wonder if she headed straight there to visit them. It seems like something she'd do—she strikes me as fiercely loyal, and the kind of person who's always making sure everyone else is okay.

"And you got married over the summer?" I ask.

"Yeah, we eloped in Vegas," Luke says. So he secretly married his coach's daughter and lived to tell the tale. If I remember correctly from the social media posts I saw, they were lifelong friends before that, so it's a very different situation than me and Morgan.

Stop thinking about Morgan, I have to remind myself.

"Surprised the shit out of all of us," Drew says.

"Nah," Zach adds. "I wasn't surprised in the least. We all knew you had it bad for her. Just didn't know how bad, I guess."

"Like I said before," Luke says, and clears his throat. "Game 7 really put some stuff into perspective for me." I wait for them to give him shit, to say something like *Is 'perspective' code for you need to practice more?* But they don't, and Luke adds, "This season will be different. I'll be ready."

Colt looks at Hartmann and says, "You already are."

I wouldn't want the pressure of stepping into Colt's position, since he's the best goalie in the league, but do they honestly believe Hartmann's ready to replace him, after the way Game 7 went down?

Hartmann just nods, his jaw tight and his light brown hair flopping forward over his forehead.

Drew flips his phone over on the table, chuckles, and says, "Uh oh, I think my fiancée is a little tipsy."

"Why do you think that?" Zach asks.

"Don't ask," Colt groans and presses his thumb and forefinger across his brows.

McCabe chuckles like he knows where this is going.

"Audrey sends very . . . flirtatious text messages when she's had more than a single drink," Drew says with a sly smile. "I think I'm going to go get her and take her home. You guys want to come?"

I'm sitting here wondering why we'd want to go collect his drunk fiancée with him, but the other guys are nodding in agreement and downing the rest of their drinks. That's when I remember that Audrey is with the rest of their girlfriends, which means these guys all want to get back to their women.

And that's when it hits me that Morgan said these women were her best friends. Suddenly, I'm setting my glass on the table and shrugging. "Why not?"

As we stand to leave, McCabe says he's going to get home to AJ and Abby, and Walsh says he's headed home to his family too. But Walsh falls into step next to me as we head down the brick sidewalk in Beacon Hill toward the Boston Common.

"Did AJ talk to you about the alternate captain position?" Walsh asks quietly.

My brows wrinkle together. "Yeah, did she talk to *you* about it?"

"Yeah. I told her I thought it was a great idea."

"Why's that?" If there's anyone on the team who *shouldn't* want me to take that leadership role and potentially move back up to the first line, it's our other alternate captain Patrick Walsh, who spent last season in my old position.

"Because AJ wouldn't make that offer if she didn't think

you'd develop into a good leader on this team. Whatever she sees in you, focus on developing that. She doesn't try to change players, just wants them to be better versions of themselves—whether that's how they play, or how they act. Usually both."

No one is a bigger shit talker on the ice than Walsh, which is pretty ironic because he's such a stand-up guy. But he almost never gets in fights, no matter how much he chirps at other players. It's like it's part of his charm. But when I shit-talk people on the ice, they start throwing punches.

"Hmmm." I let the sound rattle around in my throat as I give him a nod. He could easily come across as condescending in this conversation, but that's not Walsh's style. "And what if I take your spot on the first line? You still going to feel that way?"

"If you take that spot, it'll mean you've earned it. I want what's best for the team." He claps his hand on my shoulder and gives it a squeeze before saying, "Have a good night guys. I'm headed home!"

Chapter Twenty

MORGAN

Tonight has been the girls night that I truly needed to get out of the vicious cycle of thinking about Danny/Aidan and the reality that he's in my life for the foreseeable future. I'm just finishing up my dinner, laughing at the way Jules just says whatever the hell she wants and how it almost always horrifies Audrey, when my phone buzzes on the table. I flip it over to see a text from my mom.

MOM

Hey, Max and I will be in Boston in a couple weeks. He'll be busy at a conference most of the time. Would love to grab dinner or something if you're around!

I set my phone face down again, wishing that my dinner didn't suddenly feel like it was turning sour in my stomach.

As far as I know, Mom hasn't been back to Boston since

my high school graduation—which means I haven't had to see her on my turf since I became an adult. There's something comforting in knowing she hasn't been around to ruin any of my favorite Boston places for me, unlike the way she ruined my favorite restaurant in New York City, the best coffee shop in Park City, and the view of Los Angeles from the Griffith Observatory.

So many bad memories are tied to her that I wonder why I even agree to see her anymore. But, she keeps making the effort—she calls or texts often enough that I know she hasn't forgotten me, but not often enough to consider it a meaningful relationship. And here she is, wanting to see me again because she'll be in town with Max. She's trying, even if her efforts all feel half-assed. Maybe that's all she's capable of?

"You okay?" Lauren asks, nudging me with her elbow from the seat next to me.

"Yeah," I say, realizing I'd been staring at my glass sitting on the table in front of me with such intensity that she probably thinks I was trying to make it levitate. "Just got distracted by a text."

"Your mom?" Clearly she saw my screen.

"Yeah, unfortunately."

Lauren's arm sweeps around my shoulder as she pulls me into a side hug. While technically they're my cousins, she and Paige are more like the sisters I never had. I used to spend a month every summer up in Maine with them, and my dad and I have spent every Christmas with them since my mom left. So I developed a very close bond with the two of them even though we lived over three hours away growing up. It's nice that we all live in the same city now, even if Paige is almost always traveling for work.

"You good?" Eva asks, brows scrunching as she assesses me from across the table.

"Yeah, I'm fine." Just embarrassed that I've made a bit of a scene when I'm supposed to be having fun with my girlfriends. "I just got distracted by my mom texting me."

Audrey leans back as the waiter clears her empty plate. "Did you ever ask her about your stepbrother's last name?"

Jules's eyebrows lift in anticipation of my response.

"No. I'm putting the past in the past, where it belongs," I say, wishing that this was true in my mind as well.

Now that I know who "Danny" is, and that we work together and my dad is his agent, I need to stay far away from him.

Despite being a great father to me, my dad is a great agent because he has no issue being a cutthroat asshole. Sleeping with his daughter is not something Aidan can risk in a contract year. It's not an understatement to say that his entire future rests in my dad's hands.

Unfortunately, it seems that the more I've tried to avoid Aidan this week, the more he's been on my mind. And flashbacks from Bermuda—the easy flirting the first night in the bar, how protective he was at dinner and on the boat, the way our bodies came together even when we knew they shouldn't—hit me at the most unexpected times. I can't stop thinking about our time together and wishing we could turn back time, even just for a night.

"Oh, come on, Morgan," Audrey says with a groan, as she rests her elbow on the table and cradles her chin in her palm. "You said it was the *best sex of your life*, remember?"

Her voice is quite a bit louder than I'd like in the glass-encased rooftop restaurant, so I lift my gaze to see if anyone else heard her. And of course—*of fucking course*—who is standing right behind her, but half of the Boston Rebels.

Drew smooths his hand over the top of his fiancée's dark hair with a shake of his head, like he's realizing she's had too much to drink. But Drew is not who catches my eye.

No, it's Aidan Renaud, standing slightly behind him, a goddamn smirk plastered across his perfect face and eyes dancing with amusement as he stares at me like he just *knows* I was talking about him.

How do these moments, where I just want the earth to open up and swallow me whole, always happen to me? Dad used to laugh and say, "Stupid shit really does always happen to you." Things like starting my period at the tennis club while wearing a white skirt, or tripping right before I got to the sand pit at the long jump the one year I did track in high school, and instead landing face-first in the sand.

My cheeks are on fire, so rather than respond to Audrey and potentially make the situation worse, I tilt my champagne glass up and take a sip. But of course, the French 75 only reminds me of being at the club with Aidan in Bermuda before he fucked me up against the wall outside, and now I can feel the flush creeping down my neck and chest.

Luckily Eva's phone rings then, so loud that all our heads are turning toward her. Eva snatches it up and mutes it saying, "Sorry, it's the nanny."

Luke is already at her side, and they step over to a quiet corner of the restaurant to take the call. This is the first night they've both been out at the same time; they wanted to do a trial run with the nanny to see how Gigi does with neither of them home. Eva's still got another few weeks before she can lace up her figure skates and start training for the Olympics again, but it coincides with the start of Luke's season, so they'll both go back to work at the same time.

The guys start pulling up chairs from empty tables, and I don't know why I didn't anticipate that they would show up here. It's happened before, more than once. But somehow, I hadn't really considered that the next time it happened, Aidan might be with them. Running into him is going to be part of the new normal. Even if I could somehow back out of working with the Rebels, which is not something I'd do, he'd still be around because his teammates are my friends.

"Best sex of your life, huh?" he says, leaning toward me from where he's planted a chair at the end of the table next to me, his voice low enough that I'm sure I'm the only one who can hear him.

"I was talking about someone else."

I glance away and don't miss Lauren's gaze focused on me. There isn't much she doesn't notice, and I don't want her to start putting any puzzle pieces together, especially since she works with us.

His low rumble of laughter is a caress running along my skin, and I shiver in response. It's like he knows that what we had together in Bermuda was the most amazing sex. I might have even said that to him at one point, and maybe he said it too?

Above us, the string lights that run from one side of the rooftop restaurant to the other sparkle against the glass walls and ceiling, creating a glowing ambiance. All around us, lush plants provide enough greenery that you feel like you're eating outside. The whole space has an ethereal glow, and it's giving me flashbacks of the grove of trees and bushes we retreated into as we left the club our last night in Bermuda.

I don't want this beautiful space to remind me of that night with him. I don't want my body to crave my stepbrother's the minute I see him. I don't want to know that under this broody exterior lies a guy who brought me coffee because he knew I wasn't a morning person, who drove a boat slowly and near the shore so I wouldn't be afraid, who refused to let me celebrate my birthday alone in my hotel room.

"Sure you were," he says, his voice low and soft as he reaches under the table. My entire core clenches when his callused hand lands on my bare knee, and another shiver wracks my body when he slides his hand halfway up my thigh. "That's why you looked like you wanted to disappear as soon as you saw me standing there."

He's teasing me, and I'm not sure how I feel about that. I'm a conflicted jumble of emotions and have been since finding out who he is earlier this week. My body wants to lean into him, give in to the attraction. But my head tells me I need some distance so I can figure out how I feel about all of this.

"Maybe you could teach me how," I say. Then I raise my voice quite a bit louder when I add, "I hear disappearing is your specialty."

From the other side of Jules, Colt's laugh rings out. "Way to put him in his place, Morgan."

Our group starts talking animatedly about Renaud's absence last season, and how much better the team will be now that he's back. But I'm barely listening because I'm so distracted by his hand, now resting on his own thigh beside me, and the way he keeps flexing his fingers, splaying them wide before relaxing. I remember him doing something similar under the table at dinner after the wedding, the last time we sat side-by-side like this. I wonder if it's a coping mechanism? And if so, what exactly is he dealing with right now?

We don't stay much longer because Eva and Luke come back to the table to tell us Gigi woke up and they're headed home, and it's obvious the staff is getting ready to close for the night. So we all pile down the stairs of the restaurant and everyone sets out in their own directions after we say our goodbyes. I turn to walk home because we're only a few blocks from where I live, and suddenly Aidan's walking beside me.

"What are you doing?" I ask him.

"Walking you home."

"I'm perfectly capable of walking myself home. I do it all the time." If he's concerned for my safety, he needn't be. It's a busy Saturday night, and the two streets I need to walk down to get to my place are well lit and will be packed full of people.

"As a *friend*, I feel responsible for making sure you get home safely." His teasing floods me with memories of just how friendly we've been in the past. "If you prefer, I can walk behind you and pretend like I don't know you."

"How do you even know you're headed the same way?"

"Besides the fact that we're walking in the same direction, you mean?" His tone has a bit of a bite to it, like it always does when he's uncomfortable. I don't know why I know this about him, but apparently I do. Now I'm wondering why he's uncomfortable.

"How do I know you're not following me?" I tease, just to lighten the mood.

"Relax," he says, and runs a hand up my back. I glance sideways and note the way his eyes are dark orbs as they study me, his olive skin bathed in the light of the street lamps. "I live over on Marlborough Street. You?"

"Newbury," I tell him, wondering why he has to live three blocks from me, on one of the nicest streets in all of Boston, when he could live anywhere in the whole damn city?

"I met with your dad earlier today," he says, and my gaze snaps up to his face. "Just a standard check-in before the season starts. But obviously he knows that we work together."

"Yeah, I told him about the media piece I was writing about you."

"Does he know . . . anything else?" Aidan asks.

"How the hell would I have broached *that* topic with my father?" I ask, glancing over at him. "I can't even mention that I met you in Bermuda, or that you're my stepbrother, since we don't talk about my mom."

"Ever?"

I nod. "He's always been supportive of *me* having a relationship with her. But for obvious reasons, he doesn't want to know about her life after she walked out on him."

His hand curls around my hip as he moves me in front of him to avoid a big group of drunken guys heading toward us, two of whom are walking backward and yelling to the others. Once we pass them, he doesn't let go, even as he steps up beside me.

"It seems like she walked out on both of you, no? Why do *you* still want to have a relationship with her?" He asks the question with obvious curiosity instead of the judgment I would have expected.

My lips turn down at the corners as I swallow the lump in my throat. "It's complicated."

I think about the text from earlier tonight and how, after her last wedding, it was nearly two years before I saw her in person again. This time, I'll be seeing her twice within a month, and that feels like maybe it's progress?

I glance up at Aidan as we walk, but apparently he's decided to hold on to his thoughts. Finally, as we turn the corner onto Newbury Street, he says, "You seem like you have a good relationship with your dad?"

"Yeah. I know his reputation as an agent, but he's a great father."

Most of what I know about Dad's professional reputation is from Lauren's husband, Jameson, who was my dad's client when he played for the Rebels. When he retired early to raise his little sisters, Audrey and Jules, after their mother died and their father left, Dad gave him his first job as an agent. Dad's basically the reason Jameson and Lauren missed their chance together and didn't reconnect until five years later. Jameson has told me a few horror stories about how Dad has screwed over his clients if he thought they weren't being loyal to him.

"He's been a great agent for me. He took me on in college and convinced me to enter the draft while I was still in school. I got to play two more years of D1 hockey knowing that I had a spot lined up already. It's funny that he never mentioned having a daughter."

I scoff out a laugh. "Why would he mention his teenage daughter to his client?"

I barely hear Aidan's low chuckle over the sound of a

driver laying on the horn at a guy who's double-parked. "Fair point. Were you always such a daddy's girl?"

"Yeah. I don't know if it's because he traveled so much for work when I was younger, or because my mom was never particularly warm and fuzzy, but when Dad was home, I always gravitated toward him. After my mom left, we became more like partners, figuring out how to exist without the person who'd made us a family in the first place. Since then, Dad's always treated me more like an equal than his child."

Aidan's hand squeezes my hip, and it feels like he's giving me a supportive hug—a shared recognition of what we've both been through with our parents.

"Was it like that with your mom after your dad passed?"

"No, because Max was always around for us. He was basically a surrogate dad to me, even before he and my mom started dating. He took me to hockey practice, he took us out to dinner . . . that type of thing. I think he was just checking in on us as much as he could, because he knew it's what my dad would have wanted."

I chew my lip, wanting to ask him so many more questions, but not wanting to pry. "Max seems like a really good guy."

"He's the best." There's no hesitation when Aidan says this, and it makes me realize how hard it must be for him, watching Max marry a new woman every few years. It's hard for me with my mom, but she was never the kind of parent to me that Max has been for Aidan. The irony—that they're not even biologically related—isn't lost on me.

I slow and turn onto the brick walkway that leads to the steep stone steps of my brownstone. This walk back from the restaurant is so reminiscent of the times we walked back to our hotel rooms in Bermuda, but it feels platonic enough that it makes me wonder if we can fall into a friendship after all the lines we've crossed together. This would be so much easier if I could just think of him as one of the guys on the team, if we could hang out without it being awkward or without bringing up memories from Bermuda.

"Thanks for making sure I got home safe," I say as I start to turn away.

"That's the least I could do for a *friend*." His emphasis on the word has me wondering whether he's really able to think of me as a friend.

The way his eyes flick down to my cleavage, visible in the V-neck of my sweater, makes me think not. But I don't ask. Like me, he's probably trying to figure out how to do this whole friendship thing with someone he's already slept with.

"All right, well, thanks, *friend*."

Turning away from him, I take the stairs up to my front door two at a time. After I slip inside, I turn to shut the door behind me and through the large glass pane, I catch sight of Aidan standing on the walkway. My stomach swoops low in my belly as our gazes lock, and the smirk on his face as he shakes his head slightly tells me he thinks I just ran away like a scared little kid.

And maybe I did. Because what I said to AJ back in her office before I went to Bermuda—that if there's one thing I excel at, it's attracting assholes—is still true.

Whether Aidan Renaud is *actually* an asshole, or he's just really good at pretending he is, remains to be seen. But the fact that I'm wondering what it would take to unravel that mystery is, in itself, the problem.

Chapter Twenty-One

AIDAN

"How'd that feel on your hand?" Jared asks as I finish my last set of triceps pushdowns. The last few weeks have been more than my body has been accustomed to but it's left me feeling high on endorphins every single day. I'm finally back to doing what I love, and now that we've all passed the grueling physical tests they put us through, tomorrow will be our first day back on the ice.

"Felt fine. No pain at all." One of the only lingering issues with my hand after reconstructive surgery is that when I bend my wrist a certain way *and* put pressure on it, it aches. So we've been doing different exercises over the past week and a half to rebuild my strength and get my hand ready for the force I'll need to exert on my stick.

Given how extensive the injuries were to my bones, I was incredibly lucky that there was no nerve or tissue damage in my hand. I certainly learned my lesson about trying to break up someone else's drunken fight in a crowded bar.

Maybe that's why AJ asking me to serve as the other alternate captain rubs me the wrong way—last time I tried to do the right thing, I got a year on IR.

"That's great," Jared says, glancing around the empty training room. It was packed earlier, but we're the last ones here. "You ready to be back on the ice tomorrow?"

"Beyond ready." I've skated more this past summer than any summer before. I worked on my stick handling skills and practiced shooting until I felt as confident as ever, and did skating drills until I thought my legs would give out under me.

Yet I haven't gone up against other players, because that was considered too dangerous to my recovery—one wrong hit to my hand before I was done rehabbing it would have ensured I was out another season. So facing off with my teammates at training camp tomorrow will be the true test of whether I'm as ready for my return as I told AJ I was.

"Good. Leave that kinesiology tape on it overnight to keep it stable. Then see me first thing tomorrow morning and I'll retape it for practice."

We decide on a time to meet, and I turn to head out of the room so I can go shower, only to find Morgan standing in the door to the hallway. She's wearing a dress that hits just below her knees. It's a deep green that plays off the golden streaks in her hair, which hangs in loose waves around her shoulders, except for the pieces of hair above her ears that are braided and pulled back behind her head. She's gorgeous standing there looking fancier than I'd expect for work, but incredibly pissed off, too.

Jared gives her a nod and heads into the office off the training room, shutting the door behind him. I run my palm up my forehead and push my hair off my face because the sweat is starting to drip into my eyes.

"Why do I feel like I'm in trouble?" I joke. It's been nearly two weeks since I last saw her, despite looking for her every time I'm here. The less I see of her, the more I'm thinking of her.

Morgan rolls her eyes. "*Should* you be in trouble?"

"I usually am. And you just look so . . . pissed off?" *Well, this is awkward.*

"Go ahead, tell me to smile," she says, lifting her chin. "It's been a while since I had a reason to punch anyone."

"Someone's feisty today." My chuckle does not seem to relax her.

"I don't have time for this right now. I need a quick video of you to add to the *Renaud Returns* compilation we're posting tomorrow." Morgan emphasizes *Renaud Returns* like it's the most ridiculous thing she's ever heard. "Can you just . . . pretend to be working out, or something?"

I lift an eyebrow at her. "What's really going on here?"

"Nothing. Is a girl not allowed to be in a bad mood?" Her tone is flippant and I have to bite back a smile because she's adorable when she's pissy like this.

"Am *I* the cause of your bad mood?"

"No." She takes a deep breath like she's grounding herself. Then she shakes her head slightly, lets out her breath, and admits, "I agreed to have dinner with my mom tonight."

"Is she here with Max?" I met him for coffee yesterday morning before his conference started, but he didn't mention Anne being here too. Then again, I didn't mention working with Morgan, either. It was a very quick visit and he was mostly peppering me with questions about how I'm settling back into my place in the city, how my hand is doing now that I'm training more intensely, and whether I'm looking forward to being back on the ice.

"Yeah, for that conference."

"Why did you agree to dinner with her if you didn't want to go?"

She sighs and says, "Because she's making an effort to see me."

I cross my arms over my chest and note the way her eyes track the length of one bicep, along my folded forearms, and up the other bicep.

I think of all the ways I saw Morgan trying to be a good daughter in Bermuda, when Anne was so clearly not being a good mother. "I've seen the *effort* your mom makes and how she treats you."

Her laugh is humorless. "You should see how she acts when it's just the two of us."

"Morgan. Why do you keep doing this to yourself?" I try to keep my tone from sounding patronizing, but really . . . why?

She reaches into the pocket of her dress and pulls out a package of Nerds Gummy Clusters. She shakes the bumpy rainbow-colored candies into her cupped hand and holds it out to me. "Want some?"

I generally try to avoid things that are artificially flavored and colored, but our nutritionist isn't around to reprimand me, so I reach out and take a few, popping them in my mouth and trying not to make a face at the overbearing sweetness. "Haven't had Nerds since I was a kid."

"These are like little stress relief pills for me. Not the healthiest choice, but better than some other alternatives, I guess. So, anyway, can you go and pretend to lift some weights or something so I can snap a few photos to send off to Natalie for tomorrow's post?"

"Sure," I say, turning to survey the equipment and figure out what I can use that won't require a spotter but will still make for a good photo.

Ten minutes later, I'm even sweatier, and she's got the photos she needs. She turns to leave, typing on her phone as she sends the photos off. Her shoulders are a tense line as she heads into the hallway. And then I head into the locker room to find my phone.

Max might think this is an odd request since I just saw him yesterday, and I know he has plans tonight. Not to mention that never once in the past have I tried to get to know his new wife—they're never around long enough to bother. But the thought of Morgan having to face her mom alone means I'm just desperate enough to risk raising some suspicion.

Carson's warning flits through my mind, but I push it away quickly. This isn't a distraction; this is looking out for his daughter since she obviously hasn't told him how her mother treats her.

Yeah, that's all this is.

AIDAN

Hey, I hear Anne's in town with you, and she and Morgan are going out to dinner. Maybe you can cancel your plans and we can surprise them, so I can get to know my stepmom and stepsister a little better?

MAX

Why do I feel like you're up to something?

AIDAN

Can't a guy get to know his new stepfamily
without an agenda?

MAX

I know you so much better than you think,
son. But sure, let's go with your reason.

Chapter Twenty-Two

MORGAN

I pull open the heavy glass door of Evolve, the new restaurant right near the Public Garden that my mom chose for dinner tonight. There are heavy mustard yellow curtains hanging on either side of the opening, and a big dark host stand set back in the center.

Going out to dinner tonight is the last thing I need. I'm struggling to keep up with all my clients' needs given how much I've taken on with the Rebels. One of my highest-priority clients has a big social media announcement coming tomorrow about the launch of a new brand partnership. Given that dinner will take hours, I'll probably be up until two in the morning double-checking everything and getting all the media scheduled to post tomorrow. Then I have to be back at the Rebels practice facility in the morning for the first skate of training camp.

The only bright spot in all of this is that Natalie has turned out to be much more competent and capable than

Tatum when it comes to social media management, so I'm already working on a plan to delegate more to her and pull back slightly. I also need to have a conversation with Patrick because he needs to know that his intern is more qualified than the person she'll be reporting to when Tatum returns.

"Can I help you?" The hostess asks when I approach the large piece of carved black walnut that serves as the host stand.

"I'm meeting someone with a reservation. Anne . . ." I pause for a moment, barely catching myself before I almost used my mom's *previous* married name. ". . . Heinberg."

"Ah yes, I just seated Mrs. Heinberg. Follow me."

I walk behind her through the glowing restaurant. The walls are painted black with evenly spaced pieces of polished dark wood running vertically from the floor to the loft-style ceiling, with everything painted black. The lights that hang from the ceiling give everything a golden tint. The restaurant is crowded and loud, with every table full and waiters bustling around.

My mom sits at a four-person table near the back wall, made up of vertical slats of wood, evenly spaced to divide the kitchen from the dining area without actually blocking the view. I take the seat opposite her.

"Hi, honey," Mom says, a smile plastered on her face. Her skin is so tight from her facelift that her smile looks forced. She must have gotten some sun on her honeymoon because I notice the tightness even more than I did three weeks ago. "Don't you look lovely today."

"Thanks, I came straight from work."

"You wore *that* dress to work?"

I lift my eyebrows and give her a small smile. "Yes?"

I'm not sure how she can find fault with this outfit. It's a dark green poplin dress that hits right at my knee, paired with a wide woven belt that matches the tan wedges I'm wearing. It's classic and professional.

My mom gives a slight laugh and says, "Honey, I forgot you worked from home. I thought you were going into an office or something."

"Actually," I say, realizing that I never got a chance to tell her I was working for the Rebels part-time. "I just started—"

"There are our girls," a man's voice booms from my right, and Mom and I both look over. But whereas she jumps out of her seat, exclaiming what a great surprise this is, my blood runs cold because Aidan is standing next to Max. I don't understand what the hell is happening right now.

He *knew* I was going to dinner with my mom, so showing up here can't be an accident. Was he roped into this by Max? Or did he suggest it?

Max takes the open seat next to my mom, and Aidan pulls out the chair next to me. *Shit, Danny. I need to remember to call him Danny.* Am I supposed to pretend I haven't seen him since Bermuda? That we don't work together? Or are we going to tell them?

My mind is reeling with questions and trying to figure out how we've found ourselves here together, when my mom says, "To what do we owe this surprise?"

I lift my water glass and take a sip, hoping it'll help my suddenly dry mouth and throat.

"It was Danny's idea," Max says. "He wanted to get to know his stepmom and stepsister better."

My throat contracts as I swallow, pushing some of the

water into my lungs. I cough into my napkin, then barely manage to excuse myself before getting up from the table.

I slip into the women's room, and with one hand on the side of the sink and the other holding my hair back, I cough so hard I nearly throw up. I manage to clear my lungs, but when I'm done and glance up into the mirror, I look like some sort of Halloween doll meant to scare children. My nose and cheeks are bright pink, and there's mascara smudged under my eyes.

Grabbing a couple squares of toilet paper from one of the stalls, I set about cleaning my face, and then my phone buzzes in my pocket.

The first text came in about two minutes ago, and I probably didn't notice because I was too busy hacking up a lung and wondering if I was going to pass out in the process.

UNKNOWN NUMBER

Are you okay?

Morgan, do I need to come in there and
make sure you're alive?

I glance at the heavy wooden door. *What the hell?*

MORGAN

How did you get my number?

UNKNOWN NUMBER

It's your contact number on your company
website.

MORGAN

Why were you on my website?

UNKNOWN NUMBER

I was curious.

I save his contact, take one last look in the mirror to ensure I look presentable-ish, and pull open the door. He's standing there in dress pants and a button-down shirt, and the way the top two buttons are open and his sleeves are rolled up, showcasing his bronze skin and muscular fore-arms, has my mouth watering.

I run through the laundry list of reasons I need to stay away from him, the same as I do each time I think of him.

"Are you okay? That was quite the choking incident back there."

My bark of laughter is sharp. "You said you wanted to *get to know your stepsister better?*"

"Maybe I do." His smirk just about does me in. Half the time I can't decide if I want to kill him or kiss him.

We're close in this narrow hallway, and I'm surrounded by his scent. I swear this man wears pheromones as cologne. "You've known me in the biblical sense."

"There's still *plenty* of ways I'd like to know you." His voice is husky and rough as his breath meets my face and he brings his hands to my shoulders like he's trying to keep me close to him.

"Aidan, why are you here? I thought we were keeping our distance."

"When did we decide that?" His tone is cajoling, a clear indication that he doesn't think he agreed to that.

"That night we walked back from the restaurant." I've been going out of my way to avoid him in the two weeks since, which only means he's constantly on my mind.

"No, that night we decided to be friends. So I'm being a good friend and not letting you have dinner with your mother alone."

He's seen how truly shitty my mom can be to me, and he's shown up so I don't have to weather that alone. I'm not sure what to make of it. It *is* something a friend would do—maybe it really is as simple as he's saying?

I glance away, and that's when I notice my mom and Max watching us closely through those wooden slats. "Fuck. We have an audience."

Aidan turns and follows my gaze, dropping his hands from my shoulders as he does. "We probably need to tell them we work together."

"Probably." I look back at him, chuckling before I say, "Funny how you assured me in Bermuda that there'd be no awkward family dinners in the future, and then you went and orchestrated one."

I turn and walk away, expecting that he'll follow.

"You guys okay?" Max asks when we get back to the table.

"Yeah, Danny was just making sure I was still breathing. I told him I was fine, but apparently he had to see for himself."

Aidan's posture is rigid when he takes his seat next to me. "Seems she's okay after all."

"Oh, good," my mom says. "I was afraid we might have to skip dinner and rush you to the hospital or something."

I don't know what to focus on first—the fact that missing dinner was the first priority in that sentence, or that she thought I might need to be rushed to the hospital and didn't even bother to come check on me? I try to give her the benefit of the doubt because, knowing Aidan, he probably jumped up first saying he'd make sure I was okay.

"I'm fine," I say, picking up my menu. "Also, you married a doctor, so he probably could have stepped in before the hospital was necessary."

Max lets out an amused chuckle and says, "Seems like Danny had it under control. Speaking of," he turns toward Aidan, "how's training camp going?"

"Training camp?" Mom asks, tilting her chin as she looks at her stepson.

"I'm a professional hockey player. I play for the Rebels."

"No way," my mom says. *My god, how does she not know this about her husband's son?* It makes me wonder if she and Max talk about anything meaningful at all.

Aidan sends Max a questioning look, and I assume he's wondering the same.

"I'm sure I told you that, honey," Max says to my mom.

"You probably did," she says, rubbing his arm. "Sorry, I'm just so forgetful lately." She throws in a giggle that makes her sound like a teenage girl still trying to figure out if playing dumb is the right way to flirt with boys.

"It's funny," I say, "because after we got back from Bermuda, Danny and I actually realized we work together."

"Imagine my surprise, sitting in a meeting in my GM's office, only to have Morgan walk in."

"You work for the Rebels, too?" Max asks, saving my mom the trouble.

"Just part-time," I say.

"*That's* what you're using your MBA for?" Mom asks. "A part-time job for a hockey team?"

I know Mom's views on hockey and how much she hates the sport. I think she hates it just because my dad loves it so much, and maybe also because it took him away from her more than she wanted. Retrospectively, I'm guessing their unhappy marriage was half the reason Dad traveled so much for work. Once she left and it was just him and me, the travel virtually stopped.

"Actually," Aidan's voice rings out protectively, while his hand moves beneath the table to rest on my thigh like he's worried I'm going to jump across the table and strangle her. I'm not. Sadly, I'm used to my mom knowing virtually nothing about my life, whether I've kept her updated or not. "Morgan owns her own boutique PR firm and is just helping out on a special project with the Rebels."

I glance over at him. I know Colt, McCabe, and I essentially had that conversation in front of him in AJ's office, and he just admitted to searching up my company's website, but somehow I'm still shocked.

"Tell me more," Max says.

"In the early summer, I was brought on to create a new social media vision for the team, and train their social media manager on how to execute it," I tell him. "Then she went out on medical leave, so I agreed to help out until she's back." I glance at Aidan and then back at Max. "So it's kind of funny that I didn't realize *Danny* is Aidan Renaud."

Max chuckles. "Yeah, I guess, why would you have? You probably assumed he was Danny Heinberg?"

"Exactly."

"Your teammates must have been surprised that you two are related," Max says to Aidan.

Before he can respond, I say, "We haven't said anything to them, and we don't plan to."

Next to me, Aidan stiffens but I'm not sure why. This is exactly what he said in the elevator that first day in the Rebels' office: that there was no reason my friends needed to know he's my stepbrother. And if he told his teammates, my friends would all know too, and they'd quickly put two and two together. The only way for no one to find out we've slept together, is to keep our stepsibling status a secret.

Aidan's grip on my thigh tightens. Just like on the walk back from the restaurant the other night, he can't seem to keep his hands off me.

But we're only friends, so I glance at him, hoping he understands my meaning loud and clear when I say, "I don't like to blur personal and professional lines."

Chapter Twenty-Three

AIDAN

"Renaud!" Our head coach, Charlie Wilcott, motions me over to where he's standing at the edge of the rink, clipboard in hand, as he watches us doing drills. Behind him, AJ stands at our bench.

I skate over, coming to a stop in front of him, and pull off my helmet. "Yeah, Coach?"

"You think anymore about the alternate captain position? We need to make an announcement soon."

My gaze flicks to where AJ stands next to him.

"Honestly, I'm still conflicted."

"Why's that, son?" he asks. He's the kind of coach who makes you feel like you're part of the family. I came on the team at the same time he did, and even though he was also new, he made me feel welcome from my first day. I improved more as a player in the years I played for him, before my injury, than I'd developed in all the years before that.

There's been a lot of speculation over the years about

what the media calls "The Wilcott Effect"—why his players develop so quickly and his team makes it to the Stanley Cup Playoffs yearly. But the answer is simple, really. He encourages you to be a better player, and then refuses to let you settle for anything less than your best. It makes me think of what AJ said a couple weeks ago: *Sometimes, all people need in order to reach their potential is an invitation.*

"I've been so focused this past year on getting back to playing, and I promised myself that there'd be no distractions. That I'd be singularly focused on being the best player I can be."

"What if being the best player you can be means stepping up in other ways, too?" Coach asks, his head cocked as he watches me consider his question.

"I'm just not sure if being in a leadership position, being a role model on the team, is the kind of player I am."

"That's too bad," he says, my response clearly disappointing him. "Because, especially with Colt retiring at the end of the season, our team could use more leaders. We can always find someone else to take your position, but we'd really like it to be you."

I glance between them, trying to figure out if by "your position" they mean my position on the team, or the leadership position they've already decided should be mine. Could be either, honestly, since I'm in the last year of my contract. I'd really like to re-sign with the Rebels, and not have the long, drawn out contract process McCabe had last year.

"You're already going to have to change your brand of playing, Renaud," AJ says, and I can tell just by her voice that she's trying to deliver this news gently. "Being the best hockey player you can be, and being a good teammate at the same time, will mean you're *already* right for the alternate captain role."

I wonder again if this is AJ's way of keeping me in line, and I'm tempted to tell her that the real reason I'm so hesitant here is that I don't know if the guys on the team see me as captain material. It's hard to know. While they've welcomed me back enthusiastically, the vibe of the team has shifted in a way that leaves me feeling like the ice is shifting beneath my feet.

Perhaps this is my coach and GM's way of smoothing that transition, making me feel like an integral part of the team rather than an outsider stepping back in? Or maybe I'm just overthinking the fuck out of this, as I'm liable to do.

"All right," I say, hoping I don't regret this choice.

Coach claps a hand onto my shoulder pads, giving me a shake. "Good choice, Renaud."

"We'll tell the team at the end of practice today," AJ says, "and announce it publicly right after." She glances across the ice where Morgan is standing with the social media intern, and motions her over. It's taken every ounce of my willpower not to glance over at her every time I'm not involved in a drill or a play, but I keep reminding myself: *No distractions.*

Now that they're making me a captain, it's more important than ever.

"I should get back to practice," I say, shaking the sweat from my hair before putting my helmet back on.

"Yep," Coach says. "And you're looking good out there, keep it up."

Practice ends about fifteen minutes later, and I'm relieved when AJ announces the captain positions for this season and

I skate forward to stand next to McCabe and Walsh to the cheers of my teammates. We stand there together so photos can be taken, and then our teammates pile in behind us for one big group photo.

I take my time after that, as we file off the ice, just absorbing the feel of the place. A few weeks ago, this rink felt different—unfamiliar, though not unwelcoming. Now, it's starting to feel like home again.

———

"Good choice today, man," McCabe says, knocking his shoulder with mine before he hands me a beer. Thankfully, tonight we've picked a proper bar to celebrate the end of our second week of training camp, so I'm not stuck drinking a fucking margarita.

Though if I'm being honest, the level of discretion at The Neon Cactus was nice. Whether they realize we're professional hockey players or not, no one bothers us there. But at this place, people keep coming up and asking for pictures.

After a year without this kind of notoriety, I'm torn between annoyance at the constant interruptions while I'm trying to hang out with my teammates, and being grateful people remember I exist. With the announcement the Rebels put out this afternoon, naming me as the new alternate captain alongside Walsh, and renaming McCabe as our captain, I guess I shouldn't be surprised that I'm at the forefront of Boston sports fans' minds.

"Fucking finally," Colt says.

"What do you mean, finally?" I ask. For at least the last

decade, Colt's been the unofficial captain on this team, since he's a goalie and can't wear the *C* on the ice.

"It's about time you stepped up. You could be a leader out there and instead you spend half your time in the penalty box."

"Pfft. You sound like AJ," I say.

"Because I'm always right?" Colt smirks. "This is a good move for you," he says, more sincerely. "I feel good about this."

I wait for him to say something sarcastic, but it doesn't come. "Are you getting sentimental in your old age, Colt?" I ask, tipping my beer back as my gaze catches behind him where Morgan has walked in with Jules, Audrey, and AJ. McCabe and Colt had said "the girls went over to visit Eva" while Hartmann came out with us, but I hadn't realized that his departure half an hour ago meant they'd be showing up here.

I see what she means about how intertwined she is with my teammates.

I can think of at least five reasons I shouldn't be thinking about her. But no matter what I tell myself, she's always running through my mind. I look for her every time I'm at the Rebels practice rink. I picture her every time my hand is around my cock. I haven't thought of or looked at another woman since I met her.

It's been so long since I've felt this way about anyone that I almost don't recognize the feeling. But when I do, I also remember all the heartache that came with the one and only time I let myself fall for someone. I don't want to be infatuated with my stepsister, but I think I'm quickly heading in that direction.

"Dude," McCabe says as his elbow digs into my side, "you're staring. And I'm going to guess you're not eying my girlfriend or Colt's fiancée, so why can't you take your eyes off Morgan?"

Fuck. Fuckety fuck. I forgot that under that scowl and his hardened exterior, McCabe is incredibly observant. It's a skill I'd like him to lose at the moment, especially since I'm not thinking as quickly as I should after these last few beers.

"Just . . . thinking that I never thanked her for the write up she did on me coming back this year."

On either side of me, my friends snort out laughs that let me know they're not buying that story. Luckily, there isn't time for them to comment on my lie before the women are right in front of us.

Her friends cozy up to my friends, and when she glances at me, she looks a bit uncomfortable. She takes in the drinks in our hands and says, "I'm going to go get us some drinks. AJ, Jules, what do you guys want?"

She heads to the bar with her friends' drink orders, and I give myself a moment to watch the sway of her hips as her short skirt highlights her thick, toned thighs. Then I snap my gaze back to my friends before I let myself remember what those thighs felt like wrapped around my waist in that cave and around my head in that hotel room. But as I chat with them, listening to all the updates on Luke and Eva's baby, my eyes are already scanning the crowd because I've lost sight of Morgan.

When I find her, she's down toward the end of the bar ordering her drinks, and beyond her, on the other side of the bar, sits some random finance bro who can't take his eyes off her. The lecherous look on his face as his gaze travels over her has a tight coil winding around inside me. He says something to the guy sitting next to him, then slides off his barstool and heads around the corner of the bar.

I know the second Morgan spots him, because her spine stiffens and she angles her body the opposite direction like she hopes he won't see her there. Obviously she knows him.

"Be right back," I say, handing Colt my beer as I push through our small circle and weave my way through the crowd. I hear murmurings around me as I jostle people out of my way to get to her. He gets there first.

She turns slightly toward him, says something, and then tries to turn away but his hand snakes around her waist. "I have nothing to say to you, Carter," she says as I come up behind her, settling myself up against the bar on her other side.

"This guy bothering you?" I have to raise my voice to be heard over the loud music from the speakers directly above the bar, and a few people near us turn their attention in our direction.

She turns toward me, looking immensely relieved at my presence. "He was just leaving."

"Babe," this asshole, Carter, draws out the word like he's trying to coax her to give him a chance. "Come on, I miss you."

The fuck? I need someone to tell me she didn't have a thing with this guy. He sounds like a used car salesman who knows he's fucking you over and has the slightly disheveled look of someone who just lost an important business deal. A few locks of greasy hair hang down his forehead, and his cheeks are pink in the way that happens to some people when they've drunk too much.

"You are, quite literally, the last person on the planet that I want to talk to right now," she says, her voice so full of disdain that I actually chuckle.

"You heard the lady. Time to run along," I say, with a little flick of my hand like I'm shooing away a bug. Because that's what this guy is, an annoying bug.

"Hey, man," he says, looking up at me from the other side of Morgan. "I'm trying to talk to my girl and I don't know what your problem is—"

I keep my voice a whole lot calmer than I feel when I say, "My problem is that, *a*, she's not your girl, and *b*, she's asked you to leave her alone multiple times."

"Maybe you should mind your own business?" he says, taking the hand that was resting on Morgan's hip and pushing it into my chest.

I don't move an inch. "I suggest you not touch me, or her, again."

"Yeah? Or what?"

Chapter Twenty-Four

MORGAN

Here I was, thinking this situation couldn't get any worse, and then Carter had to open his big mouth and utter the stupidest words you could say in this situation. I suspect he's the only guy in the bar who doesn't recognize Aidan. A few weeks without a haircut or trimming his beard, and he looks every bit the hockey player he's known as and almost nothing like the guy I flirted with at a bar in Bermuda.

"Let's not find out." Aidan is eerily calm, his voice making him sound almost bored, and that seems to ramp Carter up even more.

I have no idea what Carter is thinking—Aidan is easily six inches taller than him, with about fifty pounds more muscle. And despite his calm voice, I can tell Aidan is wound tight, ready to beat Carter's ass if he makes the wrong choice here. It's like he's just waiting for Carter to throw the first punch so he can show him what *or what* looks like.

"Hey," a sharp voice comes from my left, and we all turn to see the bartender setting three drinks on the bar top. "Cool it, you two, or I'll have security remove you."

"I didn't do anything," Carter's voice rings out like a petulant child, "this asshole is bothering us."

Standing between these two men—so different in every way—it's unbelievable that I ever fell for one, and unfortunate that I can't have the other.

No, you don't want Aidan, I remind myself. We had a great few days in Bermuda, back when I thought he was someone else. Nothing about us together makes any sense.

Carter steps past me, as I stand with my back against the bar, and shoves Aidan again. It's like he has zero self-preservation instincts.

When Aidan barely moves despite the way Carter throws his weight into the shove, Carter instead cocks his elbow back like he's winding up to punch him. I don't move away fast enough, and his elbow connects with my cheek. I yelp in surprise as I press a hand to my cheek, and then the pain strikes and my eyes instantly fill with tears. *Fuck, that hurt.*

Stepping toward Carter, Aidan pulls me behind him. Over the shouts of everyone around us, I have to strain to hear Aidan's words. "You're going to apologize to her, and then you're leaving."

"The hell I am," Carter says, and he must make a move toward Aidan because when I peek around his side, Aidan's fist connects with Carter's nose and the sound of crunching bone silences everyone in the immediate vicinity.

"Aidan," I gasp, "your hand—"

"Is perfectly fine. See?" Instead of showing me his hand, he punches a stunned Carter a second time, this time connecting with his jaw. And a third time, right on the side of his face.

Carter's head snaps back each time, but he stays upright, and as Aidan goes to punch him again, my voice rings out sharply. "Aidan. Stop!"

He stills instantly, and we watch as Carter stands there swaying side to side before he steps back, slips, and falls on his ass.

"Enjoy your broken nose, asshole," Aidan says as he grabs my hand and drags me through the crowd toward the door.

On the sidewalk outside, Aidan moves so quickly I'm nearly running to keep up with him. About a block down, he pulls me into the alcove that houses the recessed doors to a shop. The light above us shines in my eyes as he tilts my chin up, moving it to the side as his fingertips lightly skim my cheek. "That's going to leave a bruise."

"No shit." I wince at his light touch, but am not in the mood to listen to him state the obvious. "What the fuck was that all about? I had things handled, and you made it worse."

His fingers steer my jaw upward, making me meet his gaze. "He had his hand around your waist and wouldn't leave you alone. That's not *handled*."

"Oh, so the big hockey player has to come throw his weight around? How fucking predictable."

"Nooo," the word is slow and deliberate leaving his lips. "You just needed backup."

"No, I didn't. In case you hadn't noticed, I'm an adult and can handle myself."

"He was not leaving you alone, despite your telling him multiple times."

I don't know what bothers me more—the way he stepped

in and escalated things, or the fact that he saw me as weak and needing rescuing from the confrontation with Carter.

"I don't need you inserting yourself into situations I already have a handle on. Or any situations, for that matter. I'm going home to put some ice on my face."

"I'm coming with you."

I step past him onto the sidewalk. "No, you're not. Go back to your teammates, Renaud." Using his last name doesn't dismiss him the way I intend it to, because as I head down the street, he steps up beside me.

"I'm not going back in there."

"Why not?"

"Aside from the fact that they probably wouldn't *let* me back in, I can't be held responsible for what else I'd do to the asshole who was harassing you." He shoves his hands in his pockets as we walk.

Half a block later, when it's apparent he's intent on following me to make sure I get home safely, I say, "Are you sure your hand is okay? That was such a stupid thing to do after having multiple surgeries."

He chuckles. "That was my right hand. If I'd used my dominant hand, he would've been on the floor. I went easy on him."

I shake my head at him and his ridiculous bravado. "What is it about men that makes them think fighting is the answer to everything?"

"Maybe brute force is the way we protect people when words don't do the job."

I huff out a laugh. "Not every problem requires your fists to solve it."

"That one did."

———

My phone rings before I've even closed the door to my apartment, and AJ's number flashes on my screen.

I barely even have time to say hello before she's talking, "Morgan, where did you guys go? McCabe and I tried to follow you out, but by the time we were on the sidewalk, you were already gone." We must have been standing in the recessed doorway at that point, so they didn't see us when they looked down the street. "Are you okay?"

"Yeah," I say, glancing over the island into my kitchen where Aidan is fishing around in my freezer. "Just about to get some ice on my cheek, but I'm fine."

"I'd like to know what the fuck Renaud was thinking," she says. I'm holding the phone out from my face so it doesn't touch my cheek, and since he looks over at me with a smirk, he must be able to hear her even across the room.

"You know what, me too. He's right here. Hold on, you can ask him yourself." I'm laughing silently as he glares at me, but I'm enjoying this too much. Getting in trouble with his boss would serve him right for involving himself in my life when I didn't ask for his help, and for fighting after she told him that he needs to stop.

He hands me a bag of frozen corn as I set my phone on the island and put the call on speakerphone. His lip curls up into a subtle smile, and he shakes his head at me like he's already thinking of a way to repay me for putting him in this position.

"Hey, boss," Aidan's voice is apologetic. It's the kind of tone you use when you know you're in trouble.

"No less than five hours after we announce you as the alternate captain, and you're already fighting? And not even on the ice, where it's legal?" AJ is pissed and not doing anything to hide it.

"That guy was harassing Morgan and refused to take his hands off her after she'd asked him to. What kind of an alternate captain would I be if I didn't stand up for people who work for the team?"

AJ's silent for a moment. "That's really what started that?"

"Yeah."

With the frozen corn held against my face, I shake my head at him trying to charm AJ. I can't help but smile when he grins and gives me a wink, like he knows he's saying the right things. This playful side of him is so much more like the version of him I saw when we were alone in Bermuda than the hockey player I've seen since we returned to Boston.

And truthfully, he does seem to keep showing up when I could use some backup—first at that dinner with my mom a week ago, and then tonight with Carter. He's being a good friend, which is what we've agreed to since there's no way we can actually avoid each other.

"You didn't have to punch him. I specifically told you not to risk your hand by fighting," AJ says, and I nod in agreement with my eyebrows lifted, but that motion hurts and I wince.

"I hit him with my *other* hand. I'm not stupid enough to risk my career like that. Besides, he pushed me twice and threw the first punch," Aidan says, and my chest shakes with silent laughter because, standing behind him, I didn't even realize Carter hit him. I thought it was just a shove, since Aidan didn't even flinch. "I was defending myself."

"Bullshit. Maybe that first punch was self-defense, but the second and third certainly weren't. And you wouldn't have stopped there, either, if Morgan hadn't told you to."

"What can I say . . . she's a good influence on me."

"Hmmm." The sound rattles around in the silence of my apartment. "Speaking of which, are you at her place?"

He looks at me like he's not sure how to respond, so I nod that he should tell her. "Yes, I walked her home. Wanted to make sure she was okay and that asshole, Carter, didn't follow her from the bar."

"That was Carter?" AJ's voice is the perfect mix of *oh my god* and *I'm going back there to rip his balls off, myself.*

"Yeah," I say with a deflated sigh. "In the flesh."

"Oh, Morgan. I'm so sorry you ever wasted your time on him."

Hearing her confirm that I'm too good for him, and knowing that he *still* didn't want me, makes me feel even worse. So does the smug look plastered across Aidan's face.

"He's a mistake I'd really like to keep in the past." I need to turn this conversation away from my love life. "Okay, so I'm safely home, which means Renaud is about to leave. Before he goes, how are we going to handle the PR nightmare that's probably already unfurling on social media?"

"I'm going to need you to put together a statement from the Rebels, and while Renaud's there, could you please help him craft an appropriate response, too?"

"No problem, boss," Aidan says with a sly grin in my direction. "I'll stay as long as it takes."

"Which won't be long," I add emphatically. I need him out of my space so I can think about what just happened back at the bar, why he followed me home and insisted on coming in, and whether either of those things means something.

We disconnect the call and he opens the fridge, pulling out two cans of seltzer and then looking around the living area of my apartment. "Give me a tour?"

"Aidan, what was supposed to be a fun night out with friends has now turned into more work and a black eye, thanks to you. Let's just get this over with."

He sets the cans on the counter and moves toward me. He rests his hand over mine where it holds the bag of frozen corn against my face, then leans in. With his voice low, he says, "Hey, I'm sorry about both, but I'm *not* sorry I hit that douchebag who clearly deserved it. And I'm even less sorry now that I know you and he had something together in the past."

I shake my head slightly. "Can we please forget about that part of it?" Now that I've seen Carter and Aidan side by side and experienced how they each treated me, I'm actually embarrassed that I ever gave Carter my time and attention.

"Trust me, I'm trying to wipe it from my memory. I don't want to think about you with anyone else."

A shiver racks my body at his possessive tone, but I ignore it. Instead, I lift an eyebrow. "Or with *you,* right? Since we're just friends?"

He nods, but there's nothing *friendly* about the way he's eying me.

"So, about that tour, friend?" He heads out of the kitchen and starts walking through my living room, and I follow behind him, trying not to focus on the way his pants cling to his ass.

I know I should get him to focus on the statement we

need to write, but seeing him relaxed and borderline flirtatious reminds me how much I like this side of him.

Friends, I tell myself as he heads down the hallway to explore the rest of my place. *Just show him around first, and then you can get him to focus.*

Chapter Twenty-Five

MORGAN

"**A**re you sure you're going to make it through this meal?" Audrey asks after the waiter brings our food. The wait today was torturously long, as everyone in Boston has apparently decided to enjoy this beautiful fall day by going out to Sunday brunch. I'm exhausted, and brunch has now run into the midday nap I was planning to take in order to make up for my lack of sleep this weekend.

I stayed up half the night Friday writing a statement from the Rebels and helping Aidan craft one he could post as well, despite the way he tried to get us off track every chance he got. Then the story of Aidan's "violently aggressive" return to Boston flooded the media on Saturday morning based on some videos people took at the bar the night before.

I spent most of Saturday at the Rebels practice facility working with the PR team on how to handle this and crafting the story we wanted to tell on social media. AJ made a public statement about Aidan defending a fellow member of the Rebels staff who was being sexually harassed, so now I'm officially part of the story because I was in the video.

I had to fend off my dad's questions about why Aidan and I were at a bar together, and then Natalie and I spent the rest of the day responding to comments on our social media platforms. The girl's good, I'll give her that. We decided on a tone—*we protect our own*—and she went with it. People were reposting our cheeky responses and, in general, the consensus was that Boston fans are glad Renaud is back, and everyone outside of Boston hates him.

I have a feeling he feeds off that energy, so maybe his return to the ice will be spectacular and this will all be okay for him, after all? It doesn't change the fact that I'm annoyed I had to spend all weekend dealing with his inability to avoid fighting. I've asked myself many times if I'd be this frustrated if it were a different player, and the honest truth is, I don't know.

There's something mysterious and frustrating about how closed off Aidan is now that we're back in Boston. Every once in a while, like on Friday night at my place, I see the briefest glimpse of the man I met at a bar during a tropical storm. But that persona seems buried deep down beneath whatever Aidan is working through right now.

"I'm fine. It was just a long weekend of work. I hate to say this because I know you both are probably dreading it," I glance between Jules and Audrey, "but I'm glad the team's on the road this coming week. I need some time to focus on my other clients too. This has already been a lot more than I agreed to, and even though it will mean larger paychecks, it's exhausting."

"At least they're only gone for a night this time," Audrey says, looking at Jules. "The long road trips are the hardest."

The rest of the world thinks Colt and Jules were secretly dating all of last season. But we know the truth . . . that what started out as a fake engagement during the playoffs quickly turned real. Since travel during the playoffs is different from the regular season, she's never had to be without him for more than a couple of nights.

"I'll be fine," she says breezily, sweeping her long blond hair over her shoulders. "I've got plenty of work to keep me busy."

Jules may look like Barbie, but she runs an all-female construction crew, and the design and build firm she co-owns with Audrey has a nearly yearlong waitlist at this point. We've been working on a plan to hire more female contractors by partnering with some of the local trade schools on a mentoring program that is near and dear to Jules's heart, and we've made good progress but there's still a long way to go. Especially because I don't have enough time to devote to it now that I'm working part time for the Rebels.

"I'm so glad you don't have to travel with the team," Audrey says to me. "Girls nights to watch the away games are the only thing that gets me through the time that Drew is gone."

"I will absolutely be at your place for every away game," I say.

As if we summoned her by talking about the Rebels, my phone lights up with a text from AJ.

AJ

Are you around? I need to run an idea by you. And I really need you to say yes.

My deep sigh has my friends asking me what's wrong, and when I tell them about AJ's text, Jules says, "Morgan, whatever it is, if you don't want to, or you can't because it's too much, just say no."

"It's just work," Audrey says.

"Easy for you to say, when your company is well established. I'm still in the building phase of my PR firm. And currently, the Rebels are my biggest client." Yes, my company is growing and things are going well, but it's still new and nearly half of small businesses fold within the first five years. I don't want to be a statistic.

Besides, I'm not the kind of person who can just say no when a friend needs them. I know that my response should be based on my capacity at the moment and *not* on my friendship with AJ. But I also don't want to let her down.

And honestly, the longer I'm with the Rebels, the more I realize how much they need someone with more knowledge and skill than Tatum has. It can't be me because I'm not looking for a full-time job with them, but it could be Natalie after she graduates, if I can get her ready by then.

"Still, you are only one person, and there are only twenty-four hours in the day," Jules says.

"I know, I just need to remember that when I talk to her."

"If this helps at all," Jules says, "when AJ first found out about *Our House,* she was very interested in having us do a remodel for her. But we didn't jump right in and say yes or drop everything for her. We simply told her we had a waitlist, and she understood. It's a good thing we didn't drop everything back then, because we're now slated to do a much larger project for her and McCabe when they combine their two condos."

I lift an eyebrow. "They're already planning that?" The way they went from not knowing they lived right next to each other to practically married over the past three months is kind of wild.

Audrey laughs and says, "Well, at this point she has nine months to make sure, because that's how far out she is on our waitlist right now. People wait for things they think are worth waiting for. You don't need to drop everything or prioritize everyone else over yourself."

It's exactly the type of advice that I'd give a friend, and yet it stings being on the receiving end. Because I *do* drop everything to help everyone else, all the time. Deep down, in places I don't like to explore often, I know that this stems from a fear that if I don't prioritize other people, they'll leave just like my mom did. So I try to be whatever other people need me to be, instead of doing what's best for myself.

I nod in agreement, because there's a lump in my throat as I let this realization wash over me again. It's not new information. Years of therapy as a teenager and a degree in psychology have made the source of my people-pleasing traits abundantly clear. But all the knowledge in the world doesn't make it easier to change my behavior.

So while I'm finishing up my omelette and then saying goodbye to my friends, I'm mentally preparing to say "no" to whatever project AJ wants to give me. I don't have time for more than I've already taken on, and the dark circles under my eyes are proof.

———

"No. No, no, no." I shake my head like she can see me on the other end of the phone, while I pace back and forth in front of the large bay windows in my fifth-floor condo overlooking Newbury Street.

"I wouldn't be asking if I wasn't desperate, I promise you."

"AJ, your desperation doesn't magically create more hours in the day. When you add in Friday night and all day yesterday, I spent over thirty hours last week working on projects for the Rebels. That's twice what we agreed on, and I still have my own company to run."

"I swear, I don't need you to be working for us the whole time we're gone. I just need you to be with us to keep Renaud in line."

"As appealing as being a traveling babysitter for a professional hockey player sounds . . . I can't. You're going to be there. *You* keep him in line. Or put his teammates on the job."

Her sigh is deep and deliberate. "Colt, McCabe, and I were all at that bar Friday night, and that didn't stop him from fighting. *You* did."

"AJ, I fear your logic is backward. He wouldn't have gotten in that fight if I hadn't been there."

"I don't think that's true. I think Renaud's a loose cannon and Carter's harassment was an *excuse* for him to let it all out. If it hadn't been that situation, it would have been another."

I think back to the way Aidan examined my face, searching for injuries, and how he seemed so pleased with himself when he had to stay longer at my place so we could craft an appropriate statement.

He wasn't pleased with himself for getting in a fight. He was pleased that it gave him a reason to be around me. And sure, we're friends now, so spending time together shouldn't be a problem. But spending time *alone* together definitely has me needing to remind myself why nothing can happen . . . because when it's just the two of us, he's a different person.

But I can't tell AJ any of that.

"What if I get him to promise that he won't do anything stupid on the road this week?" I ask.

AJ's laughter is deep and almost sultry. She reminds me so much of my former boss, Petra Ivanova. Petra is one of Lauren's best friends, and the biggest badass I know. Which is saying something, given that I know AJ.

After I graduated from NYU, I moved to Park City, where Lauren and Petra were both living, to be Petra's personal assistant at her event planning company. She eventually ended up hosting a TV show in LA, then moved the show to New York so she could be with her now-husband, hockey player Aleksandr Ivanov.

The only reason I would consider saying yes to AJ's request is that we're playing in New York and I might be able to catch up with Petra. In fact, if there is anyone I could tell about this whole situation with Aidan, it's Petra. She would keep my secret and it would be so nice to talk to someone removed from the situation.

"I really need you to be there to make sure this doesn't go sideways for him," AJ says. "His contract is up at the end of the season and I'd like to keep him. But, if he can't rein in the fighting, I won't renew his contract."

That stops me in my tracks. "Does *he* know this?" I ask.

"He sure does."

Damnit. He knew that fighting Carter would get him in

trouble with AJ, and he did it anyway because he was protecting me. Now, the guilt weighs on me and I feel like I owe him this.

"Fine," I say with a sigh. "Just for this *one* game."

"Excellent," AJ says. "He won't even be playing in the following game, so that buys us some time."

I don't fully understand the rules around these preseason exhibition games, but I know that there are usually no more than eight veteran players participating in each game.

"The following game is at home. Let's make sure this is figured out before the next *away* game." My tone is a tad flippant because being at a home game is no big deal, but giving up multiple days to travel for away games is.

"Will do," AJ says. "And truly, thank you for doing this."

"It's no problem."

"We both know that's not true. I'll make sure you get time and a half for the trip since it's outside your contracted hours."

"I appreciate that," I say, thinking how maybe, once my business is solid and I've saved a little money, I can finally move out of the condo I spent the first decade of life in. Dad and I moved out to the house he still lives in, in Brookline, after Mom left, but he held onto the Boston condo and rented it. And then I returned to Boston and needed a place to live.

As convenient as it is to live on Newbury Street, I don't like to be a person who relies on Daddy's money. I don't think I'll feel truly grown up until I'm entirely self-sufficient.

MORGAN

Hey, any chance you're free Wednesday
night before the game to have dinner with
me? I'll be in town with the Rebels.

PETRA

You traveling with the Rebels doesn't even
make sense to me, so obviously we need to
catch up! I'll make a dinner reservation for us
close to the arena.

Chapter Twenty-Six

AIDAN

NERDGIRL

We need to come to an agreement about something important . . .

I have to travel with the team for the New York game because AJ thinks I can "keep Renaud in line." I'm not your goddamn babysitter, so could you please agree to behave yourself on this trip so I don't have to travel to the next away game?

AIDAN

If I do fight, does that mean you'll come on all our road trips? 😏

NERDGIRL

I don't have time for these games, Aidan. I have my own life and a business I'm trying to run.

AIDAN

Let's just hope I don't play better with you
there, or AJ will be REALLY determined to
have you keep traveling with us.

NERDGIRL

Don't you dare suggest that! This is all
because you got it in her head that I'm a
good influence on you.

AIDAN

Maybe you ARE a good influence on me.

NERDGIRL

Grow up and be a good influence on
yourself.

I laugh to myself as I sit on the plane, waiting for everyone to finish boarding, and read through our text messages from Sunday. I remember the way my dick jumped at the idea of whatever "agreement" she might be proposing, and the letdown when I realized that she was basically just asking me to act like a fucking grown-up.

Now that I know fighting makes it more likely she'll travel with us, I'm tempted to keep doing it just to keep her around more. But as much as I like to rile her up because she's cute when she gets feisty, I don't want to take a step backward in our friendship. I also don't need to be pissing AJ off by fighting, so, as tempting as it may be, it's not a road I can go down.

"Who's NerdGirl?" McCabe's voice surprises me, even though he's sitting right next to me.

I glance over at him as I turn my phone screen off. "No one."

His gaze moves to the open door of the plane, a few rows in front of our seats, where Morgan's boarding the aircraft. She's looking down with a small smile as she reads whatever's on her phone. Her other hand holds the Nerds Gummy Clusters I dropped into her bag with an "I'm sorry" note as I boarded the plane, and she's currently tapping them against her shoulder as she chews on her lip like she's deep in thought.

Her thumb flies over the screen as she stands there, waiting to make the turn toward the front of the plane where she'll sit with the other staff members.

I glance over at McCabe and watch him notice the pink packaging of Morgan's candy, then back at my phone when it buzzes in my hand.

NERDGIRL

I appreciate the candy. I would appreciate it
more if you could stop fighting so I don't
have to do this again.

McCabe clears his throat, then with his gravelly voice barely audible, he tells me, "I gave AJ a nickname in my Contacts at one point. Didn't do it because there was nothing going on."

Fuck. I shouldn't have had that text thread open on the plane. It's a recipe for getting caught, and I'm normally smarter than that.

"Giving her a nickname doesn't mean anything."

"Hmmm." The sound rattles around in his throat. "I'm going to tell you what I'd tell anyone in this situation. She's your agent's daughter and she works for the team. Don't touch her with a ten-foot pole."

"That's exactly what I would have told *you* about our boss if I had been here last season."

I don't know what possesses me to compare the two situations. What Morgan and I had in Bermuda was casual, and nothing's happened since. McCabe's already made it clear that AJ is his endgame. The two situations are not even in the same ballpark.

"You're serious about her, then?"

I scoff. "I'm not serious about anyone. I just gave her some candy to apologize that she has to travel with us."

His brows dip. "She's traveling with us because of *you*?"

Oh shit, I shouldn't have assumed he knew. "AJ didn't tell you?"

He keeps his voice low. "Why would she tell me something that's going on with another player?"

"She thinks Morgan's a good influence on me, because the other night when I got in that fight, I stopped when she asked me to."

McCabe's chuckle lasts longer than I'd expect. "Maybe you should change her contact name to *Nanny*, then?"

I thought I'd like having Morgan here in New York with us, but I was wrong. Watching her talk to my teammates, and seeing how close she is to them, does nothing but light my jealousy on fire until it's a burning pit in my stomach. Maybe I need to talk to AJ, insist that Morgan's presence isn't necessary, and beg my boss to send her home?

Of course, then she'd ask me why, and I haven't been able to think of a good reason. I've been sitting here at the bar nursing a single beer for the last hour, watching her laughing with Drew and Colt, and trying hard not to glower in their direction. It almost feels like they've already caught on and are being extra friendly with her just to piss me off.

I ask the bartender to close out my tab and head over to tell my friends I'm leaving. Coach wants us in our rooms by ten o'clock the night before games anyway, so it's not like I'm heading back early enough that it's going to raise eyebrows.

"Hey guys, I'm going to walk back to the hotel. See you at morning skate tomorrow."

"I'll head back with you," Morgan says. "I have some work I need to finish up anyway."

After we've made our way outside, I turn toward her. "You afraid I can't make it back to the hotel without getting in a fight?"

She starts walking so I fall into step beside her. "I'd better make sure, since that's the whole reason I'm here."

I shove my hands in my pockets as we walk so I can fight the temptation to wrap my arm around her waist and hold her close to me as we navigate the New York City sidewalks. At least this late on a weeknight, it's not super crowded.

"How's your face feeling?" I ask. She ended up with a nasty bruise on her cheekbone, but luckily not a black eye. She's covered it with makeup so it's not very noticeable.

"Not as good as it felt before I got elbowed. How's your hand?"

My knuckles are bruised and they still ache. "It's fine. Listen, I'm sorry that you ended up having to travel with us when you didn't want to. I'll be on my best behavior this trip so it doesn't happen again."

"I think you need to extend that promise to the whole season, not just this trip. AJ *wants* to keep you on the team, Aidan. You just have to stop giving her reasons not to."

"Did she say that?" My curiosity is piqued. "Or did your dad tell you that?"

She swallows. "My dad never talks to me about contract negotiations, but it's possible AJ may have said something that led me to draw that conclusion." We walk in silence for a minute, before she says, "Can I ask you a question?"

"Should the fact that you're asking permission make me worried?"

"I don't think so. I just keep wondering why you virtually disappeared last year? I know you were on IR and it's not uncommon in a long-term situation like that for players to return home to complete their PT and recovery. But you were less than an hour outside of Boston. Why didn't you stay in touch with your teammates, or come to any games or anything?"

On the surface, it's an innocent enough question. And it's certainly the one on everyone's mind. But it picks at old wounds in a way she can't possibly understand . . . unless I tell her.

We stop at an intersection, waiting for the light to change, and I mull over how to respond. I like that she doesn't press me for an answer as we stand there. It makes her that much easier to talk to, and it occurs to me that I haven't had anyone I could talk to about things like this since Hayley. That should put me on edge, because I almost lost my first NHL contract thanks to that breakup, but somehow it doesn't. It just makes me want to keep talking.

Once we're crossing the street, I say, "Last year was one of the most difficult years of my life. I was in constant pain after each surgery because I refused to take any of the hard-core painkillers, given what happened with my dad. I couldn't play the sport I'd devoted my entire life to, and had to watch my teammates live out my dream instead. I just . . . wasn't in a good place."

"I get that," she says, and although I feel like anyone else would follow it up with a *but,* she doesn't.

"I wasn't trying to be a bad friend or teammate. I was barely holding my own shit together, and I didn't have the capacity to be there for anyone else. And then when I was finally feeling more myself, my best friend's wife died and I had to be there for him and his son."

I glance at her when she doesn't respond. She nods, chews on her lower lip, then says, "I'm sorry you had to go through all of that. I bet your teammates would like to know . . . especially the ones you're close to."

"I don't really know how to do this whole talking about my feelings thing."

"The thing is . . . the more you do it, the easier it becomes." She turns toward the entrance to the hotel and we walk through the doors into the lobby without talking. I'm still mulling over her words, and she's good at giving me space to think.

"Are you letting your beard grow back in?" she asks when we stop in front of the bank of elevators. It's short and neatly trimmed now, and my hair's a bit longer than it was when we met at the end of the summer. I wonder if she'd have recognized me then, if I'd looked like I do now?

"I normally do, during the season. But I can keep it short if you prefer."

She coughs out a laugh as we stand there waiting. "My opinion shouldn't matter any more than anyone else's who you work with."

"But it does," I say, turning to look down at her where she stands next to me.

"Don't do that." She reaches out and pushes the elevator button again, like that might make it arrive sooner.

"Don't do what?" As if I don't know what she means.

"Don't treat our friendship any differently than any other friendship."

I shouldn't be trying to make space for her in my life. I shouldn't be thinking about her nonstop. I shouldn't be craving her company. But I do.

Pursuing her might be my most reckless idea yet—it could lose me my agent, and piss off my GM—but somehow I'm no longer sure I care.

We step into the elevator when the doors open, and as soon as we've tapped the numbers for our floors and the doors close, I admit, "I don't really have any female friends, so I'm not sure how to act."

"You have *no* female friends?"

I shrug. "Not really." How do I admit that every woman in my life is either dating or married to one of my friends, or trying to sleep with me?

"Sounds like a big red flag to me," she tilts her chin up like she's challenging me to prove her wrong. But she's not wrong, necessarily.

I step closer, forcing her to tilt her head back to look up at me. "I think red might be a great color on you."

"Stop pursuing me, Aidan." She's so close that her breath warms my face.

"Stop giving me reasons to, Morgan."

Her chest heaves with a surprised gasp. "I most definitely have not given you reasons."

But we both know that's not true. Our bodies have an inexplicable pull toward each other, even though we both know this is a bad idea.

"So the way you were just looking at me, leaning in like you wanted me to kiss you . . . that's how you look at all your *friends*?"

Her breathing is heavy, and she doesn't step away. I'd like to say the sexy off-the-shoulder sweater she wore tonight is what's been driving me crazy, but that's not it. It's the way I can't see her freckles through her makeup, and every time I try to remember what they look like, visions of us together in Bermuda flash through my mind. Hell, those memories are *always* in my mind, driving me crazy.

"You know," I say, when she doesn't respond, "we have a great track record in hotels. We could keep our streak going."

She crosses her arms and shakes her head as she steps back. "I don't know how to do the whole casual thing . . ."

"The thing is . . . the more you do it, the easier it becomes."

"Don't use my words against me, Aidan."

"Hey, we could be on the same team here," I say. "We have amazing chemistry, and you could use some practice keeping things casual. I volunteer as tribute."

My suggestion isn't just reckless, it's downright stupid. I

could lose my agent and my career because of this woman. It's the exact path I promised myself I'd never travel again.

"Such a noble sacrifice," she says with an eye roll, right as the elevator dings our arrival at her floor.

"Friends with benefits would allow us to still have our friendship *and* reap the benefits," I blurt out as the doors open. It's the desperate need to be around her that makes me suggest this, *not* the fact that it's a good idea. In fact, friends with benefits is probably the worst idea I've ever had.

At least I can rely on her being logical about this and rejecting me, so I can get back on the path where I'm focusing on nothing but hockey this season.

My breath hitches when she freezes, one foot in the hallway. The fact that she doesn't turn and roll her eyes over her shoulder as she walks away has me panicking a bit.

Finally, she glances over her shoulder at me then and huffs out a small laugh. "You know what, I'll think about it."

My head falls back against the wall of the elevator the minute she's out of sight, and as the doors close, I groan out, "Fuuuuuuuck."

Chapter Twenty-Seven

MORGAN

"Only you, Morgan." Petra's husky laugh is legendary and has people sitting at nearby tables turning to glance at her, obviously recognizing the voice of one of America's favorite talk show hosts.

"You sound just like my friends when I told them what happened in Bermuda."

"Trouble sure has a way of finding your love life," she says, shaking her head. Her bright blue eyes are sparkling and her wide mouth is spread into a grin, but she's not laughing at me. She drops her voice low and says, "So no one else knows that Danny is Aidan Renaud?"

"Just me and him. And now, you."

"Your secret is safe with me. I'm a vault."

"Which is why I told you." I take the last sip of my wine and set the glass back down. "I need advice. I have absolutely no idea how to proceed here. Our chemistry is great, but for all the reasons I already mentioned, I should probably stay away. I need a nice, stable guy I can settle down with, and Aidan's neither of those things."

"See that's the thing," Petra says. "He just suggested you should be friends with benefits, and you're already thinking long term."

"I knoooow. It's because I have no idea how to do this whole casual thing. I'm a relationship kind of girl."

Before Petra reconnected with Aleksandr, she was the queen of one-night stands. I'm not sure why, but casual relationships were kind of her personal brand.

"Okay," she says hesitantly. "But you've already decided that Renaud's not the type of person you want a long-term relationship with, so that makes him kind of perfect as a friend with benefits. You know the sex will be great, and the more you see him, the more you'll remember all the reasons he's *not* relationship material. It's actually perfect."

"I don't know if that sounds perfect, or terrible."

"What could be terrible about having great, no-strings-attached sex?"

"Because when the sex is that good, I bet I'd overlook a lot to keep it going longer."

"You don't have to overlook anything, Morgan. That's the thing with casual, you don't have to see a future with the person or try to change them. You just enjoy it for what it is: good sex."

She must see the doubt on my face, because she winces and adds, "Maybe you'd be better off finding a guy who's looking for a long-term relationship like you are."

"And therein lies the problem," I say as the waiter approaches and Petra hands over a credit card before he can even give us the bill. "I don't generally have trouble attracting guys, it's keeping them interested that's the issue. It could be that I'm attracting the wrong guys, but it doesn't seem to matter how different they all are, the one constant is that they don't want to stay with *me* long-term."

I'm so used to this that I've accepted it as fact. I don't even get teary-eyed about it the way I used to. I'm pretty freaking great at my job, I have amazing friends who are all badasses themselves, I'm attractive enough, I do nice things for people whenever I can. There's no reason I can identify that I'm not attracting the right type of guy.

"Yeah, that doesn't make sense to me," Petra says, folding her napkin and setting it next to her empty plate. "You're talented, successful, beautiful, and nice—everything a guy *should* be looking for."

"And yet, I'm never quite what they want."

"Maybe the problem is that men in your generation are all overgrown children," she says.

"You're like six years older than me," I say with a laugh.

"Maybe you just need an older man, then?"

"Funny, Aidan is your age. And he doesn't have any female friends, aside from me."

"Maybe this situation could be mutually beneficial, then," she says, with a lift of her dark eyebrows. "You learn how to do casual, he learns how to be a good friend to a woman."

My bark of laughter is louder than I'd want in a restaurant, and my cheeks turn pink as people turn to stare. I lower my voice when I say, "I think trying to have sex with your female friends is exactly what *not* to do if you're being a good friend."

She lifts one shoulder in a shrug. "Yeah, but your situation is different because you slept together before you were friends. Besides, given everything you told me about work, you don't have time for a relationship right now anyway. So in the meantime, why not have great sex?"

The idea has merit, especially when she points out that I truly don't have time for a relationship right now. Growing my business and furthering my career shouldn't stop me from having great sex, too. And who better to do that with than the guy who I already know will fulfill my needs?

———

The game is tied 4-4 halfway through the third period. The way the teams are so evenly matched between their veteran players and guys from the AHL affiliates who are trying to secure a spot on their team, means the game has been both exciting and frustrating. High-scoring games always are.

When Alex Ivanov steals the puck right off the stick of one of our rookie defensemen, spins behind the goal, and passes it to New York player Owen Jimenez, who slaps it into the net before our minor league goalie can get to it, I groan. From my spot in the media room, I watch Petra in the stands, jumping up and down and hugging another player's wife.

I don't know how her husband is still this good. At thirty-six, he's approaching records that have been held by some of the all-time hockey greats, and he's showing no signs of slowing down. If anything, he's better than he's ever been. A couple years ago when New York re-signed him, there was talk of his current contract possibly being his last. Now, I can't imagine him retiring any time soon.

Coach Wilcott sends in all new players for the face-off, and Aidan is among them. While we lose the face-off and New York brings the puck across the neutral zone into our defensive zone, he swipes the puck as it's passed and takes off with it. Watching him navigate his way around New York's defense, his skill and speed are evident—it's exactly what everyone needs to see from him tonight to show that he's back and as good as ever.

When he fakes a shot, spins, and then sends it top shelf in the other direction, lighting the lamp on New York's goal, his face is plastered on the Jumbotron, right at eye level up here where I'm working. A coast-to-coast goal like that doesn't happen often, and I love that he gets to celebrate on the ice with his teammates in this way.

Obviously, I love it just like I'd love it for any player on our team who was coming back from injury. Nothing more.

The way the announcers are talking about that play, combined with the enthusiastic response from our players and the fans who traveled to New York for the game, tells me this is a good live update for our social platforms. I shoot a text off to our photographer asking her for any photos she got just now, and then I grab some clips of the video stream so I can get a post lined up.

Though New York comes back to score two more goals and we end up leaving the arena as the losing team, there's an energy as we get on the bus to head to the airport for our late-night flight home. Even though we lost, our veteran players were on fire and one of our rookies, who was drafted a year ago and just got pulled up from his college team, had two goals. Both of these things bode well for the comeback season everyone expects us to have—because if there's one thing I've learned since taking on this position, it's that everyone in this organization expects us to bring home the Cup this year.

I settle into my seat while people are still loading onto the bus, and watch Aidan as he walks down the aisle. When our gazes meet, there's a familiar heat in his eyes, and it has me crossing my legs to quell the ache there. Petra's words ring in my head: *You don't have time for a relationship right now anyway. So in the meantime, why not have great sex?*

Before I can lose my nerve, I pull out my phone.

MORGAN

> I've given your proposition some thought and I'm in, as long as we establish some clear rules.

From where he sits, across the aisle and one row in front of me, next to McCabe, I note that he doesn't take out his phone on the drive to the airport outside the city. As much as I am dying to see his response, it's probably better that he doesn't look at my text while sitting so close to his teammate.

Half an hour later, I'm walking across the tarmac toward our plane, and he's several people in front of me waiting to walk up the steps to the jet. That's when his text comes through.

AIDAN

There's only one rule for friends with
benefits . . . don't catch feelings.

MORGAN

That won't be a problem.

AIDAN

Perfect.

Chapter Twenty-Eight

AIDAN

I'm walking out of the locker room after Thursday's practice when I see Morgan chatting with the social media intern in the hallway.

"You're going to be great," she says, reaching out and giving the younger girl's shoulder a squeeze. "We've gone over what types of things to post during the game, and I'll only be a phone call away."

"You're right, I don't know why I'm nervous to do this without you," the other girl says, and I take this to mean that Morgan's not planning on being at this weekend's home game.

"Being nervous is a sign that you want to make sure you do a good job," Morgan says. "And you will, so stop worrying."

"Thanks. But I have you on speed dial, just in case."

Morgan laughs and tells her again that she's going to be great. The girl thanks her and turns to open the door to the staircase behind her, leaving Morgan in the hallway where she glances down at her phone, not having noticed me yet.

It's been almost a week since she texted me about my offer, but in that time, we've barely seen or talked to each other. And the last text we shared was me saying that our arrangement was "perfect."

I've been telling myself that I'm waiting for her to make the first move. But the truth is, I've opened that text thread a hundred times a day and each time I overthink the hell out of what I'd say and end up closing it without reaching out. Knowing her, she's expecting me to make a move, since I'm the one who offered our little arrangement in the first place.

Her dad's warning to stay away from her echoes in my head, but it doesn't stop me from walking toward her when I could just as easily have turned and gone in the other direction. Now that the offer is out there, and she's agreed, I'd be a dick to keep avoiding her. This isn't about my mild infatuation with her; it's about not wanting to make her feel like I changed my mind because she wasn't worth the time or effort.

That's what I tell myself, anyway, as I walk down the hall.

"Hey," I say as I approach, and she jumps in response to my voice before glancing up from her phone. "I haven't seen you around this week."

"I've mostly been working from home," she says. "The only reason I'm here today is that my AC is broken and the repairman can't come until Monday, which does me no good because these temperatures are going to continue into the weekend."

We're having a record-breaking heatwave right now, the warmest weather Boston's ever seen in October.

"I have air-conditioning," I tell her with a wink.

She shakes her head at me like I'm being ridiculous. "I'm not staying with you."

"You sure? I'm headed down to the beach for the next couple days. That seems like a much better place to ride out this heatwave than a fifth-floor walk-up with no AC."

"My dad has AC and a pool," she tells me, "so I was thinking I'd just stay there. But then I found out he's doing his annual guys' weekend where all his college friends come into town and they go golfing and stay at his house. He started it when I left for college, and I've been banned from ever attending."

I cough out a laugh. "I'll bet. Men are pigs."

"Ew," she says, scrunching up her nose. "Those are my dad's friends. I've known them my whole life. They're like uncles to me."

"Morgan, you're a grown-ass woman. You go parading around in front of them in a bathing suit, and they're going to be looking at you just like you're any other hot woman in a bikini." Does she really not see that *this* is the reason her dad hasn't allowed her to be around on this weekend every year?

"So instead you want me to come to the beach with you and parade around in my bikini there?" Her tone is teasing, but I have a feeling it's a genuine question.

I lift an eyebrow. "Obviously."

She leans against the wall behind her, folding her arms across her chest. "A weekend away together seems like it's veering into relationship territory. Doesn't sound very casual to me."

"If you think one weekend away together is a relationship, then I have my work cut out for me," I say, shaking my head.

"Seriously?" She tilts her head and narrows her eyes, like she can't quite determine if what I'm saying is true.

It's not. I'm speaking utter bullshit right now. I've literally *never* taken a woman away for a weekend because I don't want to give the wrong impression. But Morgan doesn't need to know that.

"I have so much to teach you." I shake my head at her like she's missing the whole point, when really I'm the one twisting things so I can spend more time with her. "That's it, there's no other choice, you're coming with me."

———

"I can't believe how pretty this place is," Morgan says as we sit on Old Pilgrim Beach watching the pink, orange, and purple shades of the fall sunset behind us play out on the waves in front of us. Everything else around us is a deep blue as the darkening sky bleeds into the ocean where they meet on the horizon. "I had no idea this was even here."

"This beach is the best-kept secret on the South Shore, and we like to keep it that way. That part over there," I say, pointing south along the beach where the houses are built right up to the shore, "is Pilgrim Beach. It gets super crowded because of all the cottages packed in there. This part, Old Pilgrim, used to be a private beach, but when I was a teenager, there was a big lawsuit between the town and the residents of the houses behind the dunes." I point over my shoulder and she turns to look, even though you can't see the houses through the tall grass lining the sandy hills.

"So now it's public, but it never really gets crowded down here."

"This feels like being on Cape Cod without having to sit in three hours of stop-and-go traffic to get there," she says with a sigh.

"Exactly, which is why the first rule of Ember Cove is: you do not talk about Ember Cove."

She huffs out a laugh. "Like Fight Club?"

"Exactly. And now that I've shared it with you, you're sworn to secrecy. We don't want it to be like the Cape."

She laughs and pulls the hem of my hoodie over her knees so she's balled up inside of it. Now that the sun is almost set, it's gotten cool on the water. It's a welcome reprieve from the heat wave we've been having.

"I see why you came back here last year," she says, gazing out at the waves.

"Just wait until morning. There's nothing like a run on the beach followed by a cup of coffee while watching the waves."

"Sounds great . . . if you're a morning person, which I'm not."

"Mornings on the beach are the best," I tell her, swinging an arm over her shoulder and pulling her against my side.

"I don't know," she says, doubt ringing out in her tone. "I think *this* is the best time."

"Sunset?"

"No, like half an hour ago, during golden hour. It's actually my favorite time of day anywhere. It's gorgeous at the beach or on a lake, and even in the city, when the setting sun ricochets off the brick buildings and makes them glow."

"Speaking of, we've got about half an hour of light left.

Want to grab dinner at the clam shack and eat it on the jetty? They use a separate fryer for shellfish, so it should be safe for you to eat there."

Her lips part as she pulls away and turns her head to look at me. I'm not sure what I see on her face. Confusion, maybe? "You . . . looked into that for me?"

"I didn't bring you all the way down here to kill you, Morgan," I say, my voice dry as I roll my eyes in her direction.

"Oh yeah? Why did you bring me all the way down here?" Her tone is slightly mocking, because we both know that she's going to end up in my bed tonight, despite the fact that she left her bags in the guest room.

"Couldn't have you dying from heatstroke back in Boston, either." I let out a deep sigh as I stand and reach my hand down to pull her up. "I didn't realize keeping you alive was going to be so much work."

She looks up at me and laughs. "You're doing a stand-up job," she says as I pull her up from the sand.

I press my lips to her hair where it meets her forehead, but as soon as the scent of her hits my nostrils, I know it was a mistake. Like always, she smells like vanilla, cinnamon, and sugar . . . like a delectable treat I can't wait to devour.

"All right," I say, clearing my throat as I pull away, "let's go get dinner before it's too dark to see our food."

Chapter Twenty-Nine

MORGAN

From the front seat of Aidan's Jeep, we watch the waves crash into the long rock jetty that juts out into the ocean, protecting the mouth of the river and the harbor on the other side of it. We'd attempted to take our baskets of fish and chips down to the jetty earlier, but the combination of gusty wind and a lot of sea spray from the waves meeting the rocks, drove us away. Instead, we've got the top of the Jeep down and the windows up to block the wind as we eat and chat while watching the ocean.

"Did your mom say anything to you about Thanksgiving?" Aidan asks, and my head swivels so fast I probably look like I'm possessed.

"No, why?"

"Max said something about him and Anne maybe coming to Tampa for the holiday. We play Carolina the night before, so we'll probably land in Tampa on Thanksgiving morning, before our game the next day."

"She hasn't said anything." I'm not sure how I feel about the idea. Last year, I spent Thanksgiving with Lauren and Jameson, Audrey and Drew, Jules and Colt. My dad—who I normally spend the holiday with—was on the West Coast for work. I hadn't really thought yet about this year, but my plans definitely do not include my mom. "But I love Thanksgiving and, I don't know…I worry that she'd ruin it for me somehow."

"That sounds exactly like something she'd do."

"Listen," I say, reaching across the gearshift and resting my hand on his forearm. "Don't dislike her on my account. I understand that she's just not capable of being the kind of mom I want her to be, and that's made all the difference in how I view her."

"You mean *lowering your expectations* has made all the difference." It's harsh, but he's not entirely wrong.

"I don't know why *you* sound mad about that? Setting realistic expectations, based on who she is, not who I want her to be, has saved me a lot of heartache."

He wipes his fingers on the napkin sitting on his leg, and then puts his free hand over the back of mine. "All I see is the way you keep giving her chances and she keeps showing you that she doesn't deserve them," he says. "And I keep wondering, why?"

"She's my mom."

"Morgan, you shouldn't lower your expectations for how *anyone* treats you, but especially not family. They're the ones who are supposed to have your back no matter what."

"I have my dad for that," I say, and Aidan lets out a sound that's half laugh, half scoff in response. "What was that?"

"Nothing. Just agreeing with you."

Goose bumps rise on the back of my neck, and it's not from the cool air outside the Jeep. I lift an eyebrow, and my tone is suspicious when I ask, "Why do I feel like you know something about my dad that I don't?"

"He basically told me to stay away from you."

Of course he did. My dad is nothing if not overprotective of his only child.

"Good job with that," I say with a laugh, thankful that I didn't mention to my dad that I was headed down to the beach. I don't need to raise his suspicions.

"I'm not always good at taking orders," he says, and gives me a sly smile.

"I'm not sure you're *ever* good at taking orders, but you do *not* want to piss my dad off right now," I assure him. "He can be absolutely ruthless if he thinks you've crossed him."

"Don't I know it," he says, reaching his arm above him and holding onto the roll bar to lift and reposition himself so he's facing me fully.

"Then what are we doing here?" I tuck my hair behind my ear, trying to ignore the way my stomach flips over when I'm asking hard questions but he's looking at me like he wants me naked.

"We're just two friends who went to the beach for the weekend, *as friends do.*"

"Uh huh." A smile curls my lips, and it has him leaning toward me over the console between our seats. His gaze is focused on my lips, so I wet them with my tongue, and he groans before he leans in further.

"I think friends should take care of their friends' needs."

"Always?" I tease.

"Always if it's you and me."

His lips meet mine tentatively, with small kisses that have my pulse racing and my body leaning toward him, wanting more. I don't know what it is about his physical proximity that lights me up, makes me want to be playful and sexy in a way that wouldn't feel comfortable with anyone else. The only reason I'm not climbing over the center console and straddling him in his seat is that I'm aware we're exposed in this parking lot. A fact that is confirmed for me when there's a rapping on the window and we spring apart.

"Dude, really?" Aidan groans as he looks over his shoulder to find a guy with floppy brown hair and a big goofy grin standing there.

"Sorry to interrupt. Just wanted to tell you that you better stop by and see my brother."

Aidan sighs. "Why's that, Finn?"

"Because when I saw your Jeep and texted him saying I didn't know you were in town, he was pissed you're here and didn't tell him."

"Well, if you hadn't gone spreading the news and then interrupted my date," Aidan says, clearly annoyed, "he wouldn't be pissed off, would he?"

Finn shrugs. "Just go see him. He needs that." Then he glances up at me and smiles. "Hi, Finn Walker, and you are?"

"Oh my god," Aidan groans, starting the car before I can respond. "Mind your fucking business, kid." And then he's backing out of the spot and pulling toward the road.

"Well, that was rude." I can't help but laugh, because that was the most classically male interaction I've ever witnessed.

"He's always in my business like only a little brother can be."

"I thought you were an only child?"

"Remember when I told you I knew how to drive a boat because my best friend's family owns the local marina? That's my best friend's little brother. They grew up across the street from my house, and we were basically all inseparable. So now, we have to go make a quick social call. But then," he turns and glances at me as we sit there, waiting for a break in traffic so we can pull out onto the road, "we're finishing what we started."

"We'll see how I feel," I say with a shrug, for no reason other than it's fun to be contrary around him. Aidan practically growls in response, which has me holding in a laugh, and then holding onto my basket of food as he turns out of the parking lot faster than I was expecting. He's clearly in a hurry to get this visit over with so we can get home, and I'm okay with that.

"You were down on Old Pilgrim and didn't tell her about the time the harbormaster had to rescue us from Shepherd's Rocks?" Liam asks.

Next to me, Aidan's chuckle shakes the couch. "You'll tell it better," he says with a grin.

I've never seen him this relaxed. When we first arrived, we were greeted by his best friend's five-year-old son, Jack, who we could hear through the door as he thundered down the stairs inside, yelling, "Uncle Aidan's Jeep is outside." He then proceeded to throw the door open and jump into Aidan's arms, wrapping himself around the man's torso.

Aidan jokingly called him "my little barnacle," and the only thing that could have possibly shocked me more than how relaxed he was around a child, was seeing Jack's dad walking out of the kitchen behind his son. Because standing right in front of me was the most recognizable face in professional football: Liam Walker.

Given my dad's profession, I'm not normally starstruck in front of athletes. But there was a moment there where I was rendered speechless.

I should have pieced that puzzle together sooner—Aidan's best friend's wife dying, his little brother, Finn Walker. There's no sports fan in the country who doesn't know the story of Liam Walker, America's favorite quarterback, whose wife, Kelsey, suffered a brain aneurysm while home alone with their son. Liam was away, and Jack had to call 911 because his mother was on the floor unresponsive.

The recording of the call was all over the news, and although the funeral was supposed to be a private affair, the media turned it into a spectacle with helicopters and camera crews. And Liam decided to take this season off to stay home with his son as they adjusted to this change.

Right now, though, Liam is all grins as he says, "So, about twenty yards off the beach, there are these four rocks called Shepherd's Rocks. It's one big rock, and three smaller ones around it, right on this point where a marsh river meets the ocean and two tides converge. At high tide, you can barely see the top of the largest rock, and the others are submerged. We were probably eleven or twelve when we had the bright idea to put a lobster trap out there and see what we could catch. So the next afternoon, we waded out to see if there was anything in the trap, but it had gotten kind of wedged in between two of those smaller rocks and it took us a while to get it loose."

"Oh no," I groan, already sensing what happened.

"Yeah," Liam laughs. "So the tide came in faster than we realized while we were busy trying to free the trap, and by the time we'd hoisted it up onto the largest rock, we had to climb up there too because the water was too rough to swim back to shore."

"Our moms were on the beach yelling at us the whole time, and we didn't hear them because of the waves, but once we were up on the rock and saw them frantically waving at us," Aidan says with a chuckle, "we knew we were in big trouble."

"We weren't out there that long before the harbormaster showed up in his boat," Liam says. "Not only was he a grumpy old bastard about having to come fish us off the rocks, but he was also like, 'You boys have a permit for that trap?'"

Now I'm laughing too. "Did you?"

"Since we'd *borrowed*"—Liam throws up air quotes—"the trap from our neighbor's backyard . . . we most definitely did not."

"Did you at least catch any lobsters?"

"Yeah, but the Harbor Master threw them back in the ocean because we caught them without a permit."

"Were you in trouble?"

"Not as much trouble as when we stole a boat," Aidan says.

"Oh my god, please tell me you weren't twelve for that one, too?"

"No, we were sixteen," Liam says.

"Old enough to know better," Aidan adds. "That one

would have been *really* bad if it hadn't been Bob who caught us."

"That was my dad," Liam says, and I note the past tense. "He stopped by the marina to drop off some bait for a charter boat leaving the next day and saw us pulling out into the open ocean."

"You at least knew how to drive a boat, right?" I confirm.

"Yeah, but we were too young for a boating license and if my dad hadn't hopped into our other boat to come after us, we actually could have gotten in big trouble if we were caught."

"We were both grounded for a month for that one," Aidan says. "Luckily, they didn't find the beer we'd hidden on the boat earlier that day when we hatched the plan."

"You guys were such idiots," I say with a laugh.

"Just normal teenage shit," Liam says, shaking his head. "Sometimes I wonder how we survived half the stuff we did. God help me when that one is a teenager," he says, nodding his head toward the ceiling where we can still hear Jack moving around his room even though Liam put him to bed nearly an hour ago.

I glance at Aidan and notice his Adam's apple bob. I wonder if he's thinking about Liam being a single parent, and if that brings back memories of his own father's death when he was a kid.

"Speaking of," Liam says, when the silence grows heavy because neither Aidan nor I know what to say about the prospect of Liam being a single parent, "I better go check on him. I'm glad you guys stopped by. It's been . . . different without you right across the street." He and Aidan exchange a look I can't quite read.

"You guys should come into the city and catch a game," Aidan says.

"Yeah, maybe if we got a box or something it would be possible," Liam says. I know he can't go anywhere without the media hounding him these days. He's been radio silent about his life since his wife passed, and while I respect that he needs his privacy, I also see it through the PR lens of "the less you say, the more people wonder."

"Anytime," Aidan says. "You just let me know. You're welcome to stay at my place too, if you don't want to trek back down here late at night."

"A sleepover with Uncle Aidan would be the highlight of Jack's life, I'm sure," Liam says with a small smile as he stands to walk us to the door.

As we walk down the stone path that cuts through the front lawn, I don't miss the way Aidan's whole body seems less tense. Despite the heaviness of the losses both he and Liam have experienced, he's at home here—relaxed and comfortable in a way I haven't seen since our first night in Bermuda.

"You could have told me your best friend was Liam Freaking Walker," I say when he takes my hand as we cross the street.

He gives me a little squeeze and says, "It was more fun to see how you'd react."

"Gotta be honest, I was a little starstruck."

His chuckle rumbles over the sound of crashing waves down at the end of the street. "Most people are."

"How does the whole world not know you two are childhood best friends?"

"The world doesn't need to know everything about us.

Liam, in particular, is extremely private," he says, and it's funny to think that his best friend is the one professional athlete who might be even more closed off than he is. Which is why seeing them together in Liam's home, totally at ease, was such a treat. "No one expected him to be the star he is today, honestly. Least of all him."

"Why not?"

"Not an exceptional college quarterback, middling performance at the Combine, fourth-round draft pick, traded after two years of riding the bench in San Francisco, and after three years as the backup here, he only ended up playing because our QB got injured mid-game. But he rose to the occasion, and the rest is history."

I didn't know all of the "history," only that people are saying he might be the greatest quarterback of all time, which is why taking this year off, at his age, has everyone speculating about whether he'll be as good when he comes back next season.

Aidan sharing this side of him, bringing me to his childhood home, introducing me to his best friend, and trusting me with all of this when I know how private he can be . . . all of it feels significant.

Which is why, as he lets us into the house, turning and boxing me in against the closed front door, I have to remind myself that none of it means anything, even if it feels like it does.

When he dips his head and trails kisses along my jaw, telling me that he's been thinking about getting me alone for weeks, I have to remind myself that this is the moment where I might start thinking it all *means something*.

I'm not going to make that mistake this time.

Not even when he scoops me into his arms and walks us up the stairs. Not even as he gently removes each item of my clothing in his bedroom. Not even as he lays me down and props himself over me, while his hands roam my body and he tells me I'm perfect. Not even as our bodies are joined and he's saying that the best part of being home is having me here with him.

This is just how he does casual. Friends with benefits, and nothing more.

Chapter Thirty

AIDAN

I am so unaccustomed to waking up with someone in my bed that the feel of soft hands stroking my skin sends a shot of adrenaline flooding through my system.

My eyes jolt open. The soft light of early morning filters through the curtains, illuminating my room, and memories of Morgan and me here last night flash through my mind. I'm not sure if it's those memories, or the way she's curled up against me on her side as she trails her hand along my abdomen, sinking perilously close to my dick, that has me so hard.

With her eyes still closed, she lets out a soft groan and her knee slides over my quad as she brings her center right up against my thigh, leaving a trail of wetness along my skin. As tempted as I am to see where this leads, I'm pretty sure she's still asleep and I don't want her to wake up mid-thigh ride, humiliated that I watched her do something she wasn't aware she was doing.

"Hey," I say, bringing the backs of my fingers to her cheeks and running them across her freckles I'm always so desperate to see.

She freezes right as her hand slips onto my cock, and I can't stop the way my hips press up into her waiting hand. She opens her eyes, her gaze locked on mine before her cheeks turn pink. *I fucking love it when she blushes.*

"Oh my god, was I just . . ."

"Desperate to be with me, even in your sleep? Yeah, I think so," I tease.

She groans and goes to roll away, but I curl my arm up and around her back, holding her to my side. "Don't worry, baby, I'm feeling the exact same way. I already woke up hard for you. You're just helping me along."

The way she stares at me without blinking makes me wonder if she's never woken up to morning sex with someone. To be fair, I haven't either, not for about a decade. But it seems like a really good idea right about now.

"Don't tell me you're not turned on," I say, letting my fingers trail along the ridge of her cheekbone before I tuck her strawberry blonde waves behind her ear. "You're so wet it's all over my thigh."

"Well, that's humiliating," she says.

"You can call it humiliating, but I'm going to call it my favorite way to wake up."

"Yeah?" she asks, one eyebrow lifted.

I pull the sheet back so I can see her naked body pressed up against mine. "Yeah," I say, tilting my hips up again so my shaft runs right along her palm.

Her fingers tighten around me, smooth and soft as she strokes me slowly with just the right amount of pressure. My head drops back to my pillow.

"Seems like it would be uncomfortable to wake up with a raging hard on." There's the small, teasing smile that's so reminiscent of the easy way she flirted with me at the bar in Bermuda. But the way she's gripping my shaft, tugging up and around the head of my cock before sliding back down, is confident and determined.

"It's *terribly* uncomfortable," I say with a small chuckle.

"How *ever* could we make this better?"

In less than two seconds, I've flipped her up and over my hips so she's straddling me, and her squeal of surprise, followed by laughter, spurs me on. I grip her hips, and she slides her wet center along my shaft with a sigh.

"Seems like you have an issue we need to make better too," I tell her.

"Yep. Such a problem," she says, tilting her hips to slide along me again.

I reach over to the nightstand and grab the strip of condoms. There are only a few remaining after the ones we used last night. As I tear one open, I tell her, "I want to watch you ride me."

She glances down at our joined bodies, and in the early morning light, she crosses her forearms over her stomach. She looks self-conscious in a way I haven't seen before.

"You are so fucking hot right now," I tell her as I roll on the condom, "above me like this. I want to watch the way you take me when you sink onto my cock, and I want to watch your tits bounce as you fuck me."

"Jesus, Aidan," she says with a slight gasp.

I lift an eyebrow. "Oh sorry, am I not supposed to be honest right now?"

I'm hoping that knowing how turned on I am by the sight of her body will help her regain whatever confidence she just lost, but she's frozen with the corner of her lower lip between her teeth instead.

"Tell me what the problem is so I can fix it," I insist.

She huffs out a laugh. "You can't fix my body, Aidan."

"No, I can't. Because it's already perfect as is." I slide my hands up her thighs and over her hips, then behind her to cup the globes of her ass.

"I think you'd say anything right now that would result in sex."

"I'd say anything right now that would make you *comfortable*. Because whatever issues you see when you look at yourself are the exact things that are turning me on. Your body is lush and strong and soft. It's perfect."

She sighs and lowers her arms, but the hesitation I'm seeing on her face still bothers me. "Stand up," I say, nodding my chin toward the side of the bed.

"What? Why?"

"I want to show you something."

She scoots off me and mutters something I can't quite make out, so I stand quickly and take her hand. With a gentle tug, I walk her over to my closet door and pull it closed so that we're standing in front of a full-length mirror.

"What the fuck," she whispers, her arms wrapping around her midsection as her gaze meets mine in the reflection. "This is my worst nightmare."

I step up so I'm right behind her, so close my dick presses into her back. I drop a quick kiss on her shoulder before my lips move to the shell of her ear. "I'm going to show you what I like about your body. And if that doesn't make you more comfortable being naked in front of me, we'll stop."

"Couldn't we just . . . do this with our eyes closed or find somewhere dark?"

At this point, my body knows every inch of hers, but this is the first time we've been together in full daylight when I can see her so clearly.

"And deny us both the pleasure of watching while you come? I think not."

I slide my hands up the outside of her thighs and over the curves of her hips. Her skin is tight and smooth as it hugs her curves. I settle my hands at the narrow curve of her waist, which highlights her hourglass shape, and her breath catches when my fingers curl into her hips. "Put your hands on the doorframe."

"What?" she squeaks the word out.

I take her hands in mine and guide them to the trim around the door, placing them slightly higher than her shoulders so she'll have an unobstructed view.

"Like this." The position causes her to bend forward slightly, and her full breasts sway with the movement. My hips press up, grinding my dick into her back. "Fucking hell."

I stay leaning over her, so my lips are right at her ear as my hands trail up her arms. "Your skin is like silk, I've never felt anything so soft." I graze my knuckles along her triceps and then along the sides of her breasts.

She sucks in a breath when I cup the underside of each one in my hands, and the way she spills over my fingers, her hardened nipples straining for my touch, has a moan of desire slipping out of the back of my throat. In response, her breathing grows quick and shallow. "Do you see how fucking sexy your tits are, Morgan? Do you see the way your nipples are begging me to play with them?" The sweep of my thumbs across the pebbled mounds has her moaning this time, then her lips part and she closes her eyes.

"Open your eyes, baby," I say as I spread my legs on the outside of hers, bringing our hips to more of a level height. Then I stand up, grasping her hip in one hand and my cock in the other as I slide it along her dripping seam. "Even through the condom I can feel how wet you are for me."

She licks her lips as she glances down, watching me use the head of my cock to rub circles on her clit. I slide my other hand over her soft stomach and then back up to her breast where I toy with her nipple, sliding it between my fingers until she can't hold in her moans.

"Do you see how fucking sexy your body is now?" I say. "The way it turns me on? The way I can't wait to slip into this tight little cunt of yours?"

"Do it," she says on an exhale. "Please."

"What's that, baby? Begging now, are you?" I tweak her nipple harder between my fingers and her responding moan is guttural.

"Yes," she hisses out the word.

"Ask me again, and make me believe you really want this."

"Please fuck me, Aidan. Please . . . don't make me wait—"

I shove inside her in one long push before she can finish her sentence, and she cries out in pleasure as her fingers curl into the wooden door frame. With each thrust, her breasts sway forward and her lips part a little more until she's gasping for breath as she watches me fuck her.

Listening to her beg for it and then watching her take my

dick like this has me ready to come way too quickly, so I slip my other hand down her abdomen and find her clit. I press small, tight circles over it as I increase my pace until her entire body is shaking and I suspect my arm around her rib cage is the only thing holding her up.

"Oh god," she gasps, pressing her head back into my shoulder and squeezing her eyes shut.

"Don't you dare shut your eyes, or I'll stop." My words are a rough demand and her eyes fly open in response. "I want you to see how fucking beautiful you are when you fall apart on my cock."

"Oh shit . . . oh my god . . . I'm . . ."

"I know, baby." Every muscle in my body tightens with the effort of holding my release until she's done, and I watch in fascination as her mouth drops open and her tongue sweeps along her lower lip and she nearly screams with the force of the orgasm that shakes her entire body.

I hold her upright while she climaxes and then pour myself into the condom as her inner walls squeeze my cock, wishing there was no barrier between us. My body curls around hers protectively once we're both done, and after removing the condom, I pull us back onto the bed where she cuddles into me. And the whole time, all I can think of is one singular word. The one that can never apply to her: *mine.*

Chapter Thirty-One

MORGAN

Aidan is in the kitchen pouring batter onto the waffle iron when I walk in after a shower. My hair is still wet, but I've French braided it to keep it off my face, and I'm wearing one of his Rebels T-shirts. It hits mid-thigh and is soft and cozy.

He glances over at me, and I don't miss the way his eyes widen. "Damn," he breathes out the word. "You look way better in that shirt than I do."

I know my smile is tentative. "I hope you don't mind. My suitcase was in the other room, and this was the first thing I found in your closet."

"I don't mind at all. I hope you like waffles?"

"Love them. But . . ." I stop myself, because I've already made my body insecurities into way too much of a thing. And he's already given me many reassurances that he loves my curves—in fact, he's the only man I've ever been with who has specifically addressed the size of my body and why it turns him on. The way he just proved it to me, in front of that mirror, will live on a loop in my head for the rest of my life.

I'm not sure other sexual experiences in the future will ever compare to what we've shared, and it actually makes me sad to think that the best sex of my life will end at some point and I'll have to settle for someone else.

Maybe not, I assure myself. *You could still find someone just as amazing.*

"Don't you dare tell me you're going to deny your body something this delicious," he says, and I sigh in response, my shoulders sagging.

"My body likes to turn everything I eat immediately into fat."

He flips the waffle iron over and resets the timer, then rounds the island to where I'm standing. Wrapping his arms around my back, he pulls me close and tilts my chin up.

"Morgan, you've got curves, and as I think we've already established, that's part of what's so appealing about your body. You're strong, but also soft and sensual . . . you're fucking *luscious.* Literally, every guy's wet dream."

My chest shakes with a silent chuckle. "Maybe yours, but definitely not *every* guy's."

His jaw clenches, like he wants to say something about that. Finally, he says, "If a guy is looking for some kind of a stick figure, he doesn't know what he's missing out on."

"So guys don't care about things like a woman having a thigh gap? That was always a huge focus for my friends when we were teenagers."

His laugh is husky and sensual. "Baby, the only thigh gap I

care about is that there's enough room for my face when your thighs are spread."

I can feel the flush creeping up my neck and into my cheeks.

"Have you always felt this way about your body?" he asks.

"I mean, just since puberty." My laugh is humorless as I remember back to those days. Then I rest my head on his chest so I don't have to look him in the eye as I say, "As a kid, I was already used to being bigger, but that also meant I was faster, and stronger, and a much better athlete. By the time we all hit seventh or eighth grade, those things started mattering less for girls and more for boys. All my friends were focused on fashion, makeup, and having the perfect body."

Not that I'd tell Aidan this, but puberty is also when my mom's behavior toward me began to change. As I became more full-figured and my breasts and hips developed, giving me an hourglass figure, my mom became more and more critical. Now that I'm an adult, I can see how my mom projected her own body insecurities onto me. At the time, it just felt like I was a disappointment. Is it really a surprise that I grew into a people pleaser?

He presses his lips to my forehead. "Teenage girls care about the stupidest shit."

"Maybe, but you also have no idea how hard it was to be a size eleven, when all my friends were a size three or five. My friends' favorite pastime was going to the mall. Watching them pull cute crop tops or super short skirts off the rack and knowing I'd never be able to pull off something like that with my body . . . it was just hard."

"I get that. But you do realize that the size of your

clothing has absolutely no bearing on who you are, your value, or what's really important in life, right?"

"Objectively, yes. But after a lifetime of being told *You have such a pretty face* or *Maybe you should hit the gym a bit more*—"

His hands grasp my shoulders as he steps back slightly so he can study my face. "Who the fuck told you to hit the gym more?"

Now that I'm not tucked into his chest, this whole conversation has me feeling much more exposed and vulnerable. I look away rather than answering.

"Your mother?" His words are ground out through clenched teeth.

"Among others," I say before looking back at him. "And yes, I know that the size of my clothing is the least important thing about me, but it's hard to undo decades of growing up in a society that tells women certain bodies are more desirable and then treats them differently if they don't fit that mold. I don't blame my mom for repeating learned behavior."

"You don't repeat learned behavior if you know it's wrong," he insists. "Which means your mom obviously buys into that shit."

No doubt she does. But don't we all, to some extent? Even when we know it's wrong, even when we're trying to undo the stigma of not being thin, we're constantly having to remind ourselves that bodies come in all shapes and sizes and that one size isn't better than another.

"I have no idea what it's like to be a woman looking at other women and judging them for their size," Aidan continues, "but I can tell you this, as a man: there's nothing you need to change about your body. Your curves are delicious." He slides his hands from my shoulders, down my arms, grazing the sides of my breasts with his palms as he does. A shiver runs through my body, and then he's running his hands along my waist and settling them on the curve of my hips. "I literally can't look at you without getting hard."

I shake my head as I look up at him, and a knowing smile spreads across my face. It's not just the way he affirms my body both in and out of the bedroom, it's the way it feels like he's revealing small pieces of himself each time he does. For someone who claims he's not good at emotions, he has a natural way of showing that he cares. Not that he cares about me like *that*.

"Why are you looking at me like that?" he asks.

"Because . . . you continue to surprise me."

"What fun would it be if I was predictable?" He presses a quick kiss to my nose as the waffle timer beeps and he turns to walk around the island. I take a seat at the counter and he slides a plate over to me, next to the butter and syrup he's already set out. Then, moving over to the coffee pot, he asks, "Milk and sugar, right?"

"How'd you know that?"

"I got you coffee in Bermuda, remember?"

"Yeah, but how'd you know that's how I'd take my coffee in the first place?" At the time, I needed caffeine so badly it didn't occur to me that it might be more than a coincidence that he got my coffee order exactly right.

"Lucky guess. I actually got two that morning, one black and one with milk and sugar, figuring those were the two most likely options."

"So you normally take yours black?" I ask and then watch as he pours milk into both mugs.

"I hate black coffee." He drops a couple teaspoons of sugar into both cups, gives them a stir, and turns to hand me mine.

So he gave me the coffee we both preferred that morning in Bermuda, and drank the black coffee instead. It's not a huge sacrifice, but I think it says something about the kind of person he is. Or, maybe I'm reading too much into it?

"Honest question," I say, taking the mug from him in both hands and then dipping my head to breathe in the scent. "Do you always make breakfast the next morning when you're keeping things casual?"

"Sure," he says with a shrug, but the creases at the edges of his eyes match how tight his voice is, and I'm not sure what to make of that.

"And cuddling after sex?"

"Why not?"

"I'm just trying to understand where I keep going wrong with relationships. So, cuddling after sex and breakfast the next morning doesn't mean anything?"

I watch the column of his throat bob before he visibly relaxes. "The general rule of thumb with a casual relationship is that there's no expectation of monogamy or long-term commitment. I don't think making someone breakfast changes that?"

I can't tell if he's totally full of shit, or if guys and girls think differently about this type of thing. Maybe it's just me who wants to grab on to small gestures like this breakfast and think they mean more than they do? In this case, I'm staying at his house, so I guess it only makes sense that he'd make me breakfast while making some for himself, too. So yeah, I guess that actually doesn't mean anything.

"Hmmm," I say as I cut a small piece of my waffle and take a bite, chewing slowly as I mull over my thoughts. "I always kind of assumed that going on multiple dates and sleeping with someone multiple times, even before talking about making it official, at least made it exclusive. I guess it didn't really occur to me that, in that situation, a guy might also be seeing other people at the same time."

"It doesn't necessarily mean he is, but he could be, unless you'd agreed to make it exclusive."

"Okay." I guess that explains a bit of the disconnect I've had with guys before, where I apparently thought things were more serious and more exclusive than they actually were. For example, Carter flying me to Miami at the beginning of the summer while he was there for work because he didn't want to go that long without seeing me apparently didn't mean that he was seeing *only* me.

We're silent for a minute as he gets his waffle off the iron and spreads butter on it before drenching it in syrup. He keeps casting quick glances at me and looking away when he finds my eyes still on him.

"So now, for example," I say, just to make sure I have some clarity on what our friends-with-benefits situation entails, "I should be open to meeting other guys, since we're keeping this casual?"

"Yep." His one-word response comes out tight, reminding me of the post-wedding dinner in Bermuda. He turns away, but his body doesn't block the way his hand grips the glass handle of the mixing bowl so hard that the whole thing is shaking as he moves it aside and pulls the waffle iron plug out of the wall.

"Okay, good to know."

There's nothing about his physical response that leads me to believe he meant what he just said. I'm torn between wanting to ask him about it, and needing to take him at his word. Because reading too much into things is exactly my problem . . . trying to find reasons that what's happening is more than casual, even when a guy is telling me he doesn't want more.

I have to trust what he's telling me, even if everything about being here in Ember Cove with him feels like more than just sex.

Maybe going on a date with someone else is what I need to do to practice this whole casual relationship thing? The idea makes me feel sick because Aidan has made me feel more important, more desired, and more cherished than any guy I've ever been with.

But, just like almost every other guy I've been with, he doesn't want a real, committed relationship with me, so I guess I need to keep searching until I find someone who deserves me *and* wants a relationship.

Chapter Thirty-Two

AIDAN

"So this thing with Morgan," Liam says, nodding his chin toward the edge of the water where she and Jack are searching for sea glass among small rocks and shell fragments left behind when the tide receded. She's wearing the same yellow bikini she wore in Bermuda—which makes me damn glad I didn't steal it as a keepsake—and my unzipped hoodie over it. "It's serious?"

I cough out a laugh. "No. I don't do relationships, you know that."

He turns and gives me the exact same look his dad used to give us whenever we tried to lie to him about where we'd been or what we'd been up to. Liam's so much like his father, and there's no better man to be like. I'm hit with a painful wave of nostalgia for our childhood, back when things were easier . . . before I'd lost my mom, and he'd lost his dad and wife. I'm pretty sure the only reason Liam is holding it together is because he needs to be there for Jack.

"Right. You always bring girls back to Ember Cove and introduce them to your best friend when it's not a relationship." His sarcastic tone matches the side-eye he gives me.

I think about the fact that the only other woman I've brought here is Hayley, when we stayed at my house for my mom's funeral. I never planned to bring another woman here, but I'm breaking all my own rules—rules that were carefully crafted to avoid the pain, heartbreak, and devastation I've experienced all my life, losing almost everyone I've loved—for Morgan.

"To be fair . . ." I cross my arms over my chest and glance at Morgan. The sight of her in my clothes is quickly becoming a fetish. ". . . I had no intention of introducing you until Finn saw us and told me I better get my ass over to see you."

"Still, a whole weekend away with a woman, in your childhood home, means something."

"Yeah, it means I'm getting laid."

I feel guilty once the words leave my mouth, as if that's all this is between us, and clearly Liam sees right through me because he just chuckles. "Dude, be fucking for real right now. You have feelings for her. You might not even realize it yet, because you haven't had an actual relationship since Hayley—"

"And I won't, again. It's just not worth it." My throat tightens at the memories of my ex and the grief I sank into when our relationship ended. If it hadn't been for hockey and a particularly astute coach, I would have lost my first NHL contract. I swore off relationships after that, focusing on nothing but hockey. It's worked well for me . . . until now.

I fought so hard to return to my team this year—the surgeries, the grueling and painful recovery, the training—I can't risk getting distracted, especially given how much I want my contract to be renewed. Somehow, though, Morgan doesn't feel like a distraction.

Liam looks over at Jack, knee deep in the water, trying to kick the waves onto Morgan, who's playing along by jumping back with a yelp every time.

"Yeah it is, man. It's worth all the pain."

I press my lips together, wanting to tell him he can speak for himself, because I've lost enough people in my life and don't want to risk hurting like that again. But the way he's looking at Jack, the way he's still living and loving even after losing two of the people he loved most in the world, makes me wonder—for the first time in forever—if that could be me some day.

"Besides, you and Hayley were young and dumb. Just because that ended badly doesn't mean you and Morgan would make the same mistakes. Don't miss out on actual happiness," he says, giving me a quick glance, "just because you're scared."

"I'm not scared."

Liam gives me a nod. "Sure you're not."

As I look back toward Morgan, I realize that I may actually be telling the truth. Because I'm not scared, *I'm fucking terrified*. Terrified that I'm already starting to develop feelings for her when I know I can't have her, and terrified that eventually I'll have to watch her be happy with someone else.

I should run, as fast and as far as I can, before this gets any more serious in my mind.

But I already know that I can't do that. If there's anything these last twenty-four hours have shown me, it's that I like my life a whole lot better when she's in it. Even if it can't be forever, I'll take whatever we can have together for now.

———

"I would never have thought to have pizza delivered to the beach," Morgan says as we sit on the blanket with the fire crackling in front of us and the waves crashing beyond. I built us a makeshift fire pit in the sand, just like the kind Liam and I made when we were teenagers.

"It's quite the hack when it's been a perfect beach day and you're not feeling ready to leave the ocean."

She relaxes against my chest as she takes another bite of her pizza. Sitting between my legs, she's basically using my body as a chair, and there's nowhere I'd rather be right now. Sitting here talking about my childhood and what it was like spending the summers down here as a kid, then moving here permanently after my dad died, and having Max move down here once he and my mom got married, has been therapeutic.

I never talk about my past with anyone but Liam or Max, but Morgan makes me want to open up about everything. Sharing the good memories I have of my dad before his addiction changed his personality and made him into someone I didn't know was freeing, like I finally let go of a heaviness I wasn't aware I was carrying.

"So do you use the place here as a summer house, like your mom did when you were a kid and your family still lived in Boston?"

"Yeah. When she left the house to me, I think she hoped I'd raise my own family here."

"Do you think you will?"

I take a deep breath. "I don't think I'll get married or have kids."

"Oh yeah? How come?" Her curiosity is a nice change. Usually that statement sparks a response more along the lines of "You'll change your mind one day," or "You just haven't met the right person yet."

"Honestly?" I ask as her head sinks back into the crevice between my chest and shoulder. "I watched how losing my dad, first to his addiction and then to death, almost wrecked my mom. I watched how losing my mom almost destroyed Max, and I've watched him chase those memories ever since. I watched what losing Kelsey did to Liam. And . . . I just don't think I'm cut out for that."

"Cut out for losing people you love?"

I swallow down the lump in my throat. "Yeah."

"But two people you loved very much both died, and you're still here, living. You'll be here, whether you let love into your life, or not . . . you just won't get to experience that kind of happiness."

"I thought I was in love, once." The admission is so quiet I'm almost surprised she hears it over the sound of the waves.

"Yeah? What happened?"

"She left me. I got called up to the NHL and we were supposed to move together, but she ended things rather than coming with me." I still can't bring myself to speak her name or talk about her reasons for not moving with me.

"I'm sorry that happened," she says, turning on her side and nuzzling her face into my chest. "You know, lots of people have relationships that end badly, especially in their twenties. It doesn't mean you can't try again."

"That one wrecked me," I say, holding her close and thinking about the darkness that overtook me after I moved into a new apartment, in a new city, by myself. How truly alone I was. How I almost succumbed to that darkness. How I almost lost my career because of it. "The only thing that saved me then was hockey, just like it did when I lost my mom. But the thing is, my hockey days are numbered."

"Why's that?"

"I'm thirty-three. They don't let you keep doing this forever just because you love it. Eventually, there are younger and better players who rise up to take your place. It's the nature of professional sports."

"And you ... think you're past your prime?"

"Not yet. But last year was a wake-up call. It made me realize that I don't know who I am without hockey." I don't know what possesses me to admit this, but there's something about her, something about the way she listens, that makes me feel like I can say the quiet parts out loud.

Her arm slips around my waist as she gives me a squeeze and says, "Maybe the problem is that you're giving one-hundred-percent of yourself to hockey, so there's nothing left for other aspects of your life? And like you said, hockey's not forever."

"I promised my coach, my GM, and my agent that I'd focus on nothing but hockey this year. No distractions." I sound like a fucking broken record, but I need these reminders.

"Am I a distraction?" she asks.

Only if you count being on my mind every second I'm not on the ice. "You easily could be, if I let that happen."

"So tell me, would you be a better hockey player if you were sitting home by yourself right now?"

Her and her fucking logic.

"If I wasn't here with you, I probably would have gone to the gym this morning and tomorrow morning too, getting my body ready for the season." Of course, given how many calories sex burns, I can probably count all the times I've fucked her this weekend as at least as much exercise as I'd have gotten otherwise.

"You did go for a run this morning after breakfast. And you were already coming down here without me, weren't you?"

My chest shakes with the low rumble of laughter that escapes. "Not exactly."

"What?" she practically shrieks, turning her head to look up at me. "You said you were coming down here and I should come with you since my AC was broken."

"You said you wouldn't stay at my place in Boston, so I came up with an alternative plan that you seemed more likely to agree to." I give her a sheepish smile.

"I can't believe you . . ." she says with a laugh, but I silence her with a quick kiss.

"Can you blame me for wanting to spend more time with you?"

She sighs as she looks at me, so close I can feel her breath on my face. "Aidan, I know you're supposed to be the expert here, but if I didn't know better, I'd say that this doesn't feel very casual."

"There are no rules, baby. This can be how *we* do casual."

The *hmmm* that rumbles in her throat lets me know she doesn't fully agree, but before she can respond, her phone starts buzzing loudly where it sits on the blanket next to us. We both glance down to see *Dad* lighting up her phone screen with an incoming call.

"You going to answer that?" I ask.

"He'll worry if I don't. But I don't want him to get suspicious when he hears the waves."

"Just tell him you're at the beach watching the sunset with friends."

She snatches up the phone before it goes to voicemail. "Hey, Dad."

With the phone pressed against her left ear, she turns toward the ocean and settles back against me, using me as her chair again. I can hear Carson's voice but can't tell what he's saying. She leans her head to the left and glances up at me, and I press a kiss to her cheek, then trail my lips down to her jaw and press kisses along the column of her neck down toward the slope of her shoulder. The way she relaxes into me with a small sigh turns me on, so I slide my hand around her bare thigh.

"Yeah, just watching the sunset at the beach with some friends." I have to hold in my laughter when she says, "Yeah, up in Newbury Falls with Eva."

I know she's on the phone with her father—the one person who truly can't know what's happening between us—so I shouldn't tease her, but I can't resist. Maybe it's knowing that she wants to be here with me badly enough that she's willing to lie to him that spurs me on? Or maybe it's just that I always want her, no matter what the risk is?

Whatever the reason, I trail my fingers from her thigh across the fabric of her bikini bottom and her legs fall open as a shiver wracks her body. I take that as an invitation, and slip my fingers between the fabric and her skin, trailing them along her seam and up to her clit. I rub small circles that have her arching her back and pressing her head into my collarbone.

"Uh huh," she says to her dad as she tilts her hips to give me better access.

I glance around the beach to make sure no one else is around, even though, with my legs bent on either side of hers, no one would be able to see my hand in her bikini bottoms unless they were right in front of us.

I toy with her clit until her breathing grows rapid, and then I slip two fingers into her, easily sliding in through the moisture that's pooling between her legs. She lets out the slightest moan, so I whisper, "Shhh," directly in her ear, before I slide my other hand up her abdomen, under my hoodie, and find her bikini top so I can move it aside and give myself access to her nipple.

She lets out a small gasp and says, "Hey Dad, I think we're leaving the beach. Gotta go, I'll call you tomorrow."

She presses the screen to disconnect the call and tosses her phone onto the blanket as she tilts her hips further to give me more access, whispering, "Holy shit, Aidan. I was on the phone with *my dad*."

"You were the one who spread your knees and invited me in," I say, my voice low, my lips by her ear. "Admit it, you wanted me to get you off, regardless of who you were talking to."

"Oh shit," she whispers as I tweak her nipple while I fuck her with my fingers.

"Tell me it's true," I say, "or I'll stop."

"Please don't stop."

"Then tell me what I want to hear."

Her breathing is so heavy it almost sounds like she's panting. "Yes, I w-wanted you to get me off."

I sink my fingers into her harder and faster.

"Good. Now beg for it."

"What?" Her surprised gasp follows as I press the heel of my hand to her clit so it grinds against it as I sink into her over and over.

"I want to hear you beg me for this orgasm." My voice is a low growl in her ear and I rub my thumb over her nipple again.

She moans, then says, "Please . . . oh god . . . please, Aidan."

I roll her nipple between my thumb and forefinger and she presses her head back into me as her hips rise to meet my fingers. "Attagirl. Look at you asking for what you want."

"Oh fuck . . ." She moans again. "I'm . . ."

"I know, baby," I say as she looks up at me, her big blue eyes wide in surprise as the orgasm rips through her. I smother her moans with a kiss as she pulses around my fingers. When her moaning stops and her body stills, I pull my fingers out and slip them between my parted lips, licking them clean as she watches me.

"Let's go," I say. "I need you naked and in my bed."

I fix her bikini bottoms and lift her hips so she stands. Then I move around to the far side of the dying fire, where the waves are approaching as the tide comes in, and kick wet sand onto the embers while she gathers up the pizza box, our phones, and the blanket. And then I reach for her hand and lead her up the beach toward the street, wishing that every night could be as perfect as this one.

Chapter Thirty-Three

MORGAN

"Can you do me a favor?" I ask the woman at the reception desk when we check into the hotel in Denver two days later. "Would you mind putting me in a room close to a stairwell?"

"Sure, let me see what I have," she says, tapping her mouse a few times.

I'm trying not to lay my head down on the wooden counter while I wait. Our flight was delayed because of some thunderstorms in Boston, and while we all got our keys from operations as we entered the lobby, I decided to stop at the front desk to see if they might be able to switch my room.

"You good, Morgan?" I hear AJ call from behind me, and turn to find her and McCabe standing there. Everyone else seems to have headed up to their rooms already.

"Yeah, just seeing if I can get a room closer to the stairs. I have this weird anxiety about needing to be near an exit in hotels. You guys go ahead."

"All right. You can make that request with operations for future stays, so you don't have to wait when we arrive," she says. I already did that before my last trip, but given that I wasn't supposed to travel for this game, I'm stuck with the room that was originally booked for Natalie. "Call if you need anything."

"Will do," I say, turning back to the front desk and briefly closing my eyes as I stand there waiting for a new room assignment.

I wouldn't be so dead tired if I hadn't been up half of last night dealing with yet another PR emergency. While this one cut my beach weekend with Aidan short, at least this time it wasn't his fault.

Instead, my darling, talented social media intern fucked up big time and now her future with the team is quite uncertain.

When I'd told her I'd be "on call" if she needed me during Saturday night's game, I certainly didn't expect to get a text from her saying: *I'm so sorry. I messed up so bad.* Nor did I expect a text from AJ, explaining the situation, to follow.

Apparently, while I was busy getting railed by Aidan in the shower after our beach dinner, Natalie was distracted during a game and accidentally posted a picture of her and our superstar rookie, Jake MacIntyre, in bed together rather than the image the team photographer had sent her.

Why she had the team's social media account open on her personal phone instead of the one we gave her, is a mystery I may never know the answer to because AJ and Patrick are dealing with this, and I've been instructed not to speak to her while HR "investigates" the situation.

I feel partially responsible for not properly talking to her about etiquette around the players. I can't help but feel like I should have been the kind of mentor that sat her down and said, "Hey, here's what you need to know about being a woman in professional sports." I should have explained to her that as an intern, it was imperative that she not sleep with anyone on the team. I assumed that HR had talked to her about how to remain professional around the players.

When Aidan and I first realized we worked together, I set up hard and fast professional boundaries . . . but then I crossed them. Normally, my sense of right and wrong is a little too strong, but around him, it completely fails me.

I've given myself all kinds of reasons why our situation is different—that we'd already had sex before we knew any of the ways we were connected, that our relationship is entirely outside of our professional commitments, and that because we are keeping things casual it's okay.

But did I hold back because it would have felt hypocritical to have that talk with Natalie? And if so, is what happened to her partially my fault?

"I've got a room that's across from the stairwell on the fourth floor," the front desk employee tells me. "But it's on the side by the road, so it may be loud in the morning."

"That's fine," I say, knowing that I'll sleep through the traffic, but I may not go to sleep at all if I'm anxious.

With my key in hand, I make my way across the lobby toward the elevator, moving slowly because I'm so tired. When I get to my room, I almost pass out face-first on the bed, and the only thing that saves me from that fate is my bladder and my phone buzzing in my bag.

I grab my phone on my way into the bathroom, but it's Aidan with a video call, and I'm not answering it while I'm peeing. Apparently he's impatient, though, because he sends a text immediately.

AIDAN

Why aren't you answering your phone?

MORGAN

Sorry, I was peeing. Didn't think you needed to see that.

AIDAN

I wouldn't have minded.

MORGAN

Well I would have. What's up?

AIDAN

What's your room number?

MORGAN

Why?

AIDAN

I want to see you, obviously.

MORGAN

I'm exhausted and can't afford another night of no sleep.

Even as I text it, though, a thrill runs through me at the thought of having him here with me.

AIDAN

I'll be sleeping tonight too, you know. I can just as easily do it in your bed as mine.

MORGAN

I fear we won't actually get any sleep.

AIDAN

I consumed about five pounds of pasta tonight, in preparation for tomorrow's game. I'm going to sleep like a baby, but I'd really prefer to do it with you in my arms.

MORGAN

And this is what you call casual?

I'm sure he's getting tired of me questioning him on this, but he's confusing the fuck out of me. He wants to fall asleep with me in his arms, even if we don't have sex first? Absolutely *nothing* about that seems casual to me.

If this is how guys think, then no wonder I'm perpetually confused about them sending the wrong message!

AIDAN

Give me your room number so we can both go to sleep. Please.

MORGAN

Well, since you asked nicely, it's 4312. I'm right across from the stairwell at the end.

AIDAN

Be there in 2 min.

Sure enough, I've barely finished brushing my teeth when he's knocking on my door. A quick kiss to my forehead, and then he's stripping my clothes off and pulling his own T-shirt off to slip it over my head before he drags me to bed. Nothing shocks me more than the way he wraps his arm around me and pulls my back against his chest, and says, "Goodnight, baby."

His steady breathing is instantaneous, and grows slower and deeper against my hair as he drifts off to sleep. I know it in the way his arm relaxes around me, and his body softens behind mine. I wish I was half as relaxed as he is, but his presence has me so keyed up, I'm not sure how long it will take me to fall asleep.

———

I don't know if my own moan wakes me up, or the intense throbbing between my legs. But as I crack my eyes open, letting them adjust to the dim light filtering through the edges of the curtains, it's instantly clear to me why I'm so turned on. Aidan's hand is in my underwear, his fingertips resting against my clit. I'm not sure if he's even awake, but when his hand twitches and rubs right across that sensitive bundle of nerves, I can't control the way my hips jerk in response, or the breathy sigh that escapes.

"Well, good morning." His voice is rough and low. Tendrils of his breath caress my skin behind my ear and coast over my cheek as his hand freezes.

"Morning," I croak out the word through a throat already tight with longing.

He slides a finger along my seam, where it easily glides through the moisture pooling there. "You always wake up so wet and turned on?"

"Only when someone's hand finds its way into my underwear in my sleep."

"That happen often?" There's an edge to ›his voice that makes me think he doesn't like that idea.

"There's a first time for everything." I've never woken up turned on like this, except with him.

"Good," he says, pressing a kiss to the back of my head as

the pad of his finger meets my clit, circling over it and drawing another moan from the back of my throat. I'm so turned on, I'm already halfway there.

"I'm already close," I say.

"I can tell." He increases the pressure and my breathing grows shallow and quick as I chase that orgasm. When it doesn't come immediately, he flips me onto my back and spreads my knees, settling himself on his stomach as he dips his face to my center. "God, I missed this."

I can't even respond because he slips two fingers into me and curls them up as his tongue toys with my clit, stealing my breath. The sensations are too strong, too good, and the heat spreads from my core through my veins until it feels like electrical pulses are shooting through me, exploding every nerve in their wake. My whole body feels weightless, like I'm floating through space while disintegrating, turning into stardust.

My legs collapse to the side as my orgasm subsides, and he looks up at me with a shit-eating grin.

"Get up here," I mumble, my eyes half-closed. "I want to taste you, too."

"Can't. My alarm is about to go off—"

"How do you know?"

"I always wake up ten minutes before it's set, no matter what time that is."

"You're a freak of nature," I say, the words slow as the tiredness overcomes me.

"I'm your freak though," he says with a laugh, and my eyes fly open at the implication that he's mine. That can't be what he meant.

"You have . . ." I circle my finger in the air, vaguely in the direction of his face. "... *me* all over your beard. You should probably wash your face before you see your teammates."

"No way. I want to be tasting and smelling you all morning."

My core clenches at the thought of him thinking about this even when we're apart, no matter how gross the idea of what he's suggesting actually is.

"That sounds like exactly the kind of *distraction* you're not supposed to have this season."

"All right," he says, like he's about to broker some sort of deal. "I'll wash my face so your scent isn't a distraction, if you let me do this again tonight."

I was surprised when I heard we weren't headed back to Boston after the game, but AJ explained that the team tries not to do that unless it's a short enough flight that they can get back to Boston by midnight, or a longer overnight flight where everyone can just sleep on the plane.

"We'll see. Maybe if you're good, and don't get in any fights during the game or afterward, that can be your reward."

His eyebrows lift as he gives me a smirk. "I do love a good incentive."

"At this point, whatever it takes to keep you focused and not on AJ's shit list," I say, reaching out to tap his nose. But he grabs my hand, pulling it out of the way and bending down to kiss me goodbye.

"I can't promise I won't be thinking about my head between your legs through all of morning skate." He pushes off the bed and stands there staring down at me.

"Use all that focus and put it toward hockey," I say with a laugh.

"Maybe. I can't really leave here without my shirt though," he says, and when I sit to pull the hem up and over my head, he groans. "I really wish I didn't have to leave."

"Go," I say, handing him his T-shirt and pulling the sheet up to tuck it under my armpits. "You're not going to let me be a distraction, remember?"

"Hmpf." The sound rolls around in his throat, but he turns and grabs his phone and his key card off the nightstand. And then he slips out the door, shutting it quietly behind him.

My phone buzzes a minute later.

AIDAN

Made it back to my room without running into anyone. Can't wait to see you again tonight.

My head crashes back into my pillow. *It's not serious. He just wants sex.*

But even as I tell myself this, I realize that *he* wasn't the one who just came so hard he felt like he turned to stardust. In fact, the only thing he got out of that was pleasuring me. And somehow, that was enough.

Chapter Thirty-Four

AIDAN

MAX

Good game tonight! Those two assists were great. I think I'm going to catch a flight up to Boston for Friday's game. I don't want to miss opening night.

AIDAN

Thanks! But you don't have to do that, it'll be on TV.

MAX

I know I don't have to. I want to.

I stand outside her hotel room door waiting for her to answer, and my stomach is twisted in knots. I'm half terrified that one of my teammates is going to walk out of his room and see me here, and half excited at the thrill of sneaking around.

"We can't keep doing this," Morgan says as soon as I've stepped into her room and the door is shut behind me. She's looking up at me with those big blue eyes that make me want to agree with anything she says. But I can't agree with that.

I step toward her, and watch her step back. "Yes, we can."

My arm shoots behind her and I plant my hand against the wall, halting her progress. "Aidan, this is too risky. AJ told me tonight that they're still not sure if they're going to keep Natalie on as an intern, and if they don't, she may not be able to graduate in May since this internship is a graduation requirement. I tried to take the blame, telling her that I hadn't talked to Natalie about the etiquette around having a relationship with a player, and if I had, this might not have happened."

"And what did AJ say about the whole not having a relationship with a player thing?" I'm particularly curious about her reaction given that she's living with our captain.

"Obviously the relationship isn't ideal, but that's not the real problem here. It's that she posted it on our socials accidentally."

"I don't think there's anything you could have done about *that*." I dip my head closer to hers and drop my hands to her waist. "So tell me why that means we can't keep doing this?" I run my thumbs along her abdomen as my fingers curl into her ass so I can bring her closer to me. Even six inches away is too far.

I am so fucked.

"I feel like such a hypocrite." Her words are whispered and her chest heaves with a deep breath as her tongue darts out to wet her lower lip.

"Baby, we're not two kids in our early twenties fucking

around and taking pictures of ourselves in bed together. That was a whole level of stupidity and if Natalie didn't know better, MacIntyre sure should have. McCabe's talked to him, and it won't happen again."

"Meanwhile, Natalie's the one who looks like a fool and might lose her job, while he gets a slap on the wrist and a talking-to from the captain."

"He wasn't the one who posted the picture on the team's social media," I remind her. "It was an accident and it sucks that it happened, but there are professional consequences for things like that."

"What do you think would happen if people found out about us?" she asks, and I pull back a bit at the worry in her voice.

"Your dad would kill me."

"It's cute that you're scared of my dad," she says, walking her fingers up my chest before she slides her hand around my neck like she's already forgotten she just told me we can't do this.

"I have a *very* healthy respect for how he could destroy my career if he wanted to."

"And I'm sure he has a healthy respect for the commission he earns on your contract. You're worth more to him than three new players would be."

"You think he wouldn't be willing to forsake his percentage if he found out I was fucking his daughter?"

She bites the corner of her lower lip, and the way her teeth sink into the full pink flesh has my dick jumping. "Fair point. So, again, maybe we shouldn't be doing this."

"Or maybe we just need to make sure we don't get caught."

"Aidan, that's a dangerous game when your career is on the line."

"I think we're just going to have to be careful, because I'm not going to stop seeing you just because your dad warned me off." My heart feels like it seizes in my chest as the realization of what I just admitted washes over me. *Fuck man, this is not just friends with benefits.* "Unless you honestly want me to leave?"

At this point, I don't think I could stop pursuing her, unless she is adamant that she doesn't want me. After only a few days of getting to spend alone time with her again in Ember Cove, I'm full-on infatuated. Being with her is addictive. I like myself better when I'm with her—she smooths out my rough edges, and I polish up the parts of her that she's tried to make dull in order to fit some mold that others have set for her.

"But, I think you promised me a reward if I was a good boy tonight?" I say when she doesn't respond. I dip my head down to hers and trace the shell of her ear with my nose as I say, "I was *such* a good boy, just so you'd let me taste you again."

Her whole body shudders. "Oh god."

"Nope, just me, baby. And I plan to do *ungodly* things to you tonight. So if that's not what you want"—I trail one of my hands up her side, along the curve of her breast, and then rest my palm against the front of her neck, using my fingers to tilt her head up—"you should say so. Otherwise"—I press wet kisses along her jaw—"I'm going to get on my knees right now."

"Fuck . . . yes . . ." She whispers, and I'm on my knees in front of her before she even finishes hissing out the *S*.

"That's my girl," I say. "Let's see how wet the thought of us together made you."

I reach under the hem of her tank top and pull the elastic waistband of her sweats down her legs, leaving her underwear in place. There's a distinct wet mark where her arousal has soaked through her thong. From my knees, I lean forward, lapping my tongue against her.

She moans and presses her head against the wall behind her. I pull her thong down and drop it at her feet, where she kicks her clothing away. Reaching behind her knee, I bring her leg up over my shoulder. "Lose the shirt."

"So bossy," she says in mock outrage.

"I'm sorry if you thought that was bossy. Let me rephrase. *Lose the fucking shirt*, Morgan, or I'll edge you until you're crying and begging me to make you come."

She huffs out a laugh. "You drive a hard bargain."

"There's nothing hard about it. You do what I say, and we both end up happy."

Her eyes widen a bit at my statement, but she pulls the tank top over her head and whispers, "You really are ruining me for anyone else."

I look up at her, my sexy fucking girl with her curves and her insecurities. She has no idea the power she holds over me.

"That's the plan." And before I can think too much about what that means or she can ask me to elaborate, I dip my face to her center. I lap up every bit of her I can get my mouth on until she has to bite the heel of her hand to keep from screaming as she comes undone on my face.

And when I stand, still holding her up with my hands on

her hips, I lean in close, telling her, "You've soaked me in your cum and now I want you to taste yourself."

Her lips part with a surprised gasp. "Why?"

So many reasons. "I was good tonight because I wanted *this.* And I want you to know what it is I'm so obsessed with."

"You're obsessed with the taste of me?"

I'm obsessed with you.

"Among other things." I kiss her hard, and she doesn't pull back. Instead, she parts her lips, running her tongue along mine.

"Kind of salty," she mumbles between kisses. "Is that how you taste?"

"Someday you'll find out," I say, "but not tonight."

"Why not tonight?"

"Because if the option exists to fuck you, I'm not going to choose coming in your mouth instead."

She gives me a lazy half smile. "What if the option doesn't exist to fuck me?"

I know she's teasing, but I can't help the growl that rattles around in my throat. "Then I guess you can get on your knees. But that wouldn't be my first choice."

"What would be?" she asks, lifting her chin slightly like she's challenging me to say something completely out of pocket. But I don't want something wild, I just want to keep myself joined with her as often as possible.

"I'd really like to fuck you from behind," I say, sliding my sports coat off and unbuttoning my dress shirt. "I'd like to watch myself sinking into you while I'm gripping your hips so hard I leave handprints behind."

"That's oddly specific," she says with a slight eye roll.

The slide of leather against metal as I unbuckle my belt

precedes the scraping of my zipper, and then my pants land at my ankles. I step out of them, leaving them on the floor with the rest of my clothing.

"I've had a lot of time to picture all the ways I want to be with you."

"Oh yeah, and where are you when you're picturing this?" She takes my hand, leading me over to her bed.

"Where *aren't* I?" My laugh is husky and loud in the quiet room. I reach for her, letting my hands glide over every part of her bare skin. "In the shower, at the grocery store, during my workout, while skating laps to warm up. Every night before I fall asleep."

She doesn't say anything, just presses her lips between her teeth like she's trying to hold back a smile. Maybe she's finally realizing just how perfect I think she is.

Reaching out, she slides my boxers down my legs, tugging on them to get them down my thighs. Then she sits at the end of the bed, legs spread so I'm standing between them, and grips my shaft. "I just want a taste."

She wets her lips as she stares at my cock, parts her lips, and slides me into her mouth. With her tongue pressed against the underside of me as I slide along the roof of her mouth, I can't hold back my groan. My hand instinctively moves to the back of her head to help her set the pace, while being careful not to push in enough to choke her.

"My god," I sigh. I'm not sure a blow job has ever felt quite like this. It's not that she's doing anything special, it's just that it's *her* doing it.

You are so fucked. That phrase rattles around in my psyche, uninvited but ever present.

She pulls back, looks up at me, cocks one eyebrow, and

throws my words back at me. "God's not here. But you promised to do ungodly things to me, no?"

"All right, smartass, let's see you on all fours on the bed."

She gulps audibly, like it's just occurred to her how revealing that position will be. But she tilts her chin up with a defiant glint in her eyes.

"Good fucking girl," I practically purr as she does what I ask. It's not that I'm proud of her for following orders; I'm proud of her for not letting her insecurities get in the way.

She looks over her shoulder at me.

"Fuck," I groan, "hold on, I need to grab a condom." Two seconds later I'm back and rolling it down my dick. "How gentle do you want me to be?"

After a game, I'm always keyed up. There's still so much adrenaline running through my body, even after a shower and the ride back to the hotel.

She licks her lips again. "You decide, and I'll let you know."

I line myself up behind her, guiding the head of my cock through the slickness at her opening and down to her clit. She moans the minute I rub myself against her, like she wasn't expecting me to be working her up again. "I'm always going to make sure you're taken care of first. You know that, right, Morgan?"

Her eyebrows knit together and she arches her back, shoulders up, to get a better look at me. "You did take care of me."

"And I'm going to keep doing that, even while I'm inside you." I pull back, then slip into her in one long, slow motion until I'm buried so deep there's nowhere else to go.

She grunts out a sound that's neither pleasure nor pain—

just an acknowledgement that she's reached her limit for how much of me she can take. But as our bodies move apart and together, as I watch myself pushing into her, as my hands explore her body, as her grunts turn into moans and her sighs turn into pleas for more, I realize I'm way too close, too soon.

I slow the pace, taking a deep breath to calm my body as I reach forward and cup her breasts in my hands. She turns back to look at me over her shoulder again, saying, "Please don't stop."

"I'm too close," I tell her. "I'm not coming until you do, so you tell me what you need to get there."

She puts her weight on one of her arms and lifts the other, guiding my hand from her breast to between her legs. "Just touch me, I'm so close."

With my finger gliding over her clit and my other hand toying with her nipple, her breathing turns ragged and her movements become frantic. She's slamming herself back against me so hard and so fast while chasing her orgasm that there's nothing I can do to hold myself back. Her inner walls grip me through the waves of her orgasm, triggering a tsunami of sensation throughout my body.

I move my hand from her breast to her shoulder, pulling her up so her back's against my chest as my orgasm rips through me. My entire body shudders as I come and the sheen of sweat between us has her sliding against my chest as I continue moving inside her.

"I'm so sensitive," she says, bringing her hand to my wrist and holding it in place like she's afraid I'll stop toying with her clit. "I think I'm going to . . ."

"That's my girl," I say. "Give me one more."

"I can't . . ." she stops on a gasp, and her shoulders and head slump forward. "Oh shit . . ." Then her words are a jumble before she cries out her pleasure.

When she's finished, I pull her back against me and press a kiss to her temple. "Have I ruined you yet, or shall I keep trying?"

Her shoulders shake with a single bark of laughter. "Do you have any idea how hard it is knowing that I'll never have sex this good with anyone else?"

My voice is low and almost sad when I tell her, "I know *exactly* how that feels."

Chapter Thirty-Five

MORGAN

"This is so fun," Lauren says as we stand at the back of the club seats, looking down toward the ice at our home opener. Everywhere we look, people have McCabe and a dark blue 9 on their backs.

"This was brilliant marketing," I say. "Jersey sales must have skyrocketed because of this."

Her smile is the small, private kind, like she's proud of herself for creating this event but doesn't want to come off as gloating. "I'm still surprised he agreed to it."

"I'm not. He's like a different person now that he and AJ are together."

"Yeah, but he's still really private," she says.

"All he's got to do is hand out pictures he already auto-graphed to any season ticket holder wearing his jersey after the game, *if* he scores his 500th goal," I say. "It's not like he's going to be chatting up the crowd. It'll be late, and people will be in a hurry to get their picture and get home."

"Yeah, I would have loved to set it up as a meet and greet," Lauren says, "but after we saw how many people RSVP'd that they wanted to participate, and now seeing his jersey on so many fans, I'm really glad we didn't go that route. We'd be here all night."

I laugh. Even though season ticket sales are limited so not everyone wearing his jersey will be waiting for a photo . . . she's probably right. I'm not sure if McCabe has the patience to chat and take a picture with thousands of people, especially when I'm sure he'd rather be celebrating with his teammates. Scoring his 500th goal will put him in an elite group of NHL players who have reached this milestone. Even if it doesn't happen tonight, it's going to happen soon.

"All right, I have to get downstairs so I can take some video of the team as they take the ice for warm ups," I say. "I'll see you at the end of the game, hopefully to celebrate McCabe's 500th goal."

After I flash my Rebels ID for the security guard, I take the elevator to the lower level where the locker rooms are and find the spot where I know Tatum always stood to take photos before games. But as I stand there waiting, I realize I could get much better shots if I were closer to the ice, right where the hallway opens to the rink. The lighting is better, and the players will be lit up as they come out of the tunnel.

I move in that direction and immediately realize there's a distinct disadvantage to this spot. In order to be out of the way as the players come through the tunnel, I have to stand in view of the entire arena, fully exposed to the crowd. No wonder Tatum preferred the alcove off the hallway.

But there's no time to move back there now. The lights behind me have already dimmed and the white and blue spotlights are flashing across the ice as a single bright beam settles on the opening in front of me. The announcer tells the crowd to give it up for last season's Division and Conference Champions, and the cheers are deafening.

The players come out one-by-one, each giving me a smile or a thumbs up for the video they know I'll be posting. But when Aidan steps forward, just out of the spotlight as he waits for his name to be announced, he glances over at me. His eyes land on my chest, where the *C* on McCabe's jersey is prominently displayed near my shoulder.

His entire face hardens. "Take. It. Off." His words aren't audible over the noise from the crowd, but I know exactly what he's said. *Is he jealous?*

That thought has my eyebrows dipping together in confusion, and he must think I didn't hear him, because he steps toward me, leaning down to talk directly in my ear. "If you're trying to make me jealous by showing up in my best friend's jersey, you've got my attention. So take it off, or I can't be responsible for how I play tonight."

"No way. It's McCabe's celebration tonight. *Everyone* is wearing his jersey."

"*Except you.* Take it off, or whatever happens out there on the ice will be on your conscience."

"Bullshit. You're an adult and in control of your own actions."

"Not with you, I'm not."

His name is announced, but he doesn't make any move to step into the spotlight.

"Go," I insist, trying to push him away.

"Tell me you're going to take it off."

"Oh my god, you jealous fool," I keep my voice low. "Fine. Now, *goooo*."

He turns and steps onto the ice, and my attention focuses on McCabe, who was right behind him. I can tell by the way he looks at me that he hasn't missed what happened. The funny thing is, he doesn't appear even a little bit surprised. If I didn't know better, I'd say he's amused.

Hartmann and Colt follow behind McCabe, and then the lights come back on. I shield my eyes from the sudden brightness. When I turn back toward the tunnel, AJ's receding figure is at the end of the hallway. Which means she probably just saw what happened with Aidan also.

Well, shit.

―――――

We're only halfway through the second period when McCabe sinks the puck into Buffalo's net. Coming around the back of the pipes, he sinks to his knees and slides until he's nearly at center ice. His teammates surround him, celebrating his 500th goal, and then he skates toward the edge of the ice to high-five the entire bench before hopping over the boards so the next line can come on for the face-off.

By the time the period ends, we're leading by three goals. The team is on fire, except for Aidan, who's playing like shit. I've spent the last two periods up in the media booth wondering if I caused that, but also trying to figure out why it bothered him so much that I was wearing McCabe's jersey just like thousands of other people here.

No distractions. That's what he promised AJ, Wilcott, and

my dad. And here I am, distracting him. I didn't do it on purpose. It honestly never occurred to me that he'd mind.

I'm chewing on my lip, wondering if I should go down and try to get some photos of them coming back out before the third period, just so Aidan can see that I've taken the jersey off. Of course, I wasn't planning to walk around the arena in leggings and a tight long-sleeve shirt without having the oversized jersey on, so now I'm super self-conscious. But it seems entirely selfish of me to let my own insecurities keep me up here in this room when I could go down there and set his mind at ease.

I take the jersey and fold the top over so that the only thing visible is the Rebels logo on the front, and tie it around my waist. Then I head down to the lower level, positioning myself near the tunnel that leads to the bench. I'm set up with the video recording as the players enter the hallway single file, each of them with hard looks of determination on their face. Unlike before the game, no one acknowledges me this time. Not even Aidan. But I still notice his eyes sliding over to me as he approaches and his lips curving up as he passes me. At least I won't have to practically edit him out of the footage this time.

When he goes on to get an assist and a goal in the next period, AJ finds me in the media room. "Make sure you post about that goal," she says. "A veteran player returning from injury to score a goal in the home opener is newsworthy."

"It's already set up. I'm just waiting a little longer to post it, so people don't miss the post about McCabe's 500th goal," I tell her.

"All right, good. What do you think got into him this last

period?" she asks. Her tone is completely neutral so I have no idea if she's insinuating something.

"I'm not sure," I say. "You'd have to ask him."

"Oh, I will," she says with a small laugh. "I heard you were down in the tunnel getting some footage before the third period. Maybe seeing you was what turned things around for him?"

"AJ, I really don't think—"

I'm interrupted by the screaming of the crowd, and we both turn to see a fight breaking out on the ice. I'm half-expecting Aidan to be at the center of it, so you can imagine how surprised I am when he's the one holding Jake MacIntyre back, head bent as he talks him down and keeps him from joining in.

I glance over at AJ and don't miss the self-satisfied nod of her head. She didn't miss that either, thankfully.

———

"We missed you at Sunday dinner last week," Lauren says. Sunday family dinners were always a big thing at the Flynn's brownstone in South Boston back when Jameson, Audrey, and Jules all lived there together. Things have changed a lot in the nearly two years since Lauren and I moved back to Boston and she reconnected with Jameson, but the family still tries to do dinner as often as possible, and I'm always included.

"Yeah, sorry, I was dealing with the whole Natalie-posting-the-wrong-photo situation."

Lauren shakes her head saying how terrible she feels for her. "It seems like you've been MIA a lot lately."

I huff out a laugh. "My life feels like it's been in overdrive since my mom's wedding."

"Maybe two jobs is too much," she says. "Orrrr . . . is there *someone* else taking up your time?" Her eyes flick across the wide expanse of the club level, where Aidan waits with Walsh and Colt. The three of them came up about twenty minutes ago and have been shaking hands with fans after getting their autographed photo from McCabe.

"Literally just overworked," I say, hating the lie that springs to my mouth. But if I do decide to tell my cousin everything, it's not going to be at our place of employment with him standing right across from us.

Aidan's gaze flicks toward me, and then away when he sees Lauren and me looking his way.

"Mm-hmm. I already heard about the jersey situation in the tunnel before the game. So whenever you want to talk about how . . . *overworked* you are," she says, lifting both eyebrows, "just let me know. I'm always here."

I roll my eyes at her but don't respond, while she snickers like a child. It reminds me a lot of how Audrey, Jules, and I used to tease her about how obvious Jameson's feelings for her were, while she kept denying it and insisting they were just friends.

But that's a ridiculous comparison, because Aidan doesn't have *feelings* for me. Sure, he brings that same big dick energy to our situation that Jameson did with Lauren, but that's *all* it is. Jameson was determined to wife her up the minute Lauren was back in his life, and that's the furthest thing from Aidan's mind.

While Jameson was hanging out with Lauren's kids and basically stepping in as a father figure from the start, Aidan doesn't even want kids. Not that I have any or am even certain I want them. But not only is settling down with a family *not* on Aidan's to-do list . . . it's the antithesis of what he's looking for.

My heart races as I watch him joking around with his teammates. *What am I even doing?* Why am I spending every second of my free time with him? Why am I investing so much emotional energy into him when all he wants are hangouts that end with sex and absolutely no commitment?

I know that's what friends with benefits entails, but I can't help but feel that our "relationship" has evolved beyond that.

Maybe . . . maybe I really do need to see other people, too? I wonder how Aidan would react to that, given what happened when I had McCabe's jersey on. That was probably only because McCabe is one of his best friends and they're on the same team, though. It's not like I'd go out with one of his friends.

"You sure you don't want to talk about this?" Lauren asks, and I glance over at her to see concern written across her features.

"I'm good," I lie.

I'm pretty sure I'm spiraling, falling into the same pattern I always do when I start dating a guy and think it's more serious than it is. Aidan has told me—repeatedly—that he doesn't want anything more than this with me, but then he makes me feel so goddamn special, so cherished.

But I'm not. I'm not special *or* cherished. I'm just someone to have around when he wants a woman to spend time with. Yeah, the sex is amazing, but I'm starting to feel like a dirty little secret. The woman who's good enough to fuck, but not good enough for anything more serious.

I know that things are way more complicated than that, and it's the circumstances, not him, making me feel this way, but I can't help wondering if this is just going to end in heartache for me.

He suggested this arrangement because I needed to practice keeping things casual, but if this *practice* has taught me anything, it's that I don't want this to be casual. And he doesn't want it to be serious.

So it seems that we're in a no-win situation.

Chapter Thirty-Six

AIDAN

I haven't seen Morgan all weekend—not since after the game Friday night, where she essentially ignored me in favor of talking to her cousin the entire time. Once the last of the fans had left, we invited them out with us to celebrate winning our home opener, but they both politely declined. Lauren, because her twins would be up at six-thirty no matter how late she went to sleep, and Morgan, because she was "tired."

When I reminded her that she was supposed to be making sure I didn't get in any trouble, she suggested that maybe AJ could pay Colt to babysit me instead. Lauren had coughed to cover her laugh and said, "I'm going to go thank McCabe." Then she left us standing there alone.

"What's wrong?" I asked.

"I'm just tired and I don't have the energy to keep you in line tonight."

I'd been so tempted to ask her just to come back to my

place instead, but I was meeting Max the next morning for breakfast and I've literally *never* had a woman over here before. My home is too much a part of me to share with strangers, so hookups always happen elsewhere. But Morgan's not a stranger, nor is she just a hookup.

This morning when I was making myself breakfast, there was a moment when I wondered what it would be like to look over and see her sitting at the table in front of the window overlooking my small backyard space.

I wonder what she's doing now? I glance out the top of my living room windows, the part that isn't blocked with the privacy shades that rise from the bottom. It's dark, and across the street on the second floor, a couple walks into their living room with bowls in their hands, before sinking down onto their couch. Blue light from a TV glows in the room, and I wonder what it would be like to grab a bowl of ice cream and settle into watching a show with Morgan.

The way I'm craving her presence, the sound of her voice, and the sight of her here where I've never brought another woman, feels way more intense than the sexual connection I initially thought this was. I don't just crave her physical presence; there's a closeness there that I haven't felt in forever. She's making me want things I've been certain, for the past decade, that I don't want.

Yet somehow, I think maybe I want them with her?

I pick up the remote and pause the video footage of Washington's preseason games that I'm supposed to be watching but have completely zoned out on. Before I can think too much about all the reasons this is a terrible idea, all the things that stand in the way of Morgan and me being together, I pull out my phone.

AIDAN

Hey, what are you doing?

NERDGIRL

Working. You?

AIDAN

Same.

NERDGIRL

Oh yeah? You out on the ice already
warming up for the game two days
from now?

AIDAN

No, smartass. I'm watching some footage of
Washington's last few games.

NERDGIRL

Smart.

AIDAN

How would you feel about working over
here? I've gotten used to having you around.

NERDGIRL

And the solution to that problem is to have
me around more?

AIDAN

Maybe I don't see it as a "problem."

NERDGIRL

Maybe you should. It feels like you're
breaking a lot of your own rules here.

AIDAN

How so?

NERDGIRL

Having me around all the time sounds a lot
like monogamy.

AIDAN

Would you rather I call someone else to
come over?

I regret that text the minute I send it, but she starts to respond before I can unsend it, so I know she's seen it.

I don't want someone else. I only want her. But we're supposed to be keeping this casual. It's how we ensure neither of us gets hurt. It would be wrong for me to switch things up, especially because we can't be together in the long term, and the last thing I want to do is hurt her.

NERDGIRL

That choice is really up to you, isn't it?

I can hear the snark in her tone even through text, so I hit the button to start a video call instead. It rings enough times that I'm initially afraid she isn't going to answer, but she eventually accepts the call.

"Yes?" Her tone is dismissive, which is probably what I deserve after that message.

"I'm sorry." I sigh as I sink back into my couch cushions.

"For what?" She pulls her hair back, winding it into a bun that she secures on top of her head. She's in a tank top, and I think her laptop must be open on her thighs with her phone propped up on it.

"For making you feel like you were replaceable. That isn't what I meant. I . . ." I don't even know what I want to say next.

"You . . . ?"

I run my hand through my hair and sigh. "I don't know what we're doing here."

"Yeah. Me either."

"I just wanted to see you."

She gives me a shrug and a sarcastic smile. "Well, here I am."

"I'd like it a whole lot better if you were *here*."

"If you're so desperate to have me around, maybe you should come over here?"

I sigh again, feeling like I'm fucking everything up. "I can't. McCabe is picking me up early and I'm riding to the airport with him and AJ."

"I didn't hear myself asking you to spend the night."

I huff a laugh. "We both know what will happen if I come over."

"Well, you'd best stay there then. I have so much work to do and now I have to pack, since apparently I'm going to Washington tomorrow." She doesn't sound happy about that, so I try not to let her see how excited this news makes me. The chance for more time with her is always a good thing in my book.

"Any word on whether Natalie's going to come back? Or are they going to replace her so you don't have to be at every game?" I see how overworked she is. Even last weekend in Ember Cove she was working while I went on my run, and then we had to head back to Boston that night so she could help fix the crisis Natalie created. It makes me wonder when she ever has time to rest.

"I'm not sure, but I can't keep doing this. I was at Lauren and Jameson's all morning with the twins because I'd promised to babysit so they could go to brunch with Jameson's college roommate and his wife who were in town for the weekend. And then what was supposed to be a quick phone call with AJ this afternoon somehow turned into me flying to Washington with you guys tomorrow."

She sighs wearily, and her eyes close as she leans her head back against the top of the couch cushions. I wish there was something I could do to help lighten her load, but I also wonder why she offers or agrees to do things for other people when she already has so much on her plate.

"Is there anything I can do to help?"

She opens her eyes and looks back at the screen. "Yeah. Don't do anything stupid that would require me to travel with the team beyond the game against Washington."

"*I* didn't do anything—"

"This time," she interrupts.

"I told you I'd be a very good boy if you reward me," I say with a wink.

She rolls her eyes, but her face lights up with the smile she's failed to hold back. "I think you're confusing yourself with a dog."

"I think you'll find that with the right kind of rewards, I'm *very* trainable."

This time she doesn't hold back her laugh, and I love the way her cheeks push up and her eyes crinkle. "You're exhausting, you know that?"

"Maybe you ought to come over and tire me out then?"

"I can't, Aidan," she says, with a sigh. "I have to finish my work and get some sleep. Tomorrow's going to be a long day. You should get some sleep too. It's going to be a long road trip."

"It's only five days," I say. That's actually on the shorter side. The thought of her not staying with the team beyond the first game, and me not seeing her at all during that time is . . . not preferable.

I'm starting to see what Drew meant when he told Hartmann that it was going to be hard to be away from his wife once the season started up. Not that *this* is that serious, but given how much I already know I'll miss seeing Morgan, I can only imagine how the guys with families feel. Ironically, after over a decade of playing professional hockey, it's the first time I've ever felt like I "get it."

"Even so, rest is recovery. Go get some sleep," she says. "Good night."

Before I can respond, she's already disconnected the call. I sit for a minute trying to figure out what that dismissal means.

The fact that she's not prioritizing spending time with me, given everything else she has going on, should be a *good* sign. It means she understands how this whole casual thing works.

I'm no longer sure I want to be the one she practices being casual with. Maybe I never really did. I suggested the friends with benefits situation to spend more time with her, not because what I felt toward her was simply friendship mixed with sexual attraction.

Being with her has filled cracks in my life I didn't even realize were still there—loneliness, grief, abandonment—and I worry that once this is over, those cracks will open right back up, leaving painful wounds in their wake.

Even as hard as I've tried not to, I'm getting emotionally invested. And the way she's pulling back right now makes me remember the concern I had back in Bermuda: *I'm more worried about you breaking me.*

———

"All right, boys," Wilcott says as he claps his hand against his clipboard. "One more period to go, and you all know what I'm going to say."

"Do. Your. Job." Our shouts fill the locker room.

Apparently this is what Coach said to the team at the beginning of Game 7. Since we went out there and *didn't* do what was needed to bring home the Cup, we've adopted it as our rallying cry this season—a reminder that should probably feel ominous, but somehow feels empowering instead. The one thing we can control on the ice is ourselves: how much energy we bring to the game, the precision with which we perform, and how we react when things don't go our way.

I always thought my reactiveness on the ice was what fueled me. But it became clear during the preseason that controlling my reactions on the ice actually makes me feel more powerful, instead of letting my emotions get the better of me, which only resulted in too many power plays for our opponents. I think *that* might be the lesson AJ wanted me to learn, and the reason she gave me the alternate captain position.

We line up to take the ice, and behind me, Colt and Hartmann are talking about the goalie hug they have planned after we win.

I look over my shoulder, saying, "Let's not start the celebration too early. We still have an entire period to play."

"Dude," Colt says, "winning is the only option we picture."

Hartmann claps his hand on my shoulder. "Just imagine it. It's the last minute of the game. We're up by one. Washington's on fire, taking shot after shot, but Colt blocks or saves every single shot. You've got to *picture* it to believe that's what's going to happen."

Goalies are always a little out of their mind—you'd have to be, if you're willing to stand between the pipes while people shoot ninety-mile-per-hour pucks at you. Still, visualizing the win is something I've done for as long as I can remember. I just never pictured it so specifically.

"Maybe we should do a better job of keeping the puck down near Washington's net, instead," I say.

"Sure, *you* visualize that," Colt says, then coughs a laugh. "Meanwhile, I'll be picturing myself saving your ass when that doesn't happen."

I swallow as a lump suddenly appears in my throat at the familiarity of it all—the ribbing and shit-talking and camaraderie amongst my teammates.

This. This right here is what I missed more than anything last year. Not the ice time, I got plenty of that once my hand healed. Not the travel, because it was actually kind of nice not being in a new city every couple days. It was the sense of belonging, of being around *my people*. And instead of showing up, being there to support them last year like a teammate should, I succumbed to bitterness and licked my wounds in private. Alone, as always.

I see now why so many hockey players get married young, like Hartmann did. The travel and the unpredictability of the sport is so much easier when you have a family support system. It's something I didn't even realize was lacking until I got injured, and for the first time ever, I'm not just wondering, but seriously considering, if that's something I'd want. Someone to come home to, a relationship built on mutual respect rather than the random hookups I had before Morgan was in my life.

"It's good to be back," I say.

"It's good to *have* you back," Colt tells me. "Really."

With that, we follow our teammates into the hallway. At home, we walk down the hallway to the rink solemnly, each of us running a hand across the Rebels logo painted on the tunnel wall as we approach the bench. On the road, we're rowdy, banging the butts of our sticks on the ground with each step as we yell out the Rebels chant.

Morgan's pressed herself against the wall near the opening to the rink so she can get video of us coming back to close out this game. Just like at our home opener a few days ago, seeing her there before third period gives me the boost I need not only to get through the next twenty minutes, but to play harder than I'm normally able.

And that goal, the one I visualized on our walk back to the ice, feels even sweeter because it plays out in real time almost exactly the way I pictured it. The way my line volleys the puck back and forth as we move toward Washington's net, the way my shot sends the puck sailing past their goalie's glove and into the back of the net. It's all exactly as I pictured it, especially when I glance up at the media booth and find Morgan at the glass looking pleased.

Chapter Thirty-Seven

MORGAN

"It's kind of funny how you keep insisting you can't travel with the team, yet you keep showing up," AJ says with a small smile.

I set my glass on the bar top on the Club Level in the Dallas arena, and level her with a look. "Because *you* keep asking me to."

"Morgan." Her tone is the kind you use when admonishing a child. "Is that really what you're going with?"

I'm not sure how to respond to that, so I just lift an eyebrow.

"I've watched you handle PR nightmares with poise and talk hockey players down mid-fight. You are *not* a person who does things she doesn't want to do."

My laugh is sharp, and my shoulders shake visibly, even through the Rebels quarter-zip sweater I'm wearing, drawing the attention of a guy sitting on the barstool just beyond AJ. He gives me a nod, which I politely return, and refocus my attention on AJ. But not before she notices and turns to see who I'm nodding at. Then she turns back and mouthes, "He's cute."

"The problem is . . ." I drop my voice so no one hears me —not that it should matter. We're in Dallas having a quick pregame chat, so it's not like I know anyone here. ". . . when people need me, I'm not so good at saying no."

It's why I watched Lauren's twins so often when we first moved back to Boston, why I took over the social media accounts for Jules and Audrey's business and helped them get their nonprofit started, why I worked with AJ and McCabe as they navigated the PR nightmare they found themselves in when their relationship was exposed. And why I flew out to LA to help Luke and Eva concoct a believable story about their sudden marriage, and then helped Luke create the nursery of his wife's dreams when Eva was hospitalized.

Sometimes, I get tired just thinking about all the ways I overcommit myself. It's not that I've minded doing *any* of these things. It's that I generally say yes because I have this perpetual need to make sure everyone around me is happy and cared for. Recognizing that this sometimes comes at the expense of my own time or well-being often comes after the fact, but I really am trying to be more mindful of it.

"And you're *sure* it's not because you like the job? Like, you wouldn't be interested in doing this full time?"

I've always known Tatum was coming back after her surgery, so the thought of this turning into something permanent hadn't occurred to me before. "What about Tatum?"

"What about her?"

"Are you offering me her job?"

AJ's rumble of laughter is deep. "I think her job is a bit beneath your skillset, Morgan."

"Ironic, since I'm doing her job right now. So, what are you suggesting?"

"Nothing immediately. But our Director of Public Relations is going to be moving to San Francisco. His wife just finished her residency at Children's Hospital in Boston and was recently offered a position out in California, starting in December. I'm just putting the idea out there, letting you know that the position will be opening up, and I'm always looking for motivated and competent people to join our team."

I wonder if she'd be interested in hiring me full-time if she knew about my relationship with Aidan? I'm tempted to ask her advice here, but before I can give the idea serious thought, the guy on the other side of her stands and pushes his barstool in. The scrape of the legs against the floor distracts me as he steps up next to AJ.

"Forgive me for interrupting," he says, speaking directly to me. His light hair is thick and his brown eyes are deep pools of chocolate. "And for being so bold. But, I'm just wondering if you'd be interested in grabbing a drink sometime?"

I'm so stunned he's asking, that my lips part but no sound comes out. Then AJ laughs and says, "We're actually from Boston."

"Me too. I'm a Rebels season ticket holder, so . . . I know who you are," he says directly to AJ. Then he turns toward me. "I'm actually here for the bachelor party of a friend from grad school. We're going out after the game . . ."

"We'll be at The Lamppost," AJ says, "hopefully celebrating a win. You should stop by."

He lets out a short laugh. "I'm pretty sure my friends will be wasted by the end of the game, so I'm not sure I'd want to subject you ladies to them." He refocuses his gaze on me. "But, maybe after the next home game instead?"

I nod because I'm so conflicted I can't seem to speak. Aidan told me I should be open to seeing other people, and here's a cute guy asking me out. He seems polite and respectful. I'd be a fool to say no, wouldn't I?

"Yeah, that sounds good," I say, wondering why this all feels so wrong, why I only want Aidan. *You want him because you know you can't have him,* I tell myself. Going after the guy who wants *me* but doesn't want a *commitment* seems to be my MO, after all. This could be a chance to break that pattern.

He smiles, and his confidence shines through. "Great. I'm Sean, by the way. You want to text me so I have your number?"

"I'm Morgan. And sure," I say, picking up my phone and typing in the number he gives me. I shoot him a text with my name, and his phone buzzes in his pocket.

"Perfect. I'll be in touch, Morgan. Maybe I'll even see you at The Lamppost tonight if my friends can behave themselves long enough to stop by and say hello."

Holy shit. Him showing up at the bar tonight while Aidan is there is a recipe for disaster. I think I may be sick. In fact, I just might make myself sick so I don't find myself at the bar with both of them.

I gulp, and say, "Sounds good, talk to you soon."

When he leaves, AJ just lifts her eyebrow and waits for me to say something.

"What?"

"Why did I just get the distinct impression that you were looking for a way out of saying yes to a date with a cute, available guy? Are you . . . seeing someone?"

"No," I say, and try to let out a light laugh like the idea is ridiculous, but it comes out sounding strangled.

AJ lifts one of her dark brows, no doubt scrutinizing my sincerity. "You sure?"

"Positive," I say, but she looks suspicious as hell. Time to change the subject. "By the way, have you made a decision yet about Natalie?"

AJ sighs, her shoulders sinking as she does. "I'd really like to give her another chance, but ultimately it's not up to me. She reports to Patrick. I'm only involved because a player was part of that situation."

"I say this as a friend, not as someone who works for you. But that's bullshit, and you know it. There's no part of the Rebels organization that you're not involved in. You hired Lauren and were instrumental in promoting her, even though she reports to Patrick. You're the one who suggested bringing me on as well. Why is this different?"

AJ sweeps her long, dark hair over her shoulder. "It will be viewed as me giving her a second chance because she's a woman."

"Why can't it be viewed as giving someone who's young but extremely good at her job a second chance after making an immature mistake?"

"It *should* be viewed that way, but given my vocal enthusiasm for hiring more women in professional sports, it won't be. It'll be seen through the gender lens."

"What if I talked to Patrick about it?" I ask. "I know you

guys said I should stay out of it, but I'm the one who worked directly with her and can therefore best judge her potential."

"I wouldn't be opposed to you approaching him about this, as long as Sarah from HR is part of the conversation. But you need to know, going into this, that Patrick is a huge stickler for the rules."

"Great. I'll ask them to show me where in her contract there's specific mention of her not having a relationship with one of the players."

AJ huffs out a laugh. We both know, from her own relationship with McCabe, that this language is not standard—though who knows, maybe it's been added for new employees? "People have been fired for far less."

"People are generally fired for not being good at their jobs. If that's the case, get rid of Tatum instead."

"Is she really that bad?" AJ asks.

"She just doesn't have the mindset for social media. Like, she has no sense of what will hit with our audience, doesn't follow any of the trends, and hasn't developed the right tone in her replies to comments. She just . . . she'd probably be better suited for some other position in communications."

AJ nods, and I know what she's thinking but isn't allowed to say: the Rebels can't fire Tatum because she just took a medical leave and that would open them up to a discrimination lawsuit.

"All right," AJ says after glancing at her phone. "Charlie just texted me to come down to the locker room. You coming down to get some video before they take the ice for warm ups?"

"Sure, let's go."

The Lamppost is crowded and noisy, and the only thing that seems to distinguish it from any other upscale bar in Dallas is that the owner is apparently a huge Boston sports fan. The walls are littered not only with Rebels memorabilia, but also with souvenirs celebrating Boston's baseball, football, and basketball teams too.

I chuckle when Aidan stops on the stairs to the cordoned-off VIP section that's been set aside for our team to take a picture of the huge framed poster of our esteemed quarterback, Liam Walker. I can already envision the trash-talk in the text message he's typing out as he steps onto the landing of the second floor.

"First round's on me!" Luke hollers as he hands a credit card over to the bartender.

Cheers go up around the room, drawing the attention of the crowd below—something that probably only AJ and I notice, since we're bringing up the rear. "Pretty sure everyone else should be buying him drinks after that shutout tonight," she says with a laugh.

"He can afford it," I say with a chuckle, because with his billionaire trust fund *and* his hockey contract, he's never going to hurt for money. "Man, he's been on fire this season. It's so good to see."

"It sure is," she says, sounding relieved but not surprised.

"Is it still weird for you, coming out with the team like this?" I ask. During the playoffs last season, I met her at The Neon Cactus when the team had specifically invited her out to celebrate her nomination for the General Manager of the Year award. She'd mentioned then that she never goes out with the team, but this season, now that she and McCabe are together, it seems to be happening more.

"It's getting . . . less weird," she says, right as McCabe and Colt approach. McCabe's got a cocktail in his hand for her, and a beer for himself. The way he comfortably wraps his arm around her lower back after handing her the drink, so at ease showing his affection for her in public, has a jolt of jealousy shooting up my spine. My eyes meet Aidan's gaze across the room, wishing he could be pulling me in close like that. But not only is our relationship *not* like that, it also needs to remain private.

Colt turns, his head following my gaze. Before he can glance back at me, I say, too loudly, "Oh, it looks like space opened up at the bar. I'm going to head over and get a drink." And then I hightail it out of there, hoping that Colt didn't actually notice the way I was looking at Aidan, and praying that if he did, he doesn't say anything to AJ and McCabe.

I head to the bar, and when my phone buzzes, I'm expecting it to be a text from Aidan. Instead, there's a new text from Sean, below the messages we exchanged an hour ago when I was busy finalizing the postgame content for social media.

SEAN

My friends are too drunk for a place like The Lamppost, so we're going somewhere more appropriate. 😊 I'll be in touch once I'm back in Boston.

MORGAN

No worries. We can connect then.

The eye roll emoji in that text made me think they're headed to a strip club and he wasn't thrilled with the choice.

But then there's another text, sent just now.

SEAN

Actually, I just realized we're only a block away from The Lamppost. I'm going to sneak out and come have a drink with you. Hope that's okay . . .

Shit, no, this is not good. Going on a date with someone else is one thing, but doing it right under Aidan's nose is just plain rude. If I'd thought Sean might show up here, I wouldn't have come.

I turn, leaving the bar behind to head back toward AJ. "Hey, I'm not feeling awesome so I'm going to head back to the hotel."

"You okay?" she asks, while McCabe and Colt look on with concern.

"Yeah, I just have a headache. It's probably best if I head back and go to sleep."

"Do you want someone to make sure you get back okay? I can go with you if you want," she says.

"No," I tell her, my skin itching with anxiety. I need to get out of here. "I'm fine. You guys stay and enjoy celebrating another great win. Bye."

I turn to leave, and I'm about three-quarters of the way down the stairs when I glance at the front door in time to see Sean walking in. I freeze, hoping that if I don't move, he won't see me and I can slip out. It's just my luck that his gaze lifts and our eyes lock. *Shit.*

His face splits into a huge grin and he heads straight

toward me. I feel terrible that I was trying to sneak out without him seeing me, when he's so obviously happy to have found me.

"You came to meet me at the door? That's sweet. Let me buy you a drink before I have to run back and babysit those drunk idiots I'm with," he says, placing his hand on my lower back and guiding me over toward the bar.

Shockingly there are two seats available. As we order, an odd sensation rolls up the back of my neck. I feel like I'm being watched and sure enough, when my eyes flick up to the VIP section, Aidan stands at the metal railing, his head turned away from McCabe as he watches me.

Chapter Thirty-Eight

AIDAN

Morgan's gaze lifts to meet mine, then shifts back toward the guy she's talking to. In his collared shirt and khakis, he looks like he walked out of the yacht club to come here. When she tucks her head in toward his, it takes everything in my power not to react. I can tell she's just trying to hear what he's saying, because they're sitting right by the live band that's playing tonight. But her close proximity to another guy, no matter who he is, has me feeling downright murderous.

"Nothing going on there, huh?" McCabe asks, the laughter in his low voice unmistakable.

Fuck. I forgot he was even here, much less that we were mid-conversation before I caught sight of Morgan at the bar. Morgan, who just told everyone she didn't feel well and was going back to the hotel, but is now sitting at the bar with another guy.

"Nope," I say, but with my jaw clenched as I say it, the *P* is a sharp sound that vibrates against my lips. I'm so damn annoyed that he's noticed the jealousy that's radiating off me, but at this point, who wouldn't?

"You sure? Because you look jealous as hell."

"It's not jealousy. I just don't like the look of that guy."

McCabe glances over again. "He looks perfectly harmless. Like the kind of guy who'd bump into you accidentally and then buy you a beer to apologize."

"Those are always the guys you have to worry about." What I really mean is he's the kind of guy *I* have to worry about, because he's the kind of guy Morgan *should* be looking for.

"Why's that?"

"People who seem squeaky clean like that are usually the ones hiding skeletons in their closets."

Morgan takes another sip of her drink. It almost seems like she's in a hurry to finish it. Hopefully that's because she's in a hurry to get away from this guy, but when she looks over at him and her smile turns into a laugh, I'm left wondering if she's in a hurry to leave *with* him.

"So is this why you're less of an asshole this season? Are you . . . *happy?*" McCabe spits the word out like he never thought he'd use it in reference to me.

"Am I really that big of a dick normally?"

"Yes. This season, less so. I've been trying to figure out what's different, and I finally see it. Love changes you in funny ways."

"I'm not in love," I say quickly, almost on autopilot.

"Sure you're not."

His words are followed by a low rumble of laughter that attracts AJ's attention, and she turns back to us from a conversation she was having with Colt and MacIntyre. The rookie went down to the bar, picked up six girls, and brought them back to the VIP section. AJ and Colt decided to talk to him about etiquette, but I'm not sure the kid is willing to learn.

"Morgan's still here? Ohhhh . . ." She drags out the word like she's sharing a juicy piece of gossip.

"What the heck?" McCabe asks with a chuckle.

"Oh, just . . . that's the guy who was hitting on Morgan back at the arena. I told him we'd be here tonight, but . . . I thought he told her he couldn't stop by and would see her in Boston instead."

She's made plans to see him back in Boston? I focus on taking a slow, deep breath as the edges of my vision cloud. *Breathe.*

I tell my friends I'm going to head to the bathroom, and then I bypass the bar on my way to the back hallway with the Restrooms sign hanging above it.

AIDAN

Lose that guy, and meet me in my hotel room.

Now that I'm away from the balcony, there's no way to know if she's read the message or not. But she doesn't respond, which ratchets up my anxiety. *This is why you don't do relationships*, I remind myself. *No one can leave you if you don't let them get close in the first place.*

When I make it back to the balcony, Morgan is no longer at the bar. Then again, neither is the guy she was sitting next to. There's no way I can ask AJ or McCabe if she left with that guy without completely blowing our cover, so instead I tell them I'm beat, and I'm going to go back to my room to catch some sleep before our flight tomorrow morning. AJ seems pleased with my choice, because two seasons ago, I would have been closing down this bar. McCabe, though, can barely contain his smirk.

When I exit the bar, Morgan is alone at the end of the block trying to hail a cab. Instead, I flag one down about ten yards before it gets to her, and when she turns to give me a nasty look for stealing her cab, I tell her to get in.

She bites the corner of her lip, looking like she wants to decline, but the chilly late October breeze whips down the street, blowing her hair around her face as she shivers.

"Get in the taxi, Morgan." My words are practically a growl, and I don't like that I sound as angry as I feel right now.

Her sigh is deep as she takes the last few steps toward me. I don't know why *she* seems mad at me, but I've got a few minutes alone with her in the back of this car to find out.

"What's going on?" I ask her once we're settled in the back seat.

With her eyes closed, she rests her head against the seat. It's close to midnight and I'm sure she must be tired. Unlike me, she probably didn't get to take a two-hour nap before the game.

"What do you mean?"

"You didn't respond to my text."

With the passing streetlights and headlights of oncoming cars illuminating the interior of the cab, I don't miss the way her eyelids press together tightly. "What text?"

"You really think I believe you didn't read it? That you just happened to get rid of that guy when I sent it?" I have no idea if she "got rid of that guy" or if he left on his own. But I'm determined to find out.

She's silent for nearly a full minute, long enough that we're already turning onto the street where our hotel is, when she finally says, "I—I don't know what you're talking about."

If she hadn't faltered, I might have believed her. Instead, I reach over, cupping the far side of her face in my hand and turning her head so she'll look at me. "What's really going on, Morgan?"

"All right, you two," the cab driver says as he pulls into the hotel's drop-off area, only a few blocks from the bar. "Here you are."

"Thanks," Morgan says, reaching for the door handle as I tap the card reader to pay for the ride. She hustles out of the car and walks into the hotel like she's trying to escape having this conversation. When I get to the bank of elevators, she's not there, but the doors are just starting to close on the one in the middle. Hoping it's her, I reach out and wave my arm between the doors. I don't miss the way she sighs and crosses her arms across her abdomen as I stride in.

I decide to ask the question I've been wondering about. "Are you trying to make me jealous?"

"Why would I be trying to make you jealous?" Her tone is defensive. Not like I've hit too close to the truth, more like she's offended I'd make the suggestion in the first place.

"I don't know, Morgan. For the same reason you wore McCabe's jersey a couple weeks ago?"

"That was not about you. And neither was this."

"By *this* you mean having a drink with another guy right

in front of me? You sure? Because it certainly seems like you're trying to keep my attention."

"I don't play games, Aidan, and I'd appreciate it if you didn't either."

"What's that supposed to mean?" I'm not sure what games she thinks I'm playing here.

"It means I don't want these ups and downs!" Her voice is a lot less calm than before. "That guy introduced himself before the game, and AJ mentioned where we'd be afterward. He said he couldn't come, and I wasn't expecting to see him there. I wasn't trying to have a drink with another guy right in front of you—"

"Oh, just behind my back?"

"*You* don't get to be jealous about this. You're the one who wants to keep this casual and told me I should feel free to see other guys."

"Does that mean you *don't* want to keep this casual?" I ask, stepping closer as the elevator bell announces our arrival at her floor. I don't know why I'm itching for a fight . . . probably because I just had to watch her at the bar with another guy.

She raises her hand to tuck a piece of hair that's fallen in her face back behind her ear as she sighs. "I *know* what we agreed to, Aidan. I'm not asking for more."

The elevator doors open, and when she steps out, I follow her as she speed walks down the hallway to her room. I reach out and grasp her elbow as she stops in front of her door, and as she turns toward me she stumbles, pressing her hands into my chest as she looks up at me.

"You're not asking for more because that's not what you want? Or because you don't want to break our agreement?

Or something else?" I ask the questions slowly, careful to give her options.

My heart races hopefully, thrilled at the idea that she would want me to stick around, want something *real* with me, even while the logical side of my brain reminds me that it's not possible. I don't want to be a wedge between her and her father, and she deserves someone better than me. Someone who knows what they want and isn't so damn afraid of being hurt.

"Fuck if I know," she says, clearly exasperated. "All I know is that this doesn't feel casual." She turns and taps her key card against the door, and I reach past her to push it open, guiding her into the room with my hand on her lower back.

"Why are you in my room?" she mutters as she taps the button on the wall that turns on the lights hanging on either side of the bed.

"Why wouldn't I be?"

"Because you're confusing the hell out of me," she says, annoyance ringing out. "You don't want to be apart from me, but you also don't want to commit."

"It's not that I don't want to, it's that I *can't*."

"This is all getting really repetitive. Either this isn't serious, or it is. But you can't say one thing and act differently. What the hell is it that *you* want Aidan?"

"I want you—" My words are cut off as we step toward each other, our mouths crashing together. This isn't the gentle kiss of two lovers sneaking away to their hotel room together. It's desperation and passion. Two people who know it can't work out between them, but aren't quite ready to let go.

So don't let go. Thoughts of me and Morgan in an actual

relationship have been plaguing me since we left Ember Cover two weeks ago. I can't stop picturing what we could have if I'd just stop holding back. I also can't stop imagining the devastation I'll feel when she realizes I'm *not* what she wants and leaves me. It's not rational, I know that, but I can't get over the fear of losing her. The only thing I can do is protect myself by not letting this go any further than it has.

"I need you," Morgan mumbles. "*Now.*" The last word is desperate and pleading as her hands slip along my shoulders between my shirt and sports coat, dragging it down my arms until it falls to the ground. Then she pushes up on her toes, her mouth meeting mine again with such ferocity it feels like she's trying to devour me.

Our clothes are shed quickly, littered around the floor as we move toward her bed without breaking apart from each other. Then I turn and sit at the end, pulling her down onto my lap so her knees are spread on either side of me. She slides herself along my hard length, circling her clit against the head of my cock every time she rises up. My hands and mouth are everywhere—her neck, her collarbones, her breasts—as she takes the condom from me and rolls it down my shaft. She moans when I suck her nipple into my mouth, and I move my hands to her hips, my fingers splayed across her ass as I position her right over the top of me. Then I'm the one moaning as she sinks down fast and hard.

She rises and then slides back down on me quickly, taking me deep, over and over, but her eyes never leave mine. Then she wraps one arm around my shoulders, holding our bodies tightly together like she's trying to memorize the way our bodies fit together.

One of her hands slips between us, the backs of her

knuckles pressing into my abdomen as her finger circles her clit. She's chasing her orgasm, and I can tell by the way her lips part, her breathing speeds up, and her eyes become half lidded that she's close.

And then, she whispers, "Yes, oh my god, Aidan, yes," while her inner walls throb against my dick, and she reaches her other hand behind her and toys with my balls.

That's all it takes and I'm seeing stars at the edges of my vision. My fingers curl into the curve of her ass as I hold her hips in place. As her orgasm ripples around me and the sound of her moans fill my head, I come so hard I feel like I might pass out.

My head falls forward, resting against her breastbone, and she wraps her arms around me, resting her chin on my head. We stay there, joined together as we both try to catch our breath, and all I can think is, *It's never like this.*

I clean her up and pull her against me in bed, and I'm pretty sure she's asleep before I've even thrown the covers over us. I lie there, one arm circled around her lower back as she cuddles into me, thinking how perfect she is for me. I only wish I could be perfect for her, too.

Guilt nearly overwhelms me when I remember that when she asked me what I wanted, I said I wanted *her.* The way she fucked me after that felt different than what we've shared before. It felt like she knew there was an enormous *but* coming after that statement.

I want you . . . but *I can't have you.*

And that's when I realize that this whole relationship feels like it's come full circle. It started with sex, and now I worry that it's ending with sex, too.

Chapter Thirty-Nine

MORGAN

"Please tell me that's not airport sushi," AJ says, glancing down at the plastic container I just opened in the seat next to hers on the Rebels' plane.

Even though it's midmorning, I'm still not quite awake. I fell asleep before the plane even took off, which makes sense given that I barely slept at all last night. When I curled into Aidan in bed, closing my eyes and slowing my breathing so he'd think I was asleep, it took everything in me to keep from sobbing. Despite the fact that the sex was amazing, as always, it felt like we were saying goodbye.

How could it not? When I'd asked him what he wanted, he hadn't said anything about our relationship. He'd just said *I want you*, while looking like he was feral for me, and then pulling me to him before we used each other for sex. There were no emotions, no declarations like I'd gotten used to while we were in Ember Cove. Last night, it felt like he was already pulling away.

I don't know what I'd expected. He said he doesn't do relationships. He told me, over and over again, that what we had was not monogamous nor did it imply any long-term commitment. And somehow, just like I always do, I'd convinced myself that he'd eventually admit that there were actual feelings involved, and he'd *choose me*. But he didn't. He chose sex with me, as if that was the same thing.

"It's fine," I tell AJ through a yawn. I'm having a hard time waking up after my much-needed nap, and just want to close my eyes again. Except I'm starving and won't be able to fall back asleep when I'm this hungry. "I get sushi at the airport all the time."

"You have no idea how long that had been sitting there before you bought it," she says, wrinkling her nose. "And now you've had it on the plane for hours, unrefrigerated."

"This plane *is* a refrigerator, which is why we're both bundled up," I say, indicating my zip-up cardigan and AJ's suit jacket. Then I hold the container up to my nose. "This smells perfectly fine."

"I really hope you don't regret that," she says, then goes back to working on her laptop while I eat. I should get some work done, too. I still have hours of client work to finish up by the end of the day, but I'm too tired. So, once I've finished eating, I sit back in the comfy seat, close my eyes, and let the hum of the engine lull me back to sleep.

When the wheels hit the ground about two hours later, I nearly jolt out of my seat. It's not the shock of waking up during landing, it's my roiling stomach and churning intestines. I breathe through my nose as the plane slows, and by the time we make the turn off the runway, taxiing toward the terminal, I know I can't wait to use the bathroom.

I jolt out of my seat, stepping past AJ, who looks up at me in surprise, as I make my way forward to the bathroom.

"Ma'am," the flight attendant says as I approach, "the seat-belt sign is on. I need you to return to your seat."

"I'm going to be sick," I say, throwing open the bathroom door and barely getting it closed and locked behind me before I'm on my knees, emptying the contents of my stomach into the small toilet.

I've always hated being sick, but being sick in an airplane bathroom, within earshot of my colleagues chatting right on the other side of the bathroom door as they wait to get off the plane, is a special kind of torture. I lose track of how many times I flush the toilet, because there doesn't seem to be any end to how much partially digested food wants to leave my body.

By the time I finally stop vomiting, it's quiet enough that I worry everyone may have forgotten I was in here. Am I going to find myself locked inside this plane? And if so, who the hell do I call to get me out?

I wash and dry my hands, then use the wet paper towel to wipe the dried streaks of tears off my face. I think vomiting has overheated me, because my whole body feels clammy from the thin coat of sweat covering my skin. I need to get the hell out of here and get home before I get sick again. I can tell by the gurgling in my stomach that it's only a matter of time.

When I push open the door, the plane is quiet. But when I turn to head back to my seat, I notice the door is still open, and the stairs are still pushed up against the plane, so at least

I'm not locked in. And, right ahead of me, sitting in the aisle seats in the first row, are the flight attendant, and Aidan Renaud.

Fuck my life.

He lifts an eyebrow as he says, "You survived?"

"Barely." I turn toward the flight attendant. "I think you may need a hazmat team to clean that bathroom."

She gives me a sympathetic smile. "That is the protocol in this situation."

"AJ said you ate bad sushi?" Aidan says.

"In my defense, I didn't think it was bad when I ate it."

"Let's get you home," he says. It's then that I notice my carry-on suitcase in the aisle, with my bag on top of it.

"What about my phone, and—"

"I got everything from your seat. C'mon, before you get sick again." He sounds . . . concerned? The flight attendant hands him a couple of the barf bags you normally find in the seat back pocket. "Thanks, Brenda. Hope the birthday party goes well this week."

At first I'm surprised by how familiar he is with her. Sometimes I forget that it's the same flight crew on all the teams' flights. Of course he knows her. And he just sat here for god knows how long waiting for me to finish puking my brains out.

"Thank you both," I say as I reach for the handle of my suitcase.

"I've got it," Aidan says, standing and blocking me from taking it. "You just get yourself safely down those steps. Or do you need me to carry you?"

"No," I say, suddenly realizing how weak I am. "I can do it." I turn toward the door of the aircraft, but I'm hit by a sudden dizzy spell and grab the wall of the galley to hold myself up.

"Like hell you can," Aidan says from behind me. And then he's scooping me into his arms.

"Hey, I'm sick but I can take care of myself."

"I'm sure you can," he says, walking to the plane's exit, "but I'm going to take care of you anyway. Hold onto me."

I wrap my arms around him, resting my head on his chest as he carefully descends the stairs. He walks over to his car, which for some reason is right on the tarmac of the private airport. As if he knows I'm about to ask him, he says, "McCabe brought it over. No one believed you'd be able to walk to the parking lot after . . . that."

"Could everyone hear me throwing up?" I groan.

"Pretty much. Don't worry, everyone felt bad for you. I don't think AJ told anyone but me that this was self-inflicted."

"It wasn't self-inflicted," I mutter.

"Mm-hmm." He opens the door, then sets me in the passenger seat. "I'm going to go get your bags. If you need to throw up again, try to do it outside the car, okay?"

"I'll be fine," I say, but my stomach calls me out on the lie by loudly rumbling. *I hate everything about this situation.*

He turns and bounds up the steps to the plane, leaving me to consider that this was probably how my mom was feeling the day after her wedding. Maybe I was too judgmental about her forgetting my birthday, given that I barely know my own name right now.

Aidan comes back with my suitcase in one hand and my over-the-shoulder bag in the other. After setting them both in the trunk, he comes around and hands me the barf bags

Brenda had given him, shuts my door, and then climbs in behind the wheel.

"Where's your stuff?" I ask him as I pry open one of the plastic-coated bags. Hopefully I won't need it, but better to have it ready just in case.

"McCabe put it in my car when he brought it around."

I buckle my seat belt and rest my head against the head-rest as I crack the window to get some fresh air. "Did this make him and AJ suspicious?"

"No more than they already were, I suspect."

"They already think something's going on between us?"

"McCabe does, for sure. Not sure about AJ."

I wonder again what AJ's feelings on the matter would be? On the one hand, if anyone would understand dating a player you work with, it would be her. Plus, the Rebels are a *client* of mine, I'm not even technically an employee. On the other hand, would she be mad that I hadn't told her outright?

In the end, it probably doesn't matter. This is never going to be an actual relationship, so there's nothing to share. Plus, since AJ already knows how I stupidly let Carter back into my life at the end of the summer, she doesn't need to know how I've essentially set myself up for the same sort of heartbreak with Aidan.

We drive out of the airport in silence, and before we even reach the main road that will take us back into Boston, I'm resting my head against the window with my eyes closed. The breeze on my face makes me feel less nauseous than before. I don't wake up until the car door opens and Aidan leans in, unbuckling me and picking me up like I weigh nothing.

"Where are we?" I ask, confused by the dim, unfamiliar space. I think it's a small garage?

"My place."

There are so many questions whirling through my head, but I'm mostly focused on how he can possibly have a private garage in the city, and why we are here. But I'm too tired to ask, so I just give him a nod and close my eyes, while I enjoy how comfortable I am with my head resting against his chest.

When I wake up again, the room is dim. The shades are open, but it's dark and stormy outside. It's the kind of late fall afternoon perfect for cozying up and watching a movie with a fire burning in the fireplace. Unfortunately for me, though, my stomach is once again roiling, and I rush into the attached bathroom before heaving up the contents of my digestive system until I'm so exhausted, I can't even get up.

There's a knock on the door after I flush the toilet, and I groan. "Go away."

"I'm coming in," Aidan says, and I whimper because I can't muster the energy for any more words. I hear the water running at the sink, but I can't even open my eyes from where my head rests on my arms, folded along the toilet seat. Then he squats down behind me, pulling me back against his chest and holding me in place with his knees as he gently wipes my face off with a warm washcloth. "I hate seeing you so sick like this. I wish I could make it better."

I hate him seeing me sick like this, too. I want to be the sexy, strong woman I usually feel like when I'm with him, not the wretched hag I feel like right now. But he doesn't seem to mind that the bathroom smells like a sewer and I'm sweaty and disgusting after what my body just went through, again. He just carries me to bed, pulling the covers over me again.

"I'm going to leave the bathroom light on and crack the door open in case it's dark next time you wake up," he tells me as he stands. I succumb to sleep before he's left the room.

———

"After all of that, I probably need to send him some sort of a thank you gift," I say with an embarrassed chuckle, two nights later while I'm out to dinner with Eva, Lauren, and Paige.

I spent nearly 48 hours in some sort of hallucinogenic nightmare of sickness, where I'm pretty sure Aidan not only saw me throw up multiple times, but may have seen much worse. I don't quite remember the details—my memories are fragments.

I'm finally feeling better, so when Eva asked if I felt like grabbing dinner, I jumped at the chance because two days of not eating has left me weak and ravenous.

"But," I continue, "what do you get the person who's now seen you create a biohazard on an airplane and in his home?"

"A house cleaner?" Eva suggests.

"Or a lifetime supply of air freshener," Paige says with a laugh. I haven't seen my cousin in over two months because she's a business consultant who works extremely long hours and is always traveling for work. So when Lauren said Paige was back in Boston for the weekend and invited me out, I combined dinner plans with them and Eva.

Lauren's bright blue eyes are practically twinkling with amusement when she says, "Can we just rewind time for a sec and go back to the part of the story you *didn't* tell us? Like, the part about why, exactly, Aidan Renaud waited for you on that plane, and why he brought you to his house instead of your own?"

I knew when I started this story that I'd end up divulging the whole truth, but the flush of embarrassment still creeps up my neck and across my cheeks. No one understands that reaction better than Lauren and Paige, because our shared genetics gave them the same redheaded, fair skin that I have.

"Yeah, so . . . remember when I told you about Bermuda?"

All three of them gasp so loud that other diners turn to see what's going on at our table.

"Wait a sec," I say, dropping my voice even lower. "How do *you* know about Bermuda, Paige?"

She grimaces as she glances over at Lauren with a guilty look.

"You said we couldn't tell our husbands," Lauren says, "you didn't say I couldn't tell my sister. And I only told her because I knew you'd have shared the story with her yourself, if she was ever around."

She gives Paige a pointed look, and Paige just rolls her eyes saying, "Sorry I have a demanding job."

"So, this means that Aidan is . . .?" Eva asks, eyebrows arching high as she waits for me to finish that sentence.

"My stepbrother? Yeah, sort of."

"How can he 'sort of' be your stepbrother?" Lauren asks.

"Max, my mom's newest husband, who actually is a surprisingly great guy, is Aidan's stepdad. Max married his mom when he was younger, but they're not biologically related."

Paige chews her lower lip before she says, "That's not so bad, then."

"Yeah, except he's also on the team I now work for, plus my dad is his agent and basically told him to stay away from me. And it's a contract year for him, so he *really* can't afford to piss off my dad."

Lauren gives me a sympathetic nod. In addition to him being her uncle, she's worked for Carson Kaplan, so she truly knows how he can be.

"Shit," Eva hisses out the word slowly. "That's a lot stacked against a relationship."

"No," I say with a shrug. "It's not a relationship."

"If cleaning puke off someone, and possibly seeing much worse," Paige says, "isn't a relationship, then what is it?"

"We have . . . an agreement."

Lauren winds some pasta around her fork as she asks, "What type of an agreement?"

I explain how we got into this situation in the first place, and how, of course, I still started having feelings I shouldn't have let myself develop.

"Nothing about what you've described sounds like it's not an actual, serious relationship," Eva says. "Are you sure you're not just lying to yourself to protect your heart . . . kind of like I was doing with Luke?"

"Right, but everyone knew Luke was madly in love with you," I say, shaking my head at her. "It was the most obvious thing in the world."

"And everything *you've* described," Lauren says, "sounds like Aidan's in love with you."

I bark out a laugh. "Right, except for the part where he's told me over and over that he doesn't want a relationship."

"Be that as it may," Paige says, "it *does* sound like he has actual feelings."

My stupid, hopeful heart feels like it flips over in my chest. And then I realize that of course it sounds that way, because I've told them how he makes *me* feel. The conclusion they easily jump to is the same one I drew: that he must have real feelings, or he wouldn't be doing half the things he's done. But that doesn't mean it's actually the case.

"I think the worst thing is, part of our whole arrangement was so that I could practice keeping things casual. But all this situation has made me realize is that a casual relationship isn't what I want—especially not with him."

"Sounds like you two need to have an honest conversation," Eva says.

"My how the tables have turned," I say with a laugh, thinking about how I said the exact same thing to her at the beginning of the summer.

"You were right *then*, and I'm right *now*. You have to tell him how you feel, Morgan."

"You can't keep pretending like you're okay with keeping things the way they are if you actually want more," Lauren says. "That's a recipe for getting hurt."

"It's going to hurt either way," I say, pushing the last pieces of my dinner around with my fork. I hate the lose-lose situation I'm in. I'm pretty sure I've seen a side of Aidan Renaud that no one else has ever seen. And instead of getting to nurture that part of our relationship, I have to say goodbye to the best guy I've ever had in my life.

"Better to rip the Band-Aid off then, no?" Paige asks.

I let out a defeated sigh. "Yeah, probably."

Chapter Forty

AIDAN

"No fucking way," Colt says with a laugh when Walsh tells us that his wife, Marissa, is pregnant again. "I bet it's a girl. God, Walshy, you dealing with four girls under six would be the best thing I've ever seen."

"It *is* another girl. But, there's more," Walsh says, his voice grim. McCabe, Colt, and I look at him, all traces of laughter gone. Around us, The Neon Cactus is hopping, but the mood at our table is suddenly somber. "She's almost five months along, but we didn't know she was pregnant until a few weeks ago because she has an IUD and not having a period is a fairly typical response."

"So . . . how'd she get pregnant, then?" McCabe asks.

"That's the thing. Somehow, the IUD perforated her uterine wall."

"That doesn't sound good," I say. "So . . . where is it?"

"Right now it's just kind of hanging out outside her

uterus, but there are so many possible complications." Walsh swallows, and I can tell by the way his eyes water and his nose gets red that he's pushing down a lot of emotions right now. "There's a risk it might puncture another organ or cause an infection that could lead to pelvic inflammatory disease. It also results in a higher risk of miscarriage or premature delivery."

Patrick and Marissa Walsh are a Boston institution, beloved by the fans and near royalty in this city that loves its sports teams. He's never played anywhere else,and has always said he's retiring with a Rebels jersey on. They're the most happily married couple I've ever known, and are currently raising three beautiful little girls together. They don't deserve this . . . not that anyone does.

"Shit, man," Colt says. "What can they do to minimize those risks? Can they take the IUD out?"

"Not without risking her losing the baby."

"What about Marissa?" I ask. "Doesn't leaving the IUD in risk *her* health?"

Walsh closes his eyes, taking a deep breath before he opens them again. "Yeah. Exactly. It's a no-win situation."

"So what are the doctors recommending?" McCabe asks.

Walsh looks away and then lifts his margarita to his lips and takes a sip. "We wait and see. She gets monitored frequently, and if anything gets worse, they'll have to do emergency surgery and remove it. They'd like to avoid that scenario until she's far enough along that the baby could survive because they'd have to deliver during the surgery, but we don't know what will happen. Especially as the baby grows and pushes things around in there."

We all sit there for a moment, trying to absorb the risk to

his wife and what this means for his family. They could lose the baby, or he could lose her, or possibly both.

There's a lump rising in my own throat when I picture myself in his shoes. Of course, the woman I'm picturing is Morgan, which is delusional, but also the most real fear I've ever felt. I never thought I'd have feelings like this for someone again. In fact, I did everything in my power to make sure it didn't happen, yet somehow she slipped right through every wall I put up. And the worst part is, the feelings I once had for Hayley don't even compare to the feelings I have for Morgan.

But now I keep picturing this exact scenario playing out with her, and I can't—*literally can't*—imagine how I would survive another loss like that in my life.

"What can we do?" McCabe asks. "Is there any way we can help?"

"I need to talk to AJ and Wilcott about this. I don't know if I might need to be home with her more. I certainly will if anything goes wrong, so I just need to"—another gulp—"lay that groundwork." Walsh sniffs and wipes at his eyes with the back of his knuckles. "Maybe you can talk to the guys. I want them to know what's happening, but I . . . I can't talk about it, obviously, without breaking down, and I don't want to constantly be discussing it. I'll keep you guys posted if there are any developments, but I don't want this to be part of our locker room discussion. It's hard enough at home right now . . . playing with my girls and trying to imagine what life would be like without Marissa." He sniffs again, then clears his throat. "I need hockey to be the place I go to *not* have to think about that possibility."

Using hockey as an escape from worry and grief is something I understand all too well.

"Yeah, of course," Colt says. "We'll let them know what's going on."

"And ask them not to talk about it," I add. I remember how the only thing harder than losing my dad was everyone constantly asking me if I was okay, and how my mom was doing without him. I know they meant well, but I was just trying to hold my shit together, and constantly being reminded of my dad's overdose didn't help

I imagine the same is true for Walsh. He knows what the risks are, and until they're able to safely deliver the baby and remove the IUD, he's always going to be worried. Asking him for updates constantly will only exacerbate that anxiety.

"All right, I'm going to get home," Walsh says. "I'm probably going to spend as much time as possible there for the foreseeable future. So you likely won't see me around much outside of the rink and road trips."

After he leaves, we all sit there a bit shell-shocked.

"I can't even imagine what he's going through right now," Colt says.

"Yeah, me neither," McCabe says.

They look at me, like they're waiting for me to chime in. But I just shrug, because how do I tell them that I *can* imagine it, because I lived it.

My college girlfriend, Hayley, was pregnant when I found out I was being called up to the NHL. And by the time I left two weeks later, not only had she lost the baby, but I'd lost her. In the end, she elected to stay at school so she could have a typical "senior experience" the following year, because without the pregnancy, I wasn't enough of a reason for her to uproot her life.

I'd gone from having a girlfriend I planned to marry and a baby on the way, to living by myself in an apartment in a new city and playing with guys I barely knew.

If a contract renewal with the Rebels doesn't materialize this year, or if I get into a relationship with Morgan and things don't work out, I could easily be in a similar situation at the beginning of next season.

And there's no way I can *ever* go through that again.

———

I glance at my phone as I turn the corner from Arlington Street, at the edge of the Public Garden, and walk up Marlborough Street. The bare branches of the trees that line both sides of the street are lit from below by the streetlamps, and they sway slightly in the breeze like gray tentacles over the sidewalk. It's amazing how turning just one corner takes you away from a bustling part of the city and puts you on one of the quietest, most quintessentially Boston streets. I guess that's what you get at this price point.

A text from Morgan has come through, nearly three hours after I texted her.

AIDAN

Are you alive?

NERDGIRL

Thanks to you, yes. Are you home? I'm just about to your place.

I pause halfway up my block. Less than twelve hours after

I last saw her, I already miss her like crazy, but I'm still processing everything I learned tonight about Walsh's situation and working through the painful memories it dredged up.

It's the kind of night where I need to be alone.

I start to type out a response telling her I won't be home until later, then delete it because I hate lying to her. I stand there for a moment, thinking about what to say, when I hear her call my name.

My head snaps up, and through the low black wrought iron fencing that borders most people's tiny front yards, I can see Morgan sitting on the front steps of my brownstone half a block away, one arm raised in a wave.

The temperature is cool and the breeze is light, but she has her jacket wrapped around her tightly like it's winter. Her body has probably not fully recovered from what it just went through over the last two days.

Shit. I *do* want to see her, but I know my head's not in a good place right now.

"Did you walk here?" I call out as I approach.

"No. I was out to dinner, so I had Lauren drop me off here when we were done."

"Lauren Flynn?" Why would she have someone we work with drop her off at my house? Unless . . . ?

"Yeah, she knows," Morgan says, clearly able to read my expression even in this low light.

"How?" It doesn't really matter, but I'm curious if Morgan told her or if she figured it out.

"She already suspected," Morgan says. "But I told her the truth about what was going on. And Eva Hartmann, and my cousin, Paige."

My eyebrows lift slightly as I try to process my own jumbled thoughts. Telling her best friend and her cousins feels very much like launching a relationship. And no matter how much I already think of Morgan as *mine*, I know she can't ever be.

"You're not worried about your dad finding out?"

"Why would my closest friends gossip about me with my dad?" Her tone is dry and unamused. "Are you freaking out that I told people?"

"No, not freaking out," I say cautiously. "Just trying to figure out why."

"Because I needed advice." She reaches her hand out like she doesn't have the energy to stand and needs me to pull her up. Maybe she's not as recovered as she thinks.

"Advice about what?" I ask, now eye to eye with her where she stands on the step.

"I wasn't sure what to do about *us*. The thing is, Aidan, you want this to be casual but it's *not*. Nothing about us together is casual aside from the fact that you don't want a commitment."

Tell her you're not in a good position to have this conversation right now, I scream at myself in my head. But I know that she doesn't deserve to be blocked out like that just because I'm a mess.

"Do *you*?" I ask, instead. I never envisioned her wanting an actual relationship with her stepbrother who is also one of her dad's clients, no matter how she might feel about me.

"I think if I've learned anything through this whole experience," she says, her voice quiet and sad, "it's that I already know how to do casual, and it's not what I want."

That doesn't really tell me how she feels about *me*.

"And the thing is," she continues, "I know you don't want a relationship. But I don't want to be with someone who's just with me to pass the time."

"You know that's not what this is for me."

Her full lips flatten into a nearly straight line as she watches me, her eyes scanning my face like she's looking for something. Whatever it is, she must not see it because her lips turn down at the corners for a moment.

"Do I? Then what is this between us?"

I want to tell her how I really feel. I want to suggest that we give it a try. But I can't overcome my fear of her eventually deciding I'm not enough, or of something bad happening and me losing her.

And mixed into those fears in the back of my mind, I also can't quite escape considering how her dad would react to this relationship, or what he might do in response. After the last year without hockey in my life, I know I can't do that again—not right now, anyway. Plus, her dad is the only parent Morgan has a good relationship with, so I wouldn't want to be the reason that there's any kind of a wedge between them.

I gulp, and the words don't come.

"That's what I thought," she says, tilting her chin up as she looks up at the streetlamps that line the picturesque street. Then she looks back at me. "I guess we're at an impasse then."

My chin falls to my chest, and it feels like the muscles of my heart all contract at once. I want to tell her she's wrong, that I can be the person she needs me to be.

But I know in the end, one of us will get hurt. I'm not

willing to hurt her, and I sure as hell don't want her to hurt me, so maybe this is how it has to be?

"I want to be with you, Morgan," I say, looking back up at her. "I just can't be the person you need me to be."

"You already are, that's the sad part. Being with you is like being seen for the first time. It's being appreciated for who I am, not who I could be. It's unconditional acceptance and unequivocal support. How do you give that to someone, and then still tell them you can't be with them? That you're not right for them?" Her voice cracks with the question, and it breaks my heart wide open. "You showed me what we could be, and now you're letting your fear get in the way of the future. And I'm not sure I can ever forgive you for that."

Before I can respond, she turns and walks away. And, idiot that I am, I stand there and watch her go.

Chapter Forty-One

MORGAN

I manage to use my food poisoning as an excuse to avoid going into the office and attending the next two home games. I also begged out of the four-day road trip that followed. It hasn't been ideal, but we've figured out a process for our photographer to send me pictures and me to craft our social media posts from home while watching the games live.

With any luck, I'll have convinced myself I'm over Aidan before seeing him in person again, which I know will happen at tonight's home game.

It's been almost two weeks since we broke things off, and the only thing that's gotten me through it is burying myself in work. After telling my friends what happened, Eva and Lauren keep checking on me, and even Paige has been sending me messages from Indianapolis, where she's working with a new client for the next month. Audrey and

Jules still don't know what happened, but even they can tell something is wrong.

I'm sleepwalking through life. Nothing makes me happy. There's nothing to look forward to. I'm just . . . numb.

I'd do anything to rewind time to the first weekend in September so I could talk myself out of sleeping with that cute guy at the bar in Bermuda. I'd tell myself exactly how much it would hurt months later, after he'd shown me what it felt like to be loved and accepted, only to deny his own feelings and rip it all away. I'd tell myself that it wouldn't be worth the fallout.

But, I don't know . . . maybe even *that* would be lying to myself. I might save myself some pain, but at the expense of finally knowing what it felt like to experience unconditional love.

Though I guess it wasn't so unconditional, since he ended it for reasons that I still don't understand—because, in the end, he didn't even deem me worthy of an explanation.

As I pull the door to the practice rink open and head across the lobby to the elevator, I'm so lost in my own thoughts and focused on holding back the tears that spring up at inopportune times, that I don't even notice AJ until I've practically walked into her.

"Hi, stranger," she says, and I almost jump out of my skin.

"Hey," I give her a forced smile, and I'm sure she sees right through it.

"Are you finally feeling better?" She reaches out and pushes the button to call the elevator.

"I'm still not a hundred percent." It's an honest response, because even though I'm entirely over the food poisoning, I'm in no way myself.

AJ looks confused, probably wondering how I am still suffering from food poisoning I had two weeks ago. "What are you doing here, then?"

"Meeting with Patrick and Sarah about Natalie."

"Ohhhhh." She drags the word out as her eyebrows knit together, and it's obvious she doesn't know about this meeting.

"Patrick didn't tell you?"

"No. But I need you to know, going into this, that his mind is pretty solidly made up."

"I'll do my best to change it, then," I say, lifting my chin and letting my face convey my determination. "It feels hypocritical that she's been put on leave from her internship, while Jake has had no consequences whatsoever."

"I wouldn't say that's entirely true," AJ says cautiously before the elevator doors open and two of our players walk out, nodding at us as they continue toward the doors to the street.

Their presence here startles me. I checked to make sure the team wouldn't be here before scheduling this meeting. Some of the guys could have hung around after morning skate, but I figured they'd all leave right away to rest up for tonight's game.

As the elevator doors shut behind us, AJ drops her voice and says, "Between you and me, Jake's on very thin ice here."

"Why are you whispering in an elevator when we're the only two here?" I ask.

She huffs a laugh. "I don't know, being discreet never really stops, I guess. But just know that even though Natalie's absence has made for a much more public consequence, that doesn't mean that there haven't been other, quieter repercussions for him. You know the type of organization I'm trying to build here, and that type of nonsense has no business in this club."

"What if it was a more serious relationship?" I ask.

Her eyes narrow as she studies me, and I wonder again if she suspects something between Aidan and me. Not that there's anything to suspect, anymore. "It wasn't. He made that very clear when I talked to him. In the long run, that's probably for the best because he has a lot of growing up to do before he deserves someone like her."

"Which, again, is why it's a shame that he's still here and she's not."

"For now," AJ says, and the words hang ominously in the air as the doors open to the floor that houses both her and Patrick's offices. When we step off the elevator, AJ says, "Have a good meeting. Fight for what you think is right in this situation."

———

"Be that as it may," Patrick says after I've made my case for Natalie being far more qualified for the social media position than Tatum, "posting a picture of herself and Jake MacIntyre in bed together was the kind of mistake that ends professional careers."

"She's not a professional. She's a college intern and she made a stupid mistake, Patrick," I say.

"Which begs the question why you think she should be given another chance."

"It must be nice to be far enough along in your career that you forget about your own mistakes along the way," I mutter.

"What?" The word is sharp, and defensive in a way that makes me wonder what skeletons are in *his* closet.

"We've *all* made mistakes, Patrick. That's how we grow. That's how we learn what not to do, and how to do better. It's part of the process. Isn't that why there are internships, and why people get promoted up the ranks, instead of starting at the top?"

"Some mistakes are too grave to progress beyond," he says, and Sarah clears her throat where she sits next to me.

"I think what Patrick is saying," she says, cautiously, "is that given the nature of what happened, it's probably better if Natalie gets a fresh start somewhere else."

"Given the *nature* of what happened?" I ask.

"She didn't post it on her own personal account," Patrick says. "That would have been bad enough. But she posted it on the *team's* social media account," Patrick reminds me.

I know he has a point. I know that this is about posting the picture more than sleeping with a player. But something about it still doesn't sit right with me. Even if something happens to Jake, it'll be a slap on the wrist compared to Natalie not being able to graduate if she loses this internship.

"I'm working to help find her a new internship," Sarah says. "It's just hard to find people willing to bring someone on in November, when the semester ends in a month. She'd need more hours than most people offer for interns."

"Hold on," I say, as that sparks an idea in my head. "I think I know where she can get the hours she needs. Is it okay if I reach out to her?"

"Given that she's still technically an intern here, I'd like to be there when you contact her," Sarah says.

"No problem at all. Let's give her a call now, shall we?"

"Uhh, okay," Sarah says. "Let me just look up her number."

"I have it in my phone from working with her. Can we call from my phone and I'll put it on speaker?"

"Sure," she says.

Natalie picks up on the first ring. "Morgan?" She sounds desperately nervous and excited to be hearing from me.

"Hey, Natalie. I'm in Patrick's office with him and Sarah from HR, and you're on speaker, okay?"

"Okay," she draws out the word almost as if it's a question.

"Sarah mentioned that she was working with you on getting an internship elsewhere, and that gave me an idea."

"Oh?"

"Yeah. I don't know if I ever mentioned it, but I have my own boutique PR company with a selective client list. The Rebels are actually one of my clients, which is how I ended up taking over the social media role here while Tatum is on medical leave."

Sarah nods, clearly pleased that I haven't said anything I shouldn't have. Yet.

"Ummm, yeah, I don't think you mentioned your company."

"Well, the thing is, I've been spending much more time working for the Rebels than what I originally agreed to do"— my gaze moves between Sarah and Patrick at this reminder —"and I'm in danger of falling behind on work for my other clients. I could really use an intern to help lighten the load."

Natalie's gasp fills the office, and then she squeaks out, "Really?"

"Really. You'd be doing me a huge favor, actually. I have a

few clients whose social media accounts I manage, and I could really use your expertise there. But I'd like to hand off more than that to you, because I know you're a quick learner and think you have a bright future in PR."

"Oh my god. I don't know what to say. Thank you!"

"I'm happy to have you on board," I say. "I'll work with Sarah on how to get your internship transferred over to my company so you still get credit. I know you'll have some hours to make up given the last few weeks, and I have plenty of work to help you meet your internship requirements."

"I'm ready for anything."

"Great. Let's plan for you to start on Monday."

"I can't thank you enough, Morgan," she says before we end the call.

"Let me know what paperwork I need to do," I say to Sarah, "or if there's anyone at the university I need to speak with or anything."

I glance over at Patrick, who's wearing a bit of a dazed expression. "That was ballsy." He huffs a laugh. "Reminds me a little of AJ when she first took over here."

And here I thought he'd be pissed that I just gave Natalie an internship. If it works out as well as I anticipate, I plan on hiring her after graduation. He doesn't know what he's missing out on.

"Birds of a feather . . ." I shrug, as if being compared to Alessandra Jones isn't the most enormous professional compliment I've ever received.

"She mentioned the Director of Public Relations position?" he asks.

"She did, but I have my own company to run. If the Rebels would like to keep me on retainer for PR issues, like in the past, that's something we can discuss. But my rate is going up in the new year." I mean, that wasn't in the plans until right now, but it's time I start charging for what I know I'm worth.

"But we can't convince you to come on full-time?"

Sarah clears her throat. He's probably violating some HR policy by trying to talk me into a position that hasn't even been posted yet.

"Pretty sure I've already given you my answer, Patrick." Goddamn, it feels good to set a boundary like this. Especially knowing that I'd have said the same thing to AJ if it had been her asking. *Aidan would be so proud of me.*

I feel my nose stinging as my eyes start to water, which is what happens any time I think of him. I need to get that under control before I see him tonight.

After saying some goodbyes, I head out of the office. As I ride the elevator down to the lobby, I send AJ a text telling her how the Natalie situation resolved. I hit send as the doors open, then glance up as I step forward.

Standing right in front of me, looking shell-shocked as his jaw drops slightly, is Aidan.

"Hey." He drags the word out, and I don't miss the edge of concern in his tone, like he's worried I'm not okay after the way he obliterated my heart two weeks ago. *Fuck that.*

"Hi." My response is clipped, and my tone is as neutral as I can force it to be.

"I'm headed up to meet with AJ," he tells me as I step out of the elevator. He makes no move to get in, and the doors close behind me.

"Have a good meeting," I say and start to move past him. I

need to get out of here. I need some fresh, cold air. Maybe then I'll be able to breathe again.

But his arm stretches out quickly, his hand gripping the cuff of my jacket over my wrist. I freeze mid-step and turn my head just enough to see him out of the corner of my eye. One eyebrow arched in his direction, I wait for him to say something.

He removes his hand from my wrist and rakes his fingers through his hair. It's longer now, and so is his beard. He looks just like the guy who was staring back at me from that photo in the file Patrick handed me in his office over two months ago.

The fact that he looks so much less like the guy I was first attracted to in Bermuda should help me get over him, but it doesn't. Because I'm apparently in love with every version of Aidan Renaud—when he's flirty and bantering with me, when he's taking care of me, when he's moody and in his own head. And that's the kicker. I'm in love with him, and no matter how he feels about me, he won't let himself return those feelings.

My throat is thick with emotion, but I refuse to cry in front of him.

"Can we talk after the game tonight?" he asks.

"I can't. I have a date." I glance away from him because I don't want to know what his reaction is. I don't want to see him looking like he's perfectly okay with this information. Nor do I want to see if it upsets him, because that's exactly the kind of reaction I'd cling to, convincing myself that he still has feelings for me. But it's been two weeks of no contact, and now I just need to move on.

"You move on fast," he mutters, and the words are tinged with bitterness.

At least I wasn't the one who had one foot out the door the entire time we were together. But that's the thing . . . we were never *together*. He made me feel like we were, while telling me all along he couldn't do a relationship, and despite all his reminders, I still fell for him.

"Good luck tonight," I spit the words out and practically run across the lobby and out the doors.

I don't stop moving until I'm a block down the street, where I finally stop, lean up against a lamppost and try desperately to catch my breath and hold back the tears. At first, I struggle with both. Then, I pull myself together, vowing that he won't be the one who finally breaks me.

Chapter Forty-Two

AIDAN

I wish I could say that I channeled all my rage about Morgan's date into the game. I wish I could say that I went out onto the ice tonight and showed AJ that I'm as serious about staying in Boston for my next contract as I told her I was when we met earlier. I wish I could say that it didn't feel like every part of my life was falling apart right now. But it would all be lies.

"You coming out with us to celebrate?" MacIntyre asks me in the locker room when I return from the postgame press conference. It's the first one I've been asked to do this season, and at least I didn't fuck that up, unlike the rest of my life.

Tonight, we eked out a win with two goals in the third period. It was messy, and I definitely didn't play my best. I'm trying to be happy we won, but right now I'm a jumble of emotions that focus entirely on Morgan instead of my job.

My lips press together into a line as I consider whether

I'm better off going home or going out. I'm not sure I'll be good company tonight, but I'm equally unsure if I want to be alone with my own thoughts.

I'm a fucking disaster. Seeing Morgan earlier today, and tonight at the game, has messed with my head in exactly the way I feared it would, but still wasn't prepared for. The only thing more painful than not seeing her for the past two weeks, was seeing her again and realizing that she's moved on. Or that she's trying to, at least.

"Not sure," I tell him. "What's the plan?"

"We're headed to Dave's."

It's a trendy piano bar that's a short walk from the arena, which means it'll be filled with Rebels fans. I don't feel much like celebrating. "Nah, I think I'm going to pass tonight."

"You sure?" he asks, a note of teasing in his tone. "Because I overheard that cute social media girl telling someone that's where *she'll* be tonight."

My head snaps right as I focus my gaze on him. "What cute social media girl?" I grind out the words through a clenched jaw.

He turns and sits so he can put his shoes on. "The one that you're always staring at."

"I don't know who you're talking about." The nonchalance in my tone is so forced that he looks up at me with a smirk, letting me know I'm entirely unbelievable.

"The curvy one, with big tits?" He says it so casually I want to fucking strangle him for noticing or daring to talk about her body like it's there for his viewing pleasure. The only thing that saves him is the fact that I'm still focused on his comment about me always staring at her. Have I been that fucking obvious all along?

"Fucking grow up," I grumble. "We don't talk about our *colleagues* that way. Something you should have learned after you got that intern fired."

"Oh, did she officially get fired?" His tone is careless, just like his actions were, and I know from Morgan that his behavior ruined Natalie's job prospects here. Which is probably why I reach down, grab the collar of his dress shirt, and twist it as I pull him up to standing. The shock on his face hints at fear as he stares back at me.

"I don't know for sure. But you ruined that girl's internship and she may not graduate because of it, and that doesn't seem to bother you one bit." It all tumbles out in a low growl. "And now you're talking about another woman who works with the team like she's a piece of meat. That's not how we operate here, so you need to be a better person or find a different club to skate for."

I push him back down onto the bench right as McCabe comes up behind me, putting a hand on my shoulder.

"Listen to your captains, Rookie," McCabe says. When he glances over at me, I realize he's including me. "You might have been a first-round draft pick, but if you don't fix your fucking attitude, you aren't going to last here."

I'm not quite sure what I see flash across MacIntyre's face as our captain takes him to task. It's like humility mixed with defiance, and then he says, "Yeah, I'm sure you were both perfect angels when you first came into the NHL."

McCabe and I glance at each other, before McCabe looks back at him and says, "You don't have to be a perfect angel. Just don't be such a douche." Then my friend turns his attention back to me. "Get dressed, you're coming out with us."

I don't argue because even though I don't particularly

want to see Morgan out on a date, the only thing worse would be sitting at home alone wondering how the date is going. Some self-sabotaging part of me needs to see for myself if she's truly moved on, or if she's just trying to.

Even though I'm the one who told her I couldn't do a relationship, I'm starting to think that moving on might be impossible for me.

———

"You going to tell me what's going on there?" McCabe asks, following my gaze across the bar to where Morgan's sitting at a pub table with the same guy she had a drink with in Dallas.

"Looks like Morgan's on a date," I say with a shrug. I'm trying damn hard to sound unaffected by this, but my jaw is so tense the words sound strained.

"A second date, by the looks of it." McCabe obviously recognizes the guy from Dallas, too.

"Who knows?" Another shrug, this one smaller because my shoulders have tensed up from the way his knee just brushed hers beneath the high-top table.

"Still trying to convince me that you don't have feelings for her?" The amusement in his tone makes me want to take out all my frustration on him, since I can't do anything about that asshole sitting across from Morgan.

But I don't, because Morgan's words keep running through my head: *Grow up and be a good influence on yourself.* Maybe acknowledging that it's my fault she's on a date in the first place, because I couldn't be a fucking adult and admit I have feelings for her, would be a good place to start?

"Wouldn't matter if I did," I say. "Her dad's my agent, and he made it very clear that I was to stay away from her."

"Interesting." McCabe takes a sip of his beer, and his gaze moves past me. His lips curve up into the smallest of smiles, letting me know, without having to look for myself, that he's just seen AJ.

A part of me wants what they have. That trust, the steady confidence in their relationship, the professional respect that's morphed into something much deeper. The rest of me is terrified of having that, and losing it. I didn't realize how fucking scared I was of being hurt, until I finally allowed someone in.

Almost from the minute Morgan was in my life, I knew the potential was there for her to be *the one.* The more time I spent with her, the more those suspicions were confirmed. I miss her like hell and I know I'm an idiot for letting her go. But I can't shake the genuine fear that if I put my whole heart and my whole self into a relationship with her, I'll never get over it if it ends.

Then again, how would that be any different than the way I gave her all the emotional support she was looking for in a relationship, before ripping it away from her?

It feels like all I did was hurt us both in a quest to protect myself. *Fuck, I've made a mess of things.* The worst part is, I want to fix it, but I don't know how.

"You know," McCabe continues. "There *are* other agents in this business."

"I've been with Carson for my entire career," I remind him. "You don't leave your agent in a contract year . . ." *Even if you're in love with his daughter.*

Oh shit, that's it, isn't it? I'm in love with her. And yet I just hurt her way more than that douche, Carter, ever did.

"I got a new agent in June," he says. That would have been during the playoffs, right before his free agency period began. Which means his stellar new contract wasn't negotiated by Trevor, his agent last I knew.

"You did?"

"Yeah, Trevor was fucking me over. So I talked to Jameson Flynn, and he got me the best contract I've ever had. If you *do* have feelings for Morgan, and you worry they will impact your professional relationship with Carson, maybe you should talk to Jameson too."

"Leaving Carson without giving him a chance to be okay with this feels wrong."

"So you *do* have feelings for her." It's a confirmation, not a question.

"I don't know."

"Of course you do. And the sooner you deal with whatever's holding you back, the better. If you want to be with Morgan, and Carson is what's holding you back, why don't you go talk to him about it? If he's a dick about it, which, knowing him, you should probably expect, then reach out to Jameson."

"It's hard to imagine moving forward with Morgan if her dad is staunchly opposed to it. They're pretty close."

"I bet he'd come around eventually, if he saw that you were good for each other. In the meantime, I could put in a good word for you with Jameson."

I cock my head slightly, surprised by his offer. "You'd do that, after I ghosted you all last year?"

"You had shit going on, and so did I." He pauses, then adds, "I think we both came back as better people this year."

I cough out a laugh, thinking about how different we both are now, compared to two seasons ago. "I don't know," I say, drawing out the words slowly. "You're still kind of surly."

"And you're still kind of an asshole. But less so . . . when she's around," he nods his chin toward Morgan right as her date stands and comes around the table to her chair. He raises his hand, slipping it along her neck, and I notice the way her spine stiffens slightly. But I don't think he notices, because he's leaning in to kiss her.

I can't quite tell from where I'm standing, but I think she tucks her chin so his lips meet her forehead, and then I have to look away because my entire body floods with rage at the sight of someone else touching her. The only forehead kisses she should be getting are from me.

"Go get your girl," McCabe says. When I look back, the guy is headed toward the door and Morgan is finishing her drink. "Before it's too late."

My stomach flips over as I stalk across the bar toward her. By the time I get to the table, she's gotten her jacket on and is slinging her bag over her shoulder. She startles when I appear at her side, and that's when I realize that while I've been entirely focused on her for the last hour, she wasn't even aware I was here.

Her lips twist into a grimace, and she narrows her big blue eyes before she says, "Aidan, *please* stop showing up where you know I'll be."

"Then stop trying to make me jealous."

"I'm not trying to make you jealous!" she says, then lets out a frustrated sigh. Her full lips part as she lets out a long breath. I immediately want to pull her into my arms, press a kiss to the crown of her head, and promise her things I haven't promised anyone in a decade. "I'm *trying* to move on."

Her words are a sharp slap that bring me back to reality. And the reality is, I hurt her to protect myself.

"Well, stop that, too," I demand, even though I have no business telling her what to do.

"You don't get to tell me that you can't be with me, and then insist I not date other people."

I step closer to her. "He's not good enough for you." I don't know whether that's true or not. Maybe he's a great guy . . . but he's not *me*.

"Yeah? Then who is, Aidan?" The anguish in her voice as she looks up at me has a lump in my throat that grows so large I can't speak. "See? You can't even say it's you. So if you aren't the one for me, let me find someone who is. Or at least, someone who is not afraid of their own feelings."

She pushes me back with one hand on my chest, then turns and storms toward the door. I go to follow her, but the press of the crowd slows me and by the time I make it to the street, she's nowhere to be seen.

I'm tempted to hop in a cab and show up at her place, but she deserves more than me being reactive and jealous, demanding that she not see other people.

She deserves for me to finally show up for her, ready for a relationship. And there's no way I can do that without settling a few other things in my life.

AIDAN

Are you around tomorrow? Can we chat?

MAX

Is everything okay? You can call me now if
you need to.

I glance at the clock at the top of my phone screen. It's just about midnight, and I'm tired and unsure of what I want to say at this point.

AIDAN

Nothing's wrong, I just need some advice. It
can wait until tomorrow.

MAX

Okay. I'm on call at the hospital tomorrow
night, so I'll probably try to get some sleep
in the afternoon. Call me in the morning?

AIDAN

Will do.

Then I set off on foot. My mind is reeling too much for me to sleep, and I'm hoping that the walk home will help clear my head. I don't even know what I want to talk to Max about, specifically.

If it was just about what happened with Hayley and how to move past that, I'd call Liam. He was there for me throughout that ordeal, and given what happened with Kelsey and his belief that love is still worth it even after he lost her, he might have some good advice.

I know my issues are deeper than that one relationship. That was just the cherry on top of a shit sundae of losing people I loved, and Max will understand that better than anyone.

So I spend the thirty-minute walk thinking carefully about what I need to do to untangle my own complicated feelings about relationships and love, and hoping beyond hope that I haven't wrecked things with Morgan too badly to repair them.

Chapter Forty-Three

"You can't be fucking serious," I say with a dry laugh as I come to a stop at a stoplight. Traffic is heavier than I would have expected mid-morning on a Saturday. "*She* left *you?*"

"She sure did," Max says, sounding not the least bit sad about this.

"A two and a half month marriage is a record, even for you. What was her reasoning?"

"She determined, very correctly I might add, that I was still not over your mom."

I don't know what to say. "How do you feel about that?"

"About her leaving? Eh. I started seeing her true colors on our honeymoon. Glad I had that prenup in place."

"I meant about not being over Mom, but continuously trying to replace her."

Max sucks in a breath that's audible even over the phone. "You don't replace someone who's irreplaceable. That's not what I'm trying to do, and I hate that I've given you that impression."

Only for the past decade. "So then what are you doing marrying all these women?"

"I guess . . . I'm chasing the *feeling* I had when I was with her. Being with your mom was almost addicting. I felt like the best version of myself when I was with her."

That's hard to hear, because that's *exactly* how I feel about Morgan. Being with her is addicting, not just because I can never get enough of her, but because we bring out the best in each other.

"Then maybe you should try to find someone who makes you feel the way she did, not someone who just looks like her? Because I gotta be honest, Max. That part is creepy as hell."

He lets out a low rumble of laughter. "I think in my heart of hearts, I know no one else will ever make me feel the way she did. So I settle for someone who looks like her."

Meanwhile, I found someone who *everything* felt right with. Nothing about being with Morgan felt like settling.

"Does some part of you settle because in the back of your mind you're afraid of really falling for someone else again? Of how much it could hurt if things don't work out, or if they leave?"

"That's an oddly specific question," Max says. "You want to tell me why you're asking?"

"Answer me first, and then, yeah."

"I don't think it's that I'm worried about getting hurt, so much as it's that I've accepted I'll never get to feel that way about someone again. So I settle for less, because let's be honest, being alone at my age is a pretty bleak prospect."

I never thought about it like that. Max chose to move down to Miami once I was out of college and playing in the NHL, and I assumed it was purely job related. But maybe he wanted to escape the memories of what he had with my mom and the places where those memories existed. Maybe what he needed was a fresh start.

I don't want a fresh start, though. I want Morgan, and I want to stay in Boston. That much is now crystal clear.

"That's depressing as hell, Max," I say.

"Welcome to getting old without a partner."

"Knowing what you know now, would you do it differently, if you could go back? Would you still marry my mom, even if you knew how it was going to end?"

"Hell yes I would! There's no world in which I'd give up those years with her; no world in which that time would have been better spent alone, rather than with her and you." He says it like it's a warning, and maybe it is. Maybe, like Liam said, the heartache at the end is worth it because of the years you got to spend together. And there's no guarantee I'd lose Morgan. Am I pushing her away when we could have forever together?

I'm so lost in thought as I drive up Beacon Street into Brookline that I don't say anything in response.

"So, you going to tell me what's going on?" Max asks.

I start at the beginning, and tell him about Bermuda, and about finding out we worked together and Carson warning me to stay away from his daughter. I describe how she tried to keep me at a distance, but how I wouldn't let her. I tell him about my friends with benefits suggestion, and how every minute I spent with her made me crave her company even more. I tell him how the relationship morphed from something that was supposed to be purely physical, to something that I didn't think I could live without. And then I tell him about Marissa Walsh, and how it brought back everything that happened with Hayley, right before Morgan told me how she felt. "And now, she's dating someone else to try to get over me."

Max chuckles quietly. "I should have known, actually, based on how protective you were of her when we were at dinner in Boston. I've never seen you like that with anyone. Not even Hayley. And you took her to Ember Cove? Introduced her to Liam? Did you really believe that you didn't have feelings for her?"

"I suppose I believed it in the way you believe any lie you tell yourself to save yourself from getting hurt."

"How's that working out now, Danny? Does it *not hurt* watching her date someone else? Thinking of her finding love with someone who's not you? Have you protected yourself, or caused yourself pain in this situation?"

I let out a long, loud exhale in response to his rhetorical questions. Obviously, I did this to myself.

"You're a damn fool if you let her walk right into some other guy's arms because she wants you and doesn't think you want her back," Max says.

"That's the thing, though," I say as I pull into a parking spot along the curb on a quiet side street, in front of a large brick house with a small but manicured front yard. "She *knows* I have feelings for her."

"How could she not, after everything you just told me? And at the same time, you keep telling her you don't. How do you think *she* feels? You're probably confusing the hell out of her and breaking her heart in the process."

I rest my head on the headrest and close my eyes. "Yeah. I don't know how to make this right. I would never want her to sacrifice her career for me and don't think I should do that for her, either."

"For someone who seems to have had no trouble slipping into that gray area with your stepsister, you seem completely unable to think about her and your career as anything but black and white. Why does it have to be one or the other? Do you really think Carson would try to sabotage your career because you're *in love* with his daughter?"

"I'm about to find out."

"What do you mean?"

"I'm sitting outside his house, about to go talk to him."

"Without a plan?"

"My plan is to be honest. I don't think I realized I was in love with her until she was gone, but now that she is, I can't imagine *not* trying to get her back. I do think Carson would fuck me over if he knew about everything leading up to me falling for her—"

"Why would he need to know all of that? I think you can lead with 'I'm in love with your daughter, and I need to know how that is going to affect our professional relationship.' See where that takes you."

I'm sure he wants to see his daughter happy, and I know I make her happy. Carson knows there's no one else I've wanted to commit to in the last decade. If she feels the same way, why shouldn't he support us?

"That's a good suggestion," I say. I'll cut to the chase and tell Carson the truth and let him decide what to do with it.

I say goodbye to Max, feeling lighter now that I know Morgan and I aren't going to be stepsiblings much longer, and relieved to better understand why Max has remarried so many times after my mom's death.

Then I walk up the front walkway of the home Morgan spent her middle and high school years in, hoping I can reclaim the girl of my dreams without losing my career prospects in the process.

———

Carson is as surprised to see me at his door as I am to see him wearing flannel pajama pants and a hoodie. I pretty much thought the man slept in a three-piece suit.

His eyebrows dip and his forehead wrinkles as he looks at me, waiting for an explanation as to why I'm at his house, unannounced, on a Saturday morning.

"Sorry to show up with no warning, but I really need to talk to you."

"Oh no," he says, clearly thinking I've fucked up somehow and need him to fix my mistake.

The problem is, the only thing I've fucked up is my relationship with Morgan because I put my own fears, and my relationship with her dad, ahead of her. Now, I'm determined to either get his blessing, or end our professional relationship.

"It might not be as bad as you're imagining. May I come in?"

He ushers me through the door and leads me into a large, formal office space at the front of the house. After I'm seated across from him, thankful that there's a desk in between us so he can't easily reach me, I say, "I know you told me to stay away from your daughter, but I'm pretty sure I'm in love with her."

His brows crease and he tilts his chin, narrowing his gaze. "Can you say that again? I'm afraid I'm hallucinating."

Well, that's a great sign. "I'm in love with Morgan, and I need to know how this is going to affect our professional relationship."

He tilts his head as he looks at me, and his calmness actually worries me more than if he'd shouted at me to get out of his house before he ripped my balls off. "How, exactly, did you fall in love with my daughter? I didn't think you knew each other well."

I debate how much to tell him and settle for us meeting on vacation and finding out we worked together once we were back in Boston.

He licks his lips and his look is hesitant. "The only vacation Morgan's gone on recently is her mom's wedding."

"Yeah." I press my lips together, hoping I don't need to explain more.

"Why were you there?"

I could lie and say I happened to be staying at the same resort. But I don't want to start off by lying to him. "Because Anne was marrying Max."

"Shit." He huffs a laugh. "So you two are . . . related?"

"Not really; that marriage was never going to last. They've already separated, thankfully."

"Shocking." Carson's voice is dry. "Why didn't Morgan tell me this?"

"She said you two don't really talk about her mom?"

"It's extremely hard for me not to want to strangle the woman for the way she treats our daughter. That's one of the main reasons we separated in the first place. I couldn't be with someone who was jealous of her own daughter."

My eyes widen at that piece of information. "Does Morgan know that?"

He shakes his head slightly. "There's no way I could have told her that and not had her feeling responsible somehow. You know how she is."

"Maybe she would have felt that way when she was younger, but I think the grown-up version of her would appreciate knowing that you saw how Anne treated her, and did something about it. She's done a lot of work trying to figure out that relationship, and I think it would help if she knew the whole truth."

Carson swallows, and I watch the way his whole head bobs with the deep gulp. "She's talked to you about it?"

"I didn't fall in love with her because I barely know her, Carson. Of course she's talked about it."

"So then, you've told her about Hayley?" he claps back. *Touché.*

Fuck, this is complicated. Carson has known me since I was eighteen. He's seen me grow up, which means he's witnessed a lot of shit over the years.

"I haven't given her *all* the details yet. But I will."

He lifts an eyebrow and nods, a clear indication that he expects me to be totally honest with her. "So, if you're in love with her—and I assume she returns your feelings at some level, or you wouldn't be here—why is she going on a date with some guy named Sean tonight?"

Ouch. The fact that she's told her Dad about him after a few dates, when we never even made it out of the secrecy stage, stings even though it makes perfect sense. But that doesn't necessarily mean her feelings about this Sean guy are serious.

"I fucked up. I got freaked out by how strong my feelings were and let old insecurities and fears get into my head. When she told me how she felt, I pushed her away."

"As your agent, that's exactly what I would have expected from you. As her dad, that's exactly why I warned you off her. You never got over what happened with Hayley, and you've let it affect every aspect of your life since."

"I know." I nod in agreement as I glance down at my hands folded in my lap, almost like I'm praying. And maybe I am, in a way. Because there's never been anything I've wanted as badly as I want Morgan in my life.

"See, the thing is, Renaud, love is a *choice*. You either choose to allow it into your life, or you choose to push it away."

I know that, too, so I just nod. I understand what he's saying—I've done everything in my power to shut down the possibility of loving someone again, just so I don't get hurt. I've got no issues loving Max, or Liam and Jack. But romantic love? I've built up every wall I could to prevent that from happening.

"If you truly love Morgan, and you're willing to work to deserve her, then I'm not opposed to your being together if that's what you both want. But I *am* opposed to you hurting her because you haven't done whatever work you need to do to let go of the past."

"I'm committed to doing that work, I swear. But in the meantime, I'm also committed to making sure she knows how I feel about her and how serious I am about us. I'm not going to lose her because I'm afraid."

"I'm sure you already know this, but Morgan's not Hayley. You and Hayley were still kids, in a really shitty situation. You and Morgan are adults, and I'm sure whatever issues you two have, you can work them out with a level of maturity that wasn't present in your last relationship."

This whole time, I thought that because Carson knows what I went through with Hayley, and has seen my slightly wild side since then, he would be convinced I wasn't good enough for his daughter. But here he is, telling me that he thinks it could work?

"Does that mean I have your blessing?"

"I wouldn't have thought that you, of all people, would need it."

I lift a shoulder slightly in a shrug and tell him, "Probably not. But I'd like to have it just the same."

He gives me a nod, and says, "If you love her and you treat her right, that's what matters. All I want is for her to be happy, and loved, and secure."

"Funny, all I want to do is make her happy, love her, and give her the kind of security where she knows I'll always be there for her."

Carson nods.

"So . . ." I gesture between us. ". . . we're good then, professionally speaking?"

"I'm not the kind of guy who can separate business and personal relationships. But as long as you're good to my daughter, I'll always have your back."

"I will always treat her like she's the most important thing in the world, because she is." Treating her well was the easiest, most natural thing I've ever done—until I tried to convince myself that I didn't have feelings when they were so obviously growing out of control. Now that I've embraced my feelings for her, there's nothing to stop me from giving her the world.

"Good. I'll find out where she'll be tonight so you can go get your girl," Carson says as he stands and leans across the desk to shake my hand. Once my hand is firmly in his grasp, he squeezes, looks me in the eye, and says, "Do. Not. Fuck. This. Up."

Chapter Forty-Four

MORGAN

I choke on the protein bar I'm scarfing down as I stand in my bathroom, curling iron in hand, and stare down at my mom's face on my phone. "You did what now?"

"Don't talk with food in your mouth, darling. It's so unladylike." Mom's eyes roll like she's had to tell me this a million times already. She hasn't. Not since I was nine and she told me no boy would ever like me if I talked with food in my mouth.

I swallow and set the curling iron on the counter. "Sorry, I was just caught off guard by the whole 'I left Max' bit. It hasn't even been three months."

And besides, it's not normally my mom who does the leaving.

"Yes, well," she says, waving a hand in the air like she's brushing the memories away.

"What happened?"

"He was obviously still in love with his dead wife, and I can't compete with a ghost."

I have so many questions but don't even know where to start. Is love supposed to be a competition between you and anyone they've loved in the past? Should Max no longer love Aidan's mom just because she passed away? And how did my mom not know this about Max before they were married? And why did she just up and leave instead of trying to work things out?

I go with the last question, and she gives me a pouty sigh. "Falling in love is the best part, honey."

"No mom, *being loved* is the best part. Anyone can fall in love. It's choosing each other, over and over, that makes love worthwhile."

"I forgot you were an expert on the matter," she says snidely.

It's true, I've only been in love once before, with my college boyfriend. He broke up with me right after graduation, so instead of moving to Austin with him, I moved to Park City, where Lauren got me a job with Petra.

And now, Aidan, who showed me what it felt like to be truly accepted in a way that seemed a lot like love . . . but then *still* didn't choose me. Does that mean he didn't love me? Or he just didn't love me *enough*?

"Maybe I'll come up to Boston for Thanksgiving," Mom says, and that snaps me out of my own thoughts real fast.

I can't control the way my eyes widen and my head shakes. "What?"

"We could have a mother-daughter weekend," she says, like that's something we do. My mom's idea of bonding is going to the spa together and having treatments in separate rooms.

"I can't."

Mom looks confused and kind of offended, like I just told her that her Prada bag from two seasons ago is no longer in style. "Why not?"

"Because I have plans."

I don't, yet. But I will. If my dad is in town, I'll spend it with him. Or I'll spend it with the Flynn family again. And if neither of those options works out, I'll spend it alone. Even that is preferable to spending the holiday with my mom.

"You can't change your plans for your mother?" She sounds genuinely shocked that I won't drop whatever's going on in my life to accommodate hers, and that pisses me off.

I'm not just mad at her for always being so damn selfish, I'm mad at myself for allowing it. For being afraid to rock the boat and risk disappointing her, when all she's done, over and over, is disappoint me.

When I don't respond right away, my mom lays on the guilt. "Honey, I just separated from my husband and you can't even make time for me?"

Her audacity has me seething. It's not like separating from her husband is an uncommon occurrence, and every time this has happened, I've *always* been there for her.

"You've never *once* put me first in your life, yet you always expect that I'll drop everything for you. And that's partly on me, because I always have. But it stops now."

Mom's jaw drops and I'm pretty sure she calls me ungrateful under her breath. "After everything I've done for you—"

I swear those words have me so heated I could breathe

fire, so I interrupt her. "Mom, you left me when I was a kid and I've probably only seen you a dozen times since. You prioritized every guy in your life over me, made me participate in multiple weddings for marriages that everyone knew wouldn't last, and you only come running back to me when those marriages fail. The one thing you've done for me, my entire life, is put me last. So that's where I'll be putting you from now on. I need to go. I have to get to a work meeting."

"It's Saturday." My mom says this like she's caught me in a lie.

"And yet I'm still trying to catch up on work after being deathly ill two weeks ago. Not that you'd know anything about that. Goodbye, Mom."

Disconnecting the call feels both freeing and terrifying. I've never stood up to my mom. Never called her out on her bullshit. Never refused her anything. It feels good to finally put my foot down, but I would never have had the courage to do so without Aidan's constant reminders that I deserve better.

That's the part that hurts most, because I'm setting boundaries in my work life and my personal life based on strength I gained from a relationship that no longer exists. And maybe it never did, except in my mind.

But I don't have time to think about that, because I'll have a little breakdown if I do, and I can't be late for this meeting.

———

"Thanks for meeting with me," I say to Jake MacIntyre as I slide into the seat across from him at a coffee shop a block from my place.

"No problem," he says and looks past me out the window. His entire demeanor screams *I have better things to do right now.*

"AJ told you why she wanted me to meet with you?"

"Yeah," he says with a shrug, "but I still don't see what the big deal is." He lifts his drink and takes a sip.

"You got drunk and then posted yourself ranting about the Department of Player Safety and the Commissioner of the NHL." My voice is flat but my tone is full of judgment because who does that? Immature twenty-year-olds, I guess.

"He's an idiot. That fine and suspension the department gave me were totally unfair and the commissioner should have at least overturned the suspension when I appealed."

I tilt my chin as I observe him. He's giving off an air of entitlement that often comes from being coddled, but I have no idea if that's what this is, or if being a first-round draft pick and an instant millionaire has somehow made him think he's invincible.

"Whether you agree with his decision or not, it's binding. You'll be lucky if there aren't more fines or a longer suspension for violating 'off-ice conduct' policies."

He rolls his eyes. "I'm allowed to have and express my opinion. It's called free speech."

"Yes, but you aren't free from the *consequences* of your speech. In this case, your little rant could easily be considered abusive behavior, and it definitely makes the league look bad. Both of those things are violations of league policies, and could come with additional consequences. In this case, the best thing you can do is issue a formal apology for your behavior, and I'm happy to help you with that."

"Pfffft." He practically spits the sound out. "I'm not apologizing."

I don't know what this guy's problem is, but it's not winning him any fans right now, especially not with his team.

"Is there something else going on?" I ask.

His gaze narrows in on me. "What do you mean?"

"Your behavior is not only unsportsmanlike, but your complete lack of remorse for your actions is . . ." I don't even know the right word here. ". . . concerning."

"There's nothing wrong with my actions. Fights happen during games all the time; I shouldn't have been fined or suspended for that one. This whole thing is bullshit and reeks of favoritism."

If he doesn't understand why he went too far, that's really on his captains, coaches, and GM to inform him. Which I know they have, and he's still taking on this air of *I didn't do anything wrong.*

This kid needs to learn a little humility, and I hope someone humbles him real fast. But it won't be me, because I don't have time for his shit.

I shrug. "Okay."

He looks at me like he was expecting a different response, but I'm here to guide him, not to baby him and convince him to do the right thing when he's determined not to.

"I'll let AJ know that you don't plan to issue an apology."

A look passes over his features so quickly, I can't quite pinpoint what I just saw. But if I had to guess, it was fear. Which would make it the most logical reaction he's had during this conversation. Pissing off your GM and doing the opposite of what she's asked you to do is a bad move. But if he realizes that, he's too stubborn to change his mind. "Good."

"All right, thanks for your time," I say, standing and smoothing my skirt down. I don't miss the way he checks out my legs between the top of my knee-high boots and the hem of my short skirt. I am heading straight to a date from here, and I'm more concerned about looking good for that than looking professional for this meeting.

Based on this guy's attitude, I'm wondering what the hell Natalie ever saw in him. Maybe he was different with her? Maybe I need to have the same conversation with her that AJ had with me?

It took me twenty-eight years to finally realize that yes, when someone shows you who they are, you should believe them. That philosophy would have saved me so much heartache with my mom, and with past boyfriends. But then there's Aidan. He showed me who he was, and—

Stop it right now, I tell myself as I turn and head toward the door. Yes, his actions showed me who he was, but his words said something different. Whether he's lying to himself or lying to me doesn't matter. It's over, because that's what he wanted . . . which tells me everything I need to know.

On my way out the door, I pull out my phone and text AJ and Tucker Hartmann, letting them know how the meeting went.

AJ

I wish I was surprised.

MORGAN

I'm not sure he understands the kind of team you're building here.

TUCKER

This guy's a walking PR nightmare.

MORGAN

Truer words were never spoken.

TUCKER

Your call, AJ.

AJ

I'm on it.

Chapter Forty-Five

AIDAN

The air has that damp chill that always precedes a snowfall. Tonight's impending storm is predicted to dump half a foot of snow by morning, as winter comes in with a bang.

With any luck, I'll be watching the first flakes fall from my bedroom window, with Morgan tucked in beside me. It's a ridiculous thing to hope for, given my inability to be honest about my feelings the last few times we talked and the fact that she's meeting another guy for a date tonight.

I might be the underdog going into this, but I'm not giving up without a fight.

Small groups mill around outside the restaurant, grumbling about the wait and the weather, and blending in with them gives me the perfect cover to scan the well-lit interior of the restaurant, where I spy Morgan sitting alone along the wall.

I knew she'd be early. Banked on it, actually. Why this

asshole isn't picking her up for dates, or taking her home afterward, makes no sense to me. But tonight, it's working in my favor.

I pull my collar up around my neck and keep my head down, hoping I'm not recognized before he arrives. Luckily, he's right on time and comes strolling toward the door at a brisk pace, until I step into his path.

"Hey, man," I say, and he steps back like I'm a danger to him. Which I am, but not in the way he first thinks. But then the recognition dawns in his eyes.

"Oh, wow. Hey. You're—"

"Yeah," I interrupt before he can draw anyone's attention by saying my name. Maybe no one out on this sidewalk is a hockey fan, but just in case.

"Are you . . . eating here tonight?" His brows scrunch together, clearly wondering why I'm standing outside this restaurant talking to him.

"Depends on you, actually."

With his brows still low and one side of his mouth pulling back slightly, his face is full of confusion. "How so?"

"I have a proposition for you. What do you say I get you a luxury box for next season, and you don't show up for dinner tonight?"

"Why . . . ?" He drags out the question, clearly having trouble figuring out why I'd spend over a hundred grand to have dinner with his date.

"Because that girl you're going to meet tonight? She has my whole heart. I'm pretty sure I have hers too."

"Then why has she gone out with me several times?"

My lips twist together the same way they do when I'm physically in pain. "Because she needs a good guy in her life, and I fucked up. Now, I need a chance to make things right. Maybe she won't take me back, in which case you get the girl *and* a luxury box."

He clenches his jaw as he looks at me, clearly torn. I'd say he's a fool for giving her up for a box at the arena, but I almost gave her up because of my own damn fears, so I'm hardly one to point fingers.

"If she's not into you anymore, you'll walk away?" Sean asks.

My heart is in my throat at the idea of walking away from her for good, but if that's what she wants, I'll do what's best for her. "I will."

"I'm only considering your offer because I have no desire to be part of some sort of love triangle. If she's not over you, I don't want to be involved." He pauses. "But, she seems really sweet, so if you're not totally committed to being good to her, maybe save us both the time and walk away?"

"I'm going to give her the whole damn world, as long as she'll let me."

He gives me a quick, decisive nod. "Okay."

I get that he doesn't want to be part of a messy situation, but the fact that he just gave up so easily speaks volumes.

"Thanks, man. I'll get that suite set up. The number for the office that handles luxury boxes is online, call anytime after Monday and they'll have more information for you."

He nods, then turns, walking away, and I step into the restaurant. I bypass the host, telling her I'm meeting someone, and walk straight over to Morgan. The shock on her face is expected, but the hostility in her rigid body language isn't.

"What are you doing here?" she asks, her gaze moving

beyond me and darting around the restaurant like she's afraid Sean might walk in and find me in his seat.

"Having dinner with you," I say as I slip my jacket off and hang it on the back of the chair.

She folds her arms across the table in front of her, leaning toward me and lowering her voice as I take my seat. Her strawberry blonde hair is down in loose waves, falling forward over the expanse of bare skin in her square-neck top. "I'm meeting someone."

"Are you disappointed that I'm here instead?"

"Instead?" she asks.

"Yes, *instead.* I asked your date to bow out of dinner so I'd have a chance to convince you that I was wrong and stupid, and to tell you that I'm sorry." I take a deep breath, relieved she didn't throw her drink in my face and tell me to go to hell.

Her face softens, the slightest hint of a smile evident on those full lips. "Keep going . . ."

I pick up the straw sitting next to the glass of water that was already on the table when I arrived, and pull the paper off it, just to have something to do with my hands.

"This has *never* been 'just friends' for me. I knew from that first night in Bermuda that you were perfect for me, just the same as I knew I'd never be good enough for you—"

"Why would you think that?" she asks, before her eyes flit down to where I'm folding the straw wrapper into a thin rectangle.

"I didn't want a relationship, and you're clearly a relationship kind of girl. Then we found out we were working together and your dad was my agent, and . . . I couldn't stop wanting us to be together, but I also hated keeping *us* a secret. You are not someone to keep hidden. You shine too brightly for that. You need someone who can show you off, who can shower you with praise and affection. You *deserve* that. And I didn't think I could be the one to give it to you."

"Are you ever going to tell me *why* you're so opposed to a relationship?"

I sigh and fold the paper wrapper again before glancing up at her. "Remember how I told you about Hayley?"

She tilts her chin as she studies me. "You never told me her name, but I assume that's the college girlfriend you thought you were in love with?"

"Yeah. There's . . . a bit more to the story, though. We started dating my freshman year, and when I found out my mom died, she was there for me every step of the way. She comforted me when I completely broke down, held my hand at the funeral, made sure I went to my classes for the rest of the semester when the only thing I wanted to focus on, my only escape from the sadness, was hockey. There was so much darkness lurking in me then, and she pulled me out just enough that I didn't succumb to it. I don't know how I'd have gotten through that period without her. Going through that trauma together . . . it deepened our relationship in a lot of ways, and also filled in some cracks that would have probably made it clear we weren't right for each other. By junior year, those cracks were starting to show. I was under immense pressure to perform on the ice that year, because I'd already been drafted and there was a lot of talk about me getting called up. And then . . ." I swallow as I glance down at the paper wrapper I've now circled around my pinky multiple times. "We found out she was pregnant."

Morgan's lips part before she sinks her teeth into her lower lip and nods for me to continue.

"It was February when we found out I was getting called up to Minnesota, and the plan was for her to finish out the last few months of the semester at school, and then she'd join me in Minneapolis and we'd have the baby there. She was going to take a year off school, and then finish up her senior year once our lives were more settled. But . . . right before I moved, she miscarried."

"Oh shit, Aidan," Morgan says, her eyes glazing over with unshed tears. "I'm sorry."

"I don't think either of us was emotionally ready to be a parent, but we were committed to figuring it out. And then, once there was no baby, she decided it was better if we ended things and she stayed to finish up her degree."

"So you . . . moved to Minnesota without her, without the family you'd expected to have with you?"

"Yes, and it *broke* me. It was like losing my parents all over again but worse, in a way, because I'd spent so much time, when we found out she was pregnant, envisioning what kind of father I wanted to be. I'd catalogued all the good things about my dad before he succumbed to his addiction, and all the good things about Max, too. I wanted to be the best dad I could be, and I don't know . . ." I say, shaking my head. "I guess I was so focused on becoming a dad, I didn't think enough about how Hayley was feeling about becoming a mom. When she lost the baby, she didn't seem nearly as upset about it as I was. I think she was . . . relieved?"

"That's a terrible thing to have experienced," Morgan says, reaching her hand across the table and wrapping it around one of mine.

"Yeah. So I moved to Minnesota alone. I was in a funk, and I couldn't pull myself out of it. Eventually my coach recognized what was happening and stepped in. He made sure I got the help I needed—a therapist to talk through things with, and plenty of time with my new teammates so I didn't feel alone. He was basically another dad to me. He wouldn't take no for an answer when I tried to shut down. He pushed me but also supported me. His family became like a second family for me. I . . ." I gulp through the memories. "Not every coach would do something like that, and I don't know what would have happened if he hadn't stepped in. I definitely would have lost my NHL contract."

"So losing Hayley and the baby the way you did was what made you so afraid of a relationship?" she clarifies.

"I never wanted to give anyone that kind of power over me again. I lost the family I thought we were going to be, and I almost lost my dream of playing hockey professionally. Not letting anyone close enough to hurt me like that again became my number one priority when it came to relationships."

"I get that," she says, squeezing my hand before she pulls away.

"Because?"

She lets out the kind of silent laugh that shakes her chest slightly, and rolls her eyes. "I'm starting to think that maybe I've subconsciously chosen guys who have obvious red flags because then, when they eventually do something shitty and break things off, I can refer back to those red flags as reasons they would have been a terrible partner. I'd rather think I was lucky to escape when I did, than think that *I'm* unlovable," she says, looking down at the table.

I reach across the space, cupping her jaw in my palm and lifting her chin so that she's looking at me. "You deserve to be loved for exactly who you are, because loving you is not hard, no matter what you've been led to believe. In fact, loving you is the easiest thing I've ever done. So easy that I can't make myself stop, no matter how hard I try."

Her throat bobs as she swallows, and her eyes widen. "Did you just say what I think you said?"

"That I'm in love with you? Yes. And I want everyone to know it."

"What about my dad, and your contract negotiations?"

I give her a sly smile. "I already got his blessing. How do you think I knew where you'd be tonight?"

She laughs in response, and finally seeing her smile has me relaxing in a way I haven't been able to since I let her walk away from me that night in front of my house. "No wonder he asked where Sean was taking me tonight."

I clear my throat. "Let's agree that we're not going to talk about other men you've been with. I've met too many of them already."

"First of all, I wasn't *with* Sean—"

"Whatever," I interrupt. "I don't want to think of you with anyone but me."

She just shakes her head at me. "And secondly, your jealousy and refusal to talk about past partners are both signs of emotional immaturity. I swear, you're a walking red flag, Aidan Renaud."

Just the kind she says she always falls for.

"Yeah, but I'm *your* red flag. And I'll work on all of that . . . the jealousy, and being more open to talking about the past so we make sure not to repeat those mistakes with each other. Whatever you need from me, Morgan, that's what I want to give you."

"You already have. That's what I told you that night. You showed me what it felt like to be accepted and supported unconditionally—"

"Yes, but you need to know that this isn't just me *accepting* you as you are. These last two weeks without you, it was like part of my soul was missing. I crave your company, and the way you make me want to be a better version of myself."

"This is . . . a lot to process, Aidan." She lets her hand slip off mine. "Letting you back in after you pushed me away feels like a familiar pattern that I promised myself I'd avoid moving forward. At the end of the summer, AJ reminded me that when people show you who they are, you need to believe them."

"And what did I show you?" I ask the question with genuine curiosity, and also trepidation about her reply.

She sighs. "On the one hand, you showed me how I should be treated in a relationship. On the other hand, you played a bunch of fucking mind games, insisting that you didn't have feelings for me and pushing me away when I admitted I wanted more than friends with benefits."

"I know, and I'm so sorry. I never meant to hurt you, but the reality is that I was thinking more about my own feelings than yours. And that won't happen again."

"I'm trying to wrap my mind around this complete one-eighty from not wanting a relationship. Because it sure sounds like you do, now?"

"I don't want a relationship, Morgan. I want *forever*, and I want it with you."

"How can I trust that you're not just going to turn and run again?"

"I think the last two weeks taught me what Liam was trying to make me see back when we were in Ember Cove: that it's better to have loved and lost than to have never loved at all. I know that sounds cheesy, but while we were apart, I never once regretted us being together, no matter how badly it hurt to be without you. I only regretted letting you go."

I pick up her hand, sliding the narrow strip of paper from the straw beneath her ring finger before carefully looping the paper around itself to tie it into a knot on top of her finger.

She looks at that knot and lets out a short laugh. "You know rings are supposed to be removable, right?"

My fingers tug the knot gently, making sure it's secure but not pulling hard enough to rip the paper. "Maybe I don't want you to be able to remove it. Maybe I want a ring on you permanently."

"That's my right hand, you know." A small smirk plays at the corner of her lips.

"That's okay, this one's just a promise." Our gazes meet and her breath hitches. I want her to understand how deeply I'm already in this. "We'll make sure the next one is on your left hand."

"Aidan, this is . . ." She shakes her head. "You're here now, saying all the right things. But two weeks ago, you pushed me away when I told you how I felt."

"Which was the hardest and stupidest thing I've ever done. I was scared of how much I cared about you, and how quickly it happened. I promised myself that I'd never let anyone get close enough to hurt me again . . . but you vaulted over all the walls I'd erected—"

"Pretty sure you handed me the rope and pulled me over those walls yourself," she says with a small chuckle.

"Maybe, but it still shocked me how completely I fell for you. I was telling you that it was casual, that we were just friends, while internally I was yelling at myself that none of it was casual for me, and that I should just tell you how I felt. But I kept thinking that if I could convince myself that this was just friends with benefits, it would hurt less when you pulled away."

There's a sadness in her eyes when she asks, "Why did you think I'd pull away?"

"I was going based on past experiences, I guess. That, and thinking that there was no way I deserved you."

"You keep saying that."

"Because it's true. Look at you. You are an *attractor*. Your enthusiasm is contagious. Your friendships are rock solid. Your colleagues respect the hell out of you. Everyone loves you Morgan. I think you just don't see it because . . . maybe you don't love yourself quite enough."

"Way to take something sweet and make it an insult," she says, rolling her eyes like she so often does with me. But I hold her hand tightly, not letting her pull it away.

"I don't mean it as an insult at all. You just don't see yourself how everyone else sees you, and I'm planning to spend as long as it takes undoing all the ways your mother has fucked up your self-image. You deserve to be loved and appreciated exactly as you are, because you are already amazing and there is absolutely nothing you need to do to change yourself. I don't want to say that there's no version of you that I could love more, because I suspect that I'll love a lot of future versions of you even more—like the version where you're *mine,* where you fall asleep every night in my arms and wake up every morning in my bed, where we grow and change together as we get older, where we're sitting in rocking chairs with our gray hair, looking back on these days and talking about how far we've come."

Morgan gulps, and the tears that were pooling in her eyes spill over her cheeks. I lean over the table, using my thumbs to wipe away the tears. "Why are you so perfect for me?"

"Not sure. But I'm really glad I am."

Her cheeks push up into a small smile. "That night I came to talk to you after I was at dinner with Lauren, Paige, and Eva, what I really wanted to say was that I was pretty sure I was in love with you."

The tips of my fingers curl into the hair behind her ears. "And now?"

"Now, I think I'm even more sure."

"I'm really sorry that I hurt you, Morgan. I should never have let you walk away thinking that I didn't care. I was a mess that night—"

"Why?"

"You heard about Marissa Walsh?"

"Yeah," she nods her head in my hands, but looks like she doesn't understand why that would affect me.

I pull my hands from her face and sit back in my seat. "Hearing Walsh talk about not knowing what he'd do if anything happened to her or the baby, and talking about how hockey was his only escape from the reality of what he could lose . . . it brought back a lot of trauma, a lot of memories about what it felt like when I was in a similar place."

"You got scared." It's not a question, it's an acknowledgment that she understands what I was feeling and why I made a stupid decision because of it.

"I did. I should have told you I wasn't in a good headspace for the conversation we needed to have. No, I should have told you *all of this* then—about Hayley and the baby, about how I really felt, and about how damn scared I was. But the thing you really need to know now is I'm not scared anymore. I'm . . ." I glance away, trying to think of the right word. "I'm hopeful."

"How very unlike you," she teases, running her thumb over the scar on the back of my hand.

I focus my gaze back on her. On the small smile gracing her lips, on her blue eyes twinkling in the soft light, on the freckles that have mostly faded but are just visible enough for me to remember what they look like.

"Funny, I feel like myself for the first time in a long time."

The waitress comes up to our table then, apologizing for taking so long to get to us. I want to thank her for not showing up sooner, but that would entail some sort of an explanation I don't have time to give. Because right now, I want Morgan to have all of my attention, and to finally know that she always will.

Chapter Forty-Six

MORGAN

"I didn't realize how beautiful your house was last time I was here," I tell him as he slides my coat off my shoulders in his entryway. The living room has nearly floor-to-ceiling windows along the front that overlook the tree-lined street, and an exposed-brick wall runs along one side from the front of the brownstone all the way to the back. The living room, with its big white couch and smaller patterned chairs, opens to the dining room with a huge round table under a gorgeous chandelier and flanked by eight fabric chairs. Beyond that, it's open to the kitchen with wood cabinets, and beautiful marble countertops and backsplash. It's the perfect blend of old-world charm and modern function.

"You were too busy throwing up," he says, pressing a kiss to the top of my head before turning to hang my coat.

I sit on the bench in the entryway to remove my knee-high boots, and set them aside so I don't track snow all over his house. The walk home was beautiful, but slippery with the falling snow. And after we trudged up his stone steps to his big front door, he gently brushed the snow off my face and leaned in to kiss me.

"Did you decorate this place?"

His loud bark of laughter rings out in the quiet space. "No. I bought it fully furnished from a couple who had extremely good taste. But I don't know, sometimes it still feels kind of . . . sterile?"

I think about how lived-in my condo feels, with blankets and pillows and candles, not to mention all the photos framed on the walls and sitting on tables and bookshelves. Aidan's place looks like a photographer might show up at any minute to take pictures for a magazine. "It could use some . . . personal touches to make it feel more homey."

"I think," he says, putting his hands on my hips to turn me back toward him, "it would feel a lot more homey if you were here more often."

"Yeah?"

"Yeah. You're the only woman who's ever been in my house, and it's felt lonely since you left."

"Last time I was here, I spent two days throwing up."

"Yes, but you were *here*. I'd take cleaning puke off you over not having you here, any day."

I can't help but chuckle when I say, "That's kind of gross and oddly sweet at the same time. You're such a goner for me."

I'm teasing, but I'm not. He's shown me for months how he felt about me, despite the lies he was telling himself, and me as well. And now that his words and his actions align, I have no doubt of his feelings. Still, I'm cautious about moving too quickly given my own track record with giving second chances and getting burned.

"I really am, and I always will be. There's literally no way you're getting rid of me. Prepare for me to be clingy as hell, because now that I have you back, I don't want to be apart from you for even a second."

When he dips his head to kiss me, I rise up on my toes to meet him. My arms circle his neck and his grip tightens possessively on my hips as he pulls me against him. And when my lips part for him, he invades my mouth, our tongues tangling with desperate need.

My entire body is on fire for him, the flames coursing through my veins as I lift one of my legs, curling it around the back of his thighs and pulling him even tighter against me. But because of our height difference, I'm not getting the friction I'm looking for. He must realize this because his hands snake around the back of my legs and push between my thighs, scooping me up so I can wrap my legs around his waist. Then he spins me toward the wall, leaning my back into it so he can press his hips up and slide along my core.

I moan into his mouth and I swear the sound sets him off, because suddenly he's running his hard dick along my center, hitting my clit every single time, until we're both wild and feral and clawing at each other. But then he pulls back from our kiss, resting his forehead against mine as he holds my hips still, and I whimper with the need to feel him moving against me.

"Holy fuck, Morgan. If you don't stop making those sounds, I'm going to come in my pants. It's been too long since I've touched you and I'm not sure I can hold back."

"I don't see the problem with that," I say, bringing my

hand to his face and running my thumb along the line of his cheekbone. His beard is neatly trimmed, and I'm so used to seeing him with facial hair now that I almost can't remember what he looked like without it.

"I haven't been with you in weeks, and the first time I come is going to be inside of you, not in my damn boxers."

"Please, Aidan," I nearly whimper with need. "I need you."

"I'll give you everything you want, I promise. But I'm not rushing this." He pulls his hips away from me and as my legs fall, he scoops an arm under them so he's cradling me against his chest. Then he carries me up the stairs and down the hall. He pauses at one half-open door and presses it open with his foot.

"This can be your office. We'll set it up with whatever you need."

I'm so shocked by that statement that I can't even form the words to respond. What the hell is he talking about? Then he turns and climbs the stairs at the far end of the hall, and when we reach the top, he pushes another door open. We step into a small, empty room, and he tells me, "We can make this room into a walk-in closet for you, if you don't want to share mine."

"I just agreed to give you a second chance like an hour ago, and you're already planning for me to move in here with you? You're out of your mind." I let out a small, uncomfortable laugh.

"No, I think I'm finally in my right mind. I've been thinking about a future with you since the first night in Bermuda," he says as he turns and starts walking down the hall. "And now, I'm done fighting myself. I'm done sabotaging my own happiness. I meant what I said earlier, you're not getting rid of me."

"I don't want to get rid of you," I remind him as he heads down the hallway.

"What if I don't get another contract with Boston?" There's a deep insecurity in his question, and I want to reassure him, but it's still early in this relationship.

"I think we just take this one day at a time."

"What if you get tired of me?" he asks.

I laugh. "I'm not going to get tired of you."

"You don't know that," he says, and I look up at him as he strides through the doorway into a large bedroom at the back of the house.

"No one else has ever made me feel so seen, so supported, so adored, or so loved. Why in the world would I get tired of that?"

He presses a kiss to my forehead. "Just remind me of that sometimes, okay?"

"Remind you of what?"

"That I'm being the person you need me to be. And if I'm not being that person, tell me that too. I want us to communicate about the important things, and not let our insecurities get in the way."

I pause for a moment, thinking about how that's the most mature thing I've ever heard anyone say at the beginning of a relationship. And that's when it truly hits me: this isn't the *beginning* of our relationship. It's the beginning of a new phase . . . the one where we're committed to making this work, hopefully forever.

He lays me gently on the bed, no signs of the desperation we were both feeling downstairs, and carefully removes my bra and underwear, then strips his clothes off. When he kneels beside me, I can't resist reaching out and sliding my fist up his hard cock before circling the head with my fingers.

He groans before saying, "I want you bare."

"Oh?" I'm enjoying watching the way his abs flex every time I slide my fist down his length.

"Yes. I don't want anything between us, not even a condom."

"You already did that in a cave in Bermuda."

"Yeah, but I'm not pulling out again. So I feel like we need to have a whole conversation about what would happen if you got pregnant."

"I won't get pregnant."

"How are you so sure?" he asks.

I hesitate, not sure how he'll react because of everything going on with Marissa Walsh. "I've had an IUD for years."

"Well, fuuuuck," he draws out the word as he runs a hand through his hair. He swings a leg over my hips so he's kneeling, poised above me, as I continue stroking him. "If you don't stop that, there's not going to be any sex. I want you so bad right now."

I slide my hand off him and down his muscular thighs. Then he leans forward, planting an elbow next to my head as he repositions his legs, using his knees to spread mine apart. "Why do you have an IUD?"

"Really bad periods and no desire to have kids this young."

"Do you want to have kids eventually?"

"Eventually," I say. "But I'm not ready now."

"Good. I want to enjoy this time where it's just us for a

while first." His free hand caresses the curve of my shoulder then he trails his fingers along the side of my breast and along my rib cage.

"You're moving from 'I can't be in a relationship' to 'Let's get married and have kids together' real fast."

"It feels fast to you because you haven't been in my head for the past couple months while I fell for you. Totally and completely, even as I tried to prevent it from happening."

"Hmmm," I say as his hand continues its path down my side and along the curve of my hip. He reaches beneath my thigh and pulls my leg up and over his lower back. "I'm glad you stopped trying."

"No choice," he says, his gaze locked on mine. "I didn't want to be without you, no matter what the consequences were."

He moves his hips and glances down between us as he slides inside me ever so slowly, like he's trying to savor every second of this. My teeth sink into my lower lip as he fills me completely, and then, with his eyes locked on mine, he sets a pace that's just right.

It's not the desperate, frantic sex we would have had if he'd given in back in that hallway. It's slow and deliberate, and the reverent way he's looking at me tells me everything about what this moment means to him. Another step forward as a couple, another "first" for us together.

"God, I missed you," he says, and his lips brush the tip of my nose before he pulls his head back to look at me. I can see his emotions plainly on his face—the pain of holding back and the relief of finally giving in. "I've never felt this way about anyone before."

I know what he means . . . that while he might have loved

Hayley in the past, this is different. It's new for me too. I don't feel like I have to change myself to fit what someone else wants me to be. I'm not worried about trying to be enough without being too much, never fully able to be who I really am. With Aidan, I can let go of my insecurities, because I feel secure with him.

I bring my knee up so one foot is planted next to his hip, and use it to give myself some leverage as I rise to meet each thrust. A groan rattles around in his chest and his gaze lowers to watch the way our bodies meet. I snake my hand behind his neck, threading my fingers into his hair as I pull his head down so I can kiss him. And that's what does us both in—my nipples dragging along his skin, his tongue stroking mine in deep pulls that match the pace of our bodies meeting, his hips tilting slightly so the head of his cock presses right along the spot that he knows will bring on my orgasm. When he pulls back to look at me, my core clenches around him.

His jaw is tight, like he's holding back until I'm ready. As the pulsing in my core intensifies and my lips part in a small gasp, an electrical current flows through me and I arch my back, pressing my shoulders into the mattress and crying out.

"That's right, baby," he coaxes, moving faster until I'm gasping for breath while my orgasm rips through me. And then he's grunting, a long, low sound that escapes the back of his throat as he pours himself into me.

When we're both finished, he props himself above me on both elbows and leans in to kiss my forehead. "You're perfect. And you're *mine* now."

Chapter Forty-Seven

MORGAN

AJ looks back and forth between Aidan and me where we sit next to each other, across the kitchen table from her. She sweeps her long dark hair behind her shoulders, licks her lower lip, then says, "I didn't see this coming."

"Didn't you?" I ask. I consider how she saw him get up in my face about wearing McCabe's jersey before the home opener and wait for me on the plane when I got sick. Not to mention how suspicious she seemed when she asked if I was seeing someone.

"No. I thought the two of you were friends. I knew you only lived a couple blocks from each other, so him taking you home when you were sick didn't register as suspicious . . ." She lets out a huff of laughter and shakes her head. "Seriously?"

Aidan reaches over, taking my hand where it's resting on

my thigh, and lacing our fingers together. "Seriously. And, hopefully, permanently."

Jesus, this man . . . when he's in, he's all in.

It's been less than two weeks since he sabotaged my date to tell me he loved me. He was away on a road trip for eight days after that, and he already wants to make it official.

We're in this weird place where we can't just casually tell our friends about this, because in many cases they're also our teammates, colleagues, or boss. Lauren, Paige, and Eva already know, and now that we've told McCabe and AJ, we'll be able to let everyone else know, too.

"I called it," McCabe says gruffly, where he sits on the floor a few feet away playing with his adorable daughter, Abby.

AJ spins in her seat. "You *knew* about this?"

"I suspected."

Aidan told me that McCabe encouraged him to talk to my dad, so I think he more than suspected. But that's between him and AJ.

"And you didn't say anything?" she asks.

"That's our agreement," he reminds her as he takes the squishy ball Abby hands him and tosses it across the room so she can run and get it. "I don't say anything that I know, as a player, might impact your opinion of my teammates. And you don't say anything about other players that I shouldn't know, as their teammate."

She sighs and says, "Yeah, but Morgan's my *friend*."

"And Renaud is mine," he says, opening his arms for Abby to run into as she returns with the ball. He scoops her up and plants a loud kiss on the top of her head. "But he's also one of your players, and she's also your employee."

"I'm *not* an employee," I remind him. "I'm doing some contract work for the team, which is very different."

"And not even for much longer," Aidan adds. Even though my work with the Rebels gave us a lot of excuses to see each other over the past couple months, I think we'll both be relieved once there's a clearer separation between our personal and professional lives.

"Didn't you tell Patrick you'd be open to staying on in a consulting role?" AJ asks me.

"If you want to keep me on retainer for PR situations, I can do that. But once Tatum's back, I can't be there part-time. Natalie is the only reason I don't feel so behind these days, but I need to start devoting more time to my own business."

AJ nods. "I'm glad that's working out with Natalie. And we will absolutely keep you on retainer."

"You may not like my rates," I tell her.

"Just ask for what you're worth, Morgan, and we'll go from there."

God I love this woman. She could easily try to lowball me to save the team some money, but that's not her style. No, she'll go straight to finance or even to Tucker Hartmann to ensure I get paid what I am worth.

"So," Aidan says, "about this relationship . . . is there anything we need to do? Like do we need to talk to HR or make some sort of official announcement, before we start telling people?"

AJ's eyes slide to me like she's making sure I'm on the same page, while also trying to figure out how the hell the *always single* Aidan Renaud got to this point without her noticing. I give her a small nod.

"I don't think so. I'll check with Sarah in HR just to make sure. But I'm pretty sure there's no reason it would be a problem."

"Good," he says. "Let us know."

"You seem . . . in a hurry," McCabe observes.

"You saw what I was like for the two weeks without her, right?" Aidan responds before turning back toward me. "Now that I've got my girl back, I'm never letting her go."

"Never, huh?" I say with a chuckle as he leans in and presses a kiss to my forehead.

"Never."

"Oh my god, you two are sickening," AJ says with a laugh.

"Right, because you two aren't all ooey gooey when you're not at work," I remind her.

"She's got you there, Sunshine," McCabe says, rising and then picking Abby up so he can walk over and press a kiss to the top of AJ's head. "You two want to stay for dinner? We're ordering out."

I glance at Aidan, but he says, "Thanks for the invite, but we have plans."

"We do?" I ask.

"Yeah, we have to move some more of your stuff into my place," he says, as if this is something we've talked about before. But, given that I haven't spent a single night at my own place since we got back together, not even while he was away on his road trip, I'm not surprised.

Yes, this is moving fast. But it feels like we're playing catch-up for the months of telling ourselves this couldn't be more than friends with benefits, even while it obviously felt like so much more. "And, I think I promised you we could get a Christmas tree once I was back?"

"That's true, you did say that," I say, as we stand to say our goodbyes.

Some time, I'd love to join McCabe and AJ for dinner. But right now, I feel the same way I sense that Aidan does: I just want more time together before his next road trip.

———

I look around Aidan's home in utter shock. I lift my arm, gesturing toward the huge, fully lit and decorated Christmas tree centered on the front windows. "Is that . . ."

He just chuckles. "One of the trees you sent me a picture of? Yeah."

"That was just to see if you were okay with how I wanted to decorate, not so you'd have it all done for us while we were out." Everything, from the tree to the realistic garland draped over and hanging down the side of the mantle, to the stockings, the candle holders, and wooden holiday decorations on the sideboard that runs along the stairs, is straight out of the photos I sent him.

"Are you disappointed that you don't get to shop for everything and put all the decorations up?" he asks quietly.

"No, it's gorgeous. I guess I'm just confused. Didn't we just go pick out a Christmas tree?"

He'd found this adorable city tree lot, with lights strung between brick buildings on either side. We snapped some photos together while we walked around the lot, and found a tree that was neither as beautiful nor as perfect as the one currently standing in the living room, but we'd picked it out together.

"You said you wanted one for the bedroom too, didn't you?"

My breath hitches. I made a one-off comment a week ago that I'd always wanted a Christmas tree in my bedroom. "That's what that one is for?"

"Yeah. And there should be lights and ornaments waiting in the bedroom, but I didn't have the decorator get as many ornaments because I figured you'd want to pick some out too. And I thought maybe we could pick a special one out each year?" His voice waivers slightly as he says it, and I look up at him. "It's something my family always did growing up."

I stand on my toes so I can press a kiss to his lips. "Where are those ornaments now?"

"In a storage box in my garage."

"If you want, we could use them on our tree?" I phrase it like a question because I don't want him to feel like he has to, if he's not comfortable with it.

He gives me a small smile—the kind I'm so often giving him, the kind that says "I feel seen."

"Yeah, maybe. We can take them out and look through them at some point over the next few days."

"I hate that you're leaving again so soon," I say, "but we can make the most of the time you're home."

"By 'make the most of the time I'm home,' do you mean decorating for Christmas? Because," he says, pulling me to him and leaning in, "that's not exactly the way I want to make the most of our time together."

My chest shakes with silent laughter. "I'm sure we can decorate first, and *then* you can have your way with me."

"What about naked decorating?" he asks.

"Sounds like it would be cold."

"I'll keep you warm, baby."

I roll my eyes and push at his chest but he doesn't let me go. "You're out of your mind."

"Yes, for you." He presses a kiss to my temple and then says, "Let's take the tree up to the room and get it set up." He walks through the kitchen to the small hallway in the back leading to the door to the garage. There, he grabs the tree that's leaning up against the corner where he left it when we came in.

Throwing the six-foot tree over his shoulder, he walks toward the stairs. "C'mon. The sooner we get the tree decorated, the sooner I can get you naked."

"Way to rush it," I say, following behind him, but I'm pretty sure I want him as much as he wants me. Eight days away was hard, and we're not even halfway through the season. At least my friends are pretty much all in the same boat, and once I finally tell the rest of them about Aidan and me, we can be a support system for each other while our men are away.

I allow myself a small, private smile as I follow him up the stairs, thinking about how frequently I used to tell myself that I was a strong, independent woman who didn't need a man to be fulfilled. And while that's true, I sure do like having him around, and I sure do like how he makes me feel. Not complete . . . but supported. Like this is a partnership. I've seen it with so many of my friends, but getting to experience it myself is new.

While he sets up the tree in the stand, I unpack the strings of lights and the boxes of ornaments. I can already tell that they're all from one of the photos I sent him, just like the tree downstairs looks identical to another photo. I love that he wanted to make my Christmas decorating dreams come true, but that he also recognized I'd want to be part of it. And truthfully, I'm kind of thankful not to have to do it *all*. Downstairs probably took a team of people hours to create, but it would have taken the two of us days, and that's honestly not how I want to spend the limited time he's home.

He's left just the right amount of magic for us to create together.

It doesn't take long for our smaller tree to come together. Once it does, Aidan tosses the fuzzy white blanket that will be wrapped around the base of the tree to the floor. I bend over to get it set up, but he steps up behind me and his fingers curl around my hips possessively.

"This part, surely," he says, his thumbs hooking into my leggings, "can be done naked."

A huff of laughter escapes me. "I wondered how long you could be patient."

"I've been *so* patient, baby. Don't I deserve a reward?"

I hum my agreement as he tugs the waistband of my leggings down over my hips and drops to his knees as he pulls them down my legs so I can step out of them. Then he turns me around and stands.

"God, I missed you so fucking much." His words are half sigh, half groan, as he stares down at me, heat in his eyes, but adoration on his face.

"You missed me naked?" I say, smirking up at him.

He slides a hand up each side of my neck, cupping my jaw. "Hell yes. But really, I just missed *you*. I don't like being away from you."

"I don't like being away from you, either," I say as my fingers find his belt and start undoing it while his lips meet mine in a slow, drawn-out kiss. But the minute his belt is unbuckled and I unbutton and unzip his jeans, pushing them down over his hips, he takes control. Kicking his jeans off, he drags my sweater up and over my head before tossing it away.

Then he clasps my wrists behind me, and his gaze rakes up and down my body while I stand in my bra and thong, shoulders back and tits forward. I'm wearing a sexy pink lace set he hasn't seen yet, and it's sheer enough to drive him wild. I even teased him with that information back in the Christmas tree lot.

"Fuck me, I missed this view." He leans down to drag his lips along my cleavage, then bends down further to press his tongue against the fabric over my nipple. His hot breath and the friction from his tongue over the rough fabric have me biting back a moan, but when he clamps his lips around the stiffened peak and sucks me into his mouth, I can't hold back any longer.

"Yes," I hiss out. My hips press forward, toward him, my core clenching and my clit wanting the friction of his body. He switches to the other nipple and does the same thing, eliciting another moan and more pleading from me, which has him dropping to his knees to give my clit the same treatment.

Then he glances up at me, his full lips turned up at one side. "Tell me what you want me to do. I'm going to need a lot of directions."

"You *need* directions? Or you just want to hear me describe what I want?"

"Yes."

Before Aidan, I wouldn't have had the confidence to take

charge and voice my physical desires. He makes me want to try everything.

"Do that again," I say.

Leaning forward and pressing his tongue to my clit, he circles over the fabric so the lace grazes across the sensitive nerves before he clamps his lips around me and sucks my clit between them.

Warmth floods my body. "Without the underwear. And I want you to feel how wet I am for you." I step out of my thong after he slides it down my legs, and keep my feet spread so he has better access to me. With his mouth on my clit, he drags his fingers through my center, and I can tell the slickness there is coating his fingers.

He pulls back slightly, looking up at me. "You're so wet for me, baby. How long have you been like this?"

"Probably since you kissed me in that Christmas tree lot."

"You should have let me make you feel good as soon as we got home."

"Speaking of making me feel good," I say with a wink, "did I tell you to stop?"

His warm breath hits my belly as he laughs, and then he brings his lips back to my clit. This time, he shows me no mercy, licking and sucking the sensitive area like he's determined to make me come quicker than ever. And while I'd like that, I also like being in charge and want to prolong that.

Which is why I sink down to my knees, facing him, and pull his sweatshirt over his head, tossing it aside, and reach behind me to unclasp my bra. The minute it's off, Aidan's mouth is on me, sucking my nipple into his mouth and running his tongue over the peak fast and hard.

My core clenches tightly and I need more, so I put my hand on his chest. "Sit down."

"Yes, ma'am." His voice is tinged with amusement and longing as he leans backward and easily maneuvers his legs out in front of him, with one arm behind him holding him up. I move so one knee is on either side of his hips, hovering above him.

"Get down here with me," he growls, pulling my hips down and entering me in one fluid motion. With me straddling him, he's so deep I can hardly breathe. "You're so fucking sexy when you tell me what you want," he says, one hand on my hip and the other cupping my breast. "Keep going."

I love the way he creates a space safe enough for me to let go of my inhibitions and confidently ask for what I want. The bossier I am, the more he likes it.

"Use me. I want it hard and fast, until we're both screaming."

He doesn't hesitate. His hands and lips are everywhere, tugging at my hair with one hand while pressing into my clit with the other, sucking each nipple into his mouth with deep pulls before grazing his teeth over them, kissing his way up my neck, and whispering all the fantasies he's had about me while he was gone.

My hips are moving frantically as I take him deep and hard, and then both his hands are on my hips and he's pulling me down on him, rocking his hips into me so he's grinding against my clit. "I want to see you play with your tits while you fuck me," he says. "Can you do that for me, baby?"

"Yes," I can barely get the word out as I bring my hands to

my chest, pressing my breasts together and toying with my nipples. I'm so fucking close, I can feel my orgasm on the periphery.

"God, you're so sexy," he tells me. "I'm never going to get enough of you like this—desperate and needy for me."

I circle my hips, and he groans. "Yes, keep doing that." And then he leans back slightly, bringing me forward with him and hitting that spot deep inside me.

As he slides against my inner walls, he stokes the flames of my orgasm until they are a raging inferno that consumes me. I cry out and he showers me with affirmation, telling me how beautiful and strong and perfect I am. And when his body curls forward, I cling to him as his hands hold my hips down and he spills his release into me with a long groan.

He looks up at me afterward, his arms still wrapped around me and his head resting on my chest. "I'm sorry," the words are a whisper.

"Sorry about what?" I ask, running my palm along his jaw and then threading my fingers into his hair.

"I'm sorry we almost missed out on this. Not the sex, but the closeness, the plans for the future. I'm sorry that I ever made you feel like I didn't want something serious and permanent with you. I will never, ever do that again."

I press a kiss to the top of his head while I hold him to me. "Don't worry, I won't let you. You're *mine* now, too."

Chapter Forty-Eight

AIDAN

Four Weeks Later

"Do you seriously have to go into the office?" I grumble, pulling Morgan back against me and trailing my lips along the slope of her bare shoulder. I tuck the blankets tighter around us, trying to form a cocoon so I can keep her in bed for as long as possible.

She sighs as she snuggles into me, her back against my chest as we face the two large windows with the Christmas tree in between. It's filled with ornaments from my childhood, as well as others we've picked out together. I have no idea how it's still alive, but Morgan has been watering it daily which probably helps.

Before her, the holiday season was always hard for me. Christmas was my mom's favorite, and after my dad died, I did everything I could to make sure it was special for her. I always helped decorate the tree and bake cookies. When I was older, I'd help Max hang Christmas lights on the outside of the house. We both loved how her eyes lit up every time she pulled into the driveway.

Since she passed, the holiday season has always felt like something I had to endure. But being with Morgan, and getting to experience the joy of the holidays again, has been like a wound healing over.

"I do have to go in," she says with a sigh. She'd taken the whole week between Christmas and New Year's off, but she's on retainer for PR issues with the Rebels, and a "situation" came up. I'm pretty sure it's related to MacIntyre, because AJ finally got tired of his shit and traded him to an expansion team. As soon as he got settled in his new city, he posted another video rant, this time about his former team. But of course, she can't tell me if that's what they're meeting about. "I won't be gone long, I promise. I just have a quick meeting with Tucker, and then I'll be back."

"I just got home last night," I say, sinking my teeth playfully into her shoulder. "I'm needy."

She shakes with quiet laughter and squeezes my forearm where it's wrapped over her chest. "I miss you when you're gone. But I can't not do my job, especially with what they're paying me hourly when things like this come up."

"Baby, we do *not* need the money."

"*You* don't need the money. I, on the other hand, am still paying off my business school loans."

"Would you just let me take care of those?" This is already a tired argument, because I approach every situation—financial or otherwise—like this is a partnership. Like we're already married.

"I appreciate that you keep offering," she says. "But you know my answer. If I can't make my business successful enough to pay off my own loans, then I shouldn't have gone to B-school in the first place."

"You're ridiculous," I say, kissing her neck. "You're already successful. And wasting all that money on loan interest isn't smart. Let me pay them off, and then you can pay me back if you want, with no interest."

The *hmmmm* rattles around in her throat, and that, in and of itself, feels like a victory. She's always flat-out said "no" in the past. I'm not offering because I want to have any kind of financial leverage over her. Her loans amount to a tiny fraction of my annual salary, and I just want to do whatever I can to lighten her load.

"Just think about it," I say. "Also, your dad wants us to come over for dinner after my next road trip. Max will be in town, too."

She laughs and says, "Their bromance is my favorite thing."

I laugh at that too. Morgan wanted to spend Christmas with her aunt and uncle up in Maine, because she said it wouldn't be Christmas if she didn't see Lauren and Paige, plus she wanted to see her cousins' kids open their gifts. Her dad was going too, like he always does, and we invited Max to come along because we didn't want him spending Christmas alone.

I had no idea how rowdy the holiday would be. Lauren and Paige have three brothers, who all have kids, and they were all super into the holidays. As an only child my whole life, I'd never experienced anything like that, and that's the only way I want to spend the holidays from now on—eventually, with our own kids, too.

The only thing more surprising than how much I loved being surrounded by overexcited kids who couldn't wait for Santa to come, was how Max and Carson became instant buddies. They'd met before, of course, at the draft and games. But this was the first time they'd ever spent much time together. I don't have anything good to say about Anne, especially since she *still* hasn't reached out to Morgan after their conversation before Thanksgiving. But one thing I will give her credit for is that she does have good taste in husbands.

"Why will Max be here?" she asks, still making no move to get up though she's going to be late if she doesn't.

"I think he's considering an offer up here. The doctor who took over his practice really wants to move south, and it sounds like she's interested in Max taking his old practice back and her taking over his practice in Miami."

"That's interesting," she says. "Why does he want to be back here?"

Though I'd bet she already knows the answer, I say, "I think he's realized he wants to be around family. Hopefully, someday, his grandkids too."

"Hmmm." It's an acknowledgement without a commitment, which is fine. She's not ready for kids and I'm not in a rush. But when I do finally have children, I want it to be with her. I want what I thought I was going to have all those years ago—the chance to be a great dad. But this time it won't be because the situation is thrust on me and I'm trying to make the best of it. It will be a choice, and one I've only ever wanted to make with her.

She rolls over, facing me, and her eyes rake up from my

bare chest to my face. She runs her hand along the beard I keep short just for her . . . until playoffs, at least. Because with the way we're playing this season, there's no way we're not making the playoffs. The team is confident about that. We talk about the Cup as if it's ours for the taking. And it just might be.

Morgan leans in, kissing me quickly before saying, "I have to go shower or I'll be late."

I pull the covers back and prop myself up on my elbow. "I'll help you."

Her hand is on my chest, and she's laughing as she pushes me onto my back. "No way. I'll be even later than I already am if you get in that shower with me."

"It's *my* shower," I say, and I can't contain my smile, "and I'll get in it if I want."

"I'm locking the door while I get ready. The sooner I go to this meeting, the sooner I'll be back. We have today and tomorrow together, then your game tomorrow night, and New Year's Eve, before you leave again." She kisses the bridge of my nose before she springs out of bed and rushes to the bathroom.

I don't chase her, because I don't actually want to be the reason she's late for a meeting with Tucker Hartmann. Unlike my younger days as a player, I try not to piss off management, especially not the CEO of the team, whose signature is on my paychecks.

I lay in bed for a while with my hands clasped behind my head, staring up at the ceiling as I think about how lucky I am that our game schedule allows us to be home for New Year's Eve this year. When the shower turns off, I sit up, looking around for my sweats. I have no idea where our clothes were discarded last night—per usual, it was before we made it to the bed. I'm tempted to just go get Morgan her coffee naked, but now that it's winter, it's a bit cold for that.

I find them wadded up on a chair across the room and have just pulled them over my hips when Morgan gasps from the other side of the bathroom door.

"You okay?" I call out.

"Uh . . . yeah. I just . . . almost dropped my phone."

"You sure that's all?"

"Yeah, I'm fine. No worries." There's a tightness in her voice that has me curious, but whatever it is, she isn't ready to tell me. Or it's related to work, and she can't tell me.

"Okay, I'll be right back with your coffee," I say.

"Thanks," she calls out, but she sounds distracted. And as I leave the room, I don't miss the sound of a video or audio clip playing on her phone. It's a woman's voice, but I don't want to overhear something she doesn't want me to listen to. It's probably just one of her friends.

I return with her coffee a few minutes later, and she's wearing one of my shirts and has a towel wrapped around her head. "You wearing nothing but my shirt and telling me you have to leave for a meeting is a special kind of torture."

"Don't worry," she says with a wink as she reaches out for the steaming mug. "I'll make it up to you when I get home. We have all afternoon."

"I told McCabe we'd bring dessert tonight," I remind her.

"Good. I look forward to seeing what you make while I'm at the office, *Dear*." She chuckles as she leans up to kiss my cheek, and I smack her ass through the T-shirt before I turn to leave.

Some day, I might be able to stand in a steamy bathroom

with her in nothing but my T-shirt and not want to strip it off her and fuck her in front of the mirror. But that day is not today.

"If I hadn't come home while there were brownies in the oven, I seriously would not believe that you baked," Morgan says, licking some of the gooey chocolate off her fingers as her eyes meet mine across McCabe's kitchen table.

There's laughter in her voice and her eyes sparkle with amusement as I'm sure she's picturing how I dragged her upstairs to have my way with her the minute she got home, only for us to miss the brownie timer going off downstairs, completely burning the first batch. Luckily, I had enough ingredients that we worked together to make another batch, but we barely had time to bake them before we had to head to dinner with AJ and McCabe.

"I wouldn't have pegged you for a baker," AJ says, and as much as I'm trying to relax around her, the fact that she's my boss still makes that difficult. At least the stress of the contract negotiation phase is over, and I know I'll be staying in Boston for the next few years, at which point I'll probably retire.

The stress of maintaining both a personal and professional relationship with my boss, like I have since Morgan and I became "official," makes me wonder how McCabe was secretly dating AJ in the midst of a tense contract negotiation between her and his agent.

"I have many talents," I say.

"Most impressively," McCabe says with a smirk, "the ability to hide this relationship from everyone for months."

AJ turns toward him, tilting her head and giving him a small smile. "I feel like the pot shouldn't call the kettle black here?"

"Touché," he says. "But our reasons for hiding our relationship were obvious. Why would you two need to hide it?"

Morgan glances at me, the question obvious? Do we tell them how we originally met? I think AJ is the only friend of Morgan's who might not already know. I give her the slightest nod.

"So . . ." she starts. "We actually met in Bermuda over Labor Day weekend, not really knowing who the other was. And then . . . there was this uncomfortable situation where we hooked up, and found out the next day that our parents were getting married."

McCabe's bark of laughter is so loud it scares Abby, who is almost asleep cuddled up on AJ. Abby starts crying, and AJ hugs her closer, kissing her and murmuring, "It's okay, Daddy just thought something was funny."

She's rubbing small circles on Abby's back as I glance over at McCabe, lifting an eyebrow as I silently mouth, "Daddy, huh?"

"Dick," he mouths back. AJ's focused on Abby, but Morgan's silent chuckle lets me know she didn't miss the interaction.

"Then what happened?" AJ asks, head still bent toward Abby.

Morgan explains about Max's nickname for me and having no idea I was a hockey player. "Then we came back to

Boston and realized we work together, and my dad is his agent."

"Oh, I'm sure you backed off then," McCabe says sarcastically, glancing at me. He damn well knows I didn't.

"Obviously I did, but she just couldn't stay away. Kept coming after me, over and over."

She smacks my arm, hard, and with a laugh says, "Yeah, that's definitely what happened."

"The rest of the story doesn't matter," I say, wrapping my arm around her shoulder and pulling her into my side so I can press my lips to the top of her head. "We ended up together, and our parents are already in the process of divorcing."

AJ chuckles and says, "Only you, Morgan."

"Funny," she says, "that's the reaction everyone has regarding my love life."

"And to think you stormed into my office before that trip saying that you had a special ability to attract assholes." She lifts an eyebrow as her gaze travels to me.

"Luckily her abilities worked just fine on that trip, and she snagged me," I say.

"I hate to break it to you, dude," McCabe says. "But I don't think you were ever actually an asshole."

"Oh yeah?" I say.

"Yeah." His eyes travel to Abby with her head on AJ's chest and eyes closed. "Okay, I think we need to get Abby to bed now."

I hold in my laugh because with the way he's looking at AJ holding his little girl, I think what he means is that he wants to get *her* to bed now.

We say our goodbyes and when the elevator doors close, I

pull Morgan close. "I know Christmas is over, but I got you one more present."

She tilts her head back to look at me. "You did?"

"Yeah. I bought you my jersey. I've only ever seen you with McCabe's name and number on your back, and I'd kind of like to see mine there."

She smirks. "You really do have a fetish for me in your clothing, don't you?" I just nod, and she says, "Luckily, four is my lucky number."

"Perfect, because I'm going to fuck you with that jersey on tonight, and then watch you wear it tomorrow night at the game. And every time I put my own jersey on, I'll think about you in it."

"Sounds like a good way to be distracted," she says, lifting up on her toes to press a quick kiss to my lips. "And I'm pretty sure you promised your coach, your GM, and your agent that you'd have no distractions this season."

I can't help the way my smile spreads and laughter tumbles out. "Don't worry, baby. I'm more focused on my future than ever before."

With a new contract, a likely run for the Stanley Cup, and the possibility of forever with her, my future has never felt brighter.

———

It feels like we've just fallen asleep after staying up way too late exploring all the things I wanted to do to her in my jersey, when Morgan's phone rings. I groan and nudge her, but she's not waking up easily. So I reach over her and grab her phone off her nightstand, only to see *Preston Hartmann* flashing on her screen.

What the fuck? I can't think of a single reason that our CEO's billionaire older brother would be calling her. I can't even think of a reason she'd *know* him.

I press the screen to answer the call. "Hello?"

There's a pause on the other end. "Who's this?" Preston asks.

"Aidan Renaud."

"Oh, good. Renaud, I need to talk to Morgan. Can you put her on the phone?"

I'm not surprised he knows who I am—his family owns the Rebels. I am, however, astonished that he doesn't seem the least bit curious that I'm answering her phone at four in the morning.

"Yeah, hold on," I say and press mute. Then I give her another shake, saying, "Morgan, you need to wake up."

She groans but doesn't open her eyes. "Why?"

"Preston Hartmann is on the phone for you."

"What?" She shoots up to sitting, eyes wide, and glances down at her phone in my hand. "Oh no . . ."

I hand her the phone, unmuting it as I do, and she presses it to her ear. The look on her face is borderline panic. "What happened?" she asks. "*No, he didn't!*" There's a pause, and she sighs, folding her legs beneath her so she's sitting cross-legged. "I told Tucker to stay off social media," she says, as I reach toward the blanket at the end of the bed and wrap it around her bare shoulders. "Okay . . . yep . . . all right, I'll meet you there in an hour."

She disconnects the call, tilts her head back while letting

out a huge sigh, and then sinks back into bed with the blanket still wrapped around her. "Fuuuuck."

"Uh . . . what just happened?" I ask.

She sighs again. "We were trying to keep this quiet, but Tucker's gone and blown it all up, so I might as well tell you because it's out there now. This morning while I was getting ready to go into the office, I came across a video from Tucker's ex-fiancée, Violet Sinclaire. She was talking shit about him and their breakup last year," she says, and I realize that's probably why she gasped while getting ready this morning, not because she'd almost dropped her phone like she told me. "I sent it to the Hartmann family's PR team, and when I was meeting with Tucker this morning, Preston sent him the video. Tucker and I talked about it, I told him his family's PR team would handle it and asked him to stay off social media. I thought it was all set. But at some point overnight, he posted a video he took before they broke up. And it's not good."

"Not good, how?"

"I haven't seen it yet, obviously, but Preston said it's a video of him flying to Miami to surprise her, and then walking into her hotel room only to find her cheating on him."

"Why would he want the world to see that?"

It all happened while I was on IR, and I don't know much about the breakup, except that it was splashed all over the news for a day or two as a "mutual parting of ways." The next thing I heard, Tucker left Hartmann Enterprises and became the new CEO of the Boston Rebels. He seems good at his job, but I don't get the sense that he has the kind of passion for the sport or the organization that most people who work for the Rebels do.

"The video his ex-fiancée posted basically claimed that the breakup was his fault, and he not only left her heartbroken, but also left her family with a hundred-thousand-dollar bill for the wedding."

"And she was the one cheating on him?" I clarify.

"Looks like it, but I don't know for sure. I need to go get ready. I have to be at Hartmann Enterprises in an hour. You should go back to sleep," she says, leaning over and giving me a kiss. "You have a big game tonight."

"Aren't you on vacation right now?"

"Yeah. But when Preston Hartmann tells you to meet him at the Hartmann headquarters, you show up."

"You don't work for *him*," I remind her, still wondering why she needs to be involved in this at all. Then again, I'm pretty sure if Preston Hartmann told me to jump, I'd ask how high. He's got that kind of air about him, like *cross me and I'll bury you.* Which doesn't make me particularly comfortable that Morgan's headed to his office.

"Right, but I was the one who found Violet's video in the first place and sent it on to the firm that handles their family's PR. I was the one who was with Tucker when Preston sent him the video. And it's going to be *my* job to keep this from making the Rebels look bad, since apparently I'm their go-to for crisis situations. Sadly, it looks like I have some work to do this weekend."

"Please tell me this isn't going to affect our New Year's Eve plans tomorrow." I have a game on New Year's Day, so we're not going out tomorrow night. But I've planned dinner with all our friends followed by a romantic night in for the two of us, and I've been looking forward to several surprises I have in store for her.

"I'm not sure what's going to happen. But I can promise you this: I will be at your game tonight, in your jersey, cheering for you. And I'll make sure I'm home tomorrow night for New Year's Eve." She leans into me, wrapping an arm around my back with a quick hug. I'm proud of her for the way she's setting boundaries these days, even if they're still not quite as tight as I'd like them to be. "I'm sorry."

"You don't need to be sorry—you didn't do this. But don't be surprised if I punch Tucker in the fucking face next time I see him."

"I'm going to have to recommend against that," she says with a chuckle. "Please don't make even more work for me, trying to bury *that* story too."

"Because I love you, I'll refrain." I lean over and give her a quick kiss on her forehead.

"All right, go deal with the stupid shit. I'll see you at my game tonight, if not before."

"Love you too," she says, giving me a quick kiss before she hops out of bed.

Once she's in the shower, I get up and make her coffee, like I do every morning I'm home. While it brews, I grab a protein bar because she'll probably be hungry, and a bag of Nerds Gummy Clusters from the secret stash I keep for her stressful times, and drop them both into her work bag. Once I hear the water go off in the shower, I add milk and sugar to her coffee and bring it into the bathroom for her.

She smells like coconut and shea butter, and the scent

makes me think of the day we spent together in Bermuda before that storm rolled in.

"You know what I was thinking?" I ask her, pressing a kiss to her wet hair.

"Hmmm?" she says as she takes a sip of the creamy coffee I've handed her.

"I think that once the season's over, we should head back to Bermuda."

Her chest shakes with a quick laugh. "Oh yeah?"

"Yeah. I feel like there must be other beach caves we haven't *explored* together."

She shakes her head at me, but her smile is huge and her laughter is light. "We do like *exploring*."

"Maybe I'll look into it today when you're at work."

"I think you should do that," she says, pressing up on her toes so she can give me a quick kiss. "Maybe pick out a new bikini for me while you're at it."

"No way," I say with a laugh. "I want you in that yellow one."

"I'll wear whatever you want," she says with a chuckle. "Including your jersey at tonight's game. But I've got to get ready to go *now* or I'm really going to be late."

I give her another quick kiss, then head out of the bathroom. With the door shut behind me, I move into the closet and quietly search through her drawers until I find that yellow bikini. Then I tuck it under my pillow. After she leaves, I'll search for the brand and size online and buy her three more for when this one wears out. Because if there's one thing I love as much as her in my jersey or my clothes, it's this yellow bikini and the way it reminds me of our first weekend together.

Even though I knew back then that there was something special about us together, I never could have imagined we'd end up here. I'll always be grateful that the disaster that was our parents' marriage to each other led us to our own forever.

Epilogue

MORGAN & AIDAN

MORGAN

Almost Six Months Later

"I'm happy to hold her for a bit," I tell Marissa, as I watch the Walshes' youngest daughter squirm in the baby carrier strapped to her mom's chest.

"She's always fussy around this time of night," Marissa says. "I don't want you to have to deal with that."

"You deserve a break, and I don't mind."

We're almost into the third period in Game 5 of the Stanley Cup Final. If we win this one, we'll bring the Cup to Boston and raise another banner in the rafters. Winning tonight, at home, against the same team that bested us last season, would be such a sweet victory. And after Luke's shutouts in Game 2 and in Game 4, last night, there's an energy on the bench and in the stands—like we're all realizing how momentous that is after the way we lost in Game 7 last season. We're the same team, but better, this year.

The WAG in me can't help but think that the biggest difference is Aidan's return to the ice. He's become such a leader on the team, and even asked Coach Wilcott to keep him on the second line so that our first two lines were equally strong—something I don't think his pride would have allowed for in previous seasons.

"Are you sure?" The look of relief that crosses her face is at odds with her question.

"I'm positive. And your girls are playing with Audrey and Lauren's kids," I say, glancing over toward one corner of the suite where all the kids, including Liam's son Jack, are being entertained by someone's nanny. "You should sit and enjoy a moment of peace before the third period starts."

Marissa's eyes fill with tears as she unstraps the baby carrier. These past few months have been an emotional roller coaster for the Walshes, who had to deliver their baby girl at thirty-four weeks because the IUD was getting too close to her bladder. Luckily, both the baby and her mama were fine. But with four little girls at home now, Marissa is as exhausted as you'd expect.

I take the baby and, holding her to my chest, bounce lightly from side to side.

"You're a natural," Audrey says as she and Eva approach us.

"I got a lot of practice when Lauren's twins were babies," I tell her, eyeing the cocktail in her hand.

"This is for you," she says with a laugh as she rubs her free hand over her large belly and sets the drink on the ledge that runs in front of the seats facing the ice.

Audrey and Drew told us they were pregnant again at the New Year's Eve dinner Aidan planned with his teammates. The pregnancy put their wedding on hold indefinitely, but Drew was so eager to have another baby with Audrey and get to experience the birth since he missed Graham's. It's been adorable watching his excitement and the way he's doted on Audrey through the whole process.

"Thanks. How are you feeling?"

"Huge"—she huffs out a laugh—"and uncomfortable."

"The last month is always the worst," Marissa says.

"At least we timed this right with Jules and Colt's wedding," Audrey says. "I can't imagine if we'd gotten pregnant a month later and I'd been like this"—her hand slips over the curve of her belly—"for the wedding."

I know that the idea of being in Jules's wedding a month after giving birth has been stressful for Audrey. But Jules, being Jules, decided her bridesmaids should wear "whatever black dress you're most comfortable in."

"You're going to be beautiful and radiant," I say. "Plus, you're going to have a great rack, so pick a low-cut dress to drive Drew wild."

"Speaking from experience?" she teases as she glances at my chest. I'm wearing a scoop-neck top under the WAG playoff jacket we're all sporting this year, and it's revealing quite a lot of cleavage, which currently has a sleeping baby resting on it.

"God, don't let Renaud see you holding a baby," Eva teases. "He'll probably impregnate you on the spot."

I just laugh, because she's not wrong. Aidan's become a bit obsessed with the idea of me having his child. I know he can't wait to take that step, but it feels like there are a few other relationship milestones to hit before then. "Let's let him propose first."

It's no secret that it's going to happen. He's been talking about it since we first told our friends and family we were together, almost six months ago.

His teammates jokingly refer to me as his wife, and a few weeks ago, when Max introduced us to his new girlfriend—who thankfully looks *nothing* like Aidan's mom nor mine—he called me his "future daughter-in-law."

"I'm sorry," Lauren's voice comes from behind me, "but what is this about Morgan getting pregnant?"

I look over my shoulder to see Lauren and Paige standing there with plates of food in hand, and can't help glancing behind them to check on Liam. He seems very at home in this suite talking to the three oldest Hartmann brothers.

Audrey moves over so Lauren and Paige can join our little circle. We're missing a few of our friends. Jules decided that since this is possibly Colt's last game, she wanted to watch the game closer to the ice with AJ and Frank Hartmann, and Zach's girlfriend, Ashleigh, is also with them.

"I'm *not* pregnant," I say. "Eva's teasing me about Aidan having baby fever."

Paige laughs. "That man looks at you like you're a fucking goddess who he wants to have his babies."

I can't hold in my smile. And as I look around the suite, full of our family and friends, I'm overcome once again with how lucky I am to be at this place in my life now.

There are so many moments, personally and professionally, where I felt like a failure having to start over from scratch—moving to Park City instead of Austin with my college boyfriend after he broke up with me, moving back to Boston with Lauren after her husband died, starting my own company when Petra no longer needed me to work for her. But each of those moments, each time I had to start over and reinvent myself, made me stronger and brought me one step closer to Aidan.

Ironically, even if I never speak to her again, I'll always be grateful that Mom's brief marriage to Max allowed all of this to happen for me. Because if Aidan and I had never been two strangers in a bar during a tropical storm, if we hadn't shared that weekend together before life threw a bunch more obstacles in our way, who knows if we'd be *here*, together, today.

And here, surrounded by friends who are family, and in love with the man of my dreams, is the only place I ever want to be. Because no matter how tonight ends, no matter how this series ends, we'll all be okay because we have each other.

AIDAN

"Fuck, yeah!" McCabe yells as he skates toward the bench after Colt stops yet another puck. We entered the third period up 3-1, and a win tonight will secure what we couldn't last year—a Stanley Cup victory. As I hop the boards for our line shift, I focus on nothing but this moment and what I can do to help make a win possible.

Nothing in my entire hockey career has ever felt as inevitable as us winning the Cup feels. We've earned it . . . every hard-fought victory throughout a grueling season ended with us having the best record not only in our division or conference, but in the whole league. St. Louis making it to the Final this year was a fluke, and it shows. We've dominated the series so far, and their one win was a lucky buzzer shot before we would have headed into overtime.

Us winning tonight and bringing the Cup to Boston feels right. And if there's anything I've learned over this past season, it's to *lean in* to what feels right. Fighting against that with Morgan almost cost me my own happiness, but I learned my lesson quickly. Which is why, when I saw how much stronger our team was with me on the second line, I asked Coach to keep it that way.

I move up the outskirts of the ice, knowing that Zach's got the puck behind me and will be waiting to send it to me as soon as I cross the blue line. I hear it when he breaks through their lines, and spin as he sends the puck soaring right ahead of the blade of my stick so I can take off on a breakaway. It's a textbook-perfect play, one we've practiced hundreds of times, and as I fly up the ice, eyes focused on the goal, I tune out the roar of the crowd.

It's just me and St. Louis's goalie. I watch him commit to his butterfly position, and I'm able to deke twice before I send the puck over his blocker. The swoosh of the net and sound of the goal horn bring my attention back to the home crowd going wild in the stands.

I skate back to the bench, high-fiving my teammates along the row before I hop the boards. As I take my seat, I glance at the scoreboard. Three minutes left, and we're up 4-1. While it's not unheard of for a team to come back in the last few minutes, that three-goal lead feels damn near insurmountable.

I can tell it by how tired St. Louis seems, like they've already given their all and there's nothing left in their tanks. Which is why McCabe's able to skate circles around them, and his goal has the entire arena erupting and throwing their hats onto the ice. It's not his first hat trick this season, but it is his first in the playoffs.

5-1 with less than two minutes left, and as our third line takes the ice for the face-off, I see Colt signal to Wilcott. *What the fuck is happening?*

We call a timeout, and the six players skate back to the bench.

"What's wrong?" Coach asks Colt.

"Nothing's wrong. I want Hartmann to come in."

"Why?" half the team asks at the same time.

Colt looks at Hartmann. "You deserve to be in the crease for the last game of the series and have it be a win."

"Fuck that," Hartmann says. "I've had plenty of wins this season and two shutouts this series. This is *your* game. Probably your last game, *ever*. And there's no way anyone but you should be standing between the pipes when the buzzer sounds. Get your ass out there, and finish our season for us."

"You heard him," Coach Wilcott says. "Go get 'em boys!"

And that's what we do. We show St. Louis no mercy, not even when they pull their goalie in a desperate attempt to score one more goal. Instead, Coach makes a line change with thirty seconds left, and Drew sinks the puck into the empty net. When the final buzzer sounds, we flood the ice amid the deafening cheers of a home crowd and the championship music blasting through the speakers.

It's momentary chaos as gloves and sticks and helmets go flying before we all pile onto Colt in celebration, and then we're lining up and shaking hands with St. Louis.

The Commissioner presents the trophy for the most valuable player in the series, and it's only fitting that it goes to Luke Hartmann. He stepped into his own this season, and in the playoffs he more than proved he's ready to take Colt's spot when he retires. His two shutouts in this match-up against St. Louis really cemented that he deserves this award.

Then the Cup is brought out and presented to our team, and McCabe takes his turn skating a lap around the ice, holding it above his head.

As he hands it to me and I circle the ice, I soak in the moment. Being injured last season seemed like one of the worst things that could have happened to me. But in retrospect, maybe it was the best. Maybe everything would be different now if I hadn't missed last season. Maybe tonight's victory wouldn't feel quite so sweet.

After I pass the Cup to Walsh, my gaze flicks up to the luxury suite I know Morgan's watching the game from, but it appears to be completely empty. So my eyes search along the glass, hoping this means the families are already in the tunnel to be let onto the ice, and sure enough, I catch sight of Jules and Eva, but not Morgan.

I want nothing more than to share this moment with her now that I've had time to bask in this win with my teammates. Next to me, McCabe throws an arm over my shoulders. "Don't worry, she's probably just a few people back in that line."

"Why would I be worried?"

"You get this look when she's not around . . ."

I let myself stop searching for Morgan long enough to glance at him. "Oh yeah, what kind of look?"

"I don't know," he says with a shrug. "There's a tightness in your face, almost like you're in pain."

Funny, that's how it feels too. Her absence is a physical ache that only goes away when we're together. I assume it won't always be like this. That gradually we'll settle into being an "old married couple" and every moment together won't feel quite so precious. I kind of hope that's not the case, because I know very well that nothing's forever and I never want to stop valuing each moment I get with her.

I respond with something that sounds like *Hmpf*, and McCabe huffs a laugh.

"You ready?" I ask him.

He clears his throat, no longer laughing, and glances at the carpets laid out near the bench where AJ stands in a pale blue suit and heels, next to Frank and Tucker Hartmann, the entire Rebels coaching staff, the equipment managers, and our team doctor and trainers.

"More than ready," he says. We wait for our teammates to finish their turns with the Cup, and then the boards are being opened to let our families onto the ice.

"Give me a minute to get back with Morgan," I say to McCabe as I skate away.

"No promises," he calls after me.

The families are walking out onto the ice, and it takes me a minute to find her. But once I zero in on her strawberry blonde hair, I skate around a few people, then scoop her up into my arms before turning back toward the center of the rink. She laughs as she tightens her arms around my neck while we speed across the ice.

"Congratulations." Her voice soft as she plants a kiss on my cheek.

"Thanks. Couldn't have done it without you," I say as I navigate my way around other players.

"Yes, you could have."

"Wouldn't have wanted to, though." I glance at her quickly, hoping she can see the sincerity in my eyes before I have to focus back on the ice so we don't run into anyone.

She squeezes my neck in a quick hug. "Where are you taking me?"

"You'll see." I come to a quick stop at center ice, right near the carpets that were rolled out from the bench, just as McCabe sinks down on one knee. AJ's hands fly to her mouth and it feels like the entire arena takes one collective gasp.

"You knew?" Morgan asks as I set her on the ice to stand next to me. With me in skates and her in sneakers, she only comes up to my armpit, but she snakes her arm around my waist, squeezing me to her side even though I must smell terrible.

I squeeze her back, knowing she appreciates being here to see two of our closest friends get engaged. There's a lot we can communicate these days even without words.

AJ sinks onto her knees facing McCabe, nodding as tears

fall down her face. It's too loud for Morgan and me to hear what they're saying to each other, but we watch as McCabe unties a ring from his lace where he's tucked it into his skate and slips it onto her finger. The fans and our teammates erupt in cheers, and then I turn toward Morgan.

"I've got something for you, too."

Her eyes widen as she looks up at me. "Don't you dare."

My chest shakes with a laugh. "Not only do I know you well enough to know you'd hate a public proposal, but I had no desire to follow *that*," I say, reaching my hand up under my jersey. Her brows knit together as she watches my fingers fumble behind the fabric, and then I'm pulling out a gold charm bracelet that I'd hooked onto my shoulder pads for the game.

There's only one charm on there . . . for now. I secure it around her wrist and she lifts it to get a closer look.

"An anchor?"

"Because *you're* my anchor."

She cocks her head as she looks up at me. "Weighing you down?"

"Holding me steady, no matter what storms may come," I say, and her lips curve up in a smile. "Sometimes, I think about that anchor getting stuck in Bermuda, and how things might not have happened the way they did otherwise. We might have gotten back to that beach in time to get on that boat before it left. We might not have ended up in that cave together. And if we didn't, maybe you wouldn't have agreed to go out to dinner with me that night." I gulp as I think that, despite all the obstacles lining our path, there were also a lot of small moments that pushed us together. "If we'd been a one-time hookup before the wedding, maybe we could have kept resisting each other once we got back to Boston. In a lot of ways, that anchor led us here."

Her eyes are filled with tears as she stares up at me, and I bend to press a kiss to her forehead.

"I never could have resisted you for this long. We were always going to end up together." Her words tumble out on a choked laugh as those tears slip down her face, so I cup her cheeks and wipe them away with my thumbs.

"Maybe," I say, "but I'm glad that anchor got stuck and helped us along."

She chuckles, then presses up onto her toes to give me a kiss. "I love the bracelet, thank you."

Then you're really going to love the ring, I think to myself.

She thinks we're going back to Bermuda next week. She has no idea we're leaving tomorrow afternoon—a plan that was helped along by Eva, who secretly packed a suitcase for Morgan a couple days ago, just in case we won tonight, and Luke, who was able to coordinate the use of one of his family's private jets last minute.

She thinks we're staying at a hotel just outside Hamilton, and has no idea I've rented a house with its own private moongate that overlooks the ocean, and its own private beach with a cave that's only accessible at low tide.

She has no idea that she's leaving Boston as my girlfriend, and returning as my fiancée. Or maybe she does? I've made no secret of the fact that I want to marry her as soon as possible. Because if there's one other thing I've learned over the past ten months, it's that when you finally get what you want, you hold on with both hands. Which is what I plan to do, with Morgan, forever.

Want more Aidan and Morgan? Get their bonus epilogue, and find out what the Rebels are up to two years later, here.

Curious about Zach and Ashleigh? They have a novella, THE TRADE UP, which you can download here.

THE END

Join My Reader Group

Not ready to leave the world of the Boston Rebels? Join me in my Facebook reader group, where we're always talking about the Rebels!

Books by Julia Connors

FROZEN HEARTS SERIES

On the Edge: Jackson & Nate

Out of Bounds: Sierra & Beau

One Last Shot: Petra & Aleksandr

One Little Favor: Avery & Tom

On the Line: Lauren & Jameson

BOSTON REBELS SERIES

Center Ice: Drew & Audrey

Fake Shot: Colt & Jules

Cross-Checked: McCabe & AJ

Goal Line: Luke & Eva

Penalty Play: Aidan & Morgan

HARTMANN BROTHERS SERIES

Coming soon!

Acknowledgments

I've been itching to write Morgan's book for years. When I wrote her into *One Last Shot* as Petra's assistant, I didn't intend for her to have her own book, but by the time she moved to Boston with Lauren in *On the Line*, I knew my girl needed her story told.

Morgan has so many characteristics that make her an amazing side character: she shows up for her friends, she's a good daughter, she's successful in her career, she'll tell you the truths you need to hear. If anything, I think Morgan is like a lot of women: accomplished, but struggling to hold it all together and be everything to everyone.

What she really needed was the opportunity to shine . . . to step into her main character era. And she needed the support of her friends and a strong male lead who'd show her that she doesn't need to keep chasing perfection because she's already perfect as she is.

Enter Aidan Renaud. He's scared of commitment and doesn't want to make himself vulnerable or get hurt. But despite all the obstacles in their path, he shows up for Morgan, over and over. He's imperfect. And yet, he's perfect for her—he just needs to get out of his own way.

Getting to write these two characters—who go from fun and flirty when there are no obstacles in their path, to navigating everything life throws between them, and getting them back to a place where they match each other's energy and have an actual shot at staying together forever—was a privilege. And it was possible because of the following people:

Victoria, Jenn, and Leah — Without you ladies, I don't know what I would do. Truly. You motivate and inspire me. You keep me accountable. I hope every woman has a group of like-minded friends who are as supportive as you all are!

Keri, Jason, and Mr. Connors — Our Bermuda trip, and getting caught in a thunderstorm while snorkeling, shaped so much of the beginning of this book. There's no one I'd rather travel, or brainstorm book scenes while speeding across a harbor toward a private beach in a thunderstorm, with.

Amy — You saved me this year. From stepping in as my PA halfway through the year, to taking over the editing when otherwise this book wouldn't have met its deadlines . . . everything about working with you has made my life better.

Rhea and Rachel – Your honest critiques, and the way you're both always striving to help make my books better, is truly appreciated!

Melanie – Your feedback throughout the writing process, and the way you always keep me focused on both the big picture and the small details, helped make this story the best it could be.

Elizabeth – The way you stop at nothing to make me a better writer is so appreciated. I'm sorry that, no matter how many times you tell me the things I consistently do wrong, I keep doing them. I'm just trying to make sure you still have a job ;-)

Rachel, Melanie, Alexandra, and Elizabeth – My girls. I can only write strong female friendships and found families because I have you all in my corner!

Mr. Connors – What can I say that I haven't said with every book? Without you, none of this would be possible. Thank you for believing in me. For being supportive as I figured out how to make this my career, and for reminding me that there's more to life than work.

My ARC, Content, and ALC teams — Would anyone even know about my books if it weren't for you? Thank you for everything you do, for every release and all the months in between. There are no words for how much your support means!

And thank you, a million times over, to my readers! The way you show up for me and my books truly brings me to tears sometimes. Without you, none of this would be possible!!!

Afterword

Thank you so much for reading! If you enjoyed the book, please consider leaving an honest review. Reader reviews mean so much to authors, and your time and feedback are appreciated.

Sign up for Julia's newsletter to stay up to date on the latest news and be the first to know about sales, audiobooks, and new releases!

juliaconnors.com/newsletter

About the Author

Julia Connors grew up in California, but her first decision as an adult was to trade her flip-flops for snow boots and move to Boston. She's been enjoying everything that New England has to offer for over two decades, and now that she's acclimated to the snowy winters and finally found all the places to get good sushi and tacos, she has zero regrets. You can usually find her in front of her computer, but when she stops writing she's most likely to be found outdoors, preferably with a pair of skis or snowshoes strapped to her feet in winter, or on a paddleboard in the summer.

goodreads.com/julia_connors

amazon.com/author/juliaconnors

instagram.com/juliaconnorsauthor

tiktok.com/@juliaconnorsauthor

facebook.com/juliaconnorsauthor

pinterest.com/juliaconnorsauthor